Wall-to-Wall Dead

"A really good whodunit."   —*Cozy Mystery Book Review*

"This fast-paced, nonstop action whodunit kept me on my toes."   —*Mayhem and Magic*

Flipped Out

"Bentley's well-developed characters are what makes this cozy so endearing, entertaining, and enthralling."
     —*Blogcritics*

"The reader will be drawn in like a moth to the flame. This is probably the best book in the series to date."
     —*Debbie's Book Bag*

Mortar and Murder

"With plot twists that curve and loop . . . this story offers handy renovation tips, historical data, and a colorful painting of the Maine landscape."   —*Examiner.com*

"Mystery author Jennie Bentley has nailed together another great mystery with *Mortar and Murder*."   —*Fresh Fiction*

Plaster and Poison

"[A] thrilling story that keeps the readers guessing and turning pages."   —*Fresh Fiction*

"A believable and beguiling mystery. Each novel in the series delights, and the third installment only raises the stakes."
     —*Examiner.com*

continued . . .

Spackled and Spooked

"Smooth, clever, and witty. This series is a winner!"
—*Once Upon a Romance*

"Bound to be another winner for this talented author. Home-renovation buffs will appreciate the wealth of detail."
—Examiner.com

Fatal Fixer-Upper

"An ingeniously plotted murder mystery with several prime suspects and a nail-biting conclusion." —*The Tennessean*

"A great whodunit . . . Fans will enjoy this fine cozy."
—*Midwest Book Review*

"Smartly blends investigative drama, sexual tension, and romantic comedy elements, and marks the start of what looks like an outstanding series of Avery Baker cases."
—*The Nashville City Paper*

"Polished writing and well-paced story. I was hooked . . . from page one." —*Cozy Library*

"There's a new contender in the do-it-yourself home-renovation mystery field . . . An enjoyable beginning to a series." —*Bangor Daily News*

"A strong debut mystery . . . Do-it-yourselfers will find much to enjoy in the first of this new series."
—*The Mystery Reader*

"A cozy whodunit with many elements familiar to fans of Agatha Christie or *Murder, She Wrote*." —*Nashville Scene*

"A fun and sassy journey that teaches readers about home renovation as they follow the twists and turns of a great mystery." —Examiner.com

"A first-rate mystery and a frightening surprise ending."
—*RT Book Reviews*

HOME FOR THE HOMICIDE

JENNIE BENTLEY

BERKLEY PRIME CRIME, NEW YORK

THE BERKLEY PUBLISHING GROUP
Published by the Penguin Group
Penguin Group (USA) LLC
375 Hudson Street, New York, New York 10014

USA • Canada • UK • Ireland • Australia • New Zealand • India • South Africa • China

penguin.com

A Penguin Random House Company

HOME FOR THE HOMICIDE

A Berkley Prime Crime Book / published by arrangement with the author

Berkley Prime Crime Books are published by The Berkley Publishing Group.
BERKLEY® PRIME CRIME and the PRIME CRIME logo are trademarks
of Penguin Group (USA) LLC.

For information, address: The Berkley Publishing Group,
a division of Penguin Group (USA) LLC,
375 Hudson Street, New York, New York 10014.

ISBN: 978-0-425-26049-4

PUBLISHING HISTORY
Berkley Prime Crime mass-market edition / December 2013

PRINTED IN THE UNITED STATES OF AMERICA

10 9 8 7 6 5 4 3 2 1

Cover illustration by S. Miroque.
Cover design by Rita Frangie.
Interior text design by Laura K. Corless.

—Acknowledgments—

As always, thanks go out to a multitude of people who had a part in bringing *Home for the Homicide* to this point:

My editor, Jessica Wade, and her assistant, Jesse Feldman, along with everyone at Berkley Prime Crime and Penguin Random House. Thanks for finally giving me the opportunity to write my baby-skeleton story!

My agent, Stephany Evans, and everyone at Fine Print Literary Management, for taking a chance on me those many years ago.

The book design team: cover designer, Rita Frangie; interior designer, Laura Corless; and cover artist, Jennifer Taylor; for another beautiful product.

Berkley publicist Kayleigh Clark, without whom this book would be nowhere.

My long-suffering beta reader and critique partner, Jamie Livingston-Dierks, for reading and providing feedback on everything I write, even the neurotic and weird stuff.

The two people who graciously outbid everyone else for the privilege of becoming characters in this book: Deborah Holt for supporting FOWL, Friends of the Wetumpka Library, and Kerri Waldo for donating to the Brenda Novak Diabetes Auction.

Kelli Stanley, for suggesting the title *Home for the Homicide* for book three in the DIY mysteries, which ended up being called *Plaster and Poison* instead.

And Dean James, for suggesting the same title this time around, when we finally managed to get it approved!

All my other friends within and without the publishing industry. By now there are too many of you to mention by name, but know that I'm grateful for each and every one of you. I wouldn't be here if it weren't for your love and support.

Everyone who's read a copy of one of my books sometime in the past five years; especially those of you who liked it, and even more especially those of you who told a friend.

And last but not least my family, my husband and my two boys, who have learned to accept the fact that I spend much of my time in a world far removed from theirs, where they can't join me, and who love me anyway.

"The Christ Child is gone!" Kate announced dramatically as she flung her coat over the back of a chair.

I looked up from where I was bent over a particularly stubborn piece of interior design software on the laptop. "Excuse me?"

She dropped into the chair on the other side of the table and reverted to her usual voice. "The Baby Jesus from the manger outside the church. It's gone."

"That happens every year," my husband told her over his shoulder, from where he was on his knees in front of the fireplace, building a fire.

I looked from one to the other of them. "Really?"

Kate nodded. "Don't you remember from last year? You were in Waterfield then."

I had been, as a matter of fact. It was about a year and a half since I'd moved from New York City to tiny Waterfield, Maine, to renovate my late aunt Inga's house. It was a year and three or four months since Derek and I had become an item, personally and professionally.

Only about a month since he'd become my husband.

But I had definitely been here last December.

"We were a little bit busy this time last year," I reminded Kate. "Renovating your carriage house, remember? You didn't give us much warning, so we were scrambling through half of November and all of December to get it done before you and Wayne got married."

And in addition to the renovations themselves, and my mother and stepfather coming in from California to visit for the holidays, there had been the dead body that had been dropped into the middle of our renovations to slow things down further. If the Baby Jesus had gone missing from the manger outside the church last year, I didn't remember hearing about it.

"It's been happening for as long as I can remember." Derek left the fire, now crackling merrily, and sat down next to me. He made himself comfortable, with one ankle on the opposite knee, and stretched one arm along the back of the sofa. Right where my back would have been if I hadn't been leaning forward to place the laptop on the table. "Barry puts out the nativity scene in front of the church the first of December, and a day or two later, someone takes the baby out of the manger and leaves with it."

"You're kidding." I leaned back, and he curled his arm around my shoulders and pulled me a little closer. Between the fire crackling on one side, and the heat of his body on the other, it was like being wrapped in a warm blanket.

"No," Kate said. "It's been going on for as long as I've been living here. A lot less time than Derek can remember, obviously. But Wayne said the same thing."

Wayne Rasmussen, Kate's husband, had grown up in Waterfield, just like Derek. Kate and I were both transplants. She'd come from Boston some seven or eight years ago now, with her daughter, Shannon, and had settled right in, while I still wasn't sure I considered myself a Waterfielder. Maine was great in the summer, but now, at the beginning of December, with sunset by four in the afternoon and the nights cold enough to freeze my toes off, I had a hard time remembering what it was I liked about it.

Kate was my first friend when I came to town last summer, and it was thanks to her that Derek and I had found each other. He was a handyman, and she'd recommended I hire him to help me renovate Aunt Inga's house before putting it back on the market and—the plan was—going back to my life in Manhattan with the profits. But instead I'd fallen in love with both Derek and the house, and with life in this little town on the coast of Maine (in the warm weather at least!), and had ended up staying. And now we both lived in what used to be Aunt Inga's house, since we had plans for a family and since Derek's loft, above the hardware store in downtown, didn't have the space we needed, or for that matter a yard for the kiddies to play in, once they came along.

"Is he going to investigate?" I asked.

In addition to being Kate's husband and a native Waterfielder, Wayne was also the local chief of police.

"There's nothing to investigate," Kate answered. "Usually the baby is returned after a day or two. They're just waiting."

"Is someone going to stake out the front of the church? See who returns it?"

"Lot of trouble for a doll," Derek said, and Kate nodded.

"Besides," she said, "what are they going to charge the thief with, if they figure out who it is? Borrowing Jesus?"

"What about a camera? One of those small motion-activated ones? It would kick on whenever someone came close to the nativity scene . . ."

"A lot of people walk up to the nativity scene," Derek said. Kate nodded.

"The department doesn't have the money for something like that anyway."

After a second, however, she added pensively, "Although I wouldn't be surprised if Josh could wrangle one . . ."

Josh was her stepson, Wayne's son from his first marriage, and in a strange twist of fate, also the boyfriend of Kate's daughter, Shannon. Josh liked Shannon long before Wayne liked Kate, though, so there was nothing weird about it.

Josh was also a student at local Barnham College—same as Shannon—and his specialty was information technology. In other words, he was a geek. I had no doubt whatsoever he either had, or had access to, a motion-activated camera.

"It couldn't hurt to ask."

"No," Kate said, "although it's probably just kids, Avery. Pranks."

"For thirty years?" My husband was thirty-five, and if the Baby Jesus kidnappings had been going on for as long as he could remember, whoever had been doing it when he was a kid, had to be well beyond the age of pranks by now.

"Maybe it's a family tradition," Derek said with a grin. "Someone used to do it back then, and now he's passed the job on to his kids."

That made as much sense as anything else about this situation, which essentially was none at all. "But you said the baby is always returned?"

They both nodded. "It usually takes a couple of days," Kate said, "but then one morning it's back in the manger. That's why nobody makes a fuss about it."

"Weird."

"It is," Derek agreed. "But it's just one of those little things that makes Waterfield a great place to live."

He smiled down at me. I smiled back. I couldn't help it. Looking at him made me happy. The feeling of knowing I was married to him made me giddy inside with joy. Sometimes—like when he smiled at me—it spilled over.

And he was handsome when he smiled. He was handsome the rest of the time, too—tall, lean, with hair about midway between dark blond and light brown, and eyes the color of the sky—but when he smiled, he got dimples. I've always had a soft spot for dimples.

Kate cleared her throat, and I returned my attention to her, my cheeks hot. "Sorry."

"I'm used to it," Kate said. "Josh has been looking at Shannon like that for six years. Not like I haven't seen it before."

Right.

Derek grinned. "What can we do for you? Or did you just stop by to tell us that the Baby Jesus is missing from the manger again?"

"I actually came to ask a favor," Kate said.

Uh-oh. Derek and I looked at each other, and I'm sure the same expression was on my face as I could see on his.

Shades of last year, when she'd shown up right here at the house to beg us to turn her decrepit carriage house into a love nest for two by New Year's Eve, because her husband-to-be had decided he didn't like the idea of living in the bed and breakfast Kate runs. Something about a trip to the bathroom in the middle of the night, and two of the guests seeing him in his boxer shorts, totally unbefitting the chief of police.

"If it's renovation related, I'm afraid we already have a project," Derek said. "It'll keep us busy for a while. February, at least."

Far from being put off by this, Kate sounded interested. "Really? What are you working on?"

"The big Craftsman bungalow on North Street," Derek said.

"The Green sisters' house? How did you get your hands on that? I didn't even know it had gone on the market."

"That's because it didn't," Derek said.

Derek had been talking to me about Ruth and Mamie Green's house as long ago as last summer, surmising that it would be coming up for sale soon. He wanted it, in a bad way. It was a large Craftsman bungalow in the heart of Waterfield Village, the historical district, with all the hallmarks of the Arts and Crafts movement: a wide front porch with substantial stone and wood columns supporting the overhanging roof, broad eaves with exposed rafters, and banks of big sixteen-over-one double-hung windows.

He had hoped that not much had been done to the house, for good or for bad, since it was built in the 1920s, and when we finally got a chance to see the interior, he'd turned out to be right. It was in much its original condition, which meant scuffed hardwood floors in dire need of refinishing, and crumbling plaster walls in need of patching and sanding, not to mention two original 1920s bathrooms and an original 1920s kitchen . . . but it also meant a stunning unpainted fieldstone fireplace flanked by casement windows in the living room, and fifteen-light French doors separating the living room from the dining room, not to mention the original and intact breakfront in the dining room and the original swinging butler door into the kitchen. Unpainted, of course. The whole house had the original dark-stained woodwork on doors, baseboards, and window frames; dull and dark with age, but gorgeous.

"What happened?" Kate wanted to know.

"Ruth broke her hip," Derek answered.

That had happened sometime in June or July. And because Ruth Green was in her mid-seventies, recovery had taken a long time. After a week or two in the hospital, her relatives had arranged for her to go to a rehabilitation facility, and from there to an assisted living facility, since the hip never had healed the way it was supposed to.

"How do you know all that?" Kate asked when I'd explained.

"Derek went to school with Darren Silva. He's Ruth and Mamie's cousin or nephew or some such."

"His grandmother and their mother were sisters," Derek said. "I think. The Silva line continued, but neither Ruth nor Mamie ever had children. Which makes the Silvas the closest family to the Greens."

Kate nodded. "So Ruth is in assisted living. What about Mamie?"

"She's there, too," Derek said. "She can't live on her own, and apparently the time when she and Ruth were separated wasn't pleasant for anyone concerned."

Kate tilted her head to the side, and her riot of copper-colored curls shifted. "What's wrong with her, do you know?"

Derek shrugged. "Not sure. I never had occasion to examine her. Not sure Dad ever did, either. Not for that."

Derek's dad, Benjamin Ellis, is Waterfield's GP. For a few years, between medical school and leaving the profession to become a handyman instead, my husband worked with his dad in Dr. Ben's practice. Derek's medical knowledge has come in handy more than once, since we've had a couple dead bodies turn up during some of our jobs, and it's nice to have someone around who can pretty accurately diagnose time and manner of death. It's also nice to have him around for all those little mishaps that occur during home renovation: all the cuts and scrapes and accidental hammer blows.

"Can't you guess?" Kate said. "I mean, it's obvious she's not quite right in the head."

That much *was* obvious. I hadn't seen Mamie Green more than a few times, and usually at a distance, but I could tell that everything wasn't all right there.

She was a few years younger than her sister, somewhere in her early seventies. A small white-haired lady who liked to dress, incongruously, like a little girl, in gingham and patent leather Mary Janes, with her hair in two wispy braids.

"Some form of dementia probably," Derek said. "She had a pretty normal life when she was younger. She never married or had children—her sister didn't, either—but they both had jobs. Ruth was a bank teller and Mamie worked in a nursery."

"With little kids?" Surely that wasn't smart, with someone not right in the head?

"Plants," Derek said. After a second he added pensively, "She always did dress a bit funny, though."

Nothing wrong with that. Some people think I dress funny, too. I adjusted my tunic—green with a row of silhouetted appliquéd mice around the hem, dancing—as Kate asked, "So she and Ruth always lived together?"

"As far as I know," Derek said.

"In the house on North Street?"

He nodded.

"No wonder having Ruth taken away upset Mamie. After seventy-plus years together, I can imagine it would upset me, too."

"Darren stopped by a couple weeks ago and asked whether we'd be interested in taking the house off his hands.

Gave us a good price, too. Better than I would have expected from him."

"Does he like money?"

Derek nodded.

"Maybe he just wanted a quick sale," Kate suggested. "Maybe he needs the money to pay for Ruth and Mamie's care."

"I think he just wanted to get rid of it quickly," Derek answered. "He's not hurting for cash. All the Silvas are rich. They have been for generations."

"I guess maybe he was just doing it to be nice, then. Since he doesn't need the money."

"Or maybe Ruth and Mamie didn't want to accept charity," I suggested. "Even from family. Maybe they wanted to sell the house so they could use their own money to pay the assisted living place, instead of letting the Silvas pay for it. Ruth signed the paperwork, didn't she?"

Derek nodded. "All legal and aboveboard. There's nothing wrong with her mind. I can't imagine it was easy for her to give up her childhood home, but I guess she realized she and Mamie would be better off where they are now."

He turned back to Kate. "So what can we do for you? You said you needed a favor."

"Right," Kate said. "That."

Uh-oh.

"That doesn't sound good," I said.

"No, no." Kate shook her head. Flickers of light from the fireplace lit up her hair, making it look like her head was on fire. "It's no big deal. Really."

"You sure?"

"I'm positive," Kate said. "It has to do with Melissa."

I arched my brows. It had to do with Melissa, but it was no big deal? How was that even possible?

Melissa James was Derek's ex-wife. They'd met while he was in medical school and she was waiting tables at an IHOP nearby. They'd fallen in love—or maybe she had decided she wanted to be married to a doctor. Either way, she'd turned his head and wrangled a proposal out of him, and by the time he returned to Waterfield to join his dad's medical practice, he'd had a wife along for the ride.

The marriage lasted five years. As soon as Derek decided he didn't want to be a doctor anymore, Melissa found someone else. My cousin Ray Stenham, as it happened. Big-shot local contractor. And then she left Derek and started shacking up with Ray instead.

It was a long story. Ray was out of the picture now, along with his twin brother, Randy, and Melissa had moved on to Tony "the Tiger" Micelli, ace on-air reporter for Portland's Channel Eight News—until Tony passed away unexpectedly last summer.

She'd been my nemesis for as long as I'd lived in Waterfield. She had descended on me approximately ten minutes after I arrived in town—and no, that's not an exaggeration; it really was no more than that—to try to get me to sell Aunt Inga's house to Ray and Randy, who wanted to tear it down and build a small subdivision of townhomes on the lot.

That didn't endear me to her, or vice versa, once I refused. When I learned she was Derek's ex, I liked her even less.

"I thought she left," I said.

At least that's what she'd told me at my wedding just over a month ago. That she was leaving Waterfield and moving to Portland. A bigger pond for her to conquer. No bad memories. And—I suspected—no chance of ever getting Derek back, because he was married.

Kate nodded. "She did."

"So?" If she was gone, why did we have to talk about her?

"She has a way of lingering," Derek informed me, his lips twitching.

I squinted at him. "Like a bad smell, you mean?"

"Something like that." He gave my shoulders a squeeze and turned back to Kate. "What about Melissa?"

"She's been in charge of the Waterfield Village Christmas Tour of Homes for the past eight years," Kate said.

Derek nodded. "So?"

"Now that she's gone, someone else has to do it."

He shook his head. "Not me. And not Avery. We're busy."

"I wasn't going to ask you to be in charge of it," Kate said. "I'm in charge of it."

"Oh." Derek's face cleared. "You are? Good for you."

"Congratulations," I added.

Kate shrugged. "It's more a curse than a blessing, really."

"So what do you need from us?" Derek asked.

Kate looked around, at my front parlor, with Aunt Inga's gray velvet love seat, the roaring fire in the restored tiled Victorian fireplace, and the floor-to-ceiling arched windows. Through the door, in the foyer, was a staircase going up to the second floor and, in the middle, room for the ginormous Christmas tree we hadn't gotten around to buying yet.

She turned back to me. "I thought maybe you'd like to be part of the tour this year."

"Really?" I think my voice may have squeaked, I was so surprised. And flattered.

Kate smiled. "Sure. I was actually surprised Melissa didn't ask you last year."

I wasn't. She was Melissa, and I was Derek's new girl-friend; it was obvious she wouldn't ask me to be on the home tour. "Did she ask *you* last year?"

"She asks me every year," Kate said. "The inn is one of the nicest historical homes in the Village, thanks to your husband. She couldn't very well exclude it."

True.

"But," Kate added, "people can see my house anytime they want, just by walking in. Your house isn't open to the public. And your aunt was a bit of a loner. I know a lot of people are curious to the see the inside of this place. They'd go on the tour just for that."

"Are you sure it's nice enough?" I looked around. My somewhat quirky interior designs suddenly looked rather unique, and not in a good way.

"The guy who did the renovations is pretty good," my husband informed me.

I snuggled into his side. "I didn't mean that. The house

is beautiful. We both worked really hard on it. I was just wondering whether the decorations are good enough."

"You'll need a tree," Kate said.

I nodded. "We were going to put one up. Right in the foyer, like last year. I guess we can do it a little early. When's the tour?"

"Sunday," Kate said.

Whoa. Not a lot of time to get ready, then, especially since we were starting to work on the Green sisters' Craftsman bungalow tomorrow.

"You're sort of throwing this together at the last minute, aren't you?" Derek said.

"It's not my fault," Kate answered, a little defensively. "Everyone thought Melissa was handling it. Turns out she wasn't. When she left, nothing had been done."

Huh. "Portland's only forty-five minutes away," I said. "Maybe she's still planning to take care of it."

Kate shook her head. "She's not. I tracked her down in Portland, and she told me to do it myself, if I wanted it done." She shrugged. "Not like I could say no, was it?"

Not really, no. "I suppose we could do without a home tour this year . . ."

"People have come to expect it," Kate said. "And I'll not have it said that there wasn't one this year because *I* dropped the ball."

Right.

"Was everything all right?" Derek asked, a wrinkle between his brows. "When you talked to Melissa?"

Kate turned to him. "Oh, sure. She's just being herself. Now that she's brushed the dust of Waterfield off her shoes, she can't be bothered to be nice to us anymore. Not that she was ever that nice, really."

"She wasn't that bad," Derek said.

"Sure she was. To Avery. And to me. And Jill and Shannon and every other woman in town. She was only nice to you because you're a man."

"She wasn't always that nice to me, either," Derek said.

Kate shrugged and turned to me. "So you'll do it? The Christmas Tour?"

I yanked my thoughts away from bad things happening to Melissa. Living well is the best revenge, and I had Derek, while she didn't. Now I also had a home on the Christmas Home Tour. "We'd be honored."

"Excellent." Kate got to her feet. "Wish I could stay, but I have a lot of other people to talk to. There'll be a meeting at the bed and breakfast on Tuesday night, to decide all the details. We have a lot to do by next weekend."

No kidding. "I'll be there," I said. "Derek may have to work."

"No problem. I'll see you then. Seven o'clock." She headed for the door, snagging her coat from the back of the chair on the way.

"I'll walk you out," Derek said, leaving the sofa. "And lock the door behind you."

Kate shot him a jaundiced look as she shrugged into her coat. "I'm not coming back in. I have too many other people to talk to tonight."

"You could check with Dad," Derek said, passing from the parlor into the foyer, so I couldn't see him anymore, but only hear his voice. "The Christmas Tour was Melissa's thing. I know she asked him and Cora if they'd be a part of it the first year, and they turned her down flat. We'd just separated then, and I guess they were feeling loyal. But now that she's out of the picture and it's you running it, you could ask. It's a nice little house."

Kate lit up. "I'll do that, if you think it's all right."

"Fine by me," Derek said. "I don't know if they'll say yes, but it can't hurt to ask."

"Especially if I tell him you two are doing it." She smiled. "Good luck with the Green sisters' house."

I pulled the laptop back onto my lap just as Derek said, "Thanks. Stop by and take a look if you have time. It's pretty cool."

"I might do that," Kate said and opened the front door, "but don't hold your breath."

She passed through into the outside and Derek closed the door behind her. I heard the deadbolt click, and then he came back into the parlor. "Ready for bed?"

"It's nine o'clock," I said with a glance at my watch.

"Big day tomorrow. I need my rest."

"You can go on up. I'll be there in thirty minutes." Or an hour. Whenever I had gotten the interior design program to cooperate and the new kitchen for the Green sisters' house virtually laid out.

"A month of marriage," Derek said, "and already I'm going to bed alone? I don't think so."

He took the laptop out of my hands and put it on the table before extending both hands to me. "C'mon, Tink."

I took them and let him haul me to my feet. And then I squealed when he bent and tossed me over his shoulder. "Bottoms up," he informed me, giving mine a pat, and headed out into the foyer and up the stairs. From the windowsill, our cat, Mischa the Russian Blue, watched us out of unblinking eyes.

— 2 —

"Would be nice if we could put this house on the home tour," I told Derek the next morning, standing in the living room of the Green sisters' house looking around.

The Arts and Crafts movement was the next big thing to happen to American architecture after Victoria. You have the antebellums, the Federals and Colonials built before the Civil War, and after that, you have the Victorian movement, starting with the Italianate Victorians as early as the 1840s, in some places. The Revival Gothics came on the scene in the 1870s and 1880s, along with the Second Empire Victorians, like my aunt Inga's house. Kate's Queen Anne was an 1890s style, like the stick- or shingle-style Victorians and the Eastlake, and after that, there were the Folk Victorians, the cottages, like Dr. Ben and Cora's house on Cabot Street.

The Arts and Crafts movement started in Britain as early as the 1860s, and is credited to William Morris. In the United States, however, the style is more often called American Craftsman or Craftsman style, and is used to denote the architecture, interior design, and decorative arts that prevailed from roughly 1910 to roughly 1930: during the Art Nouveau and Art Deco periods. World War I and the Roaring Twenties, pretty much. In the thirties, the houses retained some of the same styles, with the overhanging porches and pillars, along with the six-over-one or three-over-one windows. But the scale was vastly different. Craftsman bungalows tend to be sprawling, with big rooms and tall ceilings. During the Depression, houses became much smaller in all directions. Smaller rooms with lower ceilings, cheaper to build and easier—and cheaper—to heat and cool.

But I digress. The Green sisters' house was a perfect specimen of Craftsman bungalow, with soaring ceilings—not quite as tall as the twelve-footers in Aunt Inga's house, but a good ten feet—and a lovely open floor plan, not to mention all that original unpainted woodwork.

It would look stunning all decked out for Christmas.

"I wish we could," Derek said. "But there's no way, Avery. Not in a week. It'll take that long just to clean the place out."

Hopefully not. Although the Greens had left rather a lot of junk, junk Darren Silva and his hired minions hadn't bothered to discard.

Mamie and Ruth's clothes were gone, of course, along with any personal items they owned. Family heirlooms and silver had been removed, I was sure. There was nothing of real value left. Darren had even had an appraiser from Boston in to look at what was left, just to make sure, and the guy had extracted whatever he thought merited a second look before decreeing that everything left in the house was material for the dump, not even worth the time or effort to haul to a thrift store or reuse center.

I had disagreed, and Derek had, too, so after closing on the house last week, we'd spent a few days letting people with beat-up pickup trucks and trailers into and out of the house to scavenge what they could. One of the first had been my buddy John Nickerson, who owned an antique store on Main Street. John specialized in midcentury modern—stuff from the fifties, sixties, and seventies—and he'd had a field day digging through Ruth and Mamie's castoffs.

When he left, the house had already looked emptier, since he'd grabbed quite a lot of furniture—the Formica kitchen table and chrome-Naugahyde chairs, the teak television stand, the coffee table—along with several pictures of big-eyed children from Mamie's room, most of the china from the kitchen, and a shag rug from the second bedroom upstairs.

Other people had picked over what was left, until we were looking at just the dregs: stuff of no interest or value to anyone. The only thing left to do was spend a day or two hauling it all out to the Dumpster.

No sooner had the thought crossed my mind than the squeal of hydraulics sounded from outside. Derek glanced out the window and dropped his arm from around my shoulders. "It's the Dumpster delivery. I'll go tell them where to put it."

I nodded. "I'll have a look around while I wait. Make sure there's nothing we want to keep."

"Knock yourself out," Derek said and opened the door. Cold air seeped in and wound around my ankles, much as Mischa was wont to do. "I'll be back in a few minutes."

I waited for him to close the front door behind him, and then I wandered farther into the house.

As mentioned, there was a living room in the front, followed by a dining room with a window seat and a breakfront, and a kitchen, with a tiny laundry room tacked onto the back as an afterthought. On the other side of the house, there was a bedroom and bath. The master bedroom was a good size, even by modern standards, although the master bath was pretty tight, and would require some fancy finagling to reach twenty-first-century standards. Derek had a plan, though.

A staircase in the back of the house led to the second floor, or half story really, since the ceiling sloped in both the upstairs bedrooms. There was a bath up here, too, tucked into the dormer in the front. It was no bigger than the bathroom downstairs.

I had suggested turning the entire top floor into one big master suite with a walk-in closet—keep one bedroom as a bedroom, turn the other bedroom into a bathroom, turn the bathroom into a dressing room/closet—but Derek had informed me there was a trend toward master suites on the main floor, so he wanted to keep the setup the way it was. It was fine with me. All that stuff is his department. Mine's the finishes—the tile, the paint, the wallpaper, if any—while he does all the heavy lifting: the plumbing and electrical and framing and drywall. I bow to his expertise with carpentry and construction, while he bows to mine with design.

I'm a textile designer by trade. Educated at Parsons School of Design in New York City. When I'd inherited Aunt Inga's house, I was working for a small furniture company, creating upholstery for my then-boyfriend's hand-crafted replicas. But I did go through all the requisite interior design classes at Parsons, so I do know a little about that aspect of things, too. And I have, as the saying goes, a good eye for color and texture.

As I walked through the mostly empty rooms, I let my imagination go: not to the past, and what it must have been like to live here when Ruth and Mamie were small, but to the future and what the house would look like two months from now, when we were done with it.

God willing. As Derek never tired of saying, home renovation always took longer and cost more than you thought it would.

This was our seventh project. But as I looked around, I could feel excitement bubble up inside me again at the thought of taking on something big. This house reminded me of Aunt Inga's when I'd first inherited it: old and tired and neglected, but full of potential and promise. It could be gorgeous. All the bones were there; they just needed cleaning and polishing.

And the first step was to get rid of all the junk. I filled my arms with old newspapers and circulars, and headed for the front of the house. A metallic thump from the driveway told me that the Dumpster had been—for lack of a better word—dumped, and was ready for its first deposit of junk.

.   .   .

It took all of the first day and much of the second to clear the house of accumulated junk. By the time we were finally done, it was past midafternoon on Tuesday, and my back hurt from bending and scooping. But at least the house was clean, or clean enough to start working on.

Or so I thought, until Derek looked around the empty living room and dining room with his hands on his hips and a satisfied look on his face, and said, "Only the basement left."

"Basement?" I yelped.

He turned to me. "Did I forget to tell you about the basement?"

"Yes!"

"Oops." His voice was perfectly calm. "It's no big deal. Just another hour or two of work."

Just another hour or two?

"Show me," I said.

"You haven't been down there?"

He asked the question over his shoulder on his way to the back of the house, obviously expecting me to follow.

"No," I said, trotting after him. "Before yesterday, I'd only been here twice. First, when we looked at the place before we decided to buy it, and then once with John. We didn't go into the basement either time."

"I went into the basement before I decided to buy the place," Derek said, opening a door in the kitchen and exposing what looked like a rickety old staircase leading down into stygian darkness. A draft of dank air curled around my ankles, and I fought back a chill.

"Why didn't I go into the basement while we were here?"

"I told you to keep Darren company while I looked around, remember? I didn't want him following me around looking over my shoulder."

"Oh," I said. "Right."

He had done just that, since Darren Silva had been driving him crazy, dogging his every footstep. So in a quiet moment, he'd whispered to me to get Darren off his back for a while. I had complied by asking Darren to show me the second floor, leaving Derek downstairs to look around on his own. Darren had been torn, clearly, but he fancied himself a ladies' man, so he came upstairs with me. And dogged my footsteps instead, breathing down my neck. Literally.

"You might have mentioned it was there," I told Derek now, peering down into the dank darkness.

"I forgot you didn't know. Didn't you notice the door?" He reached out and flipped a switch, and the light came on. A pale light, illuminating a rough plank staircase, tilting crazily, and a dirt floor.

I took a step back. "Dirt?" And to answer the question, no. I hadn't noticed the door. Or rather, I'd seen it, but hadn't thought to open it. I thought it was a pantry, to be honest. Tucked under the stairs to the floor above. Because he hadn't said a word about a basement and I'd figured, if there was one, he'd have mentioned it.

He glanced at me. "Sorry, Tink. They didn't finish basements in the 1920s. That came later." He started down. The staircase groaned in protest, and shimmied like a flapper girl.

"Is it safe?" I asked.

"Wait until I get all the way down," Derek answered. "That way, if you fall, I can catch you."

Great.

Derek watched me with a frown as I picked my way down. "You OK, Tink?"

"Just remembering Aunt Inga's house," I said through gritted teeth. I'd fallen down the basement stairs there shortly after moving in, owing to one of the steps being purposely sabotaged.

"Ah." His face cleared. "I don't think anyone's messed with this staircase. If anyone had, it would have broken when I came down. I'm a lot heavier than you."

He was. However, his weight might just have broken it almost all the way, and mine might finish the job. Or so I reasoned.

But it turned out to be misplaced worry and residual memory, because I made it all the way down into the basement without mishap, and stopped next to Derek to look around.

The area was smaller than the first floor, but it followed the footprint of the house roughly. And if that didn't make much sense, it was because there were low walls all around the front and sides of the basement, creating a sort of shelf. Imagine this: a roughly ten-by-fifteen-foot hollow in the ground, with five-and-a-half-foot-tall dirt walls, the tops of which extended another four or five feet toward the foundation of the house. There were grimy windows back there, which let in a little bit of light, although since there was a sprinkling of snow on the ground—just an inch or two—visibility was limited. And because of the dirt shelves, the windows were too far away to be cleaned; not that I saw any need.

At the back of the house, the basement ended in a flat dirt wall, and didn't extend all the way under the utility room. I could see the pipes to the kitchen sink cross the insulated ceiling and disappear through the planks into the kitchen floor.

"Looks like you'll be spending some time down here," I told Derek.

He shot me a distracted look, and I added, pointing to the pipes, "Galvanized iron. You'll have to swap them out where they're visible, at least."

"And everywhere else. The water pressure is nonexistent."

I'd take his word for it, since that was something else he'd checked that I hadn't paid attention to.

I turned my focus back to my current surroundings again.

The basement wasn't as scarily full of junk as I had been afraid of, from Derek's estimation that it would take us another two hours to clear it. Maybe I should have guessed, since he'd seriously overestimated the time it would take to clear the rest of the house.

I mean, there was junk in the basement, and lots of it. But it wasn't as bad as it could have been. There were plenty of boxes and crates, full of things like old Christmas decorations and chipped china. An old bicycle with flat tires leaned up against one wall, while a rusty baby carriage stood parked nose-in over in the corner. A fake pine tree still sporting a few sad-looking icicles lay sideways on top of the dirt. A pair of snowshoes and two pairs of child skis were tucked up under the rafters, out of the way. They looked ancient. There were a couple of spades and rakes and other garden implements in a corner, along with a coiled hose, probably stored for the winter. A few buckets and other things lay around: the stainless steel variety instead of colorful plastic.

Something white and skeletal gleaming faintly over in a corner caught my eye, and caused my heart to jump.

"What's that?" I asked Derek, my voice shaky, and my finger equally so.

He walked a few steps for a closer inspection. "Looks like half a moose rack."

"Moose rack?"

"Antlers," Derek said. "Maybe someone shot a moose. Or maybe not. More likely they found it lying around, since there's only one side."

"How would a moose lose only one side of his rack?"

"Fighting," Derek said. "This isn't a full half, I don't think, so chances are he got into a fight with another moose, a bigger one, and the bigger moose broke part of his rack off. It was left lying around somewhere, until someone found it, and then it ended up here."

"Oh. Good."

He must have heard the relief in my voice, because he smiled. "I don't think we'll be digging up any skeletons this time around, Tink. Once was enough."

"More than enough." I still hadn't quite gotten over the

skeleton we'd found buried in the crawlspace under the house we'd renovated on Becklea Drive more than a year ago, hence my initial reaction to the innocent moose rack.

"It doesn't look too bad down here," Derek added, looking around. "I'll get the skis and snowshoes down. Why don't you grab the spades and rakes and drag them upstairs?"

"No problem." I took what I could and stomped upstairs with it. By the time I got back down to the basement, a little faster this time, since the rickety-looking staircase had proved to be sound, he had taken everything down that had been hanging on or behind the ceiling beams.

We busied ourselves carrying, crossing paths in the living room or dining room on each trip: one of us coming upstairs with junk, the other returning empty-handed. Outside in the driveway, the Dumpster filled up. The sun set, and gray twilight began to descend. The streetlights flickered on, and Derek turned on the interior lights, too.

"Not much more now," he told me bracingly after an hour or so as he passed me with the decrepit fake Christmas tree. It looked like mice had gnawed on the branches to survive the winter. "Another thirty minutes and we'll be out of here."

"Tonight is Kate's meeting for the home tour," I reminded him. "Are you planning to come with me?"

He stopped at the bottom of the stairs and grimaced. "I love you, Avery, but if it's OK, I think I'll pass. I'll help you do whatever decorating you have to do, but I don't want to sit around all night and discuss it."

"That's fine."

"Maybe I'll go hang out with Dad. Since he's going to be single tonight, too."

"Cora agreed to be part of the home tour?"

He nodded.

"Have a good time," I said.

"We always do," Derek answered and started climbing. "You, too," he added over his shoulder.

No problem. I adored Kate, and Derek's stepmother, Cora, who it seemed would be there. "I'm sure we will."

We worked in silence awhile longer, until the basement

was as close to empty as we could get it. "I'll take the bike upstairs," Derek said, rolling it—on flat tires—over to the bottom of the stairs.

"Do you need help?"

He shook his head. "Easier for one person to carry a bike than for two. Why don't you go grab the baby carriage and pull it over here, and when I get back, we'll carry it up together. That's going to take both of us."

I nodded and watched him wrestle the heavy bike up the stairs. It looked like it might be from the 1950s or '60s, maybe, and they built well in those days. No fiberglass frames back then. "Don't put it in the Dumpster," I called after him.

He peered back down at me. "Why not?"

"I'm not sure John saw it. He might be interested. It's his time period."

"I'll put it in the back of the truck," Derek said. "If he doesn't want it, we'll just take it back over here and put it in the Dumpster."

"He'll want it."

Derek shrugged. "Get the carriage."

He wheeled the bike out of sight. As I headed into the gloom to where the baby carriage was tucked into the corner of the basement, I could hear his footsteps and the scraping of the bike's wheels up above my head.

The baby carriage looked to be even older than the bike. From the 1940s, maybe even 1930s. Big and—from what I could make out—gray, although admittedly, it was a little hard to see down here in the corner. Besides, the thing was festooned with so many cobwebs the color could have been anything. Gray, faded black, maybe even blue. Or speckled.

It had a heavy metal frame anyway and four big, solid wheels. The metal was cold against my hands when I grabbed the handlebar and pulled, to get it out of the corner before turning around and heading toward the bottom of the stairs.

The carriage responded sluggishly, the wheels not turning at all. I tried again, but nothing happened.

Maybe there was a brake somewhere?

I inspected the handlebar, but couldn't find one. Next I bent to look at the wheels, and there it was. A little metal contraption with a pedal that either lay flat beside, or poked between the spokes of, the wheel.

I fiddled with it, and after some experimentation, figured out how to move it. Once I saw how, it wasn't complicated.

The carriage rolled back, and I tilted it up on two wheels to change direction toward the bottom of the stairs. As I did it, the sunshade flopped down. I guess the mechanism created to keep it aloft had gotten soft with time.

It hit my thighs, and I squealed. But not because it hurt; because there was a baby lying in the carriage, gleaming palely in the low light.

—3—

By the time Derek had rattled down the stairs to my rescue, his face worried, I was bent over, gasping for breath.

"Avery?" He put a hand on my back and bent, too. "Are you all right?"

"Fine," I managed, laughing so hard I could barely speak, in mingled relief and hysteria.

"What's wrong?"

"Nothing." I waved him away and straightened with a little difficulty. "Scared myself half to death."

"Why?" He dropped his hand from my back and looked around.

I gestured. "Baby. Thought it was real."

He peered into the carriage and got a funny look on his face. "Whoa."

I nodded, wiping tears from my eyes. "I know. The sunshade fell back, and I looked down on the top of its head, and for a second I thought, 'Baby!'" I wiped the backs of my hands against my jeans to dry them. "It was only a second or two before I saw that it was just a doll, but by then I'd already yelled."

"You scared me half to death," my husband informed me. "I thought something was wrong."

"I'm sorry." I took a step closer to him, and he put an arm around my shoulders and tugged me close to his body. I leaned my cheek against his chest and felt the warmth of his skin through the wool sweater he had on and listened to the steady beat of his heart against my ear until I'd gotten my breath back and could step away again.

He looked down at me, his eyes bright blue even in the gloom. "You OK now?"

I nodded. "Fine. Let's just get this done and get out of here."

"Sure." But he didn't move, and his eyes took on a faraway look.

"Something wrong?" I asked.

He put a finger to my lips. I listened, and after a second I heard it, too. The creak of the front door upstairs, and footsteps on the floor.

I waited for someone to call out. Waterfield was a small town, where a lot of doors stayed open a lot of the time—ours certainly did right now, since we'd been going in and out with junk—and it wasn't unlikely that someone we knew should stop by to see how we were getting along. He or she would normally have called our names when we weren't readily visible, though.

No one called out. The footsteps walked around, slowly and deliberately, into what sounded like the bedroom and bath, before coming back around to the dining room and kitchen.

Derek made to move away from me, toward the bottom of the stairs. I held on. When he glanced at me, I shook my head vigorously.

"I wanna go upstairs."

"Could be dangerous," I whispered.

"Don't be ridiculous," my husband informed me, but he stayed where he was.

Eventually, a head appeared in the doorway. "Hello?"

"Brandon," I said, and had to take a breath before I could continue, "dammit. You scared me."

Derek chuckled.

"I didn't mean to," Brandon said apologetically.

Brandon Thomas was one of Wayne's deputies, and also the Waterfield PD's forensic expert when one was needed. He and I had gotten to know each other quite well during my first few weeks in Waterfield last year, since someone was bound and determined to chase me out of town. He was in his early twenties with a blond buzz cut, bright blue eyes, and all-American good looks. He'd been a quarterback in high school, and that was still obvious. After school he'd wanted to go away to law school, but then he'd found out his mother, Phoebe, had multiple sclerosis, so he'd chosen to stay in Waterfield and take a job with the police instead. He was a nice young man, and a good cop. And because he was dating a canine handler who worked for the state police in Augusta, Wayne lived in fear that someone would steal him away.

"What's going on?" I asked.

Brandon reached up and rubbed the back of his head. His hair probably felt like a soft bristle brush when he did that. "I'm looking for someone."

"One of us?"

He shook his head.

"Who?" I asked at the same time as Derek said, "Who else did you think would be here?"

"Mary Green," Brandon said.

It took a second. "Who?"

Derek caught on before I did. Or maybe he knew Mamie's birth name while I didn't. "What makes you think she's here?"

"She wanders off from the nursing home," Brandon said. "They take Ruth away for physical therapy or something, and Mamie gets confused and wanders off."

"But why would she come here?"

"Because it's the only home she's ever had," Brandon said patiently. "She lived in this house for more than seventy years. She's lived in the nursing home for three months. It's no wonder she gets a little turned around."

"We haven't seen her," I told him.

"You were down here. Any chance she could have snuck in when you weren't looking?"

Derek shook his head. "We've been in and out hauling junk. And we heard you come in. I think we would have heard her, too. But you're welcome to look around."

"I already did," Brandon said. "Guess I'll just have to keep driving around."

He turned to walk away, and Derek said, "Hang on a second."

Brandon turned back. "What?"

"Since you're here, help me carry this baby pram upstairs. It's heavy."

Brandon shrugged and headed down the stairs. I took the baby doll out of the carriage and watched the two of them wrestle the heavy vehicle up the stairs. When they reached the top, I followed, absently cradling the doll.

Upstairs, I turned the basement light out and closed and locked the door, before following Derek out of the house. He was wheeling the baby carriage across the hardwood floors to the front door, and bumping over the threshold. I pulled the door shut behind me on the way through.

Derek stopped before he got to the Dumpster, and looked at me across his shoulder. "You think John will be interested in the carriage, too?"

I bit my lip. "It's a little before his period, I think. And it's in pretty bad shape. Although it seems a shame to throw it out . . ."

Derek nodded. "How about we just leave it here"—he parked it beside the porch, behind a spindly and leafless bush—"until tomorrow, and decide then. They won't be picking up the Dumpster for a few days anyway."

"Sure." I dumped the naked baby—doll—into the carriage, more gently perhaps than necessary, and turned to Brandon while Derek went back up on the porch to lock the front door. "I hope you find Mamie soon. I don't like the idea of her wandering around in the cold and dark."

Brandon nodded. "Give me a call if you see her. You know what she looks like, right?"

"I've seen her a few times since I moved here. And she isn't someone you forget."

"True," Brandon said, grinning. "When I was a kid, she used to push that thing"—he gestured to the baby carriage—"around town when the weather was good. Not sure whether she thought she had a real baby or she just never grew past playing with dolls."

I didn't know, either, but either way, it spoke of someone out of touch with reality. Someone who had no business wandering around Waterfield in the cold and dark of December. "Let me know if you need me to drive around and look for her. She could die out here in the cold."

"Let's hope it doesn't come to that," Brandon said and headed for his car.

I turned to Derek. "What are you and your dad doing tonight? Do you have plans?"

He shook his head. "Just to hang out at the house. Watch TV. Talk. You don't have to feed me. Cora made lasagna."

"Yum," I said. "Maybe I'll come with you."

He shook his head. "No, you won't. You'll drop me off, pick up Cora, drive to Kate's, and come back for me. No lasagna for you."

I pouted. "Fine. Be a hog."

"Don't mind if I do," Derek said, patting his wonderfully flat stomach. "You won't starve, Avery. Kate'll feed you."

She would. "We should get home and get changed. I can't go to Kate's looking like this."

Derek shook his head. "If we hurry, maybe we can squeeze in a bit of exercise, too."

Maybe so. I smiled as I let him give me a boost up into the cab of the truck.

. . .

Kate lived in a gorgeous Queen Anne Victorian a few blocks from Aunt Inga's house—and for that matter from the Green sisters' house—in Waterfield Village. When she bought it some seven or eight years ago, it had been divided up into apartments, with crappy rental bathrooms and rental kitchens. Kate and Derek had spent the best part of a year—and all of Kate's savings—turning it back into a single-family home fit for use as a bed and breakfast.

The Waterfield Inn had taken my breath away when I'd stayed in it on my first night in town, and although I'd seen it a hundred times since, when I walked in that evening and saw it decked out in all its Christmas finery, it did it again. Kate had gone easy on the decorating last year—busy with the upcoming nuptials on New Year's Eve—and this was the first year I'd seen it in all its glory. The Victorians did tend to go a bit overboard, or at least it seems that way to our modern, more simplistic tastes, so the Waterfield Inn looked just a bit as if a stage production of Dickens's *A Christmas Carol* had exploded in the foyer. There were pine garlands, gold rope with tassels, and burgundy ribbons draping the staircase to the second floor, and the fireplace mantel was groaning under armfuls of pine boughs decorated with gold-sprayed pinecones and gold cherubs. Fat burgundy pillar candles were interspersed throughout—groupings of them, arranged on top of what must be boxes, since they were of different heights—and so were big, fat burgundy silk roses.

A grouping of carolers in Victorian garb, three or so feet tall, stood beside the fireplace, mouths open and songbooks in their hands.

And then there was the tree: a Frasier fir fully twelve feet tall, with an angel on top, decorated with ribbons and strings of pearls, more silk roses (in burgundy, pink, and off-white), and golden pinecones. And lights, lots and lots of lights.

It was overwhelming, to say the least, and I just stood on the mat, openmouthed, while Cora came in behind me and pushed the door closed.

I turned to her. "Wow."

She nodded, shrugging out of her coat. "Lovely, isn't it?"

I started removing my own, still gawking at everything. "Nobody else has a chance of competing with this. Kate's may as well be the only house on the Christmas Tour."

"It's not a competition," Cora said. "It's an opportunity to let visitors see several of our historic homes. Not just this one." She reached for my down coat.

I gave it to her and watched her lay it, along with her own, on a velvet settee by the wall. "I know that. But I don't want anyone walking into my house and thinking, 'Well, this can't compare.'"

"Of course not," Cora said calmly. "But that won't happen, Avery. You have wonderful taste. Your home will look lovely. As lovely as this, but different."

Different, for sure. Walking in here was like getting slapped across the face by Old Saint Nicholas. Overwhelming. And not just because I was having feelings of inferiority, but because there was so much of it. Christmas, Christmas everywhere, and not a drop to drink.

"I need alcohol," I said.

"I'm sure Kate has some." Cora took me by the arm and led me toward the hallway to the rest of the house. The meeting was to take place in the kitchen, since the rest of the house was decorated to within an inch of its life. From the buzz of voices, it was already under way, or at least close to commencing. I had surmised as much from the number of cars lining the curb.

(Yes, Derek and I had fit in a bit of exercise before heading out, and as a result, Cora and I were running a few minutes late.)

Walking into the dining room was like déjà vu all over again. Christmas stuff everywhere. There was a mantel in here, too, decorated with greenery, candles, and bird's nests. Fat, feathered birds sat in them. Fake, I assume, since I doubt Kate would decorate her house with real stuffed birds for Christmas. The Victorians may have done so, but we've progressed some since then. Their little black eyes felt like they were following me around the room.

The heavy sideboard was likewise decorated with greenery, candles, and gilded fruit. I'm sure that wasn't real, either—or at least I hope not—but it looked gorgeous. And the dining room table was set with china and silverware on a damask tablecloth, in the middle of which sat the biggest centerpiece I'd ever seen in my life: an urn filled with a tower of gilded fruits and a pineapple perched precariously on top, reminiscent of Carmen Miranda's headdress. The whole thing must have been four feet tall; almost big enough to brush the chandelier above the table.

"Gah!" I said, imagining my own dining room. Compared to this, it looked positively bare.

"Come along, Avery." Cora tugged on my arm and we passed through the dining room into the kitchen beyond.

Kate's kitchen was beautiful, and not Victorian at all. Updated with new cabinets and granite counters and stainless steel appliances. Everything I had wanted when I started renovating Aunt Inga's house. Instead I'd gotten Derek, who refused to allow me to discard Aunt Inga's cabinets from the 1930s. I'd told him at the time that they looked like they were made out of driftwood. It wasn't quite that bad, although they weren't what I wanted at all. I'd come around to his way of thinking over the past year, though. I love my vintage kitchen, old cabinets and all. But it didn't mean I couldn't appreciate the modern efficiency of Kate's.

I also appreciated how there were no Victorian Christmas decorations in here. Not a one, unless you counted the three-tier dessert stand on the counter: amber and heavily cut, halfway filled with gilded fruits and frosted pinecones. A decoration in progress.

The room was full of women. In addition to Kate, Cora, and myself, I recognized Kate's daughter, Shannon, a student at local Barnham College, sitting at the table talking to an old lady with gray hair and an uncompromising demeanor. Her name was Edith Barnes, and she was Derek's old history teacher, as well as the librarian at the Waterfield Historical Society, which happened to be located in the historic Fraser House. I'd seen rather a lot of Miss Barnes during my time in Waterfield, since I'd spent considerable time researching the various houses we'd worked on.

The two of them couldn't have looked any more different if they tried. Miss Barnes was the classic old maid: tall, scrawny, and dragon-like, in a twinset and pearls. Shannon was twenty-one and stunning, with her mother's height and centerfold figure, but without the freckles and with hair the color of black cherries.

Of the other women seated around the table, I only recognized one: Judy Norton, the wife of Derek's old buddy Bartholomew Norton, who also happened to be the reverend at the local church. She looked up and smiled when we came in.

"Hi, Cora. Avery."

I smiled back and found a chair across the table from her. "Good to see you, Judy."

She was eight or ten years older than me, a few years older than her husband, and a few inches taller, as well. Not that she's oversized or anything, but Barry was hardly bigger than me.

"Do you know Henrietta?" She gestured to the lady on her left, another septuagenarian by the looks of it, but a lot frailer than Edith Barnes.

"I don't." I smiled at her. "I'm Avery Baker . . . Ellis."

Judy chuckled at my hesitation. "Not used to it yet?"

Not quite. "It's only been a couple months. And I don't have occasion to introduce myself a lot."

To Henrietta, I added sheepishly, "I got married in October."

"Congratulations."

"Thank you." A lady of few words, it seemed. "So where do you live, Henrietta?"

The question wasn't as rude as it may have seemed, since I assumed we were all here because our houses were to be part of the home tour.

"Cabot Street," Henrietta said.

"Like Cora."

She nodded.

"In one of the Victorians?" Cabot Street—like a lot of Waterfield Village—was Victorian. Aunt Inga's house, Kate's house, Cora and Dr. Ben's house.

"No, it's an Arts and Crafts bungalow," Henrietta said.

"My husband and I are renovating one of those right now. On North Street. The Green sisters' house."

Her face tightened. I waited for her to say something, but when she didn't, Judy cut in. "And this is Kerri."

Kerri sat on Judy's other side: a woman a few years older than Judy, with a shock of red hair. Not the soft copper of Kate's curls, or the deep dark cherry of Shannon's, but a red nature never intended, at least not for hair. Currants, maybe. Or poppies. Ripe tomatoes.

"Nice to meet you," I said politely. "Avery Ellis."

It was easier this time, since I'd just done it.

Kerri grinned. She was a lot friendlier than Henrietta, I'll say that for her. Her voice was deep, a husky contralto, and a little hoarse. Maybe she smoked. "The pleasure's all mine. I live on North Street. I've seen you coming and going the last few days."

"We started working on the house yesterday. Just tearing out so far, but by the end of the week, we'll be ready to start putting in new stuff. Which house is yours?"

Kerri chuckled. "The ugly one."

The . . .

And then it dawned on me. "The infill?"

At some point, a house on North Street in the Village must have met with some sort of accident. A fire maybe? I had no idea really; all I knew was that there was no reason why there would be an empty lot in the middle of the block, if there hadn't at one time been a house on it, one that wasn't there anymore.

This was back a few decades, mind you. Long before my time. But it was the only way I could conceive of why there would be a classic 1960s split-level Brady Bunch–type house in the middle of a neighborhood of Victorians and Craftsman cottages. The house that was originally there must have burned, or maybe just been torn down, prior to the Village's designation as protected, and someone had erected a split-level ranch.

"It isn't ugly," I protested. "You keep it looking pretty." As nice as it could, surrounded by the older, admittedly more attractive architecture. It wasn't the house's fault that it couldn't possibly compete. "The landscaping is nice. And I noticed you've decorated the outside for Christmas."

Kerri nodded. "The inside, too. And it isn't really ugly, I guess. It just looks out of place."

No arguing with that.

She added, "Where do you live, Avery?"

"On Bayberry," I told her. "The top of the hill. I inherited my aunt Inga's house a year and a half ago."

"Of course. The pretty blue Victorian."

"Yup." Although it hadn't always been pretty—not before Derek got his hands on it.

"Are you putting the rectory on the tour?" I asked Judy, who nodded.

"The church is always part of the tour, but this is the first time we're including the rectory. The library will be open, too, along with several of the shops and restaurants on Main Street."

I had assumed as much, since the Christmas Home Tour wasn't just a way to make money for the Village neighborhood association; it was a way for the merchants to make a little extra, too, in sales of hot chocolate and handmade soaps and such. And the Waterfield Library was one of the original Carnegie libraries. Businessman Andrew Carnegie donated money to its construction, as well as to the construction of another thirty-five hundred or so libraries across the United States and the world. It was very beautiful, as well as being a national landmark. Many of the Carnegie libraries had been torn down over the years, but the Waterfield branch was one that had survived.

And then Kate cleared her throat, and the buzz of voices quieted as we turned to her and prepared to get to work.

— 4 —

The meeting was short and painless—and included pizza from Guido's. Josh arrived a few minutes after Cora and I did, with the food and drinks.

We all chomped down, and the discussion started. Mostly it was Kate wanting to get her feet under her after having the home tour dumped in her lap at the last minute, and to get everyone up to speed on what to expect, since several of us were new this year.

"Expect a couple hundred people," Kate said between bites of bacon and scallion with sour cream dressing. "You'll have to feed them something—"

"Feed them?" I blurted. We were expected to feed a couple hundred people?

Don't get me wrong, I manage to feed Derek and myself, but I'm no chef. And I don't do big parties.

"Nothing fancy," Kate hastened to assure me. *Easy for her to say*, I thought. "Just cookies or some kind of little nibble."

Cookies for two hundred–plus people was no little nibble, not if you asked me, but I nodded as if I had no problem with it. All around me, everyone else nodded, too. I wondered how many of them felt the same way I did, but were just better at hiding it.

"You can offer drinks, too," Kate continued, "if you want, but in the past, I've found that when you give people something to drink, they spill, so I prefer not to. In the summer, bottles of water are nice, of course, but cups of coffee and hot chocolate leave too much room for accidents."

Everyone nodded again. I tried to imagine a wandering guest stumbling on the fringe of the Persian carpet in the parlor and spilling a cup of cocoa on Aunt Inga's reuphol-stered love seat—dove gray velvet—and shuddered.

"Lock away your valuables," Kate went on. "Keys, money, credit cards. Bank statements. Prescription drugs. There's no telling who might come through your door, and you can't keep an eye on them all at the same time."

I raised my hand. "Do we have to keep our whole houses open, or just a few rooms?"

"In your case," Kate said, since she obviously knew my house well, "the downstairs will do. Hang a rope on the staircase with a piece of paper, and write 'Private' on it. That should keep people from going upstairs. Move any-thing valuable up there."

Most of my valuables were upstairs anyway. Jewelry in the box by my bedside, and the cough syrup in the bath-room cabinet.

"The tour starts at noon," Kate said. "Prepare to stay home with a run on the door until after four o'clock. There are always a few stragglers."

No problem.

"You won't have to deal with money. People who want to go on the home tour can purchase tickets online, at the library, at the Fraser House, or at the church. When they get to you, they should already have paid, and they should have a hand stamp saying as much."

Good to know.

"Any questions?"

I had a lot, and so did other people. After a while, the meeting dissolved into chatter, and I addressed Kate. "Where's Wayne tonight?"

She swallowed. "Working."

"Anything interesting going on?"

"Nothing you'd consider interesting," Kate said. "No murders or anything."

"I don't find murders interesting." Not particularly. "I can't help it that so many people have dropped dead in Waterfield in the time I've been here."

"You could help getting involved," Kate said, and relented. "It's the robbery season. Purse snatchings and people getting carjacked in mall parking lots."

"And Baby Jesuses going missing."

"That happens every year," Judy interjected. "It usually comes back after a few days."

"Is it back now?"

Judy had to admit it wasn't.

"How long has it been?" Two days, at least, since Kate had told us.

"Five days," Judy said reluctantly.

"Is that longer than usual?"

It was. But—"It's probably just someone having fun, Avery," Judy said. "Teenagers or something."

Maybe. I turned to Josh and Shannon, who had both grown up in Waterfield. "Did you ever steal the Baby Jesus from the manger?"

"No," Josh said, looking offended. He's a lanky guy, almost six and a half feet tall, with glasses and his father's dark curly hair. He does offended quite well. "My dad's the chief of police, Avery. You really think I don't know better than that? He'd ground me for a year."

Shannon grinned but shook her head. "Me, either. And I haven't heard of anyone else who did."

"It isn't some kind of high school tradition? Or a college dare or something?"

"Not at Barnham," Josh said. "And not at the high school, either."

"It's been going on a very long time," Judy added. "Since before Barry took over. It's just one of those endearing quirks you put up with." She smiled.

"Just as long as the baby comes back again."

"It always has before." She didn't sound worried, and if she wasn't, I probably shouldn't be, either. Even if the baby had been missing for longer this time than ever before.

The meeting broke up shortly after that, and Cora and I headed out to the car. I drive a spring green VW Beetle that my mother and stepfather had given me for Christmas last year. I'd had a license when I lived in Manhattan, but driving hadn't ever figured large in my life, since the city is all about subways and taxis. Over the last year, I'd been surprised at how much I enjoyed driving around in my zippy little Bug.

I wedged behind the wheel and Cora climbed in beside me, and we took off. Zipping around the corner. Zipping around the next.

"How is the work on the Green sisters' house coming?" Cora asked, hanging on to the edges of the seat.

I smiled. "It's coming. We've finished cleaning out the junk. You won't believe the kind of stuff we found. Old Christmas decorations, a bicycle, skis, snowshoes, an old baby carriage with a doll in it . . ." I slowed down for a stop sign—California rolling stop—and took off again as we neared the Green sisters' block. "We can stop and go inside if you want."

"It's a little late," Cora said diplomatically. "And cold."

And she wanted to get home. I couldn't blame her. I was looking forward to seeing Derek, too.

"That's fine." But the house was coming up, and I pulled up to the curb to peer at it as we got there.

It looked just the way it should. Big and imposing and dark, like a black void against the night. Derek didn't trust the electrical wiring, so we hadn't left any lights on, not even on the porch. Didn't want to come back and find a charred mess tomorrow morning.

"It's big," Cora remarked.

"Not as big as the house on Rowanberry Island."

The rambling center-chimney Colonial from 1783 had seemed to go on for days. But the Green sisters' house was certainly a lot bigger than the other two projects we'd done since then: the small condo in Josh Rasmussen's building and the even smaller 1930s cottage in the Village that used to belong to news anchor Tony "the Tiger" Micelli—until he was stabbed to death with a screwdriver in the kitchen.

"Did you leave a light on upstairs?" Cora asked, and I returned to the present, pushing the mental image of Tony and the pool of blood aside to peer up at the house.

"No. Why?"

"I thought I saw one."

I looked again, staring at the three side-by-side windows in the dormer in the front of the house. They were dark, just as they should be. "I don't see anything."

Cora shook her head. "Maybe it was the reflection of a pair of headlights up on the hill. Or a reflection from the house across the street."

Maybe. I looked to the left, at the farmhouse Victorian located there. One story tall. No second-story windows.

"I must have made a mistake," Cora said, still staring at the bungalow. "There's nothing there."

No. Although now that she'd suggested it, I was loath to leave without making sure. Even if I was equally loath to leave the car to investigate.

Cora glanced at me. "There's nothing there, Avery. I made a mistake."

"Right. It's just . . ." What if she hadn't? What if someone was inside the house?

"Why would anyone break into an empty house?"

"People do sometimes," I said. "To steal the tools. And the copper pipes." Or so Derek had told me.

"Are there any copper pipes in the house? Or any tools?"

Well . . . no. We hadn't needed tools yet. So far it had all been about hauling junk to the Dumpster. Taking stuff out of the house, not putting anything in. There were no pipes, either, for the same reason.

I shook my head.

"I really think I made a mistake, Avery," Cora said. "It was just a trick of the light. Let's go home. If you want to come back, you can take Derek with you."

That made sense. He had the key, anyway. And I'd rather have Derek next to me than Cora when exploring a creepy old house in the dark.

I put the car back into gear and rolled away from the house, with a last look past Cora and out the passenger side window. There was nothing to see. All the windows were dark. The front door was closed. There were no sinister shadows skulking around the corner. Nothing was stirring. As she'd said, she must have made a mistake.

In contrast, the small green Folk Victorian on Cabot where Cora and Dr. Ben lived was cheerfully blazing with lights. And with sound, we realized when we walked in. It wasn't just Derek and his father in residence; I could also hear the television, as well as the voices of Beatrice, Cora's second daughter—her first is Alice, who lives in Boston—and Bea's husband, Steve.

"Is so!" Steve said.

"No, it isn't!"

"Yes, it is. And if you'll give me a minute, I'll prove it to you."

There was silence apart from the TV, then a groan from Beatrice and a crow of triumph from Steve.

"Scrabble," Cora said, hanging up her coat.

I nodded, keeping mine on. "Wonder which word he spelled?"

" 'Syzygy,' " Derek said when I asked.

"Bless you."

"That's the word. 'Syzygy.' " He spelled it, and added, "It means a conjunction of three astronomical objects."

I stared at him.

"Also a metrical unit of two feet," Steve added. "In poetry."

I stared at Steve. And then at Derek again. "How do you know this stuff?"

"Just because I'm a handyman . . ." Derek began, and I rolled my eyes.

"You didn't become a handyman until you'd been a doctor for a few years first. It's not like you're uneducated. But I still don't see how you'd know about the conjunctions of astronomical objects." Or poetry. "It isn't something you'd learn about in medical school."

"I grew up playing Scrabble," Derek said. "Of course, he had to use a blank for the third Y. There are only two." He looked me up and down. "Why do you have your coat on?"

"I just came in."

"Cora's taken hers off."

She had, and sat down next to her husband on the sofa.

"We thought we saw a light in the house on North Street when we drove past," I said. "I thought maybe you'd want to come with me to check it out."

"A light?"

"It was probably a mistake," Cora said, settling into the sofa next to Dr. Ben. "A reflection of headlights from the hill. Or a reflection of light from the house across the street."

"The house across the street is only one story tall. It wouldn't reflect into the second-story windows."

My husband looked at me, and then at Cora. "You didn't stop and check?"

She shook her head.

"It's late," I said. "And dark. And Cora wanted to get home. And besides, you have the only key."

He nodded and got to his feet. "I was losing anyway. It's hard to compete with words like 'syzygy.' Say good night, Avery."

"Good night, Avery," I said, and followed him into the foyer.

"I'm proud of you," he told me a couple minutes later, when we were in the car and on our way back to North Street.

I glanced across at him for a second. "You are? Why?"

"You could have run inside the house and gotten yourself killed. But you didn't. You came and got me instead."

Right. Um . . . "I probably would have gone inside," I admitted, "if I'd had the key, and if Cora had been willing to go with me. But she insisted that she'd made a mistake and she wanted me to take her home, so I did. I'd rather go sleuthing with you anyway."

"Flattered," Derek said and opened the glove box. "Is there a flashlight in here?"

"Should be." I risked a glance in that direction as he rummaged, but I didn't want to take my eyes off the road any longer than I had to.

"Got it." He pulled it out and flicked it on. Nothing happened. "Out of batteries," Derek said, disgusted.

"We can use my cell phone instead. I have a flashlight app."

"That'll work." He returned the useless flashlight to the glove box and leaned back in the seat, folding his arms across his chest. "Remind me to get you new batteries. I don't want my wife driving around with a nonfunctioning flashlight."

"Flashlight app," I reminded him.

"Not the same thing."

Maybe not, but we had reached the house now, and the time to argue was over. I pulled up to the curb and cut the engine. Derek peered out the window. "I don't see anything."

"I didn't, either. There probably wasn't anything there. But Cora said she saw a light, and it couldn't have been a reflection from the house across the street."

Derek glanced at it. "No."

"I'm sure there's no one there at all. But just in case she wasn't wrong . . ."

"May as well take a look." Derek nodded and unlocked his door. Before he swung his legs out, he opened the glove box again and palmed the flashlight.

"I thought it didn't work."

"It's not for lighting our way," Derek said. "We have your cell phone for that. This is for protection."

Wonderful. Yet another reason to hope we'd find no one

in the house. Or my husband would be hauled off to jail for assault with a deadly flashlight.

. . .

The front door opened with that long, drawn-out shriek of rusty hinges familiar from scary movies. I hadn't really noticed it during the day—possibly because the door had been standing open most of the time—but now it sent a chill down my spine.

We stepped through and stopped to listen. Nothing moved within the living room. Nothing moved anywhere, as far as I could hear. All I could hear was Derek's steady breathing and my own heartbeat thundering in my ears.

"So far, so good." His voice was more breath than actual words, and tickled the flyaway hair near my temple. I jumped. He chuckled. "C'mon."

He moved farther into the room, old floorboards creaking under his feet. I followed, tiptoeing and holding my breath.

It was amazing that this was the same house we'd spent most of the past two days in. Other than a few exceptions—like scaring myself half to death finding the doll, and Brandon scaring us both half to death wandering around over our heads—I hadn't been aware of a sense of discomfort. It was just an old house with no particular vibe to it. Not particularly happy, but not particularly sad, either. Now, however, with the darkness bearing down on us, only able to see as far as the weak light from the cell phone illuminated, it felt like a different house. Silent, sinister, full of secrets.

There was nobody on the first floor, and no sign that anyone had been here, either. There were footprints and scuffmarks all across the floors, of course, and tracks from where Derek had pushed the baby carriage, but with as much coming and going as we'd done today and yesterday, there was no way to tell whether any of the footsteps belonged to anyone else. Certainly not in the dark.

And anyway, the light Cora had claimed to have seen—and then claimed not to have seen—had been upstairs.

I crept up the stairs in Derek's wake, keeping to the outside of the steps, where it was less likely that the wood would creak.

Craftsman bungalows could be one story, but more often they were one and a half: a first floor that looked just like any other house, and a second floor tucked under the eaves with sloping ceilings and dormers in front and back.

We went into the bathroom first, since the door stood open. There was no one in there. I hadn't expected anyone, but it was still a relief.

Derek pushed open the door on the right next, and shone the dim light of the phone into one of the bedrooms the Green girls must have used when they were small. Ten by ten or so, with heart of pine floors—not as upscale as the oak floors downstairs—and with sloping ceilings and knee walls.

"Empty," he said, flashing the right around.

"What about the closet?"

"I don't think anyone's hiding in the closet," Derek said, but he crossed the floor and yanked open the door anyway. When he jumped back, my heart jumped, too, and my voice reached up into the soprano register.

"What is it?"

He turned to me and grinned, the light from the flashlight shining up into his face giving him a sort of demonic look. "Nothing."

"That's mean."

"Maybe I was hoping for you to throw yourself into my arms," Derek said with a waggle of eyebrows. "All we need is a few thunderclaps to complete the scary-movie feel."

"I can do without the thunderclaps," I told him, but I threw myself into his arms anyway. Or not threw exactly, but I walked over to him and let him put an arm around me. When that was done, I peered into the closet. It was empty, save for a row of skeletal wire hangers on a rod.

"Let's get outta here," Derek said and pulled me toward the door. "Get home and to bed."

Fine with me. "Just one room to go." I preceded him out

onto the landing and stopped. "Have you been up here today?"

"No," Derek said.

"Do you remember closing the door?"

He shook his head. "But Brandon was wandering around. He may have done it."

"I don't think he went upstairs, did he?" I eyed the door apprehensively.

The thing about closed doors is you never know what might be behind them. Not so with open ones.

But I wanted to get home and to bed, too, so I followed Derek across the landing and waited while he turned the knob and pushed the door open. And when he jumped, I told him, "Very funny."

"No," Derek said.

No?

I peered over his shoulder and jumped, too.

—5—

For a moment, I lost my breath, and not in a good the-Waterfield-Inn-is-gorgeous sort of way.

I'm not particularly superstitious, but for a moment I could swear I was looking at a ghost: a little girl curled up on the floor, her blouse gleaming blue-white in the light from the cell phone, with two long braids wound like ropes around her throat and a doll clutched to her chest.

Then I realized what I was looking at.

"It's Mamie Green."

Derek nodded. "Brandon was right. She did come back here."

"He must be frantic." It had been four or five hours since he'd been here looking for her. If she'd been missing this whole time, Brandon—and her sister, not to mention the staff at the nursing home; the staff that had lost her—must be going out of their minds with worry.

"Call him," Derek said, handing me my phone. "I'll get her."

I took the phone, but didn't dial. "She's alive, isn't she?"

Derek glanced at me. "I hope so."

He approached carefully. Maybe he was feeling a bit spooked by the whole thing, too, even if he didn't show it.

I waited, phone in my hand, while he squatted next to Mamie and put out a hand. He was careful not to startle her, just held it in front of her face without touching. "Still breathing."

"Good." I started dialing.

"Not warm enough, though." He wrenched out of his coat. "We can't wait for him here. She'll freeze to death." He tucked it around her while I listened to the phone ring on the other end of the line.

When Brandon came on, I told him we'd found Mamie Green, asleep or unconscious, in her old house, and that we would take her back to the nursing home where she lived. "Derek says we shouldn't wait for you. She's too cold and needs to get warm quickly."

"I'll meet you at the nursing home," Brandon said. "Do you know where it is?"

I didn't, and he gave me directions. Meanwhile, Derek gathered Mamie into his arms. She didn't weigh much, she was pretty much just skin and bones from what I could see, nor did she wake up, which couldn't be a good sign. I hung up with Brandon and lighted Derek's way down the stairs and out through the front door over to the car.

"How are we going to do this?"

"I'll drive," Derek said, stopping beside the car so I could open the passenger door for him. "You'll go in the back, if you don't mind. That's easier than trying to fit Mamie in there."

"Shouldn't she be lying down?"

"We'll lower the seat once I get her strapped in." He suited action to words, and loaded Mamie carefully—and awkwardly—into the front seat of the Beetle. It was a bit like maneuvering a life-sized mannequin, one that was still clutching the doll to her chest. Now that I got a good look at it in the car's interior lights, I recognized it from this afternoon: It was the same doll that had given me such a scare in the basement. She must have found it in the carriage and taken it inside with her.

"I guess we'll have to replace the locks," I said with a glance toward the house, "if people still have keys."

"Maybe not," Derek said, leaning across the body—Mamie's body—to fasten the seat belt. "I'd rather have her inside than out. She came close enough to freezing to death as it is. If she hadn't been able to get in—if she'd decided to sleep on the porch—she'd be dead by now."

In that case, maybe we'd better not do anything about it, at least not yet. We'd have to change the locks before we sold the place, though. We couldn't expect the new owners to be as sanguine as we were about uninvited visitors. But that wouldn't be for a few months yet, so maybe by then Mamie would have gotten used to the fact that it wasn't her house anymore.

"I'll go lock up." For all the good that it would do, when there were keys floating around.

Derek nodded, fumbling for the mechanism to lower the seat. "Hurry. I want to get the car started and the heat going."

I hurried, and then scrambled into the backseat so he could drive. The Beetle took off from the curb like a rocket.

The nursing home didn't turn out to be far away at all. And Derek knew where he was going, so he didn't need my directions. Ten minutes later, we pulled in under the portico in front, behind Brandon's police cruiser. By then, the interior of the Beetle was like a sauna, minus the wet branches. Derek had kept the heat cranked to ninety degrees the whole time, as high as the car would allow.

Mamie was still out cold, or asleep, but her skin wasn't as cold and flaccid to the touch. Her death grip on the doll had loosened. When one of the nurses tried to remove it after they'd loaded her onto a gurney, she held on, though.

"Let her keep it," the other nurse advised. "We can always get it away from her later."

They wheeled the gurney into the nursing home. Derek watched as he absently shrugged into his jacket.

"How did you find her?" Brandon asked. "This time of night?"

I told him about driving past the house on my way home

from Kate's meeting, and how Cora had thought she'd seen a light. "I brought Derek back to investigate. Good thing, too, because she might have been dead by morning."

Derek nodded. "If we hadn't found her tonight, she probably would be. Maybe we need to start heating the house overnight."

Maybe so. We hadn't planned to start doing that until we were ready to begin the actual renovations, but if there was a chance that Mamie would be back, it would be safer.

"She'll be all right, won't she?" I asked.

He glanced at me. "She'll be fine. As long as there's nothing else wrong with her. If she just got confused and cold, and wandered in and went to sleep and then went into deeper hypothermia, she'll be fine once they thaw her out. If there's something wrong beyond that, then I'm not sure."

"Can you let us know how it goes?" I asked Brandon.

He nodded. "Of course. I'll stick around awhile, to make sure everything's OK. If anything changes, I'll give you a call."

"Do you want us to stay with you?"

He smiled but shook his head. "That's not necessary. I'll let you know what happens."

"C'mon, Tink," Derek said and put his arm around my shoulder. "See you around, Brandon."

Brandon nodded, and headed over to the seating area in the lobby while Derek and I walked toward the door to the outside.

He didn't call. Not until late the next morning, when we were back at the house, making inroads on filling up the Dumpster. Over the past two days, we'd dragged out all the debris: everything not nailed down. Now it was time to start on the stuff that *was* nailed down, like the unsalvageable kitchen cabinets and the chipped and rusty bathroom sink we were replacing, along with the yards and yards of rusted galvanized plumbing.

When the phone rang, I was balanced on top of the kitchen counter, holding a kitchen cabinet door steady while Derek applied the battery-driven screwdriver to the hinges.

That way he could have both hands free and not have to worry about the door hitting him in the head when he was finished.

When my pocket started vibrating, he put the drill down and fished for my phone. "I got it."

"So I see," I said, hanging on to the cabinet door.

"It's Brandon." He put it on speaker so I could hear.

"I'm just checking in," Brandon's voice told us, tinny through the connection. "Sorry I didn't get back to you last night, but I just spoke to the nursing home. Ms. Green is alive and well. Still in bed for the rest of the day, but probably well enough to get up again tomorrow. And no worse for wear."

Good to know.

"They'll keep a better eye on her after this, won't they?" If she could get up tomorrow, what were the chances that she'd be back here tomorrow night?

"They'd better," Brandon said grimly. He added, "Although it isn't a prison, you know. The residents who are well enough to come and go, can. They're not locked up."

"I guess we'd better keep the heat on from now on," I told Derek, "just in case."

He nodded and addressed Brandon. "Thanks for letting us know. I'm glad nothing worse happened."

"Me, too," Brandon said and rang off.

. . .

By the afternoon, the kitchen cabinets were down and out, along with the kitchen sink and counter. We had left the downstairs bathroom mostly intact apart from the sink—we needed a working toilet while we labored over the house—and moved on to the upstairs bath, the one shared by the two kid bedrooms. Derek busied himself unhooking the plumbing while I wandered around the upstairs trying to get a vision for the space.

It would remain as two bedrooms, it seemed. Derek had been adamant about the master suite being downstairs, and in some ways it made sense. If it were my house and I had kids, I wouldn't want them sleeping downstairs while I was upstairs, either. What if someone tried to break in?

So master suite downstairs, with two kid bedrooms and a bath upstairs.

Or maybe not kid bedrooms exactly; could be guest bedrooms. Mother-in-law bedroom. Or even an office. There was no foyer or parlor in this house. If someone wanted an office, it would have to be up here, or possibly in the nook in the kitchen.

So master suite downstairs, two other rooms upstairs. The bath would have to be kid-friendly, because chances were the house would appeal to people with children, but not so kid-friendly that it would turn anyone else off. Plain white subway tile for the combination tub-shower probably—it goes with everything—and with maybe some accents of pretty glass tiles, just to jazz things up a bit. Nothing too outré, though. Shades of brown and tan probably, to pick up the golden hues of the floors and of the dark woodwork around windows and doors. The Arts and Crafts movement was very much about the use of natural materials like wood and stone.

The bedrooms themselves were plain to the point of being boring. Two square ten-by-ten boxes with heart of pine floors and sloped ceilings, and a set of two windows looking out at the neighbors. There was more ceiling than wall in each room, which meant I could have some fun with color. At the back of each room was a small door in the knee wall, barely big enough for a person to fit through. I'm not very big, but I wasn't sure I'd be able to fit, to be honest.

Still, I was curious, so I got down on my hands and knees on the floor and pulled one of the doors open. Stuck my head through the opening and peered around. Daylight trickled through cracks in the ceiling, where the roof had deteriorated enough in places to let the sunshine in.

The pine floors continued in here, not all the way out to the edges of the eaves, but a few feet, enough to provide room to stack a few cardboard boxes. I dragged them into the room, stuck my head in to make sure I hadn't missed any, and set to investigating.

I had high hopes for something interesting, of course—something secret tucked away in the eaves, out of sight—but it wasn't anything special. One box contained a complete set of china decorated with small pink flowers: cups, saucers, sugar cup, cream pitcher, and teapot—all of it doll-sized, and all of it quite old and in mint condition.

The other box contained doll clothes, hand-knit unless my eyes deceived me: a pale blue romper, small jacket, and little cap suitable for a baby doll like the one that had scared three years off my life yesterday. The doll Mamie had been clutching last night. This was the room we had found her in, so logic dictated that this must have been her room growing up, and these were her doll's clothes. Not her own clothes, I thought; back when Mamie was a girl, they probably didn't dress little girls in blue.

If this was Mamie's room, Ruth's room must be the one across the hall.

Wonder if Ruth had tucked away small treasures behind her knee wall, too?

I wandered out onto the landing and peered into the bathroom. Derek was on his knees wrestling with the plumbing. I stood there for a moment admiring the fit of his jeans and the movement of his arms in the short-sleeved T-shirt . . . and then I tore myself away and headed into the room on the other side of the landing.

It was a mirror image of Mamie's room, only painted a different color. Mamie's room was a pale, fleshy peach; Ruth's was dull green. They were both boring as dirt. When it was my turn to paint, I might go with some nice warm goldenrod or something, to bring out the beauty of the dark wood.

There was an access door in the wall here, too, leading into the same sort of narrow little space as on Mamie's side of the staircase. I stuck my head in and peered around.

Pine floors, old insulation in the gaps, and another

cardboard box, this one flat and long. I dragged it into the room and dusted it off, sneezing. A fancy chocolates box. Hopefully there'd be something other than chocolates inside.

There was, but it wasn't all that exciting. Newspaper clippings about Elvis Presley. At the beginning of his career, from what I could make out from the dates and the way The King looked in the pictures.

Elvis was much before my time, of course, but I've heard the stories. Here they were in black-and-white: swooning crowds, cops in riot gear, mayhem never seen before or since. Or maybe since, over the Beatles. That was also before my time, so I'm not sure.

At any rate, Ruth Green must have been a fan. She might have been . . . I calculated. If she was in her midseventies now, maybe she'd been fifteen or sixteen when the King began his career in what I thought was the midfifties?

Whatever. The stuff was interesting but probably not worth anything to anyone. If the newspapers or magazines had been intact, maybe they'd be worth a few dollars—but they weren't. They were just clippings. Interesting as a cultural artifact of the time, I guess, but nothing more.

I put the lid back on the box and stuck my head back into the storage space, turning it back and forth. Best as I could tell, the space was empty.

"I found a few things," I told Derek from the doorway of the bathroom.

"What kinds of things?"

I told him. "I guess Ruth and Mamie must have put their special stuff there when they were girls."

"Guess so." He grunted as he wrestled with the plumbing.

"Do you need help?"

"No," Derek said. After a moment he added, "Is it lunchtime yet?"

"Are you hungry?"

"Always." He yanked on the wrench and swore when it slipped. And shot me a glance over his shoulder, a quick flicker of blue eyes. "I just thought I'd give you something to do."

"Are you trying to get rid of me?" That wasn't very nice.

He sat back on his heels. "No, Tink. But it must be boring for you, standing around watching me work."

I grinned. "I wouldn't say that."

He grinned back. "You can appreciate properly later. Don't you have something to do?"

"I'm doing something. I'm looking at stuff and coming up with a plan for how to make it look pretty once you're done doing the boring grunt work."

"Oh," Derek said. "Don't let me stop you, then."

"You're not. I'm thinking white subway tile for the tub and shower surround. Nice and clean and classic, with some brown glass tiles for accents."

He glanced at the tub and shower the way it was now: molded plastic. "Sure."

"Brown tiles on the floor maybe, to match the wood in the rest of the house. Easier to keep clean than white. Although white would look OK, too."

"It sounds great, Avery," Derek said, "but unless I can get this coupling off, you won't have a bathroom to pretty up."

Right. "I'll just find something else to look at while I wait for it to be lunchtime."

"You do that." He turned back to the plumbing.

Very well. I backed out of the bathroom and left him to it.

So far I had investigated both the cubbies in the girls' rooms. There was nothing interesting there. We'd cleaned out the basement, and there was nothing interesting left there anymore, either. The first floor was bare. The second floor was bare. The third . . .

There was no third floor. The second floor was the top, the attic.

Only . . . I looked up, at the flat ceiling above my head. Wandered into Mamie's room and did the same. The ceiling sloped sharply down to the knee wall, which was only three feet tall or so. But above my head, there were a few feet of flat ceiling. The roof came to a point, though, the way roofs do, especially here in the Northeast. A steep pitch makes it easier for the snow to slide off. What you don't want is a flat roof where the snow can accumulate and maybe crash through. It happens, and it isn't pretty.

So there had to be a little space between the flat ceiling and the roof itself.

"Could we vault the ceilings up here?" I asked Derek.

"Vault the . . ." It took him a second to catch up, then he shook his head. "I don't think so."

"There's space up above, isn't there? If we took it out . . ."

"Chances are the ceiling up here is supporting the roof," Derek said, "and if we took it out, we'd have a problem. This house wasn't built to have vaulted ceilings."

Fine. "Can I go look at it anyway?"

"The space upstairs?" He shrugged. "Sure. Knock yourself out."

"How do I get up there?"

"Look for the hatch in the ceiling," Derek said. "And the ladder."

There was a ladder? I hadn't seen anything resembling a ladder up here. "It isn't in the bathroom, right?"

"No," Derek said, "it isn't in the bathroom."

It wasn't in Mamie's room, either. Nor was it in Ruth's. I'd spent enough time in both to have noticed it if it were there. And it wasn't in the hallway.

As a last resort, I pulled open the door to the empty closet at the top of the stairs, cater-corner to the door to Ruth's room, and peered in. And there it was: a white square outlined against the white of the ceiling.

"How do I get up there?"

There was a pause, then Derek materialized beside me. I guess he figured he wouldn't get any peace until I had something to do. This is the boring part of renovating for me: the times when Derek is busy doing plumbing and wiring and framing, the sort of stuff I don't know enough to help him with.

"See those?" He pointed to three wooden blocks nailed to the wall on my right. "That's the ladder."

I tilted my head. "It doesn't look like a ladder."

"It is. Trust me. Here." He grabbed the top block and hung on by his fingertips while he scrabbled for purchase for his toes on the bottom "rung." Once that was done, he used one hand to push the hatch up into the ceiling before jumping down. "There you go. Let me give you a hand."

He grabbed my waist and boosted me up. I did my best to hang on to the blocks of wood on the wall—no way would I dignify them with the title "ladder"—and to move up. It wasn't easy: There was nothing to hang on to really, since the blocks were flush to the wall and only an inch or two thick. I don't think I would have made it all the way up if it hadn't been for Derek's hands on my waist—and occasionally my butt—keeping me steady.

But I did get to the top, and squirmed through the hole into the ceiling. "You want to come, too?"

"No," Derek said. "I want to get back to my coupling."

"We're a couple."

He chuckled. "I stuck my head up there the first time Darren brought us here, and from what I remember, it doesn't look like a place where any coupling should take place."

It didn't, actually. I was kneeling on a rough plank floor, guaranteed to give splinters. Not a romantic setting whatsoever.

"Have fun exploring, Tink. Let me know when you're coming down."

He walked away. I heard the sound of his steps echoing up to me, and then I pulled my head back into the attic and looked around.

In addition to the rough plank floors, there was a rough plank ceiling: the stuff underneath the shingles and decking. The points of long nails stuck through here and there, from the roofers. Like in the cubbies in the bedrooms, the plank floors only went partway to the eaves: Beyond that was old insulation, like cotton batting. There was a lot of dust—decades of it—over everything, and I could see the exposed brick of the chimney where it cut through from the living room fireplace up through the roof. It was visible on the outside of the house, too, but the interior side was visible here.

The plank floor was only about five feet wide, running the width of the house from side to side. There were a few boxes up here, within easy reach of the hole in the floor. I could stay where I was to investigate them, so I did. One contained old china, human-sized this time and carefully packed with newspapers for cushioning. It wasn't particularly nice china, so they had probably replaced it with something newer and prettier, sometime in—I checked the date on one of the newspapers—1947, and had stuffed it up here out of the way.

Several of the boxes were empty—kept for packing purposes maybe, in case whatever had arrived in them needed to be repackaged at some point? I had a few of those myself, up in Aunt Inga's attic. I hadn't brought a lot of stuff with me when I came, though, so although Aunt Inga's attic was filled with stuff, it was mostly her stuff, not mine.

There was nothing else to see really. But it was only a few minutes since Derek had tossed me up here, and he'd probably be annoyed if I called for him to come help me down so soon. So I got up on my hands and knees—there was no way to walk, even bent over—and crawled over to the chimney for a closer look at the mortar. The outside bricks could do with some tuck-pointing, and I knew Derek planned to take care of it. Since I was up here, I might as well take a look and see whether he'd need to crawl up here, too, while he was at it.

The mortar didn't look too bad, although it was a little crumbly in places. Nowhere near as bad as the outside, though. I guess it stayed together better inside, away from wind and rain and snow. Although I was able to pick out loose pieces here and there, when I rubbed my finger across the joints. It might not be a bad idea to get him up here to take a look. He was better at this kind of thing than I was.

I was just about to turn away and crawl back when I noticed, tucked into the shadowy corner of the chimney and the wall, another box.

Not a cardboard one this time. More of a crate. It was made of battered wood, with a board and batten lid—three planks side by side, two across to keep them together—and both crate and lid were printed with a faded logo in red and black. I squinted, but couldn't make it out in the dusk. There were no light fixtures up here, and no illumination other than the faint streaks of sunlight that pushed through the gaps in the ceiling at intervals.

I pulled out my cell phone and turned the flashlight app on the crate. The stamped logo became almost possible to read. "Dr . . . k MOXIE," it said in big letters, and below, in tiny ones, "TR . . E M . RK REG U . PAT OFF."

Moxie Soda. One of the first soft drinks mass-produced in the United States, a hundred and fifty years ago or so, and the official soft drink of Maine. Not as sweet as other sodas, flavored with wintergreen. Definitely an acquired taste. A taste I hadn't seen the need to acquire.

With it being tucked away here out of the way, I thought there was a chance the lid might be nailed down. I was wrong: It came off easily in my hands. At first glance and in the dark, the crate appeared to be empty. It was interesting, though, and probably worth some money to an antique dealer. I'd seen similar crates for sales in the stores on Main Street, for a lot more money than they looked like they should be worth.

I put the lid aside and grabbed my cell phone. Got up on my knees to shine the light into the crate.

And screamed.

—6—

"Avery? What's wrong?"

It took a few seconds, and then Derek was at the closet, his voice worried.

"Need you," I managed through chattering teeth.

He didn't waste time answering, just swarmed up the "ladder" into the attic and crawled toward me. "What is it? What happened? Are you hurt?"

"Crate," I said, pointing to it. I had scrabbled backward about eight feet, and was sitting on my butt, my eyes wide and staring at the crate as if I were afraid the contents were about to rise up and come after me. My pointer finger was shaking.

He looked at me for a second before heading that way on all fours.

"Wait," I managed.

When he turned back, I handed him the phone. "It's hard to see."

He raised his brows but didn't comment. I watched as he made his way over to the crate and shone the light inside. For a second there was nothing, then—"Damn."

Indeed. "It's real, isn't it?"

It would be nice to imagine that it wasn't, but we probably wouldn't be that lucky.

"Looks real." He stuck a hand into the crate, and I held my breath at the faint sound of twigs rustling. Or not twigs exactly, but the sound was the same.

He pulled his hand out and wiped it on his jeans. "Feels real."

"You'd know, wouldn't you?"

He shot me glance. "I should. Not that I've had occasion to see a lot of these. When we did skeletons in medical school, they were adult ones. Not babies. The ones with the usual number of bones."

I glanced at the crate, and at the jumble of tiny bones inside it that I couldn't see from where I was sitting. "Doesn't this one have the usual number of bones?"

"I'm sure it does," Derek said, sitting back on his heels. "At least I don't see any sign that any parts are missing. I'd have to count to be sure. But newborns have more than two hundred and seventy bones. Adult humans only have two hundred and six. They fuse."

I swallowed. "What do we do now?"

"We have to call Wayne," Derek said. "Human remains, no matter how old, always require a visit from the police."

"I'll go call." I turned to the hatch to the downstairs. I couldn't get out of the attic quickly enough, and not only because the crate and contents were beyond creepy, but also because they were so sad that I felt like I could start crying.

"We'll both go," Derek said, crawling behind me. "I'm not sitting up here waiting for them. That"—he glanced back over his shoulder—"isn't going anywhere."

I didn't imagine it would. Not if it had been up here for . . . God knew how long.

The sadness receded a little in the curiosity I felt.

How long would that have been exactly, that the crate and baby bones had been up here? The house was built in the 1920s. The Green sisters had lived here their whole lives, or so Brandon had said. Seventy-plus years.

Then again, Moxie has been produced since 1876, so the baby skeleton could have been put in the attic before the Green sisters were born. The crawl space wasn't the kind of place I imagined they'd spent a lot of time. Hard to get to, and not very useful. The Green family seemed to have preferred their basement for storage, and not surprisingly, since it was much easier to access, with the permanent staircase.

I glanced over my shoulder. "How long . . ."

"Hard to say," Derek said, swinging his legs through the hole in the floor. "I'll go first and help you down."

He wiggled through the hole and hung for a moment before dropping, without bothering to use the makeshift ladder on the wall. "OK," I heard his voice, "come on."

I stuck my feet through the opening and followed. Since I'm not quite as athletic—or strong—as Derek, I turned on my stomach and scooted off the edge that way instead. I felt his hands grab my knees and then slide up over my thighs and my butt, before grasping my waist.

"I've got you. Let go."

I let go, and dropped into his arms. He held me for a second, breathing into my hair, before letting me go so I could call Wayne and set the machine in motion.

. . .

Wayne pulled up to the curb outside ten minutes later, in a squad car but without lights or sirens. There was no hurry, after all. The body had been dead a long time and wasn't going anywhere. There was no emergency.

Nonetheless, he didn't look happy. His first words to us were an echo of Derek's. "Why does this always happen to you?"

"It's not our fault," Derek said. "We're just doing our jobs."

Wayne scowled. He looked like an older version of his son, minus the glasses: a lanky six foot five or so, with curly black hair—turning to salt and pepper now in his late forties—and brown eyes, wearing a uniform shirt and jeans under a regulation blue parka.

"That skeleton's been there for years," Derek added. "Decades probably. Long enough to decompose completely. There's nothing left but bones. It's not like anyone dropped it off for us to find."

"You sure about that?"

"There was a thick layer of dust on the lid," I said. "I doubt anyone's opened it since it was put up there."

"Show me," Wayne demanded.

"It's upstairs. All the way upstairs." Derek led the way to the staircase. "In the attic."

"What were you doing in the attic?" They both began climbing. I headed up after them.

"Avery was nosing around," Derek said.

That's right, I thought. *Throw me under the bus.*

"Good thing, too," he continued, "or we wouldn't have known it was here. It wouldn't have crossed my mind to crawl into the attic."

Wayne mumbled something I didn't catch, but which I was pretty sure wasn't complimentary.

"Someone put it there," I told him. "It didn't crawl up there on its own. That makes it a crime scene. And your jurisdiction."

Wayne sighed. "Yeah, yeah. I'm just not looking forward to this. Anything to do with children is twice as hard as anything else. And the press is going to have a field day."

"At least you don't have to worry about Tony Micelli."

"True," Wayne said and sounded a little happier.

We'd reached the second floor now, and Derek opened the door to the closet and showed Wayne the hatch in the ceiling. The chief of police contemplated it with his head tilted. "Not sure I can get through that."

"There isn't a lot of room," Derek admitted. "I left the crate *in situ*, so you could see where it was, but if you like, I can go back up and fetch it down. Take a couple pictures maybe. You can see the situation from the top of the ladder."

"Ladder?" Wayne said.

Derek indicated the blocks of wood nailed to the wall and Wayne arched a brow. "Not my idea of a ladder."

"Mine, either. But I've seen these before. They're footholds. What do you think?"

"Fine with me," Wayne said with a shrug. "You've already been up there, so the scene's already been compromised, and after all this time, I doubt we'd find any forensic evidence."

"The crate is rough wood," Derek informed him. "Too rough to take fingerprints, I think."

"Not sure fingerprints would do any good anyway. Anyone involved in this is likely dead by now. Go ahead. I'll wait here."

He nodded to Derek, who grabbed the blocks of wood on the wall and started climbing. After a half a minute, he had disappeared into the attic again, and we could hear his scuffling progress through the hatch, then the scrape of the wooden crate along the floorboards. "He has to crawl," I explained to Wayne. "He can't just pick it up and carry it, because the ceiling is low enough that he can't walk."

Wayne nodded. "Hopefully it'll hold together."

"I'm sure it will. It looked sturdy. One of those old wooden Moxie crates with a lid."

"I'm familiar with them," Wayne said as the scraping stopped and Derek's face appeared in the hole.

"I'll lower it as far as I can. Hopefully that'll be enough for you to get ahold of it."

Wayne nodded.

"I used my phone to snap a couple pictures. Once I get down, I'll send them to your phone."

His head disappeared and we heard scraping. Then the crate appeared in the hatch, supported by Derek's hands, and was lowered into Wayne's without mishap. He carried it out of the closet and put it on the floor on the landing. Meanwhile, Derek swung himself through the hatch and landed beside me.

"All right, Tink?"

"Fine," I said faintly.

"You look pale."

"It's a creepy sort of business."

Since there was no arguing with that, he didn't try, just put his hand on my back and guided me out of the closet and onto the landing.

Wayne had already taken the lid off the crate and was peering at the grisly contents. Derek and I joined him, looking down at the tiny—and very sad—little skeleton.

Up there in the attic, between the shock and the lack of light, I hadn't gotten a good look at it. That was fine with me. Looking at it now, in the light, the pitiful remnants of life were almost too much to bear.

A tiny pile of bones and a tiny skull, just the right size to fit in my hand. Or if not mine, then Derek's. Someone's hand.

If it hadn't been for that skull, I might have imagined we were looking at an animal, a cat or small dog, hidden away instead of buried after death.

But there was the skull, tiny but perfectly formed, unmistakably human even without the toothy grin.

And a blanket. I hadn't really noticed the blanket before, but it was there. Tattered and stained—I preferred not to think about with what—but there. Wrapping the baby when it was put in the crate and shoved next to the chimney. A white blanket—crocheted, from what I could see— made by hand with a scalloped blue border.

Did that mean we were looking at the remains of a baby boy?

Or was it just the luck of the draw, and nobody had had any idea what kind of baby it was until it came out, and the blue was just a coincidence?

I cleared my throat. It was remarkably hard to get the words out. "Any sign of foul play?"

Stupid question, I guess, considering that the baby was in the attic instead of in the graveyard, where it belonged. But Wayne understood what I was asking—or what I was careful not to ask. He shook his head. "Not that I can see. Nothing here indicates anything but a natural death."

After a second, he added reluctantly, "Of course, it's hard to tell just from bones. But if the skull was cracked or there was a bullet in the box with the bones, or evidence of a knife on the ribs . . ."

"Surely not on a baby!"

"No," Wayne said, and I could tell from his face that he wasn't enjoying thinking about this any more than I was. "Not a baby. I was thinking more generally. About adults. When there are dead babies . . ."

He stopped to swallow. Audibly. "We've never had a dead baby before. Not to my knowledge. Not in Waterfield. But when a dead baby is found somewhere, most of the time it was from natural causes, and the parents were afraid to report it for fear that they'd be blamed."

"You think that's what happened here?"

"I have no idea what happened here," Wayne said, and took a breath. "The further back in time you go, the more likely you'd get a stillbirth, too. There weren't the medical advances back then to know when something was wrong, and births were a lot more traumatic as well, without the medical care we have these days. Births often took place at home . . ."

He trailed off.

"What?" I said.

He shot me a distracted glance. "There's something about a baby."

"What?"

"I'll have to look up the details. But it's something about a missing baby. A long time before my time, so I don't remember, but there's something in the back brain."

I glanced at Derek, who shrugged. Whatever had happened had been before his time, too—he was at least ten years younger than Wayne—and obviously it didn't ring any bells.

"What will happen now?" he asked Wayne, who shrugged.

"I guess I'll have to send Brandon over to take a look at

your attic. Just in case there's something to be found there. But my guess is this crate has been up there for fifty years or more, and any physical evidence as to who put it there is long gone. Still, it has to be done."

Of course.

"Can we keep working?" I asked, and Derek gave me a surprised look.

"Are you sure you want to, Avery? That you wouldn't rather get out of here? Go home for a while?"

"I want to stay busy," I said, since at home, all I'd be able to do was sit and relive the moments in the attic and the sad discovery.

"Sure," Wayne said. "There's no point in us looking at the rest of the house. Not after all this time."

"What about the . . . that?" I looked at the crate, unable to call what was left inside it a baby, but not quite able to bring myself to call it a skeleton, either. "What will happen to it?"

"It'll have to go to the medical examiner's office in Portland," Wayne said. "I doubt they'll find much, but maybe they'll be able to extract some DNA or something. If we're lucky, we can come close to finding out who this is. Was."

"Surely it's obvious? The Greens have lived here for seventy years. It must be a Green, don't you think?"

"You'd think," Wayne said and fitted the lid on the crate. "I'll be in touch."

He hoisted it carefully and headed down the stairs to the first floor. I followed, so I could lock the front door behind him. With one thing and another, I was feeling just a bit spooked. "When should we expect Brandon?"

"As soon as I can get him out here," Wayne said as he passed through the front door onto the porch. He turned on the doormat to look at me. "Not a word about this to any-one, if you please, Avery. We don't need news cameras and a stampede on the doors. Let's try to keep this quiet until we know more."

"No problem." I didn't want the cameras and the stampede any more than he did.

I closed the door behind him, and stood and watched until he'd placed the crate carefully into the squad car and had driven away before I headed back to Derek.

My husband was still standing where I'd left him, in the middle of the upstairs landing, staring at nothing. I nudged him. "Are you OK?"

He jumped, startled, and then gave me a faint smile. "Fine."

"What are you thinking about?"

"That," Derek said, nodding at the stairs. There was nothing there, so I assumed he was talking about Wayne and the crate that had just made their way down.

"Do you have any idea what it was Wayne talked about?"

It took a second before he remembered what Wayne had said. Then—

"The missing baby?" He shook his head. "I think I've heard that at some point in time, someone's baby went missing. But it's a very long time ago, maybe as much as a hundred years, and I don't know any of the details. If I did, I've forgotten."

"If it was a hundred years ago, it couldn't be this baby. The house hasn't been here that long."

Derek nodded.

"Do you think I should go try to find out?"

"How would you do that?" Derek asked.

"Newspaper archives? The *Chronicle* and the *Daily* have been around for a long time. And if someone's baby went missing, I'm sure it would be front page news. Don't you think?"

"I'm sure it would." He hesitated, and then relented. I guess maybe he was curious, too. "Wait until Brandon gets here. Then you can go. You're not doing anything pressing at the moment anyway. Just let him in so I don't have to interrupt what I'm doing to do it."

"Sure," I said.

"And bring me back some lunch."

"No problem. Lobster rolls OK?"

"Fine," Derek said.

"I'll wait for him downstairs. Take a look at the other rooms and try to come up with some idea for how we can make this place shine."

"I'll be up here," Derek said, "if you need me."

I headed down the stairs again, while he walked off into the bathroom once more.

7

The *Waterfield Chronicle* has been around since 1915, while the *Weekly* has them beat by three years. *Since 1912*, it says on the plaque beside the door.

They were located across the street from each other on Main Street, just up from the harbor and down from Derek's old apartment. I'd spent quite a bit of time at both offices since moving to Waterfield. I'd done enough research at each newspaper to learn that the *Weekly* specialized in human interest stories, while the *Chronicle* was the place to go for harder news—or as hard as news got in a small, quaint town like this one. I figured I'd start there, since a missing baby had to have been news, no matter when it went missing. The *Weekly*, with its slower release schedule, wouldn't have as much information.

Of course, I had no idea what I was looking for—or more accurately, at what point in time to start looking. The archives were all on microfiche, chronologically by date, and I didn't fancy starting in 1915 and working my way forward to present day.

"Would you know anything about a missing baby?" I

asked the archivist behind the counter, a round-faced woman in her fifties who adores Derek. Most women in Waterfield do. Most women do, period.

She looked startled, of course, as well she might, after that kind of question.

I clarified. "I heard that, at some point, there was a missing baby in Waterfield. A long time ago."

She tilted her head, birdlike, dark eyes bright with interest. "Who told you that?"

"Wayne," I said, and bit my tongue, just a second too late.

"The chief of police?"

I nodded.

She waited for me to elaborate. When I didn't—because I was afraid of what else I might let slip—she continued reluctantly, "He's right. There was a missing baby. I can't remember exactly when it happened, though. A few years after World War II, I think. Late 1940s, maybe early '50s. Before I was born. Before the chief of police was born, too."

"There'll be something about it in the archives, don't you think?"

"Certainly." She sounded offended, perhaps at the idea that the *Chronicle* might have ignored such a momentous incident. Or perhaps just because I wasn't being forthcoming about why I wanted to know. She could probably smell that there was more to it than idle curiosity, but Wayne had asked me to keep our discovery quiet, and I was doing my best.

"Could I take a look at the years between 1945 and 1955, then?"

She sniffed, but brought them out. A few minutes later I was set up in front of a microfiche machine in the back, scrolling through front pages. (A missing baby would be front page news, I figured, and not something relegated to the back pages.)

There was nothing in 1945. Nothing in 1946. A headline in 1947 had me all excited, until I realized that it referred to a painting that had gone missing from the Fraser House, of a young Fraser child. I scrolled by 1948 with nothing doing. I started 1949, bored out of my skull by then, and wondering whether I would have to go back and start over. Maybe a missing baby wouldn't make the front page. Maybe I'd have to redo the search from the beginning, and scan every single page as thoroughly as I had the front ones.

I would have dismissed Wednesday, September 7, 1949, too, if it hadn't been for two other big happenings taking up the front page that day, catching my eye. First on Tuesday the sixth, Allied military authorities had relinquished control of Nazi German assets and restored them to Germany, and second, in Camden, New Jersey, a World War II veteran named Howard Unruh—ironically, his last name was the German word for unrest—had shot thirteen of his neighbors to become the first single-episode mass murderer in United States history.

Between those two headlines, Waterfield's missing baby was almost an afterthought. All the way down in the corner of the page was a single column headed by one word— GONE!!—in capital letters with several exclamation points after it.

Missing, the article said, *from North Street in Waterfield: Arthur Green, seven months old.*

The article was brief but informative enough, at least to start. Arthur Green, the youngest child and only son of Lila and Arthur Senior, had been removed from his baby carriage by person or persons unknown on Tuesday afternoon around one o'clock. The police would appreciate any information about any strangers anyone might have seen in the vicinity of the Greens' house on North Street. The matter was extremely urgent.

And no wonder. Missing children are always urgent.

Only . . . if those were the remains of Arthur Green we had found upstairs in the attic, he hadn't really been missing at all.

So had someone lied? But if so, who? His mother? His father?

And why? Had someone killed him—accidentally or on

purpose—and then lied about it, because they didn't want to pay the piper?

I forwarded to the front page for the next day, Thursday the eighth, when another big headline overwhelmed the search for the missing baby. The day before, the Federal Republic of Germany had been founded, with Konrad Adenauer as chancellor, and that was of enormous interest to the rest of the world—and probably to Germany, too— four and a half years after World War II ended.

The search for the missing baby continued, yet again relegated to the part of the front page that would have been below the fold in a normal paper, on the bottom half of the page.

On September 9, Canada was in the news. World War II veteran Edwin Alonzo Boyd committed his first career bank robbery in Toronto, while someone blew up Canadian Pacific Airlines Flight 108, killing everyone onboard: four crew and nineteen passengers, among them several children.

Scrolling forward, I looked for information about that as well as about the Green baby. And I slowed down and checked not only the front pages, but the rest of the newspaper as well.

I didn't find anything else about Arthur Green—the case just petered out, it seemed, with no new information and no discoveries—but two weeks later, there was a notice that Quebec City had arrested Albert Guay for the airplane bombing. Guay's wife, Rita Morél, had been among the passengers, and since Albert had found himself a young mistress, he wanted his wife out of the way. He took out a life insurance policy on her, adding insult to injury, and then hid the bomb in her luggage. He had planned for the bomb to go off while the plane was over the Saint Lawrence River, something which would have made it impossible for forensic scientists to discover what had happened, but because the plane was delayed five minutes, it exploded over land instead.

So that was an interesting detour, but nothing to do with

what I was looking for. I kept scrolling through the rest of the year. The People's Republic of China as well as the Democratic Republic of East Germany were recognized in October, and the Republic of Indonesia in November, the same month dancer Bill Robinson—Bojangles—died. Little Arthur Green wasn't mentioned again, at least not where I could see.

I could have kept going, I guess, on the off-chance that I'd hit on something else in 1950, but what I was doing was time-consuming, and I'd already spent quite a bit of effort on it. It was several hours since I'd left North Street. Derek must be getting hungry. I handed the microfiche back with a thank-you.

"Did you find what you were looking for?" the archivist inquired, bright-eyed and keen.

I shrugged. "Some of it. The Green baby was stolen out of his baby carriage in September of 1949. I couldn't find any mention of him being found again."

She shook her head. "It's always been just Ruth and Mamie Green, for as long as I can remember. Neither ever got married. They just lived together in that big house. I never knew anything about a baby."

Me, either.

I thanked her again and walked off, up the street and around the corner to the little hole-in-the-wall place that has the best lobster rolls in Maine, at least according to Derek. Not coincidentally, it's also right around the corner from his old place, where he lived before we got married, in a loft above the hardware store on Main Street. Very convenient location for a handyman.

I had ordered and was perched on an orange plastic seat by an orange table waiting for the sandwiches to be ready when the bell above the door jangled and Cora walked in. I guess maybe Dr. Ben had a hankering for lobster rolls, too.

She made her order at the counter and then came over to greet me. "Hello, Avery. What are you doing out in the middle of the day?"

"Lunch run," I said. "It isn't like he locks me in, you know."

"The boys do love their lobster rolls." She smiled indulgently and took a seat on the opposite side of the orange table.

I nodded. "Derek says they're the best lobster rolls in Maine."

"Voted to be the last four years running," Cora said, indicating a framed award over by the door, one I had never even noticed.

I stared at it. "Huh."

"What's Derek up to?"

I returned my attention to Cora. "Oh, he's still working. We couldn't both leave, what with Brandon—"

Oops.

"Brandon?" Cora said. "Brandon Thomas?"

I nodded. "He's over at the house."

"Uh-oh. I guess I really wasn't wrong about that light last night, was I?"

I grabbed at the excuse like a drowning person. "Actually, no. Mamie Green was asleep on the floor in her old room. Holding the baby doll I'd rescued from the basement."

And now that I thought about it, maybe Mamie's fondness for the doll had something to do with the skeleton in the attic, or at least with the fact that she'd lost a beloved baby brother at a young age. It made me wonder whether she'd always been a little touched in the head, or whether that was something that had happened after little Arthur went missing.

"Oh dear," Cora said.

I pulled myself back to the present. "Yeah. She was pretty cold when we found her. Asleep, you know, so she didn't realize it, but her body temperature was too low. We took her back to the nursing home where she lives, and dropped her off, and then Brandon took over."

"And now he's at the house," Cora said.

"Right."

"What's he doing?"

I struggled for a moment. Less than a moment—2.5

seconds maybe. When Wayne said to keep the news about the baby skeleton quiet, surely he hadn't meant that I couldn't tell Cora? I mean, she was family. Right?

I lowered my voice. "We found a baby skeleton."

Cora stared at me blankly. I repeated it louder. *"We found a baby skeleton!"*

"I heard you the first time," Cora said. "Where?"

I lowered my voice again. "Attic. In a crate. I've been down at the *Chronicle* doing research."

"What did you find out?"

"That there was a third Green child. A little boy named Arthur. He went missing in September of 1949. Or so his family said."

"And you think the skeleton is Arthur?"

"Unless you know of any other babies who have gone missing from Waterfield, who might have ended up in the attic of the Green house, I think it's safe to say that it is. Don't you?"

"I guess," Cora said.

"You weren't around in 1949, were you?" She was still in her late fifties, as far as I knew. Derek's dad was a few years older.

She shook her head. "I was born in '54. And I didn't grow up in Waterfield. I came here after I got married."

"So you don't know anything about it."

"No," Cora said.

"It must be horrible, not to know what happened. Bad enough when someone dies, you know? Especially a child, I guess. But at least you know where they are."

Cora nodded.

"Dr. Ben would be about the same age as Arthur, right? Would you ask him if he knows anything about it?"

"I can ask," Cora said, "but he'll have been too small to remember anything, Avery. Whatever he knows will be from later, things his parents told him when he was a child maybe."

"I just want to know if there were any rumors about what happened."

"I'll ask," Cora said again, and got to her feet when both

of our to-go bags landed at the cash register at the same time, "but I don't think he'll know anything that'll help."

Maybe not, but it couldn't hurt to ask. As we walked toward the front counter to pay and pick up our food, I changed the subject. "Have you finished decorating for the Christmas Tour?"

"That's what I'm doing today. This is my reward." She nodded to the lobster roll.

"I haven't started yet," I confessed.

"Oh, dear." She clicked her tongue. "You'll have a busy few days. Would you like some help?"

"I'll let you know. Thanks." I pulled out my wallet to pay.

We walked up the hill together, and parted ways on the corner of North Street and Fulton. Waterfield Village was small enough that I didn't always bother to take the car to go anywhere, at least when the weather was good. It was gray and gloomy that day, cold with the scent of snow in the air. Or so Cora told me; I hadn't been in Maine long enough to develop the ability to smell snow. We got snow in Manhattan, too, plenty of it, but Manhattan smelled overpoweringly of other things.

By the time I got back to the Green sisters' house, Brandon was gone. Derek's truck stood alone at the curb. I let myself in and called up to the second floor. "Food's here!"

"About time!" floated back to me. A minute later he came clattering down the stairs.

There was no furniture left in the house, so we sat on the built-in window seat in the dining room and ate, the lobster rolls on their waxed wrapping paper spread out between us.

"It's almost like a picnic." I smiled at him.

He smiled back. "Not as good as the real thing. Remember the last picnic we had?"

I did. We'd packed a basket and borrowed Jill and Peter Cortino's speedboat—Jill's an old girlfriend of Derek's from high school—and gone out to the house on Rowanberry Island, where Derek had proposed marriage. The ring had been stuck in a whoopie pie, and I'd come within an inch of eating it.

"I love you," he told me, just as he'd done then.

"I love you, too," I answered. "Did Brandon find anything upstairs?"

Derek shrugged, his mouth full of lobster. After he'd swallowed, he said, "If he did, he didn't tell me. I don't think he expected to find anything, to be honest. It's been too long. It was just something he had to do."

Probably. "Would you like to hear what I found out?"

"Sure," Derek said.

So I went over the information one more time, with as much detail as I could remember, and ended with, "It must be Arthur Green, don't you think?"

"Probably," Derek said.

It wasn't much of a probability in my mind—it was a virtual certainty—but I asked anyway. "Who else could it be?"

"Don't know," Derek said with a shrug. "Maybe one of the Green sisters got pregnant at some point, out of wedlock, and didn't want the world to know."

"I suppose." It was a halfway likely story anyway, as stories go. Although in my opinion, it was much more likely that the baby skeleton we'd found belonged to the missing baby we knew about.

"Of course," Derek agreed when I said so. "All I'm saying is that there could be other explanations. But Wayne will figure it out."

"How?"

He leaned back against the cold plaster wall. "I imagine he'll run a DNA test on the skeleton and match whatever he finds to the Green sisters. If they're full siblings—have the same mother and father—the DNA will show that conclusively."

I nodded. And lowered my voice. I wasn't sure why, only that I didn't want to talk too loudly about it. "What do you think happened? To the baby?"

"Could have been anything," Derek said. "Maybe he

died of SIDS—sudden infant death syndrome; they called it crib death back then—and they were afraid they'd get blamed, so they made up a story about him being kidnapped."

"Natural causes?"

Derek nodded. "Nobody knows what causes SIDS, but it happens to male babies more than female, and back then they didn't know not to put them to sleep on their stomachs. That can be a contributing factor. So can cigarette smoke."

"You're kidding."

He shook his head. "Or he could have suffocated. Gotten buried in the blankets or pillows, unable to free himself. It's sad, but nobody's fault. And it happens all the time. Or it might have been some other sort of accident. Someone picked him up and dropped him accidentally. One of the girls maybe. And the parents made up the story about the kidnapping because they didn't want anyone to take the girls away, too."

I nodded. It made sense and wasn't too deeply disturbing. Disturbing enough, of course, since nobody wants anything bad to happen to a baby, but not as disturbing as some of the scenarios that had crossed my mind—and probably Derek's and Wayne's, too. And while honesty is the best policy, I could imagine parents, in shock after the death of one child, not wanting to risk losing another.

"Or," Derek said.

"Yes?"

"Someone did it on purpose, or accidentally on purpose. The baby wouldn't be quiet so they shook it. Not to kill it but to shut it up. That happens all the time, too."

I knew it did. I'd heard about it. It was still horrible to contemplate. "And then they didn't want to own up to it, and they hid the baby and said it had been kidnapped?"

Derek nodded. "I think it would have to be something like that. Something more or less accidental. It's hard to imagine anyone deliberately killing a baby, you know? They're so tiny and helpless. They can't do anything. They can't talk. They can't move. Even if the baby saw something he shouldn't have seen, he couldn't tell anyone, and by the time he got old enough to talk, he'd have forgotten whatever he saw anyway."

Derek was right. There was no logical reason to kill a baby. So it had to have been an accident, with the hiding of the body an afterthought. I said as much.

"I hope it was," Derek said. "I don't like the alternative."

I nodded. "Do you think Mamie and Ruth knew he was up there?"

"Hard to say," Derek said, crumpling up the paper that had been wrapped around his lobster roll. "Hard to imagine they didn't, but the crate was out of the way up there. And they were old ladies, probably not likely to climb the wall up to the attic. Especially since there was nothing worth getting up there."

"They weren't always old ladies, though. When Arthur went missing—or died—they were little girls."

He conceded my point. And added, "Although their parents could have told them they weren't allowed in the attic. They may not have questioned it."

"Maybe not."

"My mother told me I wasn't allowed in the attic," Derek said.

I glanced at him. "Really?"

He nodded. "She used to hide Christmas gifts up there."

"Did you go up there anyway?"

He grinned. "Of course. But our attic had a permanent staircase, not planks nailed to the wall. And I was a boy anyway. I probably would have climbed the wall just for the hell of it, and just because I was told not to. And because I wanted to try to get a look at the presents. But two girls might not have."

Maybe not. I wasn't sure I would have. Although in my childhood it had been moot. No attic. I'd grown up in a New York apartment, and my mother hid my Christmas presents in her bottom bureau drawer.

I changed the subject. Sort of. "I met Cora at the deli.

She said she'd ask your dad whether he knew anything about Arthur Green."

"I thought Wayne told you not to tell anyone."

"I'm sure he didn't mean family," I said. "She's decorating her house today. For the Christmas Home Tour."

"When are we doing that?"

"When we have time." Sometime in the next—I gulped—four days.

He got to his feet. "Go home, Avery. Get busy. I don't need you for the rest of the day."

I peered up at him. "Are you sure?"

"Positive," Derek said. "You've caused enough trouble for one day. Go home and decorate. When I finish here tonight, we'll buy a tree."

"Cool." I got to my feet, too, and gathered the trash. "And by tomorrow we can start on some of the renovating, right?"

"Changing out the plumbing *is* renovating," Derek said.

8

Speaking of attics, Aunt Inga's had more junk than any one place I've ever seen in my life. There was stuff up there that I hadn't the slightest idea what was. I'd found her old—unused—wedding veil up there just after I'd taken over the house, and used it to update the kitchen cabinets. I'd also found a few of Marie Antoinette's things from court in Versailles—no, I'm not kidding, but it's a long story—although those had been donated to a museum, and were no longer around. Derek and I had talked about it and decided they'd be too much of a temptation for thieves.

But even without the very valuable stuff, the attic was a treasure trove. Morton heirlooms from a century back, and all of Aunt Inga's things from almost a hundred years of life. My second cousin a few times removed had been close to ninety-nine when she passed on. It took me a long time to find the boxes with the Christmas decorations. I kept getting sidetracked by interesting items: a pretty little music box that played "Some Enchanted Evening," a stack of fashion magazines from the 1950s, a basket of yarn in different colors that I could imagine turning into a blanket or maybe a few pairs of warm socks. It was cold up there.

I finally tracked the Christmas stuff down to a stack of boxes on the far side of the chimney and, in the process of dragging them over to the staircase and down, narrowly managed to avoid killing myself. Aunt Inga's Victorian has steep attic stairs, although at least there *are* stairs: The "ladder" at the Green house this morning had been a real eye-opener for me.

I hadn't done a whole lot to decorate the house last year. I still wasn't entirely sure I had settled for good in Waterfield back then. I adored Derek, and I liked the town just fine when it was warm, but the cold season had taken me aback. New York City gets plenty cold in the winter, but living in a hundred-and-thirty-year-old Victorian house on the coast of Maine was colder than I had ever anticipated. Colder than I could have imagined. I had grown up in a brick apartment building in Manhattan, with central heating and the insulation of other apartments on both sides of ours. Here I was exposed, in a wooden Victorian house with original windows and doors. They didn't insulate well back then, and Derek and I didn't rip the plaster walls out and take the house down to the studs to insulate when we redid the place, so everything was original. There weren't even storm windows and storm doors on the house, because Derek—the purist—said it would be sacrilege to deface a Second Empire Victorian with aluminum storm windows.

Anyway, I'd been too busy huddling in front of the fire to decorate the place. I was thinking of burning it down. Maybe then I'd finally be warm.

But with the home tour to look forward to, it was fun opening Aunt Inga's boxes and seeing how my aunt had liked to decorate her house.

There were a lot of balls, of course, some of them very old and quite fragile. Blown glass, sprinkled with glitter. Most of it had rubbed off over the years, but there were remnants here and there. There was a box full of miniature ornaments: a tiny little Christmas ornament tea set, with a cup, a pitcher, a sugar bowl, and a teapot. It reminded me of the toy set I'd found in the cubby in Mamie's room . . . Lord, was it only this morning? What with the baby skeleton and all, it felt a lot longer ago.

The full-sized Christmas balls were beautiful, too. Some had flowers painted on them. Some had snowflakes. A few had camels and a star: the three wise men on their way to Bethlehem to greet the Christ Child.

And speaking of the Christ Child, there were entirely too many babies in the scenario of the last few days. The missing Baby Jesus from the nativity outside the church, the baby doll that had scared the living daylights out of me in the basement yesterday, and now the missing—or not missing—Arthur Green.

Being a textile designer by trade, I don't know much about psychology. Only what I've observed myself through the years. But purely from a layman's point of view, I wondered whether the loss of her brother at such a young age might be the reason why Mamie Green still liked dolls at the tender age of seventy-plus.

I also wondered whether there was a connection between the missing baby and the missing Baby Jesus. Whether Mamie in her confusion had stolen the Baby Jesus out of the manger every year, thinking it was her baby brother.

Or was that too big of a leap?

Derek would probably know, after going through medical school. I resolved to ask him about it later.

In addition to the pretty old Christmas ornaments, there were a lot of fake fir swags and greenery in Aunt Inga's boxes. There was a long, long string of it I thought must be intended for use on the banister to the second floor. So I shook it out the best I could and went to work with a box of dental floss, stringing greenery through the spokes in the banister and over the railing all the way up the stairs. Mischa the Russian Blue contemplated me from the doormat just inside the front door, while Jemmy and Inky, the two Maine Coons I'd inherited from Aunt Inga along with the house, couldn't really be bothered. They stayed curled up on the love seat in the parlor. Inky had twitched her tail at me when I first came in, but since then, they'd ignored me. As was par for the course really. Mischa, on the other hand, had had to be dissuaded from following me up to the attic. He was a mama's boy, my rescue cat.

By the time Derek walked through the door, I had decorated the staircase with greenery and silver bows, and the mantel in the foyer with more greenery and pinecones. Aunt Inga had owned some of the stuffed birds that Kate had also had—they weren't real, by the way; they just looked that way—but I couldn't bring myself to put them out. Not only did they look too much like real birds for comfort, but Mischa was eyeing them with great interest. If I put them along the mantel, I could imagine it wouldn't be long before he was up there, traipsing through my greenery and kicking it all to hell in an effort to get at the birds.

And besides, Kate had birds. I didn't want to decorate my house the way Kate had decorated hers. I wanted mine to be unique. Like me.

And that heavy, overwrought Victorian stuff wasn't me. We had renovated Aunt Inga's house to within an inch of its life, with the old wide-plank floors and the old dark wood fireplace mantels with mirrors above them and gorgeous old tiles on the hearth, with transoms above the doors and the old brass hardware, and traditional Victorian jewel colors on the walls . . . but I still didn't want to decorate the place in the traditional Victorian way. I had hung blue velvet curtains with silver stars in the dining room, and my living room sofa, which I had brought with me from New York the second time I moved, was oyster white with cross sections of kiwis on it. Three-foot-wide sections of kiwis. The house might be traditional, but the decor wasn't.

When Derek walked in, I was standing in the middle of the foyer—right about where the Christmas tree would go—with my hands on my hips, contemplating my handiwork. The staircase looked all right, in green and silver, but the mantel was a little bare. Or not bare exactly, since there was plenty of greenery. But I needed something more than the fir and the cones. Not birds. Nor the fat gold cherubs Kate had had.

Something silver and sparkly and nontraditional.

"Looks good," Derek said over my shoulder. He wrapped his arms around my waist and rested his chin on the top of my head as Mischa twined around our ankles.

"The mantel needs something more."

He contemplated it above my head. "Candles?"

"I could get some of those." Fat, silver ones. Kate had had candles on her mantel, too, but they're sort of a given for the season, so it would be OK if I had them as well. And candle flames would look wonderful reflected in the mirror above the mantel on Sunday afternoon.

"Angels?"

"Maybe angels."

"Cats?"

"Cats?" I tilted my head to look at him.

"We have cats," Derek said, staggering as Mischa twined more enthusiastically.

We did, indeed.

I went back to contemplating the mantel. "Maybe cats. Cats are sort of Halloweenish, though, don't you think?"

Derek shrugged. "Reindeer?"

Reindeer? "Maybe reindeer. If I could find reindeer. Silver reindeer."

"Christmas ornaments?"

Christmas ornaments were an obvious solution. They would look nice, I supposed. Maybe if I kept them all in the same color scheme. Something unusual: maybe some blue and purple to go with the silver, instead of the usual red and green.

And speaking of Christmas ornaments . . .

"Is there somewhere around here I could buy Chinese paper lanterns, do you suppose?"

"Chinese paper lanterns?" Derek repeated, as if he'd never heard the words before.

"You know. Rice paper, round. Or sometimes other shapes. White or colored. Lots of wires to help them keep their shapes. You can outfit them with a light kit and make lamps out of them."

"I know what they are," Derek said, dropping his arms from around my waist. "I just don't understand what you want with them. We have a light."

We did. A rather attractive reproduction bowl pendant in white glass.

"I wasn't going to put lights in them. I was going to turn them into Christmas ornaments. Big Christmas ornaments." Stencil snowflakes and camels on them, like the antique Christmas balls of Aunt Inga's. Maybe brush them with glue and then sprinkle glitter on the shapes, to sparkle in the candlelight.

Or maybe the foyer wouldn't be the best place to hang them. Maybe they needed to go on the porch, to welcome guests when they came up the walk. A dozen enormous pseudo–Christmas ornaments in different colors, hanging from the porch ceiling. It would look wonderful.

"Sure," Derek said when I described my vision. "Your ideas always turn out great, Avery."

Is it any wonder I love him?

I was warming to my plans now. I wasn't aware I'd made any really, but it seemed my subconscious had been busy while I'd been standing here. "I want a small Christmas tree, too. A big one for in here, a ten-footer at least, but a tiny one for somewhere else. Maybe the dining room table. Or maybe two tiny evergreens, one for each side of the mantel in the dining room. We can get them in pots and plant them outside when the ground thaws."

"Why do we need so many Christmas trees?" Derek wanted to know. "Isn't one enough?"

"It would be. But I found this box of teeny-tiny Christmas ornaments, only about an inch tall. They'd get lost on the big tree. But they're beautiful, so I'd like to use them somewhere where they'll fit."

"Small evergreen it is," Derek said. "Are you ready to go?"

"I should change first, don't you think?"

Derek looked at me, in jeans and a ratty sweater, with my hair in a bun and dust on my face. "You look great."

And again: Is it any wonder I love him?

"I'd like to change," I said. "It won't take long. And don't take this the wrong way, but you could do with a shower and some clean clothes, too."

"Are you saying I smell, Tink?" He lifted an arm and sniffed his armpit.

"Not at all." I wasn't. "Just that you're dirty. We can spare fifteen minutes for you to get clean."

"Fifteen minutes?"

"Do you need more?"

"That depends," Derek said.

"On?"

"On whether you're planning to take a shower, too."

"I wouldn't mind getting clean, I guess."

"I wouldn't mind getting dirty," Derek said, and grinned.

. . .

An hour later, we arrived at the Christmas tree lot. It was a five-minute drive from the house. If it hadn't been for the fact that we had to transport the tree back, we could have walked.

It didn't take long to pick out a nice, tall Frasier fir and load it into the back of the truck, where it stuck out over the edge. Derek and the tree guy tied it down with string, and we were on our way. The two tiny trees for the dining room were next, and I picked two droopy evergreens in pots: some sort of weeping dwarf cedar, according to Derek. Not a Christmas tree per se, but nice and green and fragrant. And small. Barely two feet tall.

We loaded those into the truck as well, behind the seat with the kitty litter—in case of bad road conditions—and headed up the Ocean Road toward the Waymouth Tavern.

"Are you sure the tree will be safe while we're inside?" I asked Derek.

He glanced at me. "Sure."

"You don't think anyone will try to steal it?"

"It's a bit too big to walk away with," Derek said, "and

if another car pulls up next to ours and people start transferring the tree from one car to the other, don't you think
someone would notice?"

Sure. But that didn't mean they'd object. Or think anything of it. "It's amazing what you can get away with when
you do it with enough confidence. If I saw two people in
the process of transferring a Christmas tree from the back
of a truck to the roof of a car, I'd probably just think they
were supposed to be doing it."

"Huh," Derek said.

I shrugged. "People see what they're supposed to see.
And nobody expects someone to be bold enough to take a
Christmas tree off someone else's truck bed in a restaurant
parking lot, and drive away with it."

"Except you," Derek said.

Well, yeah. Except me.

Nonetheless, we continued on our merry way to the
Waymouth Tavern, which was located on the cliffs above
the Atlantic Ocean a few miles outside Waterfield proper,
and parked in the lot. But at least Derek consented to parking in the middle of the lot, in plain view of the windows,
and with the tree facing the restaurant.

I loved the place. The view was incredible—even if it
was impaired a little by the full winter dark at the moment.
In the summer, when the days were long and the nights
were light, it was lovely. The interior of the tavern was dark
and cozy, with romantic booths lining the walls, looking
out over the ocean, topped by reproduction Tiffany lamps
in warm colors.

"We should put a Tiffany lamp or two into the house," I
told Derek when we were seated in a booth overlooking
the . . . not water: the parking lot. With our truck and our
tree.

"Our house?" Derek said.

"No, of course not. The Green sisters' house. The style
isn't right for a Victorian."

For a Craftsman bungalow, on the other hand, it was perfect.
Tiffany lamps were Art Nouveau, the first few created in the

late 1890s, toward the end of the Victorian era, and then more into the teens and twenties. All handmade, all gorgeous; each one a work of art.

"If you want," Derek said.

"A pendant for the dining room maybe. The Tiffany Company made mostly table lamps, but there are lots of reproduction pendant lamps to be found. Just look around."

"One that says Coca-Cola might look nice. Like the ones above the bar."

I looked at the bar. Indeed, the "Tiffany" lamps there spelled out Coca-Cola in leaded glass.

"Maybe not."

Derek grinned. "I'm sure we can find something tasteful, Avery. And if not, I know someone who makes stained glass windows. Maybe she could craft you your own custom lamp."

Tempting, but . . . "That may be too cost-prohibitive. Whoever buys the house when we're done with it may not like Tiffany as much as I do. It's probably safer to go with a generic—tasteful—Tiffany lamp from a warehouse somewhere. Cheaper and easier that way."

"Whatever you say," Derek said and turned to the waitress to order a bottle of beer for himself and a soda for me. Since we'd been there enough to know what was on the menu, we took care of ordering the food at the same time.

When she left, Derek leaned back against the seat and nudged my foot under the table. "So tell me how I can help you get ready for this Christmas Tour thing, Tink."

Ah, yes. That was something else we had to do. "You can help me set up and decorate the Christmas tree. It's huge." Almost twice my size.

"Sure," Derek said.

"I can probably manage the rest of the decorating myself, as long as I have time to do it." The rest was much lower to the ground. Except for the Chinese lantern Christmas ball ornaments, but those weren't even made yet. There was plenty of time to get those hung.

He nodded.

"We'll have to figure out what we're going to serve on Sunday."

"Serve?" He nodded his thanks to the waitress for putting his bottle on the table, and continued to talk to me. "We're feeding people?"

"Just some sort of snack," I said. "Cookies, or something. Nibbly things. Not a meal."

"How many people?"

"Um . . ."

He arched his brows, and I said reluctantly, "A couple hundred. But I'm sure they won't all want a cookie."

"Oh," Derek said darkly, "I'm sure they will. If we don't have enough cookies for them all, trust me, they'll all want one."

Maybe so. "We can buy them. The cookies."

"We'll have to," Derek said, "because I'm not baking twenty dozen cookies. I have better things to do."

When he put it like that, so did I. Although the odor of fresh-baked cookies would be wonderful, permeating the house and setting the mood. Then again, maybe we could buy a scented candle.

The food came, and so, after a few minutes, did the fluttery Henrietta, from the Christmas Tour meeting last night. She was accompanied by a distinguished-looking man about the same age as Dr. Ben. I smiled at her, and she gave me a distracted look back, while the man nodded to Derek in passing.

"Who's that?" I whispered when they were out of earshot, getting settled at a table around the corner, overlooking the ocean.

Derek shot them a glance to make sure they weren't close enough to hear us talk. "Henry Silva. Darren's father."

Ah. I had thought there was something familiar about him, but I'd been sure I hadn't seen him before. That explained it.

"And she is?"

"His sister."

"Henry and Henrietta?"

"I think the father's name was Henry, too," Derek said. "I guess their mother wanted to make him happy."

Guess so. "She's on the home tour. She was at the meeting last night."

He smiled. "Oh, good. I'm glad she's feeling well enough to take part in the tour."

"Hasn't she been well?"

"She's in her seventies," Derek said, "with a bad heart. Last spring she contracted pneumonia. She spent a couple weeks in the hospital. Even had a heart attack while she was there. Dad wasn't sure she'd pull through."

"Your dad's her doctor?"

"He's everyone's doctor," Derek said with a grin. "She has a heart specialist, of course. In Portland or Boston. But for the pneumonia, yeah. Dad was her doctor."

"She seems kind of nervous."

"She's old," Derek said. "And probably worried about dying."

Probably. "Where does her brother live?"

"Same place as she does. Big house a few blocks down from Dad and Cora."

"They live together?"

"Now," Derek said. "She was married once, but he passed away. After the pneumonia scare, she moved back in with her brother. I guess he didn't want her living on her own anymore. His wife is gone, too, twenty years ago, so it's just the two of them. And Darren."

"She must have died young. The wife." Henry Silva couldn't be more than sixty-five: tall and distinguished.

"Divorce," Derek said. "She isn't dead—not that I know about—she just moved away."

Ah. Yeah, I guess not every person who goes missing is dead. "Does he have a bad heart, too?"

"Not that I know of," Derek said.

"So the house that'll be on the tour is Mr. Silva's house."

Derek nodded. "Big Arts and Crafts hall on Cabot. Makes the Green house look like a dinky cottage."

My jaw dropped. "That's their house?"

Derek grinned. "I figured you couldn't have missed that."

No, indeed. The house I was thinking of—the one that must belong to the Silvas—was a rambling Arts and Crafts mansion of about six thousand square feet. Two stories tall over most of it, it was covered with cedar shingles in the traditional New England style, painted a pale grayish green, almost like the water on a cloudy day, or lichen-covered driftwood. It looked a lot better than it sounds, believe me. The place was gorgeous. There were windows everywhere, and lots of dark wood on several open porches along the front and—I assumed—the back. The house looked like it ought to perch on the cliffs overlooking the ocean, windblown and spectacular, but instead it sat on an acre or two of grass in the middle of Waterfield Village. It made an impression there, too, or at least it had on me.

"That's their house?" I said again.

"Yup," Derek confirmed. "That's it."

"What does Mr. Silva do?"

"He inherited it, along with the family business. Something to do with logging."

Lots of logging in Maine. Not so much down here on the coast, but inland. "Good for him."

Derek nodded. "The house has been in the family since it was built, I think."

The waitress arrived with the food then, and the conversation stalled out while she deposited plates on the table— burger and fries for Derek, chicken sandwich for me—and asked if we needed anything else. When she was gone, I picked up where we'd left off.

"So what's the Silvas' relationship to the Green sisters? I thought Darren was their only surviving relative."

"Not the only," Derek said. "Just the last. At least until he gets married and produces offspring." He picked up his burger and took a bite. After chewing and swallowing, he added, "I think Henrietta and Henry and the Green sisters are some sort of cousins. They shared the same grandmother, I think."

"So their mothers were siblings." I nibbled daintily on my own sandwich. "Making them first cousins."

"I think," Derek said. "Which would make Darren a first cousin once removed or something, yeah?"

Something like that. "Do you think we'll have a chance to sneak away on Sunday to see the inside of their house?" It wasn't like I'd ever get the opportunity again probably. It wasn't like they gave tours, and Henrietta and I hadn't gotten off on that great of a foot, I felt.

"I think you'll probably be too busy with your own house," Derek said.

When I pouted, he relented. "You could ask Kate if you could tag along when she does her checkups on Saturday afternoon."

"Checkups?"

"Stopping by all the houses on the tour to make sure they're ready. Melissa used to do it."

Of course. Melissa was a perfectionist—or as Derek, more kindly disposed than I, might say it: a professional—and would have wanted to make sure that everything was tip-top and nothing would reflect poorly on her organizational abilities during the tour. I wasn't sure Kate was quite that obsessive.

Still, it couldn't hurt to ask.

"I'll do that."

"Eat your food," Derek said and devoted himself to his own.

. . .

We finished our meal before the Silvas finished theirs, and on our way out, I glanced in their direction. They had gotten their food—Henry was eating steak and his sister what looked like a salmon filet—but the food sat mostly forgotten as they spoke. Or maybe "argued" would be a more accurate term. Henry was pouting like a sulky five-year-old, sitting back in his seat with his arms folded across his chest, while Henrietta was leaning forward across the table, lecturing him in true older-sister fashion. She even stabbed the table a few times with her finger to get her point across.

"Wonder what that was about," I said as we pushed out through the door into the parking lot, and the crisp, cold air of the winter night.

He shrugged. "Family matters? The Silvas have had plenty to deal with already this year, between Henrietta's heart and Ruth's hip and helping her and Mamie sell the house. And now there's the baby skeleton. It's not strange if things are boiling over a little."

"It looked like Henrietta was lecturing Henry, though. And he couldn't have had anything to do with whatever happened to Baby Arthur. He was a baby, too."

"I don't know, Avery," Derek said as we made our way toward the truck. The tree was still there, sticking out over the back of the bed. "Maybe she's unhappy that someone else didn't find the baby skeleton before the house was sold. Or maybe it doesn't have anything to do with that at all. Maybe Henry got home late last night and she was worried."

"He's sixty-five!" Surely that was beyond the age where he had to worry about staying out late.

"Sixty-four," Derek said. "And she's still his older sister."

He opened the car door for me and gave me a boost inside. "Don't worry about it, Avery. It's none of our business, whatever they were talking about."

He closed the door. I watched as he walked around the truck to get in on the driver's side, and although I knew he was right, I couldn't help but wish I knew what Henry and Henrietta had been talking about.

9

Wayne dropped by midmorning the next day. We were back to work at the house again. Derek had started to replace the old plumbing, while I spent some more time just sitting around enjoying the view and thinking.

I probably shouldn't have been there at all, to be honest. It would have been a better use of my time to be at home decorating for the home tour. There was still a lot to be done. But I felt guilty for leaving Derek to do all the work, even when all I could do was keep him company. And then, when Wayne showed up, I was glad I hadn't gone anywhere.

"I just wanted to give you an update," he told me, stamping his feet and shaking the snow from his shoulders.

Yes, it had finally started snowing. Pretty little floaty snowflakes drifting toward the ground from a leaden sky. About time, too, in December.

"We appreciate that." I closed the front door behind him. "Let me get Derek."

Wayne nodded, and shrugged out of his parka while I stopped at the bottom of the stairs and hollered up. "Derek! Wayne's here."

"Just a minute," floated back down. We waited, and a minute or two later he came clattering down the stairs, his hands grimy from the work.

"What's going on?"

"I wanted to give you an update about the skeleton," Wayne said. "I sent it to the ME's office in Portland yesterday, and they looked it over and extracted DNA for a test. Those usually take a long time, but I was curious, and so was everyone else, so we called in a few favors and got it done."

"And?"

"Things didn't turn out the way I thought they would."

I blinked. "It isn't Arthur Green?"

Wayne blinked back. "How do you know about Arthur Green?"

"I checked the newspaper archives," I said.

"I checked the old police records." He glanced at Derek. "Arthur Green was the sisters' little brother. He disappeared in September 1949."

"I know," Derek said. "Avery told me. But the skeleton isn't him?"

"Not conclusively," Wayne said. "Most likely it is. Hard to imagine who else it could be. There have been no other missing babies in Waterfield that we know about. But the skeleton's DNA doesn't match the Green sisters' DNA."

"At all?"

"Some of it matched. Not all. They didn't have both parents in common."

"So it could still be Arthur Green. If his mother had an affair with someone else."

"It could," Wayne admitted.

This was a wrinkle. If it wasn't Arthur Green, who was it?

And if it was, why didn't he match his sisters' DNA?

But it might explain why the baby had died, I realized with a shock. If Mr. Green had found out that his wife had cuckolded him, and that Arthur wasn't his biological son, he could have hurt the baby in a fit of temper and accidentally—or deliberately—killed him. And hidden him in the attic so no one would know. The wife might have known and allowed it, out of guilt and because she didn't want anyone to know that she'd cheated. Or she might not have known and thought the baby really did get stolen.

"What was their relationship like after the baby disappeared? The Greens?"

"I have no idea," Wayne said. "But I can't imagine it was good, whether they knew what had happened or not. Losing a child is the single most traumatic thing that can happen to parents."

I could well imagine.

"So what'll happen now?"

"Not much," Wayne said. "I'm certainly not going to tell the Green sisters that their brother's skeleton has been found in the attic of the house they've lived in all their lives, and by the way . . . it seems he's only their half brother."

No, that wouldn't do anyone any good. The sisters were both fragile in their own ways: Ruth physically and Mamie psychologically. And it didn't serve any purpose to involve them, that I could see. They were in no position to do anything about anything.

"What'll you do with the bones?" Derek asked.

Wayne sighed and ran a hand through his salt-and-pepper curls. "I'll have to talk to Mr. Silva, I guess. Senior or junior. Tell him the skeleton has been found and what we've discovered. And arrange to have the bones interred somewhere. The Silvas will have to make the decision on whether that'll be in some sort of family plot, or just an unmarked hole somewhere."

"None of what happened was the baby's fault," I said, "whoever he was. He deserves a decent burial in consecrated ground."

"Of course. And I'm sure the Silvas will do the right thing."

Wayne grabbed his parka from the window seat and began shrugging into it again, preparatory to leaving.

"Are you going there now?"

He nodded.

"Can I come?"

Derek rolled his eyes.

"No," Wayne said. "Why do you want to?"

"She just wants to see the inside of the Silvas' house," Derek said. "She won't have a chance on Sunday."

"Oh." Wayne smiled faintly. "Sorry, Avery. You'll have to find some other kind of excuse for a peek. This is police business."

"I found the body!"

"I'll let them know. If they want to talk to you, they know where to find you."

He headed toward the door. "Better luck next time, Tink," Derek said and started up the stairs.

∙ ∙ ∙

So we were back where we started. He was plumbing and I was bored. I wandered around the downstairs for a bit, listening to the clanging from upstairs and trying to concentrate on imagining the house as a finished product. Dark wood cabinets in the kitchen, Shaker style probably. Espresso color. Brushed nickel hardware. Granite counter. Very Craftsman looking. Very natural. Wood floors, if the ugly old vinyl came up without leaving the floors too damaged.

That was something I could do actually. Tear up the vinyl in the kitchen. Except I didn't want to.

I headed upstairs and stuck my head into the bathroom. "Can I leave and go do something else?"

Derek turned to look at me. "What do you want to do, Avery?"

"Decorate for Christmas," I said. "Go to the crafts store and buy Chinese lanterns and paint and glitter and make my ornaments. That way I won't have to spend all evening doing it tonight."

"Are you sure that's all you want to do? Wayne's not going to be happy if he finds you snooping around the Silvas' house."

"I won't go near the Silvas' house."

He squinted at me.

"I swear. I'll just go to the crafts store and home." With maybe a short detour in between. Not to the Silvas' house, though.

"I suppose," Derek said. "Though I'm starting to take it personally, Avery. Used to be, you wanted to spend all your time with me. Now we've been married six weeks, and you're already trying to get away?"

"Of course I'm not trying to get away." I went to drop a kiss on his cheek. It turned into something else. When I surfaced again, I added a bit breathlessly, "I'm just bored. There's nothing to do."

"You could start taking up the vinyl floor in the kitchen," Derek said as if he'd read my mind.

"I'll need a spade for that. We don't have one." Believe it or not, a spade is often the best tool for taking up glued-on vinyl. Sometimes you have to chip it away, bit by tiny bit, but other times, if the glue is old, it comes up very nicely, in big flakes, with a spade.

"You could go get one and come back," Derek said. He had a trace of lipstick at the corner of his mouth, and I reached out and wiped it off with my thumb.

"I could do that. Or I could wait until tomorrow."

"You could go buy your lanterns and stuff, and get some lunch and the spade, and then come back."

It was better than nothing. Just meant I had to move faster than I'd thought I'd have to. "I could do that. What kind of lunch do you want?"

"Pizza," Derek said, which suited me fine.

"Guido's?"

"Sure."

Guido's Pizzeria was in the direction I was going anyway. "I'll be back in an hour or two." I ducked out the door and into Mamie's room, where I gathered up the boxes of toys, and into Ruth's room, where I picked up the box with the pictures of The Pelvis and put it on top of the others. And then I stepped back onto the landing, only to stop in my tracks when I saw Derek waiting there, one shoulder against the doorjamb and his hands folded across his chest.

Nice arms. Nice chest.

Speculative expression on his face.

"On second thought," he said.

"Yes?"

"I think I'll come with you. I'd rather eat pizza at a table."

The dismay must have shown plainly on my face, because he chuckled. "What are you up to, Tinkerbell?"

When I didn't answer right away, because I didn't want to admit what I was planning to do, he added, "What's in the boxes? Is that the stuff you told me about yesterday?"

I nodded.

"What are you going to do with it?"

"I thought I might take them out to the nursing home," I said reluctantly. "And give them to Mamie and Ruth."

"And see if you can't turn the conversation ever so gently to their baby brother while you're there reminiscing." It wasn't a question, and his voice was resigned.

I shrugged. I couldn't deny it, and there was no need to admit it, since he already knew. "I wasn't going to mention the skeleton."

"Sure." He pushed off from the doorjamb. "I'm coming with you."

"You are?"

"I'm not sending you out there on your own to get in trouble."

"You're going to get in trouble with me?"

"With any luck," Derek said, "maybe I can keep you from getting in trouble."

He took the boxes out of my hands and headed down the stairs. "Besides," he added halfway down, "I'm hungry. If I have to wait for you to buy Chinese lanterns as well as make nice with Mamie and Ruth, I won't get fed until three o'clock."

There was a very real chance of that.

"We can stop for food first," I told him.

"Don't mind if we do," Derek answered, and made for the front door.

• • •

The first stop was at the hobby store on Main Street, a tiny little place that specialized in wooden models of sailing ships and such. They did have some packages of Chinese lanterns, though, white and colored.

"What do you think?" I asked Derek, who watched me with his hands in his pockets. He was wearing the kind of coat with a lamb's wool collar and lining, and the shoulders were wet from the snow. It was snowing heavier now than it had been just about an hour ago, when Wayne had visited.

He looked from the lanterns to me and back. "You want them to be colored, right? To look like Christmas balls?"

Of course. However—"I can spend a little more for the colored ones, and buy white paint and glitter to decorate them. But they won't be hard and shiny. If I want them to look like glass balls, it might be better to get the white ones, and paint them with high-gloss paint first, and then decorate them."

"OK," Derek said.

"They'll be a little heavier that way. And they'll cost more. And it'll be a lot more work. While if I buy the colored ones, they'll be lighter. But they won't be glossy." I gnawed my lip, while the possibilities danced like sugarplums in my head, making me dizzy.

"Avery," Derek said.

"What?"

"It's a nonissue."

"No, it isn't! People are going to come over and see them. I want them to be perfect. I don't want Kate to regret asking us to be part of the tour."

"She won't regret asking us to be part of the tour," Derek said. "Get the colored ones. Decorate them. If you don't like the result, we'll paint them and you can try again."

Oh.

I smiled. "I can do that."

"I thought you could," Derek said, and helped me carry three packages of lanterns, white spray paint, and glitter to the register. "Do you need a stencil?"

"I'll make my own." I'd done it before. Back in the spring, when we'd been working on the center-chimney Colonial on Rowanberry Island, I had discovered sailcloth rugs, and decided to try my hand at making one. Stencils played a big part. I'd ended up making several rugs, so there'd been a lot of stenciling, and I'd learned to make not only my own sailcloth rugs, but my own stencils, as well.

"Food?" Derek asked hopefully when we had checked out and put the purchases in the truck. He'd worked hard this morning, and he had a high metabolism anyway. He was pretty much always hungry.

"Sure," I said. "Let's do it."

We headed down the road toward Barnham College, and pulled into the parking lot at Guido's Pizzeria before we got there.

It was a small cinderblock building with a neon sign flashing HOT-HOT-HOT, sort of like a strip club. Derek had taken me here for the first time when we were renovating the midcentury ranch on Becklea Drive last fall—Primrose Acres, the 1950s subdivision, was just down the road—and we'd been regulars ever since.

It could get pretty busy at night, with the college students, but in the middle of the day like this, it wasn't bad at all. It was no problem getting a table. The waitress, most likely a student herself, had long, black hair in a ponytail and piercings in her eyebrow and lip. Tattoos of leaves and flowers wound up both her arms and disappeared under the sleeves of the black T-shirt.

"I miss Candy," I told Derek when she'd departed with our drink and pizza orders.

A shadow crossed his face, and he nodded.

Candy used to work at Guido's. She'd been our waitress the very first time Derek had taken me here, and almost every time since. She lived in Josh Rasmussen's condo building, and she passed away a few months ago. Derek had tried hard to save her, and had thought for a while he had. She'd made it to the hospital still breathing. But then something went wrong. It hadn't been his fault, not at all, but he still took it personally.

That made me feel bad for inadvertently bringing it up and reminding him, so I hurried to change the subject. "At least she isn't flirting with you."

"Probably noticed the ring," Derek said and twisted his hand so the wide gold band on his finger caught the light. "I didn't use to wear one."

True. I smiled at my own: a little slimmer, encircling my own finger. "Are you sure you want to come to the nursing home with me?"

"I'm sure."

"Because you could just go back to work and I could go on my own."

"No. I want to come."

I peered at him across the table. "You're curious, too. Aren't you? Go on, admit it!"

"I may be a little curious," Derek said.

"Just a little?"

"Not as curious as you."

"How do you know how curious I am?"

"I know you," Derek said. "I know you're absolutely eaten up inside right now because there's something you don't know. You're incurably nosy."

I pouted, and he grinned at me, and then transferred the smile onto the waitress when she put the drinks on the table. "Thank you."

"Food will be right out." She stomped off in some sort of military boots laced up her calf, over black stockings. She couldn't have looked any more different from the previous waitress, Candy, with her bouncy blond ponytail and pink cropped top and bubble gum.

"I wonder if David Rossini still manages the place," I said.

"Last I heard," Derek answered, "Francesca kicked him out and filed for divorce."

"Really?"

He nodded. "Wouldn't you?"

"For cheating? You better believe it. So don't even think about it."

"It wouldn't cross my mind," Derek said sincerely. "But to get back to what we were talking about . . . yes, I am a bit curious. It's an interesting story. Sad, but interesting."

Definitely. Sad and a bit disturbing. I wondered whether it might be better not to know exactly what had happened—in case what had happened was something I didn't want to know—but wasn't it always better to know the truth?

Not that I planned to ask Ruth Green whether she thought her mother was an adulteress or her father a murderer, of course. I might be curious, but there were limits to the kinds of questions you could ask. Especially of a fragile seventy-five-year-old in a hospital bed.

No, I was just going to give her the box of Elvis clippings and tell her where I found it, and see if she felt inclined to reminisce. If she didn't, we'd get out of there and look for Mamie. Give her the tea set and see if she'd be more obliging with information than her sister.

I might ask a few leading questions if the occasion seemed to call for it. But I wouldn't turn it into an interrogation. I knew my place. And if it ever got back to Wayne that I'd sprung the news of the skeleton on the Green sisters, he'd probably lock me up for interfering in his investigation. And that was the last thing I needed, with the Christmas Home Tour coming up. I didn't want to be stuck in jail while Derek had to deal with the visitors and while both he and Kate were cursing me.

"Are you absolutely sure you want to do this, Avery?" Derek asked me on the way back to the truck after we'd eaten and paid.

I squinted up at him. "Would you rather I didn't?"

"I would rather not upset Wayne," Derek said, ducking the question.

"He won't be upset. There's nothing for him to be upset about. We're just returning some of the Green sisters' things that were left at the house. Whoever packed up—and I'm sure it wasn't them, if Ruth has a broken hip—didn't realize the boxes were there. We're not doing anything wrong."

"You think Wayne will see it that way?"

"It's the truth," I said, "so why not?"

Derek shrugged and opened the door for me. I let him give me a boost up into the passenger seat, and then I watched him walk around the truck and open his own door.

"You know," I told him when he was sitting next to me, inserting the key in the ignition, "it's OK if you don't want to come. Really. You can drop me and the lanterns and the boxes off at Aunt Inga's house and I can take the Beetle out to the nursing home on my own. I don't mind. If you're worried, you don't have to be a part of it."

"I'm not afraid," Derek said, his tone highly offended.

"I didn't say 'afraid.' I said 'worried.' If you're worried, you don't have to come."

"I'm not afraid. Or worried. I just think we should leave Wayne alone to do his job."

"I'm not interfering with Wayne's job," I said. "I'm not going to tell them about the skeleton. I'm just returning their toys."

"Sure." Derek put the truck into reverse and backed out of the parking spot, then shifted and moved forward, out of the lot and onto the Augusta Highway. "I'm coming. That's final."

"Suit yourself," I said, and settled into the seat.

It didn't take long to get to the nursing home, even if Derek did stick to the speed limits today, as opposed to the other night. Nonetheless, it was no more than fifteen minutes later when we pulled up outside—in the adjacent parking lot this time, instead of under the portico—and got out. I grabbed the boxes, and we headed for the door.

A nice lady manned the reception counter in the lobby, and like most ladies of a certain age—eight to eighty—she seemed predisposed to give Derek anything he wanted. She practically preened.

As we stopped in front of the counter, she simpered up at him. "Good afternoon, Dr. Ellis."

"I'm not a doctor anymore, Wanda," Derek reminded her with that patented, dimpled Derek-grin, "but good afternoon to you, too."

"And who's this?" She turned bright eyes on me.

"This is my wife." There was a distinct note of pride in Derek's voice, and it made me blush. The nurse flushed, too, from pleasure or the effect of Derek's grin. He's a handsome devil, my husband.

"Nice to meet you," I said, putting the boxes down on the counter and extending a hand across. "I'm Avery."

Wanda took my hand and shook it. "How can I help the two of you?"

I had my mouth open to answer, but Derek got in before me. "First, I wanted to know how Mary Green was doing. We found her the other night and brought her here, and I just wanted to know if everything turned out all right."

"Oh," Wanda said brightly, "she fine. Right as rain again. If you hadn't found her when you did, it could well have gone wrong, but as it is, no harm done."

"Wonderful. Is she here?"

"She's out of bed and moving around again," Wanda said, "but if you want to see her, I'll see if I can track her down."

"A little later. First I'd like to see her sister, Ruth. Avery has something for her."

Wanda turned her attention to me, and I explained. "We're renovating the Green sisters' house, and I found some of their old things that were missed in the cleanup. Some of Mamie's toys and Ruth's teenage stuff. I thought she might enjoy seeing it."

"Of course." Wanda smiled. "She's in room 202, down the hall. Just don't tire her out. She's been in physical therapy this morning, and she might be a little worn out from it."

I could imagine. "We won't stay long," I promised. "Do you think Mamie will be with her, too?"

"She might be. But Mamie is more of a free spirit. She likes to wander."

No kidding.

"If we don't find her," Derek said, "we'll be back so you can track her down for us."

"Happy to help," Wanda said, and turned away as the phone rang. As we headed down the hall, we heard her trill into the phone, "Thank you for calling Sunset Acres. How may I direct your call?"

"Sunset Acres?" I asked Derek out of the corner of my mouth.

He shrugged. "Guess someone has a sense of humor."

Guess so.

—10—

We found Ruth Green in a room down the hall. Not knowing much about it, I halfway expected her to be in a hospital bed in one of those traction things, with her leg halfway
up into the air, attached to a wire.

She wasn't. She was sitting in a chair with her leg on an
ottoman. It was encased in a huge, puffy cast: dark blue
with white Velcro straps. A four-footed walker stood next
to her, and she was leaning back with her eyes closed, her
face pale with papery skin.

Ruth looked older than seventy-five, but maybe that was
the pain.

While I'd seen Mamie a few times in the year I'd been
living in Waterfield—she was active and physically healthy,
even if her mind had gone bye-bye a long time ago—this
was the first time I'd met Ruth. She didn't look much like
her sister, other than that they both had white hair and that
there was perhaps a similarity in facial features. But where
Mamie looked girlish and frilly in her incongruous pinafore
and braids, Ruth looked severe yet fragile, with her white

hair cropped short, sticking to her head in wispy curls, and with lines and grooves on her face.

"If she's asleep, I'm not waking her," Derek told me *sotto voce.*

I shook my head. No, I wouldn't expect him to. She looked like she could use the rest. The physical therapy must have been hard.

But she must have heard us whispering, because she opened her eyes, blinked and then focused on us. After a second it must have dawned that we were there to see her. "Oh."

She made an effort to push herself farther up in the chair, without much success. Derek went to help.

"Do you need a hand, Miss Ruth?"

She blinked up at him. "You're Dr. Ellis's son, aren't you?"

He nodded. "Yes, ma'am. I'm Derek."

"Aren't you a doctor, too?"

He shifted her a little higher in the chair and made sure she was comfortable before he stepped back. "I used to be. Now I renovate houses. This is my wife, Avery."

"Hi," I said. If I hadn't been carrying the boxes of stuff, I would have twiddled my fingers at her.

She had very cool, blue eyes. "Renovate houses?"

"We bought yours," I said apologetically. "From Mr. Silva."

Her face closed. "I see."

"I'm sorry you had to leave. You lived there a long time, didn't you?"

"All my life," Ruth said. "My father bought the house for Mother when they married."

That was quite the wedding gift. "How long were your parents married?"

"Fifty-seven years," Ruth said proudly.

"That's a long time." And it meant that whoever had done what was done to Baby Arthur—if anyone had done anything at all, and if it even was the remains of Baby Arthur we'd found—Mr. and Mrs. Green had stayed together afterward. For a long, long time.

If Mrs. Green had had an affair, Mr. Green had obviously forgiven her. And she had loved him enough to stick around after the death—or disappearance—of the baby.

"They must have been happy together."

Ruth shrugged skinny shoulders underneath a fuzzy cardigan jacket. "They had their difficulties, like everyone else."

"Marriage is hard." I glanced at Derek, who arched his brows at me. *Sorry*, I telegraphed. *Nothing personal. Just trying to get information.*

It must have transferred, because he said, "Avery has something for you, Miss Ruth."

"Right." I put the boxes down on the foot of the bed and retrieved the one with Ruth's Elvis clippings. "I thought you might enjoy having this. I found it in the wall cubby in your room. There were a couple of boxes in your sister's room, and this one in yours. Pictures of Elvis."

I took the lid off and put the open box on her lap, carefully, and watched as her thin fingers sifted through the clippings.

"How old were you?" Derek asked after a moment, his voice soft.

She shot him a distracted glance before going back to the clippings. "Sixteen. Seventeen."

She'd been around ten, then, when her brother went missing. Died.

"We found some of Mamie's things, too. In the other bedroom."

I took the lid off the box with the tea set, and showed it to Ruth. She stared at it for a second, silent, before she said, "She loved that. She used to make me take tea with her dolls long after I was too old to play with them."

"You must have been good friends. Sisters, close in age . . ." I let the sentence trail off, hoping for a tidbit of information.

She smiled. "We were. Mamie, me, and Henrietta."

"Henrietta?" Of course I knew who Henrietta was, but I wanted to keep the conversation going.

"Our cousin," Ruth said. "She's a year younger than I am, and a year older than Mamie. We were inseparable, the three of us." A shadow passed over her face.

"What's wrong?" I asked.

She shook her head, her lips pressed tightly together. "We were good friends when we were small. Then things changed."

"I'm sorry."

"It was nobody's fault," Ruth said, going back to sifting through her clippings. "Things happen."

She said it without looking up. I glanced at Derek. He nodded and got to his feet. "We'll leave you to rest, Miss Ruth. It was nice to see you."

"Didn't she want to sell the house?" I asked Derek when we were back in the hallway, hunting for Mamie's room.

"I don't think she did," Derek answered. "She must have known she didn't have a choice, but I can't imagine she was happy about it. She and Mamie lived together in that house as long as they've been alive. It's the only home she's ever had. And now she's here, with no privacy, unable to take care of herself, unable to take care of Mamie . . ."

He shook his head. "It happens to a lot of people as they get older, you know? They get to a point where they can't live on their own anymore. Just look at Henrietta. With the hip, Ruth would be out of commission for a good long time, and of course Mamie couldn't stay in the house on her own. This was the best thing for them. The only thing for them. But I imagine she'd have preferred for it not to be this way."

Probably so.

Mamie's room was empty, except for the two dolls and one teddy bear on the neatly made bed. The bear was a dirty yellow and was missing one black button eye and half an ear. One of the dolls was the baby I'd found in the basement of the house a few days ago. The other was tucked carefully under the blanket so only the top of the head was visible. I guess maybe it was Mamie's favorite.

I took an impulsive step forward, but Derek held me back. "She isn't here."

"I just wanted a look at the doll," I said.

He shook his head. "She might be able to tell if someone has disturbed the 'baby.' Better leave it alone."

I figured I'd probably be able to put the blanket back over the "baby" to make it look like no one had touched it, but it wasn't important, after all. Just idle curiosity on my part. So I backed out of the room and we wandered on down the hall looking for Mamie.

We tracked her down to a chair in the common room, by the fireplace. Maybe she was still feeling chilled after the ordeal the other night, or maybe someone else had put her there and she just hadn't gotten around to wandering off yet.

She had no idea who we were, of course, and didn't seem to understand when we explained it. But she was beyond excited to receive her tea set. Her face cracked in a wide grin, and she hummed as she pulled each little cup and saucer out and caressed them before putting them on the table beside her.

"Who gave it to you?" I asked, pulling up an armchair and leaning forward to watch as she put it all together perfectly on the table.

"I got it for Christmas. From Mama and Papa." Her voice was high, girlish.

"That's a great gift." I found myself talking to her as if she were seven instead of seventy-some. "How old were you?"

She wrinkled her brows at me. "It was last Christmas."

Of course. "Seven maybe? Or eight?"

"Seven," Mamie said. "I was seven last Christmas. I'm eight now."

I made sure not to look at Derek. "Eight is a great age. Do you and Ruth play tea party a lot?"

"Ruth and I and Henrietta," Mamie said. "Henrietta is my cousin."

"I think I've met Henrietta once."

"She's nine. But she still likes tea parties. Ruth doesn't."

"Why not?"

"She has to take care of the babies," Mamie said, fiddling with her teacups. "The babies are too small for tea parties."

"Do you like babies?"

"I like *my* baby," Mamie said. "I don't like Henrietta's. He cries all the time."

"But your baby doesn't cry?"

She shook her head. "He's good." She looked up at me. "Do I know you?"

"My name is Avery," I said.

She shook her head. "I don't know you. And I'm not supposed to talk to strangers. You'll have to leave."

"Of course." I got to my feet. "Enjoy your tea set."

She looked down at it, and her face softened. I don't think she even noticed when we walked away.

. . .

"Something wrong?" Derek inquired when we were outside again, crossing the parking lot and breathing deeply of the crisp, cold winter air with a hint of snow.

It wasn't that it had smelled bad inside the nursing home. It hadn't particularly. I hadn't even noticed being bothered by it inside. There had been a medical, sort of antiseptic smell, overlaid by some mixture of baby powder or vanilla and lavender. But it hadn't smelled bad.

But now that I was outside, I noticed I was gulping deep mouthfuls of cold air, as if I couldn't replace the air in my lungs fast enough.

I shook my head. "I'm fine."

"Dizzy?"

"No. Just . . . the air feels good."

"Close in there." Derek nodded.

It had been, yes. And hot, not just in front of the fireplace, but everywhere. I guess it's true what I've heard, that old people feel the cold more.

"We didn't really learn anything."

"I wouldn't say that." He unlocked the car door for me and boosted me inside. "We found out that Mamie liked her own brother, but didn't like little Henry."

"So?" I said, but he had already closed the door behind me and was on his way around the truck. That gave me a little time to think about what he'd said before I had to respond.

"Do you think that's significant?" I picked up the conversation when he was sitting beside me.

He glanced at me in the process of inserting the key in the ignition. "Hard to say what's significant and what isn't. I don't imagine it is. But it's something."

"If it doesn't mean anything, I don't really care."

"It's too soon to know what means anything," Derek said and put the truck in reverse. "You also found out that Ruth, Mamie, and Henrietta were close friends when they were small, but that something happened to change that."

I nodded. "Do you suppose it was Henrietta who killed the baby?"

Derek stared at me. "I wouldn't think so."

"What are you saying, then?"

"I'm not saying anything. Just telling you that you found out some things."

"Useless things."

"That happens," Derek said and headed out of the parking lot.

I waited a few minutes, while he navigated back toward Waterfield proper, and then I broke the silence again. "Where are we going?"

"Home," Derek said.

"To Aunt Inga's house?"

He nodded. "You can drop off the lanterns and paint, and I'll find a spade. Then you can spend the afternoon taking up the floor in the kitchen."

"Fine." I folded my arms across my chest.

He gave it a minute and then looked at me. "Don't you want to take up the kitchen floor?"

"I want to make my Christmas ornaments," I said.

"The lanterns?"

I nodded.

"Why don't you do that tonight? I'll help you. We can spend all night getting ready for the tour. I'll even cook."

"Cook what?"

"Dunno," Derek said. "What do you want?"

"Tikka Masala."

He stared at me. "Indian?"

I nodded.

"I don't know how to cook Indian food."

"Then you shouldn't offer," I said.

"Can you cook Indian food?"

"I can barely make sandwiches. You know that."

"Then you have a lot of nerve criticizing my abilities." He was silent for a moment. "Do you really want Tikka Masala?"

I shook my head. "Not really. Spaghetti would be fine. Or cheese sandwiches. Or chili. Something simple."

"Stir-fry?"

"Stir-fry would be great." He made a good one.

"We'll have to stop for a few supplies on our way home. So you'll come back to the house with me and work on the kitchen floor if I promise to make you stir-fry tonight?"

"I guess," I said.

"I appreciate the rousing enthusiasm," Derek answered and stepped on the gas.

．　．　．

I ended up spending the rest of the afternoon shoveling vinyl in the Green sisters' house, while Derek clanged and banged the plumbing all around me. After finishing upstairs, he came down to the first-floor bath and went to work there. Meanwhile, I pried up big flakes of mustard yellow vinyl and dragged them out to the Dumpster. Every so often, I took a break and went to watch Derek work. Shoveling is hard on the arms and shoulders, whether you're shoveling snow, dirt, or old flooring, and the view was quite nice. Derek in faded jeans that pulled nicely across his posterior as he knelt on the floor, and in a plain blue T-shirt that showed admirable musculature as he wrestled with the pipes . . . definitely worth taking a break for.

Until he sent me a pointed look over his shoulder and inquired whether I didn't have something more useful to do, whereupon I toddled back to the kitchen and my spade.

By five we called it a day and locked up. The vinyl was gone, and Derek had determined that most of the hardened glue cemented to the old floors could be sanded off and the hardwoods rescued.

We stopped at Shaw's Supermarket—a Maine institution since 1919—to pick up supplies for the stir-fry. And no sooner had we walked in than Derek nodded a greeting. "Darren."

Darren Silva nodded back. "Derek." He glanced at me, but either he couldn't remember my name, or I just wasn't worthy of his attention.

I didn't like Darren Silva. It could have been shyness on his part, I suppose—maybe he just wasn't used to women, or something like it. Derek had another friend like that: Ian Burns, up in Boothbay Harbor. The first time I met him, Derek warned me not to look directly at him and under no circumstances talk directly to him. Just pretend he wasn't there unless he spoke to me.

Maybe Darren Silva was the same way.

It was hard to reconcile that kind of person with the picture in front of me, though. While Ian was a big, burly lumberjack-looking fellow who kept a full beard because it made him feel safe, and who ran his family's salvage yard and shot moose in his spare time, Darren Silva was nicely groomed and dressed in an expensive designer suit with a starched shirt and tie under an elegant cashmere coat . . . looking for all the world like he had just stopped at Shaw's on his way home from the office.

He looked normal. Gainfully employed. Well off. Secure of himself and his position in the world.

In other words, I suspected he was just being rude.

"How's everything?" Derek inquired politely.

Darren snorted. "Going to hell."

All righty, then.

"How so?"

Darren rolled his eyes. "You know. The police showed up at the office this afternoon to tell me there'd been bones found in the house. You found them."

"Yes," Derek said.

"Couldn't you just have left them where they were? Or put them in the Dumpster, or something?"

There was a pause. I was too flabbergasted to speak, and Derek must have felt the same way, because it took him a minute to find his voice. When he did, it was mild. (I'm pretty sure I would have been shrieking like a banshee by then, had it been me.) "Not really, no. Human remains are a police matter."

"If they'd been there for over sixty years," Darren said with an annoyed flick of his neck, "a few more years wouldn't have mattered. You know, I have half a mind to tell you to stop renovating."

There was another pause. I waited, interestedly, to see whether Derek would lose his temper this time.

He didn't. "You can't tell me to stop renovating," he informed Darren, his voice as smooth and polite as before. "It isn't your house anymore. I paid for it."

"I'll buy it back!" Darren said.

"I'm sorry, but it isn't for sale." Derek took my arm and nudged me sideways. I sidled to my right.

We'd taken only a few steps when Darren called us back. The high color was gone from his face, and he looked sheepish. "Listen," he told Derek, "I'm sorry. I didn't mean it. It was just a shock. You know?"

"To us, too," Derek said, obviously not entirely ready to forgive and forget yet.

Darren glanced my way. "I thought we'd cleaned out the whole house before you took over."

"It wasn't your fault," I said, since he'd acknowledged me. Sort of. "The crate was up in the crawl space under the roof, wedged beside the chimney. Unless you were up there, you wouldn't have noticed it."

Darren shook his head. "I asked Aunt Ruth, and she said there was nothing in the attic. That it was too hard to get to."

"I'm sure she didn't know, either."

There was a pause.

"Did the police say anything else?" I asked.

Darren looked at me. He had very pale blue eyes, several shades lighter than Derek's. "Like what?"

"I don't know. I thought maybe they'd asked you questions."

"Questions about what?"

"About the skeleton," I said patiently.

He sounded mighty defensive for someone who hadn't even been born yet when Arthur Green died, and moreover, wouldn't be born for another thirty years, give or take. It wasn't like I was accusing him of anything.

Unless he was feeling defensive on someone else's behalf. Not his father, since his father had been just a baby. But maybe Darren's aunt Henrietta . . .

"What about the skeleton?" Darren said.

"I thought maybe they'd asked you about it. What you thought happened to it. Whether there were any family stories."

"Family stories?"

I gave up. "I'm sure things will calm down shortly. And at least the news channels haven't gotten hold of it."

Darren paled at the thought.

"Excuse us," Derek said and gave me another push. I stumbled off and he followed. Darren didn't say anything to stop us this time.

"That wasn't very nice," I told my husband when we were out of earshot.

"He wasn't very nice."

No, he hadn't been. "I guess it must have been a shock. He might feel guilty for leaving it there for us to find, even if he had no idea it was there. And it was a relative. It's personal. Not like it is for us."

"He still didn't have to be rude," Derek said, and dropped my arm to start picking through the vegetables.

We got what we needed along with some steak and dessert—rice I already had, in the cupboard at home—and then we headed out. Once we got to Aunt Inga's house and had greeted Mischa—who wound around our ankles with abandon, purring hysterically—and Jemmy and Inky, who favored us with an open eye and a twitching tail respectively, from the velvet love seat in the parlor—Derek got busy chopping on the kitchen counter, while I laid old newspaper all over the dining room table and began preparations for creating my oversized Christmas ornaments. Soon, the sound of oil popping from the wok mingled with the carols on the radio, and the odors of browning beef and broccoli mixed with the sharp scent of spray paint. I was humming along with Bing and "White Christmas" when there was a knock on the door.

Mischa, ever my guardian, shot out from under the table and streaked for the door, the better to protect me from whoever was outside. I took a few steps back from the table and peered through the foyer.

"Brandon's here," I informed Derek as I turned down the music. "I'll let him in."

"Go ahead," floated back to me. "I've got my hands full."

"He might want to talk to you."

"I can't imagine why," Derek said, "but if he does, he can come into the kitchen."

Right-o.

I snapped the latex gloves off my hands and went to answer the door. "This is a surprise."

"Sorry," Brandon said.

"Something wrong?" I waved him inside. He stamped his feet on the mat and moved into the foyer so I could close the door behind him.

"This looks nice." He looked around at the decorations.

"It will, once we finish."

"You can stay and help if you want," Derek said, sticking his head out of the kitchen for a moment. "There's plenty of food."

Brandon's nostrils quivered. "Smells good."

"Stir-fry," I said. "You're welcome to stay."

He shook his head. "I wish I could, but I need one of you to come with me over to the house on North Street."

"Our house?" Derek and I exchanged a glance. "Is something wrong?"

"Not with the house. Miss Mamie is missing again."

"The nursing home lost her?"

"They didn't lose her," Brandon said. "She left. She's not a prisoner there."

Right.

"You go," I told Derek. "If she's hurt or something, you'll know what to do better than I will."

He nodded. "Just turn the heat off and put the lid on the wok to keep the food warm." He paused next to me for long enough to drop a kiss on my cheek.

"No problem. Be careful." I watched him snag his coat from the foyer and follow Brandon out into the night. Then I locked the door behind them and headed for the kitchen to make sure the food didn't overcook. There's nothing worse than soggy Chinese food.

Or rather, there are plenty worse things than soggy Chinese food, but as far as Chinese food goes, soggy is the worst.

Derek came back after thirty minutes, his face somber. By then I had set the enameled-top table in the kitchen with plates and silverware, and had started worrying that the food would be inedible by the time he returned.

I was also worried about Mamie. After such a close call just two nights ago, it was amazing to me that the nursing home staff would allow her to wander off again. Sure, she wasn't a prisoner. They couldn't keep her chained to her bed, I understood that. But if she wasn't capable of keeping herself safe, surely there was something they could do to keep her inside when the temperatures dipped down below freezing.

"Was she there?" I asked Derek.

He shook his head. "No sign of her. We went through the whole house, top to bottom. I even stuck my head up into the attic. She wasn't there."

"That's not good, is it?" I got busy filling the plates with rice.

"No," Derek said. "Because it means she's somewhere else. Hopefully somewhere safe. More likely somewhere that'll kill her."

"Outside, you mean." I ladled still-warm stir-fry over the rice.

He nodded. "I told Brandon that if he couldn't track her down in the next hour, I'd help him look."

"Of course." I put the wok back on the stove and went to get the water pitcher out of the refrigerator to fill the water glasses. If Derek was headed out again, I'd better not get him a beer.

"This is good," he told me when I took a seat across from him at the table.

"You're the one who made it." I lifted my fork.

"You kept it warm," Derek said.

"And a great big job it was. So the house was empty? No sign of her?"

He shook his head. "None. No sign that she'd been there, either. Everything looked just the way it did when we left."

"She must be somewhere else." I forked up some food and chewed. Mmm. Good. "Her cousin Henrietta's?"

Derek shook his head. "Brandon had already been there. Henrietta hadn't seen her."

"What about Henry?"

"Brandon didn't mention Henry," Derek said. "I guess he wasn't home."

At this time of night? "Maybe Mamie is with him."

"I'm sure Brandon will track him down and ask," Derek said.

"There's no other family. Does she have any other friends?"

"None we know of," Derek said. "She and her sister kept to themselves. I never saw them talk to anyone else. They'd chat with Dad if they met him outside, but that was it."

"So she's wandering."

He nodded. "Most likely. That's what she likes to do. The baby carriage is gone."

"Our baby carriage? From outside the house?"

"That's the one. Would you happen to remember whether it was there today?"

"During the day, you mean?" I thought back. "I'm not sure."

"I didn't go to the Dumpster a lot," Derek said. "You took the vinyl flooring out there."

"I'm aware of that." I scooted the stir-fry around my plate while I thought. "I was out there several times in the afternoon. Do you think it went missing earlier?"

"I have no idea. All I know is it's missing now. It could have disappeared anytime between yesterday when we put it out there, and this evening." He forked up another mouthful of food.

"Does it matter?"

"I don't guess it does. I just thought you might remember."

"I'm sorry," I said, wracking my brain in an effort to recollect whether or not I'd seen the carriage when I'd taken the vinyl flooring out to the Dumpster earlier. It had been cold and dark, I hadn't been wearing a coat, I'd wanted to get back inside as quickly as possible . . . "I didn't notice. That doesn't mean it wasn't there, just that I didn't happen to see it."

He nodded. "Don't worry about it, Avery. I was just trying to figure out whether she'd grabbed it and is taking it for a walk, or whether someone else might have found it and taken it with them."

"I suppose someone else could have. It was just sitting there, next to the Dumpster. I guess it looked like it was trash."

"It *was* trash," Derek said and stood up. He grabbed his plate and took it over to the sink. "Dessert?"

"Sure."

We indulged in dessert—whoopie pies, another Maine staple: the state snack, not to be confused with the state dessert, which is blueberry pie—before I went back to my Chinese lanterns and Derek went to work stringing Christmas lights around the tree. It had settled into the shape it would hopefully stay now, after twenty-four hours inside in the warmth, and it looked wonderfully tall and broad in the middle of the foyer. It managed to make the foyer look small, which was no small feat. No pun intended.

Brandon did call while he was in the middle of it, and told Derek he hadn't found Miss Mamie, so if the offer of help was still open, Brandon would be delighted to take Derek up on it. The search party was meeting outside the church in twenty minutes.

Derek said he'd be there and then he finished hanging the lights before grabbing his coat. "C'mon, Avery."

I stopped in the middle of blowing glitter at a lantern to stare at him. "You want me to come with you?"

He stared back in the process of shrugging into the sheep's wool. "Don't you want to?"

I blinked. "I don't mind, I guess." The idea of wandering through Waterfield in the dark and the cold wasn't all that appealing, but Miss Mamie had to be found.

"Good," Derek said. "Get your coat on."

"Just a second." I put the latest lantern, aka Christmas ornament, down carefully and made sure it wouldn't roll over and ruin my glittery camel stencil before it could dry. "I didn't realize I was included in the invitation."

"You're always included," Derek said, digging hats and gloves out of the basket next to the door. Meanwhile, I pulled on my puffy down coat, the one that went all the way down to my calves, and shoved my feet into heavy fur-lined boots. Manhattan had been plenty cold enough in the winter, but I'd never spent a lot of time outside. It was easy to grab the subway or a cab from home to school or home to work—or home to dinner—when the weather was too bad to want to venture outside. I'd had to update my entire winter wardrobe for Maine, including a pair of boots I'd never want to be caught dead wearing in Manhattan. There was nothing sexy or fashionable about them, but they kept my feet warm, and for that I adored them.

Derek wound a scarf around my neck before squashing my hair up under a hat. I'd made both scarf and hat myself. The scarf was your average knit-one, purl-one construction with fringe on both ends, but the hat—a tam-

o-shanter—was my own design, teal and white, with a
lotus leaf design adapted from a vintage pot I'd found in
Aunt Inga's kitchen, from a Norwegian company called
Cathrineholm. I loved it, and when I'd gone to look for
more, I'd discovered that so did a lot of other people. eBay
did a brisk business in Cathrineholm midcentury enamel-
ware, and John Nickerson had informed me he couldn't
keep it in stock.

Anyway, I had adapted the lotus leaf design from the
pot to the hat. And the result was, if I did say so myself,
rather attractive. If nothing else, the teal brought out the
washed chlorine color of my eyes.

Derek pulled the hat down over my eyes, and I had to
reach up and push it back out. "I have to see to search."

"You can hold my hand," Derek said and grinned. "I
just don't want you to lose any exposed parts, Tink."

"I'm more worried about Mamie's exposed parts," I
said. "Was she at least wearing a coat when she left?"

"I didn't ask," Derek said and pulled on his gloves.
"Let's go."

We went.

.   .   .

The crowd outside the church numbered about a dozen
people. In addition to Derek and myself and Brandon, there
was Wayne—in civvies, so he must be off-duty tonight—
and Josh. Barry Norton, the reverend, was there—Judy's
husband and Derek's old buddy from school—but Judy
herself was absent. Darren Silva had shown up, still in his
fancy cashmere coat, and someone—Darren or Brandon—
must have managed to track down Henry, because the older
man was also there. He looked like he'd dressed hurriedly,
his thick, gray hair a little tousled and the shirt misbut-
toned at the collar.

Kerri—she of the Brady Bunch house—was on the other
side of the crowd, just about as far away from Darren and
Henry as she could get, and she had been joined by a friend.
The friend was tall, skinny, and blond, huddled inside an

oversized green cape. The long hair, round glasses, and cape made her look something like Professor Trelawny from the Harry Potter movies.

Peter Cortino, another friend of Derek's, who married Derek's high school sweetheart, Jill, a few years ago, was there as well, and so was Dr. Ben.

Derek immediately headed for his dad. "You shouldn't be here."

Dr. Ben arched his brows at him. "I hope you're not telling me I'm too old, son."

Derek opened his mouth, and closed it again.

"I'm sixty-four," Dr. Ben said. "That's hardly death's door."

"It's not that you're old . . ."

"I'm not ill, either." He thumped his chest. "The old ticker is just fine. I don't even have a cold."

"We won't be tramping through the wilderness," I said, tucking my arm through Derek's and smiling at my father-in-law. "Just walking around Waterfield Village. I'm sure he'll be fine."

Derek sent me a less than loving look. Dr. Ben, meanwhile, smiled back. "Precisely. And if we find her, and something's wrong, I might be able to help. You"—he nodded to his son—"can't be everywhere at once."

No arguing with that. And at any rate, that was when Brandon cleared his throat and then, when we all looked at him, shot a guilty glance at Wayne. "Did you want to do this?"

Wayne shook his head. "Carry on."

Brandon raised his voice. "Thanks for coming. As you all know, Mary Green—Miss Mamie—is missing again. We've looked in all the logical places, and haven't been able to find her. The next thing to do is a canvass of the Village. If we don't find her here, we'll reassess what to do next."

We all muttered and nodded, stamped our feet, and blew into our mittens.

"We'll break up into pairs," Brandon said, looking around

at all the pairs already formed. "Ms. Holt and Ms. Waldo, are you going to feel safe together, or would you like to pair up with Mr. Silva Junior and Senior?"

There was a moment of silence.

"I feel safe," Kerri said with a glance at Henry and Darren. Henry glanced back at her. Kerri turned to her friend. "Dab?"

Professor Trelawny shrugged.

"Whatever you want," Brandon said. "Dr. Ben, you can go with Mr. Cortino, and Reverend Norton, you can come with me."

All three of them nodded.

"I can go with your dad," I told Derek, "if you and Peter want to hang out."

He glanced down at me. "You think I'd rather spend time with Peter Cortino than my wife or my father?"

"We have spent rather a lot of time together lately . . ."

"Oh," Derek said, "so it's you who'd rather spend time with someone other than your husband. Are you sure you wouldn't prefer to go with Peter and have me go with Dad?"

"Just because he's gorgeous . . ." I began. He gave me the evil eye, and I grinned. "You and your dad can't go together. Sending the only two doctors out together doesn't make any sense. You'll do more good separately, assuming we'll need a doctor at all. But I wouldn't mind spending some time with my father-in-law. And I actually thought you might enjoy hanging out with a buddy, now that you're an old married man."

"I can go with Peter if you'd rather," Derek said with a shrug. "It makes no difference to me."

"Then go with Peter. It'll be good for you. And your dad and I will have fun together." Or as much fun as we could have, walking around in single digits looking for a lost old lady.

"Whatever you want," Derek said and headed for where the other two had gravitated together like two magnets. "Excuse us. Change of plans."

They both looked up politely and Derek added, "Avery wants to go with you, Dad."

"That's fine with me," Dr. Ben said with a shrug. "That way those of us with short legs don't have to try to keep up with the two of you with long ones."

My father-in-law was a few inches shorter than his son. Not short by any means—Derek tops out at six feet or so—but not overly tall, either. Peter was almost as tall as Derek.

They were about the same age, and with all due respect to my husband—quite attractive in his own right—Peter was the best-looking man I'd ever seen. He looked like one of Michelangelo's statues come to life, only in jeans and a puffy parka, or one of those Greek gods of legend. Almost too handsome to be believed, with glossy black curls, melting chocolate brown eyes with cow lashes, and a face that might as well have been carved in marble. One of those guys who quite simply take your breath away upon first sight.

More important, he was a very nice guy who adored his slightly-less-than-perfect wife and their four children.

Yes, four. In six years. Peter Junior, Paul, Pamela, and little Pepper, only two months old.

"Is Jill home with the kids?" I asked.

Peter nodded. "No sense in her walking around in this. Besides, Sneeze will want feeding."

"Sneeze? Is that your new nickname for the baby?"

"It seems fitting."

It did, seeing as a sneeze—brought on by the pepper pot at dinner—was what had sent Jill into labor in the first place.

"How is the baby?"

"She's fine," Peter said. "They're all fine. And luckily Jill's nursing, so I don't have to partake in the middle-of-the-night feedings." He grinned.

At that moment, Brandon came over to us with Darren Silva trailing him, and gave us our assignments for the next couple of hours. We informed him of the team change, and he assigned Derek and Peter the area around Main Street in downtown, while Dr. Ben and I were told to stay in the Village, and search the six square blocks between North Street and Birch and between Cabot and Fraser. It was an area that included not only the Green sisters' house on North Street and Dr. Ben's house on Cabot, but also Barry's church and the rectory.

"Does everyone have a flashlight?" Brandon wanted to know when the assignments were done and it was time to head out. "I brought a few extras."

Some people didn't—the Silvas, for one—and after the oversized Waterfield PD regulation Maglites were distributed, we wandered off. Derek and Peter headed down the hill toward downtown, while Wayne and Josh walked toward the other side of the Village, and Brandon and Barry set out in the direction of Aunt Inga's house. Henry and Darren headed north, while Kerri and her friend sidled over to us. "This is Deborah," Kerri said by way of introductions, "but you can call her Dab."

Dab? Not Deb? "Hi, Dab," I said. "Nice to meet you."

Dab ducked her head and muttered something too softly for me to make out.

"She's shy," Kerri said.

Ah.

"We have the quadrant next to yours. Same cross streets but south of Cabot. Do you want to do all of Cabot, or only the north side?"

I looked at Dr. Ben. He looked at me.

"We can do all of it," I said, "if you prefer. Or you can take one side and work your way south, and we'll take the other and work our way north."

"That works," Kerri said, since obviously it was what she'd been aiming for all along. "We'll take the south side."

"We'll take the north." Which would include Dr. Ben's and Cora's house, but not the Silvas' big compound.

"We'll see you in two hours." They set out, presumably for the south side of Cabot, which was the closest point to us, as far as their quadrant was concerned.

Meanwhile, Dr. Ben and I were standing right smack-dab

in the middle of our section, outside the church. North Street was two blocks in one direction, Fraser a block in the other.

I looked around, at the church, the rectory, and the graveyard. "Let's start with the churchyard." Before it got too late. Wandering among the old gravestones is creepy anytime it's dark, but at least I wasn't too cold and tired at the moment. Two hours from now, I definitely wouldn't want to do it.

Dr. Ben nodded, so maybe he was thinking the same thing. We headed for the entrance to the graveyard, between two low stone walls.

"I'll go this way," he said when we were inside, gesturing left.

Fine with me. It was eerie either way. I went right, over to the corner of the stone wall, and started there: walking the paths between the graves, shining my flashlight back and forth, over and behind the leaning stones.

A few of the graves had been decorated for the season, with wreaths and candles and little lanterns. Aunt Inga was buried here, and I passed her grave: just blanketed with a couple inches of snow. I brushed the snow away from the top of the stone, making my mitten wet in the process, and stood for a second looking at it. Inga Marie Morton. Lived and died and left me her house and her cats, and gave me a new life with a new career and a new husband in the process. I made a mental note to come back with a wreath and a lantern just as soon as I could think again. Just let us find Miss Mamie and get through the Christmas Home Tour, and I'd be back with some greenery to make things look more festive.

From the other side of the graveyard, I could see Dr. Ben's flashlight beam cut through the darkness. We weren't very far apart at all, and when he raised his voice, I had no problem hearing him. "Anything?"

"Nothing. You?"

"No. I'm almost done with this side."

I wasn't, so I left Aunt Inga's final resting place and

hurried up. By the time I had searched my half of the graveyard with nothing to show for it, he was waiting for me by the front entrance. "Nothing here."

I shook my head. "The church is closed, right?"

"I'm sure it is," Dr. Ben said, "but we should check." He made for the front double doors of the church, which—surprise—opened. We stuck our heads into the small narthex and looked around.

It was nice and warm, and would make a fine place for someone to curl up out of the wind and snow. That might have been why it was open: Barry or Judy had decided that if Miss Mamie needed shelter, she might find it in the church. I crossed the small space and tried the doors into the nave itself, but they were closed.

The narthex was empty, though, so we ducked back out and made our circuit of the church itself, shining our flashlights into the bushes growing around the old brick structure. We found a few items of trash, which we picked up and hauled back to the front and the trash cans, but there was no sign of Mamie.

We ended up back in front of the church, in front of the nativity scene.

"Ready to move on?" Dr. Ben asked.

I nodded. "Just a second." The nativity was rather lovely, actually. It looked old, and was almost life-sized. The camels towered over me, and I could look Melchior—or maybe it was Caspar—right in the eye.

The sheep were about the size of Jemmy and Inky, covered with flaking white paint, and Mary and Joseph were kneeling behind the empty wooden trough that should have held the Baby Jesus.

I don't think the trough was very historically accurate, because it looked like it would leak like a sieve. Any water or grain poured into it would trickle out through the cracks between the planks. But it looked appropriately rustic and atmospheric. It would have looked even better with a Baby Jesus inside, draped in swaddling cloths, but alas, such was not to be. The only thing there was a bunch of hay.

"The baby goes missing every year," Dr. Ben said, coming up to stand beside me to look at the manger, too. "It usually comes back after a few days, though."

I glanced at him. "How long has it been?"

"More than a few days. I think maybe we're not getting it back this year."

"Is it valuable?"

He shook his head. "The figures are old, certainly. They could use some work, too. Maybe Derek would like to take that on once the two of you are finished with the house. Get the figures ready for next year's Christmas season."

"Maybe." He'd probably enjoy it. He likes doing restoration. "I'll run it by him."

Dr. Ben nodded. "But to answer your question, no. The figures are sixty or seventy years old and, as a set, might be interesting to someone collecting that type of thing. But they're not antiques, and they're not made by anyone of any importance. And there's no reason at all why anyone would want just the baby."

"Derek told me that this has been happening for a long time," I said, turning away from the nativity scene. We had a big section of Waterfield Village to search, and no time to waste. I didn't want to have to meet the others in—I checked my watch—an hour and forty-three minutes now, and tell them we hadn't gotten to everything we were supposed to.

Dr. Ben fell into step with me as we set off down the sidewalk, flashing our lights over fences and into bushes. "That's right. As long as I can remember anyway. Or at least I can't remember a time when it didn't happen. When Derek was ten or eleven or so, he and some friends made a plan to hide in the churchyard overnight to see who took the baby."

"Really?" He hadn't told me about that. "How did it go?"

There was a rustle in the bushes in the yard we were passing and I slowed down to flash my light in that direction. A pair of glowing eyes stared back at me for a second before they translated themselves into the sleek shape of a cat, slipping through the snow.

"Not well," Dr. Ben said. "They scared themselves half to death being in the graveyard in the first place, and then it got late, and they got cold and uncomfortable. On top of that it began to snow. And because they hadn't gotten permission to be out, we all got worried when they didn't come home. The bottom line was that one of us found them and dragged them home before they could discover anything at all. I grounded Derek for a week."

"Oops." That was probably why he hadn't told me.

"And if we'd only let them alone," Dr. Ben said, "they would have seen who took the baby. It was gone by the next morning."

"Did you think they took it?"

"The thought crossed my mind," Dr. Ben said, "but there were five of them, and they all swore up and down they hadn't."

These were Derek's childhood friends I had met a few months ago when one of them got married, I guessed. Ryan, Alex, and Zach. And Barry Norton, of course.

"He never told me about this."

"Nothing much to tell," Dr. Ben said, flashing his light into a Jeep parked at the curb. It was empty. "The baby was returned the next night. Same as always."

"And no one has any idea who takes it and brings it back?"

Dr. Ben shook his head. "We assume it's some sort of joke. They don't keep the baby. They just borrow it for a day or two."

"Is it different when it comes back?"

"No," Dr. Ben said and shone his flashlight into the bushes behind a mailbox. "It's the same as it always is. It just goes away for twenty-four or forty-eight hours, and then it shows up in the manger again, just the same as it was when it left."

We got to the corner. "Do you want to keep going straight down Cabot," I asked, "or turn here?"

"Let's go one more block before we turn. That way we can check my house."

"Your house?" Why would Miss Mamie be there?

He glanced at me. "I'm the town doctor. She knows me."

So she might decide to stop by, if she was out, wandering, and realized she needed help. "Were you alive when Baby Arthur went missing? In September of 1949?"

"Just barely," Dr. Ben said. "But I heard stories when I got a little older. Every parent in Waterfield, including mine, was afraid to let their children play outside or sleep alone at night. Arthur Green was our Lindbergh baby, and Waterfield wasn't the same afterwards." He pushed open the gate into his own yard and held it for me. We headed up the walk to the front door.

While Dr. Ben went inside to tell Cora that we were here and that she didn't have to worry about the dark figures skulking around her yard flashing beams of light into the bushes, I walked around the house looking for Mamie.

Cora was an avid amateur gardener, and in the summer, the yard was ablaze with colors and varieties of flowers and grasses. Now it was all hidden under a few inches of snow, and I did my best to remember where the beds were, so I didn't accidentally stomp all over some rare variety of perennial.

The yard was empty of little old ladies. I stopped outside the potting shed in the back and flashed my light at the latch. There was a padlock hanging from it, but it was open.

I hesitated before reaching for it. I had a bad experience with a garden shed once. The one on Aunt Inga's property specifically. It had gone up in flames with me inside it last summer, and I barely made it out with my skin intact. Ever since then, I'd been a little leery of sheds.

I looked around, and flashed the light around, too, for good measure. There was no one in sight. Nobody was likely to rush up and push me inside and then light the shed on fire.

With all the snow, it probably wouldn't burn anyway. And my feelings were illogical; I knew that. Just residual fear. The chances that the same thing would happen again were slim to none.

Besides, I hadn't upset anyone at all lately, so there was no reason why anyone would want to kill me.

Nonetheless, I had to force myself to unhook the padlock and pull the door open. "Hello?"

There was no answer. Of course not. I hadn't expected one, but my heart was still beating double-time when I stepped forward into the doorway, shining my light into the interior of the shed.

It was small, and looked a lot like Aunt Inga's shed used to before it was immolated. Shelves, pots, garden implements, bags of dirt.

Over in the corner was something that looked like a huddle of fabric, and my heart skipped a beat. "Miss Mamie?"

There was no answer, but if she were asleep, there wouldn't be. I forced myself to step forward into the darkness.

I had only taken a couple of steps when the doorway darkened.

—12—

I jumped and squealed and dropped my flashlight. The beam bounced a couple of times, and then settled on the floor to illuminate a pair of sturdy brown boots, the soles and tips wet with slush.

"Goodness, Avery," Dr. Ben's voice said, "you scared me half to death."

It took me several seconds to find my voice. "Likewise."

"What are you doing?" He flashed his light around the interior of the shed.

I bent to pick up my own flashlight before I answered. "I saw this bundle of . . . stuff." I pointed at it.

"Fertilizer," Dr. Ben said, focusing his flashlight beam on it. "And Cora's gardening coat."

Of course. Now that I was standing closer, it was easy to see. A couple of big bags of fertilizer, with a coat on top; a coat whose sleeve had accidentally gotten hung up on a nail, so it looked like someone's arm was inside it.

"There's nobody here," I said, stating the obvious.

Dr. Ben shook his head. "Let's go."

Our next focused stop was Miss Mamie's old house,

now Derek's and my renovation object on North Street. On the way there, we shone our lights into cars and bushes, but saw no sign of Miss Mamie. And we discussed my brush with death in the garden shed in July, since Dr. Ben had obviously noticed that I was still jumpy.

"It's normal," he told me. "It's only been a few months. You'll be more comfortable in time. The more garden sheds you visit without incident, the better you'll feel."

Sure.

"Derek hasn't built you a new one yet, has he?"

I shook my head. "We were busy with the TV crew when it burned, and then there was the condo to renovate, and the wedding, and by then it was too cold to start building. He told me he'd build me a new one when the weather gets warm again."

Dr. Ben nodded. "That'll help, too. Get involved in building it. It'll be yours and you'll feel more confident about it."

Good advice.

"Feel free to come hang out in ours anytime you want," Dr. Ben added.

"Thank you." I smiled. "I might take you up on that when the weather gets a little better."

We stopped on the sidewalk outside the house. It was dark and creepy, just as creepy as it had appeared that first night when Cora and I drove past.

"I don't have the key," I said. "And anyway, Derek and Brandon already checked here."

Dr. Ben nodded. "Let's just take a look around the yard. If they've already checked the inside, there's no sense in doing it again. This is taking more time than I thought."

It was. We had already used up half our allotted time, and we hadn't patrolled anything even close to half our section. Hopefully the others were making better time. I kept hoping my phone would ring with a report that someone had found Miss Mamie, but so far, no luck.

"I'll go this way," Dr. Ben said, and headed left, across

the snowy grass in front of the house. I went straight, down the driveway and around the Dumpster to the opening.

There was nothing inside it that shouldn't be there, at least as far as I could determine in the beam from the flash-light. And Derek was right; the baby carriage was gone. We had parked it between the house and the Dumpster, and now the space was empty. I shone the light on the ground to see if I could determine which way it had gone—it couldn't have flown, after all; someone had had to wheel it away—but between the hard-packed snow from before and the new dusting over top, I had no idea.

I continued down alongside the house, flashing my light to and fro.

It was dark back here, the only sounds my footsteps crunch-ing on the snow. A square of light shone on the ground up ahead, out of the basement window. Derek and Brandon must have forgotten to turn it off when they searched the house earlier.

I squatted in front of it and peered down, just in case it wasn't Derek's or Brandon's doing, but Miss Mamie's. There was no reason to think she'd be in the basement—if she were inside the house, it was more likely she was upstairs in her old room again. Not that she was in the house, because Derek and Brandon had checked.

Anyway, I squatted and peered in. And saw nothing. Everything looked empty and quiet, just as it should.

But just in case, I pulled out my phone and dialed Derek. A few seconds passed and then I heard his voice. "Avery?"

"Did you check the basement when you were over here at the house earlier?"

"Hello to you, too," Derek said. "Yes, we did."

"Is it possible that you forgot to turn off the light?"

There was a beat. "I don't think so," Derek said.

"Not the big ceiling light. The small one under the stairs. The bulb hanging on the string."

"Oh." He sounded relieved. "Yes, we might have forgotten

to turn that off. I don't recall turning it on, but Brandon may have, and I may not have realized it."

Good enough. "I just wanted to check. It's on now, and I wanted to make sure we didn't have to go back inside. I don't have the key, so it would involve breaking a window."

"Don't do that," Derek said. "I take it you haven't found her yet."

"Afraid not. I guess you haven't, either."

"No," Derek said. "No sign of her down here."

"No sign of her up here, either. We'll keep looking."

"Us, too," Derek said. "See you at the church in an hour."

I told him we'd be there and continued on my way into the backyard. From the other side of the property, I could hear Dr. Ben's footsteps crunching and see the beam of his flashlight moving to and fro.

It wasn't a terribly big backyard. Smaller than Aunt Inga's, and about the same size as Dr. Ben's and Cora's. But where Cora kept her yard in immaculate shape, and where Derek and I had slowly but surely managed to tame Aunt Inga's mess, the Green sisters' yard was a nightmare. It was a good thing it was winter and there were no leaves or grass, because we wouldn't have been able to get around during the warm season. The backyard would have been a jungle. As it was, I kept brushing against snow-covered bushes and trees, making my pants and my mittens wet.

I found Dr. Ben standing outside a small, rickety structure that looked more like an outhouse than a potting shed. It leaned. It was built from what looked like driftwood—and I know I'd once said that about Aunt Inga's kitchen cabinets, but this really did look that way. There was evidence that the planks might at one point have been painted a dark green, but all that was left now were a few flecks here and there; the rest was a silvery gray. It had small windows with small window boxes underneath, and a small door that showed evidence of red paint, and the whole thing was, in a word, small.

"Playhouse," Dr. Ben said.

I nodded. So it seemed. The structure certainly hadn't been built for anyone adult-sized. I'm short, but even I would have had to bend my head to get under the lintel. "I didn't even know this was here."

"In the summer you probably can't see it." He nodded to the overhanging branches, dipping low over the roof and doorway, threatening us with snow showers. "Unless you knew it was back here, you wouldn't notice."

"It must be the girls' playhouse from when they were small."

"I expect so," Dr. Ben said. "We should check inside. Since we're here anyway."

"Of course." I stood back and watched as he struggled with the latch. "Is it locked?"

"I don't think so. But it may as well be." He grunted, jiggling the mechanism back and forth. "It must be rusty. Here."

He handed me his flashlight so he could use both hands on the handle. I juggled it and my own flashlight for a second until I could get one of them pointed at the lock so he could see what he was doing. The other waved around wildly while I did it, and that's when I saw them. Two thin tracks, as if from bicycle wheels, through the snow. Parallel tracks, a couple feet apart, disappearing around the corner of the shed.

I followed.

"Where are you going?" Dr. Ben asked from behind me. "I can't see."

"Just a second." I ducked around the corner and flashed my light around. The baby carriage was there, parked beside the wall. Empty, of course.

I stomped back to Dr. Ben and focused the light on the handle again. "The old baby carriage from the basement is parked next to the wall. We didn't put it there. I think maybe Mamie did."

Ben refocused his efforts on the door. "Give me the flashlight," he said after a minute's struggle.

I handed it over and watched as he hefted it and brought it down on the latch. There was a tinkle of glass as the flashlight shattered, along with the sound of metal screeching. The latch bent.

Dr. Ben worked it loose and pulled the door open. We both bent low and leaned into the doorway, playing our single beam of light around the tiny interior.

It wasn't much to look at. Built-in benches around the perimeter, with a table in the middle. On it sat the doll-sized tea set I'd given Mamie yesterday. The doll from the carriage was propped up against a little chair on one side of the table, while on the other, a different baby doll stared out at the world through painted blue eyes. Mamie lay on the bench by the wall, curled on her side the way she had lain two nights ago when Derek and I had found her upstairs in her old room.

Dr. Ben pushed ahead of me into the tiny space, and straightened up. There was just enough space under the ceiling for him to stand upright. I followed and straightened, too, carefully, while he moved the couple of steps over to Miss Mamie. I watched as he put his hand against her cheek, against her back, and then against her chest. I already knew what he was going to say when he turned to me and opened his mouth.

"She's gone."

· · ·

Things slipped sideways after that. I called an ambulance, and then I called Brandon and finally Derek, while Dr. Ben started lifesaving measures. We both knew she was dead, but I guess he felt he had to try.

The ambulance arrived within a few minutes, and right on the heels of it came Brandon's patrol car with Henry Silva in the passenger seat and Darren in the back. By then, I was up at the front of the property, greeting people as they were arriving and telling them where to go. "Past the Dumpster, into the backyard, far left corner."

"Wheels?" one of the paramedics asked, and I shook my head.

"You'll have to carry her. But she doesn't weigh much. Dr. Ellis is back there."

They headed into the backyard, and that's when Brandon and the Silvas arrived. I gave Brandon the same directions I had given everyone else, and he loped off. Henry followed, a little more carefully. Darren hesitated.

"I'm sorry for your loss," I told him.

He glanced at me. "Excuse me?"

"She's your aunt, isn't she? Or something like that? Second cousin a few times removed?"

"Oh," Darren said. "Yes. Distantly related."

It struck me that we were both talking about Mamie as if she were still living. "I take it you weren't close."

Darren shook his head. "This'll really upset my aunt Henrietta."

No doubt.

"I should go back there. See her. Make sure my dad's all right."

He didn't wait for me to answer, just walked off past the Dumpster, his hands in the pockets of his cashmere coat. He had dress shoes on, I noticed; shiny and black. He must have run out without taking the time to change when he realized Mamie was missing.

I was just about to follow when I heard the sounds of running feet. A few seconds later, I saw Derek and Peter jogging up the street, at a pretty good clip, too, considering that they both had heavy winter boots on their feet.

They skidded to a stop next to me and took a few seconds to catch their breath. "You found her?" Derek managed after a while.

I nodded. "She was asleep in the playhouse in the yard."

"There's a playhouse in the yard?" He glanced at Peter, who was just straightening after getting his own breath back. Being winded and disheveled and sweaty did nothing to diminish either of their good looks.

"That's what *I* said. It's down in the far corner, overgrown by bushes and overhung by trees. In the summer, it probably isn't visible at all. It wasn't very visible now, either."

"What was she doing in there?"

"Having a tea party," I said. "With the doll from the basement and the tea set we found upstairs."

An expression of shocked pity crossed Peter's features. "Did the cold get her?"

"Must have. She wasn't wearing a coat again. Just the dress and pinafore."

They both shook their heads. Down the road I saw bobbing lights.

"The others are coming, too," Derek said. "I called them after you called me. Well, Brandon called Wayne, I'm sure. But I called Kerri and Dab."

"You know Kerri and Dab?"

"Of course I know Kerri and Dab," Derek said. "Remember when I told you I knew someone who makes stained glass?"

"Sure."

"That's Dab."

"She makes stained glass?"

He nodded. "Her father did the restoration of the stained glass windows in the Cathedral of the Immaculate Conception in Portland. Remember when we were there for Ryan's wedding, I told you I'd asked him advice on restoring the windows in Barry's church? I met Dab then, three or four years ago. She came out to look at the church and decided she'd like to live here."

"Huh."

He nodded. "She has a cabin and a little studio outside town."

"Do you think she might teach me how to make stained glass?"

"I suppose she might," Derek said. "We can ask her. Only not right now."

No, right now wasn't a great time.

Kerri and Dab reached us at the same time as another police cruiser with Wayne behind the wheel. He must have stopped at home to pick it up. And to drop off Josh at the same time, because Josh wasn't with him. "I sent him inside to give Kate and Shannon the news," Wayne explained when I asked. "He can't do anything here."

None of us could really. Yet we were all standing around in a huddle under the streetlight. It wouldn't be long before the neighbors started peering out their windows, too.

Footsteps crunched on the snow in the yard, and we all turned to watch the paramedics navigate around the Dumpster with their stretcher. Miss Mamie looked very small and cold. Henry Silva followed behind, his face pale, while Brandon and Dr. Ben trailed him. Darren made up the rear. Wayne gave us all a nod and went to talk to his deputy while the rest of us stood aside and watched as the paramedics loaded Mamie into the ambulance. Henry crawled in behind. Kerri took a step forward, maybe to offer her condolences, but when one of the paramedics closed the doors, she stopped. The paramedic went to join his partner in the cab, and the ambulance drove off. Silently, with no lights or sirens, while we all stood there staring after it.

Kerri turned to Darren, who was staring after the ambulance, his face blank. "Is your father all right?"

He turned to stare at her. A second ticked by, then another. "Yes," he said eventually. "Fine."

That couldn't possibly be true—this wasn't how any of us had wanted the night to end obviously. We'd all—I know I had—expected to find Mamie alive and well, if a bit cold, pushing her baby carriage around the Village with her "baby" inside.

A baby I noticed Dr. Ben had carried up from the playhouse, and which he was showing to Wayne.

I watched, forehead wrinkled, as Wayne nodded and looked around. He studied the group of us for a moment, but none of us must have passed muster—or maybe he didn't see who he expected to see. Maybe he was looking for Henry.

He passed the doll to Brandon, who went to put it in his patrol car. After a moment's hesitation beside the trunk, Brandon ended up putting it on the backseat.

Meanwhile, Wayne approached those of us standing in a silent cluster by the edge of the road. "Sorry."

We all nodded.

"There's nothing more any of us can do."

Right. Time to go home.

He turned to me. "Dr. Ben told me what happened, but you'll have to do a report, too, Avery."

I nodded.

"It's standard procedure," Wayne added, "in an unattended death."

"Of course."

An autopsy was also standard procedure, I knew, but I refrained from asking whether one would be performed. Not while Darren was standing right there.

"You can do it now or tomorrow."

"Is it OK if I leave it till the morning? I had to stop in the middle of a project when we left the house earlier."

"Sure," Wayne said. "Just come to the police station in the morning, give a statement, sign it, and you'll be done. Thirty minutes, tops."

I told him I'd be there, and he turned to Darren. "Can I give you a lift? To the hospital, or maybe home to pick up your car?"

"The car's parked at the church," Darren said.

"Get in. I'll take you there."

They drove off together. Brandon was already gone. The handful of us who were left stared at one another blankly.

"This is horrible," Kerri said.

We nodded.

"Poor Henry."

Poor Mamie. And Ruth. And I suppose Darren.

We stood in silence a bit longer.

"So how are the renovations coming?" Peter asked in an attempt to change the subject to something a little less disturbing.

"They're coming," Derek answered. "Slowly. We haven't started the cosmetics yet."

"So far it's just been hauling junk and working on things like the plumbing," I added. "The functional stuff that doesn't have to be pretty, but has to work. Derek's domain."

My husband turned to Dab. "Avery was just saying the other day how she'd like a stained glass lamp for the dining room. Any chance you can show her what you've got?"

"Or show me how to make one," I added.

He glanced at me. "You want to make your own?"

"Why not?"

"No reason." He turned back to Dab. "Any chance you have time to give Avery a crash course in stained glass making?"

Dab nodded. "I'd be happy to."

Her eyes were pale green behind the lenses, quite pretty, and her face wasn't unattractive, either.

"Maybe I can stop by this Saturday?"

"That would be fine," Dab said. Derek told her we'd see her then, and we stood in awkward silence for a moment. Dr. Ben stamped his feet in the snow.

"Cold," he told me when I glanced at him. "It's all right for you, you're young, but people feel the cold more when they get older."

"We should go. There's nothing more we can do here."

We walked up the street together. Kerri and Dab went inside Kerri's split-level when we passed it, and the rest of us parted ways outside the church. Peter got into his van and drove away, home to Jill and the kids, and Dr. Ben said good night and headed back to Cora. I glanced at the church, and the light glowing through the stained glass windows. "Someone's inside."

"Barry," Derek said. "Lighting candles or praying for Mamie."

I nodded. "We probably shouldn't disturb him."

Derek shook his head. "No."

"Is Brandon lighting candles and praying, too, do you think?"

"What?" Derek said.

"That's his car, isn't it?"

I pointed to it, parked at the curb a few yards away.

Derek contemplated it with his head tilted for a few seconds. "Yes."

"What's he doing here?"

"No idea," Derek said.

"Maybe he's just filling Barry and Judy in on the details. I'm surprised Barry didn't come over to the house with Brandon after I called him."

"There was nothing anyone could do," Derek said. "And Barry has things to do here. Light candles, activate the prayer chain, make sure Ruth is taken care of and has someone with her when she gets the news . . ."

"When will Wayne tell her, do you think?"

"Not until tomorrow," Derek said. "He's not going to wake her up for this."

Of course not. "Should I go out there?"

"You don't know her," Derek pointed out. "It's not like you'll be able to give her a lot of comfort."

Maybe not, but I had found her sister. And she might have questions.

"Why don't you ask Wayne tomorrow morning?" Derek suggested. "When you go to give your statement. If he thinks there's anything you can do, he'll tell you."

I nodded. And glanced at the church again.

"You said you had work to do at home," Derek reminded me. "You left your Chinese lantern Christmas ornaments unfinished, remember?"

"I remember."

"The home tour is only two days away."

Yikes.

"We'd better get home," I said with a last lingering look at the lighted stained glass windows. I was really curious to find out what Brandon was doing here, but Derek was right: The home tour was drawing near, and I had to finish getting ready.

So we got into the Beetle and drove home. I went back to work on my Chinese lanterns, and Derek watched for a bit before he asked if he could help. We finished the ornaments together, and hung them to dry on two big portable clothes racks I had brought from New York when I moved, and stored in the attic. It kept the ornaments apart enough that they wouldn't touch each other and possibly smear the paint, and it kept them inside in the warmth, where they'd dry faster than if we hung them on the porch.

They'd turned out pretty nice, I thought. I planned to wait until they dried, though, to determine whether I needed to start over. They weren't shiny, the way Christmas balls are, and I wasn't sure whether I was going to be happy with that. I might just have to spray paint them all with high-gloss paint and decorate them again, but that was for another day. Today had enough troubles of its own, and I was beat. I took Derek's hand and we headed up to bed.

—13—

The new police station—built long before I relocated to Waterfield, but new compared to the old police station they had before it—was a brick building located on the northwest side of downtown, on the Augusta Highway. Not too terribly far from the condo Derek and I had renovated in Josh Rasmussen's building, which made a lot of sense, considering that Wayne had lived there with Josh before he married Kate, and he had bought the condo after his wife died because it was close to work.

When I walked through the police station's door, Ramona Estrada, the police secretary, recognized me. "Morning, Avery."

"Good morning," I said.

Back when I first moved to town, Derek had given me the impression that Ramona was some kind of gorgeous, nubile Jennifer Lopez lookalike in a police uniform, and I don't mind telling you I'd been jealous. In actuality, she was a plump and grandmotherly woman in her sixties, who might have been quite a looker in her youth, but who was old enough to be Derek's mother by now. It had amused

Home for the Homicide   151

him rather a lot, too, when he realized I'd fallen for his lie, hook, line, and sinker.

"Wayne said you'd be in. He's in his office." She waved down the hallway. Security at the Waterfield police station is, to say the least, lax. I thanked her and headed down the hall toward Wayne's office. I'd been there before, too.

He was sitting behind his desk with a pair of reading glasses perched on his nose when I arrived in the doorway. The door was open, so I cleared my throat to let him know I was there, and he peered at me above the glasses and told me to come in and take a seat. "This'll only take a minute."

He continued signing off on paperwork for another short while and then he capped the pen and took the glasses off and looked at me across the desk. "You all right?"

"Fine," I said.

"I know we all hoped for a different outcome."

"I thought we'd find her rolling the baby carriage down a street somewhere, with her doll inside. Not that she . . ." My voice gave out. Guess maybe I was more upset than I'd realized.

Wayne didn't say anything, just waited, and I got myself back under control. "She froze to death, right?"

"So we assume," Wayne said. "There's no reason to think otherwise. Unless you know something I don't?"

I shook my head. "I can't believe they let her wander off again like that. After what happened two nights ago, you'd think they'd be a bit more careful."

"They didn't," Wayne said.

"They didn't?"

He shook his head. "Mr. Silva picked her up to take her to dinner with his aunt."

By elimination, this was Darren, since Henry Silva didn't have an aunt, at least not one I knew about. "Henrietta?"

Wayne nodded. "They stopped outside the liquor store on Broad Street so Mr. Silva could pick up a bottle of wine for dinner."

Wine? For Mamie? Wasn't she tipsy enough without that?

"She stayed in the car," Wayne continued. "Or so he thought, until he came out and found her gone."

"So he's the one who called you?"

"After he drove around for a bit looking for her. He didn't think she could have gotten far. But when he couldn't find her, he called us, and Brandon went out to have a look around. When he couldn't find her, either, and it got late and it started snowing, we decided we needed to do a search."

So it was Darren's fault. If he hadn't picked her up—if he hadn't left her unattended in the car—she would have been safe and warm inside the nursing home.

No wonder he'd looked grim last night. Guilty conscience, no doubt.

"He must feel terrible," I said, unwillingly sympathetic. I didn't like Darren, but God . . . what a horrible responsibility.

Wayne nodded. "Tell me what happened last night."

I went through the events of the evening—from the start of my search with Dr. Ben up until we found Mamie's body—in detail. "She was curled up on one of the wooden benches. They're built in, and there's a little table in the middle. It was set with the doll-sized tea set I found upstairs in her room, that I'd brought to her earlier."

"Earlier?" Wayne said.

I squirmed. I had hoped he'd miss that. "Derek and I went out to the nursing home in the afternoon, to bring Mamie and Ruth some things we'd found in the house that we thought they might enjoy. The tea set and some doll clothes for Mamie, and a box of newspaper clippings about Elvis Presley for Ruth."

Wayne's lips twitched. "Were they the same clothes the"—he hesitated—"the doll was wearing last night?"

I hadn't noticed the doll wearing anything, to be honest. It had been naked the other two times I'd seen it. "Blue wool?"

Wayne nodded. "So you opened the door to the playhouse and saw Mamie."

"That's correct. Dr. Ben went to check on her. He told me to call nine-one-one and to wait for the ambulance. I did. And you know the rest."

Wayne nodded.

"What happens now?"

"I'll have Ramona type up a statement," Wayne said. "It'll take her a few minutes. Then you can sign it and leave. Thanks."

"No problem. But I meant, what happens to the . . . to Miss Mamie."

Wayne's lips tightened. "She was taken to Portland, to the medical examiner's office. Dr. Lawrence will look at her."

Dr. Lawrence was the medical examiner. She was a few years younger than Dr. Ben, who knew her well. As she said once, doctors of the dead are doctors, too. We'd met a couple of times, and she was rather nice.

"Will there be an autopsy?"

"If Dr. Lawrence thinks it's necessary," Wayne said.

"It isn't required?"

"It is if she thinks it's necessary."

Right.

"For now, she'll just take a look at the . . . at Miss Mamie and determine whether there's any reason to do an autopsy. I'm sure I'll hear from her in the next few hours."

I wanted to ask him to keep me in the loop, but there was no reason why he would, and if I asked, he'd tell me so. "I guess the Silvas will arrange for the funeral and all that?"

"I imagine they will," Wayne said. "Darren arranged for Mamie and Ruth's accommodations at Sunset Acres, and for the sale of the house. I'm sure he'll arrange for the funeral, too."

"Let me know what you find out, would you? I don't think he'll call us, and I don't want to call him."

Wayne nodded and got to his feet. "Let's go see Ramona, and then you can be on your way. What are you and Derek working on today?"

I told him what Derek was doing while I was here— regrouting the lovely ribbon tile in the downstairs bathroom—and we wandered down the hall toward Ramona making small talk about renovating. Then his phone rang, and he loped off toward his office to answer it, telling me to go the rest of the way myself. I settled beside Ramona's desk and told her my story, and watched her type it all into the computer. Five minutes later I was out of there.

The rest of the day went by in a blur. We spent the time working on the house, and the evening working on Aunt Inga's, getting it ready for the Christmas Home Tour. Derek decorated the big tree with all of Aunt Inga's vintage glass ornaments, while I decorated the small ones with the miniatures. They were an unpleasant reminder of Miss Mamie's tea set, but there was nothing I could do about that really, so I pushed the thought aside and focused on what I had to do instead.

The dining room mantel was next, and I laid it out like a little winter wonderland with drifts of white snow—pristine cotton batting sprinkled with a little glitter—arranged with Aunt Inga's little group of pixies. I had found them with the ornaments: an old cardboard box that had the words *"Norwegian Nisser"* written on it in my aunt's spidery but elegant hand. I had assumed they were simply more ornaments—until I opened the box and realized that they were little figurines instead. Vintage, about two inches tall, little red-cheeked, red-hatted pixies in the process of sledding and skating and skiing. I gave them cotton batting to ski and sled on, and a mirror for a skating pond, and arranged them all over the mantel. *Nisser*, it turned out, were creatures of Scandinavian folklore: protectors of the farm or homestead, particularly at night when the family was asleep. In Scandinavia, families would put out a bowl of porridge for their *nisse* at Christmas, just so he wouldn't feel slighted and perhaps cause trouble.

These *nisser* looked adorable, if I did say so myself. Quaint and quirky and cute.

The Chinese lanterns hadn't turned out quite as nicely as I had hoped, so I ended up spray painting them with quick-drying enamel in bright red, midnight blue, and green, and then doing the stenciling and application of glitter all over again. They just hadn't looked shiny enough the first time. I had wanted them to look like enormous glass ornaments, and they just didn't. Derek tried to tell me that I could just leave it until next year, but I wanted everything to be perfect for the home tour—if it wasn't, Kate might not ask us to participate again—so I did it over while he rolled his eyes and turned on the TV.

It was almost ten o'clock by the time I called Kate. I had halfway expected to get her voice mail, but she answered herself.

"We're ready for inspection," I told her.

There was a pause. "I'm not doing that until tomorrow."

"I didn't mean for you to come over now. Just that we're done."

"Good," Kate said. "I'll be by tomorrow afternoon."

"Can I come with you?"

"You'll already be there," Kate said.

"To the other houses. You're checking them all, right?"

"Ye-e-e-es . . ." Kate said.

"I'm not going to have a chance to see them on Sunday. And they're private homes, so it's not like I can knock on people's doors and ask to see their decorations when the tour is over. But I'd like to see my competition."

"It's not a competition," Kate said.

"I know it isn't. But I don't want to look like a poor relation by comparison. Your house looks gorgeous. If they're all like that, I don't think I'd want anyone to see mine."

Derek frowned at me over the back of the sofa. I gave him a friendly, don't-worry-about-it sort of wave.

"I'm sure it looks wonderful," Kate said. "You have a style all your own, Avery."

Which didn't necessarily sound good if you ask me. But since my whining was really only an excuse to get what I wanted, I didn't quibble. And it's true anyway. I do have a style all my own. None of the others had *nisser*, I was quite sure. Or Chinese lanterns, either.

"I'd just like to see them. I won't have a chance to leave

here on Sunday. I'll be too busy with my own house. Can't I come with you?"

"Of course you can," Kate said. "I'll do your house first, and then we'll stop by all the others. It'll take a couple of hours."

"That's fine. I'm not doing anything else tomorrow night. I'm going to Dab's house earlier to learn how to make stained glass chandeliers, but other than that I'm free."

"I'll be there at four," Kate said.

I told her I would, too, and we hung up. Derek was still frowning. "The house looks great, Avery. Don't tell me you're worried?"

I walked around the sofa and curled up next to him. "Not really. I just wanted her to agree to take me with her."

He put an arm around me and pulled me in closer. "You've done a great job. Tomorrow I'll hang the Chinese lanterns on the porch and we'll be done. And people will love it."

"I hope so."

"I know so," Derek said and turned his head to drop a kiss on the top of my head. "You have a great eye, Avery. And you've turned your aunt's house into a work of art. It's beautiful. The house itself, as well as the decorations. Everyone will love it."

I nodded, but didn't answer, since I didn't want to say, "I hope so," again. Instead I turned my attention to the TV. Someone was blowing something up. "What's going on?"

"Unrest in the Middle East," Derek said. "Or maybe it's an action thriller."

"If you can't tell the difference, do you think maybe it's time to go to bed?"

"I thought you'd never ask," Derek said and turned the TV off.

. . .

Dab turned out to live up north of town, in a small cabin set on a big, wooded lot. The house was surrounded by tall fir trees, still green now in the middle of winter and sparkling with snow.

The property consisted of the main house and a second-ary building, a bit smaller—an old garage maybe, or just a shed of some sort. It had a tall stacked-stone chimney with smoke coming out the top. Since there was no sign of activity around the main house, I headed for the smaller one, my boots crunching across the snow.

There was music coming from inside the workshop—Celtic folk, best as I could make out through the heavy door—and I had to knock a couple of times before anyone noticed. I was just about to knock again, for the third time, when the door opened.

"Oh," Dab said. "It's you."

"I hope it's not a bad time?" She had told me I could stop by this morning, but maybe she had changed her mind.

"It's fine." She waved me inside. I stepped across the threshold into a big, open space with vaulted ceilings and a couple of skylights. Not at all what I had expected from the rustic appearance.

I looked around. "Wow. This is great."

She looked around, too. "I like it. You want to take off your coat?"

I did, as a matter of fact. It was warm inside, with the wood-burning stove going. It was built into a corner of the studio, with a fire roaring inside.

In the middle of the room was a big worktable littered with stuff, and I wandered over to take a look while Dab hung my coat on a hook by the door.

The table was full of scraps of glass, in lots of different colors, along with various tools for cutting—they looked a bit like X-Acto knives, with grips and sharp points—as well as irons for soldering. A half-finished panel of something was in the middle of the table: I could make out the shape of a peacock looking at us over its shoulder, tail halfway spread.

"Wow. That's gorgeous."

"Bathroom window," Dab said.

"For here?"

She shook her head. "Victorian renovation in York."

"It's beautiful." And very intricate. I wasn't at all sure I'd have the patience necessary to do this kind of work. Each peacock feather consisted of five or six or seven different pieces of glass, and there were a lot of feathers. "How long does it take you to make something like this?"

"A while," Dab said, which didn't sound like nearly enough time. "A month or two?"

I definitely wouldn't have the patience for that.

But I was here to learn, so I smiled. "I don't think I'd be able to do anything that intricate."

"Oh no," Dab said with unconscious arrogance, "you'd have to start with something much simpler. Normally I'd recommend starting with something flat, like a panel, but Derek says you want to learn how to make a lamp."

There was a tone to her voice when she said Derek's name that gave me a moment's pause, but when I looked at her, there was nothing at all to be seen on her face. It was bland and mostly expressionless.

"I'd like to," I said.

She nodded. "Come over here." She headed for one end of the table. I mentioned that it was big, but I don't think I quite managed to convey just how big it was. Think something like a king-sized bed, stationed in the middle of the room, so she could have workstations all the way around.

The workstation over on the short end had some pretty basic tools. A couple of sheets of glass in a couple of shades of white, off-white, and brown, with a glass cutter and two copies of the same paper pattern: one taped to the table and one cut out into pieces.

Dab picked up the cutter and held it up. "This is an oil carbide glass cutter. It's a little more expensive than the steel ones, but it does better work, and it lasts a long time."

I nodded.

"Stained glass is harder than just plain window glass, and you'll want to make sure you have the right tool for the job."

Of course.

"You hold it like this." She demonstrated. "It's called a pencil grip cutter, because you hold it just like a pencil. They make fist grip cutters, too, that are better for longer cuts. But we're not going to do anything too long today, so this will be fine."

I nodded.

"Cutting glass isn't difficult once you know what you're doing."

Nor is anything else, I thought, but I didn't say it.

"We're going to start with straight cuts." She picked a piece of glass, one of the milky white ones, and positioned it on top of the pattern. "You'll know you've applied the right amount of pressure when you hear a nice, clear *zzzzzip!* as you score."

She scored—ran the cutter across the glass—and I listened for the sound she'd described.

"If you don't use enough pressure, the break won't follow the score line, and if you use too much, you'll cause unnecessary wear and tear on the cutter as well as your hand and arm."

I nodded.

"Make sure you score from edge to edge. All the way to the edge on each side. It won't break right if you don't."

I nodded.

"Position the glass with the score line along the edge of the table," she demonstrated as she spoke, "and with the biggest piece on the table and the smallest in your hand. Hold the big piece down with one hand, and fold the small piece down with the other."

She did it, and it snapped along the score line, nicely and cleanly.

I applauded.

"Depending on the size of the piece," Dab said and put the pieces on the table, "sometimes it's easier to use a pair of pliers to grip the smaller piece. You won't have to worry about cutting yourself then. And the process for cutting big sheets of glass is different. But we'll stick with this for now. Your turn."

All righty, then. I squared my shoulders and plunged in.

It turned out to be less scary than it looked, but also not as easy as Dab had made it seem. I did cut myself on a sharp edge, slicing my fingertip open, but other than that, I did all right. It took a little practice to figure out just how hard to score the glass to get that nice *zzzzzip!* sound, but once I did, the rest was a piece of cake. I cut the pieces I needed for my—very basic—lampshade in just over an hour.

"Very good," Dab said, which was nice of her, even if the tone was a bit condescending. While I'd been cutting straight pieces over on my end of the table, she'd been cutting small curved pieces for her peacock tails. She tapped them out with the little steel ball that made up the eraser end of the steel cutter. Every so often, I stopped what I was doing to watch her, amazed.

Next she introduced me to the grinder, and showed me how to smooth the rough edges of my pieces before wrapping them in foil. Finally, I got to solder the pieces together.

"If we were making a curved shade," Dab said, pointing to one that was hanging over in a corner, a confection of deep ruby reds, forest greens, and warm yellows and blues, "we'd have to use a form. Since you're just making a paneled shade, you don't have to."

I nodded, the tip of my tongue at the corner of my mouth as I tried not to resent that word "just." Yes, it was just a paneled shade, which couldn't hope to compare to the gorgeousness of Dab's creation, but I was a rank beginner. Not like I'd be able to create something like that after a couple hours' crash course. And I'd like to see her design and execute a bolt of hand-designed fabric. Preferably an intricate one.

But I didn't say anything. I just finished my paneled lampshade and took it and myself out of there. "How much do I owe you?"

"Don't worry about it," Dab said.

"That's very kind of you. Could I come back sometime? I'd like to learn how to make curved shades, too." Because honestly, I wasn't sure the lamp I had made would quite cut it in the house we were renovating. It wasn't bad—at least for a first attempt—and I was proud of it, but it didn't look like anything a professional would make. Compared to the piece of art in the corner, it made a pitiful showing indeed. In fact, compared to what I could produce in my own field of expertise, it looked pitiful as well.

"Of course," Dab said graciously enough. It was probably just my imagination that infused the two words with less warmth than she wanted me to hear.

"I don't suppose it's for sale? The lampshade over there?"

"I'm afraid not," Dab said with a glance at it. "It's a special order."

"Another house in York?"

She nodded.

"Do you have anything like it?"

She shook her head. "I work mostly on commission. And I'm booked for the next several months."

And by then we'd be finished with the Green sisters'— or Green sister's—house. Guess I was stuck with a store-bought lamp, unless I wanted to utilize the one I had just made, and I feared it wasn't up for the task.

I put my lampshade in the Beetle, turned the car toward home, and went on my way.

14

Kate rang the doorbell at four o'clock precisely, sending Mischa streaking for the door to protect me. I have to admit that my heart was thudding a little extra hard when I unlocked the door and pulled it open. "C'mon in."

She did, shaking the snow from her hair before looking around. "This looks nice."

My heart sank. "Just nice?"

"Very nice."

"Just very . . ."

Derek shot me a look and I closed my mouth with a snap. "Did you see the lanterns outside?" he asked.

"The big ornaments?" Kate nodded. "Very nice. Where did you get them?"

I explained where they'd come from and how they'd come to look the way they did.

"Smart of you," Kate said.

"This is the Christmas tree." As if she could miss it, taking up most of the space in the foyer, almost brushing the ceiling.

"So I see. Looks good."

"And the banister."

Kate looked at it, nodding.

"And here's the dining room." I walked in front of her through the door.

"You don't have to try so hard, Avery," Kate told me. "I'm not going to kick you off the tour if I don't like something."

I glanced at her over my shoulder. "I know that. I just want the place to look nice. Comparatively speaking. I don't want anyone walking in here and thinking, 'Gee, this doesn't look as nice as the others.' "

"No worries," Kate said, looking around, "it looks very nice."

"Just very . . ." I snapped my mouth closed at another look from Derek.

Kate grinned. "Are you ready to go?"

"Just let me get my coat." I headed for the coatrack in the foyer. Kate turned to Derek meanwhile.

"You aren't coming?"

"I've been inside most of these houses already," my husband told her. "I helped Kerri install a new commode once. I grew up with Darren, so I've been at the Silvas' plenty through the years. And I grew up in Dad's house."

I turned to him. "You didn't tell me that."

"That I grew up in Dad's house?"

"Of course not. That you've been inside the Silva mansion."

"I've been inside almost every house in Waterfield Village at some point or other, Avery," Derek said. "Between growing up here, being a doctor, and then being a handyman, you get to see plenty."

"You did house calls?"

"What's the point of being a small-town GP if you can't?" He bent to drop a kiss on my cheek. "Have fun, Tink. You too, Kate."

"Where's my kiss?" Kate wanted to know, and Derek blew her one from where he was standing. They grinned at each other.

Once upon a time they'd gone on a date or two, I knew. Long before I came to Waterfield. Just after Melissa left Derek, which would make it six years prior, or maybe even more. It hadn't worked out, obviously, but they'd become good friends in the process.

"How are you and Wayne doing?" I asked as we set off down the road toward downtown. The air was crisp and clear, and I could see my breath in front of me, but we were both bundled up, and it was brisk but not uncomfortable outside. The snow crunched under the soles of my boots, and I kept my (mittened) fingers in the pockets of my coat.

Kate glanced at me. "Fine. Why?"

"No reason. It's been almost a year since you got married."

Her lips curved. "I know."

"Are you doing anything special for your anniversary?"

"Champagne," Kate said and grinned, "which we'd be doing anyway."

Since they'd gotten married on New Year's Eve. Right.

She added, "We've discussed running away to New York for a couple of days. See the ball drop in Times Square. I never have before."

I had. But then I'd lived a few blocks from Times Square, in Hell's Kitchen, my whole life, so it hadn't been much of a trip. I hadn't always cared to make it, either. A few times go a long way. Times Square on New Year's Eve is a madhouse. Same as the Macy's Thanksgiving Day Parade. I did that once in a while, too, but not every year. There were just too many people in too small of an area, and you know when a New Yorker says that, it has to be bad.

Of course I didn't tell Kate so. "You should. You'd enjoy it."

"Wayne is trying to take a few days off. We'll see if it works out."

"He's the chief of police. Can't he just schedule himself off?"

"He can," Kate said, "but everyone wants holidays off. They have to make it fair. Just because Wayne is the chief and has seniority doesn't mean he can take all the holidays off. The others have to have their share, too, and someone has to man the shop."

Of course.

"He had it off last year. Along with the first two weeks in January."

"He was on his honeymoon!"

She shrugged. "Still."

Fine. "Well, I hope you get to go. If you need any help organizing the trip, let me know. I spent thirty-one years of my life in Manhattan."

"I will," Kate said.

We started our tour with the historic Fraser House in downtown Waterfield, just around the corner from Main Street. Miss Edith Barnes was the curator there, and she had it all spic-and-span and decked out the way it would have been in Colonial times.

The decorations were similar to the ones at Kate's house, yet very different from the lush style of the Victorians. The components were the same, but the execution and style vastly different. There were candles in each window, but not the fat candles I'd seen on Kate's mantels. These were slender tapers, and there was a simple wreath in lieu of a mirror above the mantel. The mantel itself was decorated with greenery and topiaries of fruit: oranges and lemons stacked in pyramids, one on each end of the mantel. Unlike Kate's golden fruit, these were natural: orange and yellow, interspersed with twigs of green. And unlike Kate's overflowing swag, draping over the edges of her mantels, the Fraser House greenery stayed on top of the mantel itself. The dining room was similarly simply decorated, the table sporting two candelabras with tall tapers, as well as a centerpiece of fir and glossy magnolia leaves, and a handful of small, green winter apples.

The effect was a bit rustic and a bit elegant at the same time, and very, very historic.

"Looks great," Kate said, and Miss Barnes inclined her head regally.

We bypassed Kate's bed and breakfast, since we both knew what it looked like, and made our way up Cabot to the Silvas' big mansion.

"Are you sure it's OK to stop here?" I asked Kate as we let ourselves into the yard and stamped up the hard-packed path toward the front door.

She glanced at me. "Why not?"

"They had a death in the family yesterday."

"This won't take long. And I don't think they were close."

"They grew up together," I said. "Miss Ruth told me. She and Mamie and Henrietta grew up together, and they were close friends when they were little. Then something happened—she didn't say what—and it changed."

"So?" Kate said, kicking the snow off her feet at the bottom step of the stairs up to the front door.

I followed suit, knocking my toes against the stones. "I wonder if it had anything to do with Baby Arthur's disappearance. Or death, now that the body's been found."

"That's only if what you found is Baby Arthur's body," Kate said with a glance at me. "Wayne said the DNA didn't match the Green sisters'."

I lowered my voice. "I think maybe Baby Arthur was conceived on the wrong side of the blanket. You know? Maybe Mr. and Mrs. Green were having problems, and she had a boyfriend."

"Do you have any reason to suspect that? Did they get a divorce or anything afterwards?"

I shook my head. "But that doesn't mean anything. Maybe the disappearance of Baby Arthur brought them closer together again. Shared grief."

"In my experience," Kate said, "the opposite would be more likely. A relationship that's already strained won't withstand adversity like that. The death of a child—or the disappearance of one—is the hardest thing two parents can go through. If they were already struggling, I don't see them making it through that and staying together. Especially if one of them did it."

"The other one may not have known."

"I'm sure she didn't," Kate said, obviously thinking along the same lines I was, "or he. But it would still put a strain on the relationship. How do you kill your child—or your spouse's child—and just carry on as if nothing happened?"

"You don't."

She shook her head. "I defy any relationship to survive something like that. I don't think you could keep it going. Especially if it was strained to begin with."

I thought for a second. "So what do you think happened to the baby, then? It was hidden in the attic, so obviously it wasn't taken by anyone else. It would have to be one of the family members who hid it."

"If it's the same baby," Kate said.

"Who do you think it is, if not Baby Arthur? There haven't been any other missing babies in Waterfield. Not that I know of."

"Maybe one of the Green sisters had a baby at some point. That would account for the DNA discrepancy. Mamie or Ruth slept with someone and got pregnant, and because it was out of wedlock, they didn't want anyone to know."

"So they killed the infant? That seems pretty brutal. I can't imagine two little old ladies doing that."

"They weren't little old ladies when it happened," Kate said. "They couldn't have been. And they may not have killed it. It could have been stillborn."

"Don't you think they would have buried it in the yard, at least?"

Kate shrugged. "Maybe it was winter and the ground was frozen."

Maybe. "That would explain some of Mamie's behavior anyway. Derek told me that she used to wheel her baby carriage around town when she was younger. If she had a baby and lost it, it would be even more traumatic than losing a baby brother."

Kate nodded, and we stood in silence for a moment, contemplating the scenario. It was sad. Almost unbearably so.

We might have continued the conversation, but just then the front door opened, and we both jumped guiltily. I'd more or less forgotten that we were standing right outside the Silvas' house. Very insensitive of us to discuss this here. Especially here.

The front door was big, a heavy slab of polished oak with panels and three small windows in the top half, and Henrietta looked especially small and frail standing next to it. Frailer than the last time I'd seen her, if it came to that. Then again, she'd lost her cousin two nights ago, and had probably received the news by now, so maybe it wasn't so surprising.

She looked from Kate to me and back without a word.

"Sorry to disturb you, Mrs. Parker," Kate said. "We're just stopping by to check that everything's ready for the home tour tomorrow."

Henrietta's dark eyes focused on her. After a moment—a long moment, as if the words didn't quite register at first—she nodded.

"May we come in?"

Another pause, while we waited for the question to hit the part of Henrietta's brain that processed. Then she nodded and stepped back. I followed Kate across the threshold and into the entry foyer.

It was fabulous. The ceilings were tall—twelve feet probably—and the walls were paneled in the same warm golden oak as the front door. Glass-fronted cabinets topped by tall tapered pillars separated the foyer from the living room beyond: a huge room with glossy oak floors that ended in a floor-to-ceiling stacked stone fireplace that took up the entire opposite wall. A wall that extended all the way up to a two-story cathedral ceiling with exposed beams. A wrought-iron chandelier that looked like it had originally been crafted to burn candles, hung from the middle beam, dark with age.

"Wow."

Kate glanced at me and grinned at my expression. "Pretty impressive, isn't it?"

It was. So impressive I hadn't even noticed the Christmas decorations.

They were there, and very tastefully done. Live poinset-
tias clustered around the bottom of the fireplace, and stockings hung from the mantel: green, red, and blue velvet with
silver ribbons and sparkling stars. The mantel was filled
with family photographs, from black-and-white and formally posed to snapshots of the current generations of Silvas in more relaxing circumstances. I recognized Darren
and the silver-haired Henry, both wearing tuxedos and
holding glasses of champagne, in one shot, and a younger
Henrietta wearing a sixties-style wedding dress in another.
A third showed a chubby baby with a shock of black hair
on the lap of a young woman with dimples. Darren and his
mother, I assumed, from the clothing and hairstyle.

A much older black-and-white photograph in a silver
frame showed what I assumed was the former generation
of Silvas. A girl, maybe nine or ten, might have been—
probably was—Henrietta as a child, in a dress and pinafore. She leaned against her father, who was tall and dark
and severe-looking, while a woman held a baby boy I
assumed was the infant Henry. He looked just like any
other baby, round-faced and toothless, with little wisps of
soft hair on his head, dressed in what looked like a hand-
knit set of short pants with suspenders and a little jacket.

"Your family?" I asked.

Henrietta nodded, brown eyes lingering on the photograph for a few seconds before we moved on.

The Christmas tree stood in a bay window in the family
room, tall and imposing, and decorated with little horses
and other wooden ornaments. There were bowls of pinecones on the tables, and old aluminum buckets of greenery
and branches with red berries on every other step of the
staircase to the second floor. Even the deck was decorated,
with Christmas-themed pillows on the Adirondack-style
furniture, and with strings of lights outlining the roof.

And speaking of Tiffany lamps, they were everywhere.
Some might even, I suspected, be original, and actually

made by Tiffany. If not, they were certainly made by someone with as much skill as Dab Holt. My own first attempt at lamp making would make a sad showing by comparison.

"This is beautiful," Kate said.

I nodded. "The sconces are gorgeous."

They were hanging on the wall in the foyer, one on either side of a big mirror facing the front door. And they were made of oiled brass, deep and rich in color, topped by warm yellow shades with filigree ornamentation. Stunning. Something like that would look fantastic in the house on North Street, on the stretch of empty wall above the stone fireplace.

Henrietta glanced at them. "Thank you."

"They look original."

"The house was built in 1919," Henrietta said.

"It's incredible." It was. Everything I had expected from the outside, and then some. "I'm sorry for your loss," I added. I mean, I couldn't really be here and not give my condolences to the family, could I?

Henrietta opened her mouth, although for a moment no words came out. Eventually, after several seconds, she managed a choked, "Thank you."

"Miss Ruth said you used to be close when you were younger."

She nodded, and by now there were tears in her eyes. I glanced at Kate, who frowned and gave a surreptitious gesture toward the door.

I agreed. We should get out of there. I certainly hadn't meant to make Henrietta cry, although maybe I should have been prepared for it. I had assumed, though, after the way Ruth spoke, that they weren't close anymore.

"We should go," Kate said, inching toward the door. I did the same. "We just wanted to make sure everything was ready for tomorrow. You'll let me know if there's anything you need, won't you?"

Henrietta nodded. We stepped out into the air and stood there for a second, getting readjusted to the cold, while the door closed behind us.

Kate shot me a look. "Awkward."

I nodded. "Bad time to call, I guess. Not that it could be helped."

Kate shook her head. "Let's do Cora and Dr. Ben's house next."

Fine with me. It was right up the road. Not that I wouldn't have plenty of occasion to see it over the holidays—Derek and I were going there for Christmas dinner—but Kate hadn't seen it yet, and should have the opportunity to reassure herself that it was ready for the tour.

Which of course it was. Cora has wonderful taste. As far as I know, it was Derek's mother, Eleanor, who furnished the place—unless it had stayed the way it was from Dr. Ben's mother; the house had been in the Ellis family for generations, and was chock full of antiques—but Cora certainly had done a great job on the Christmas decorations. They were Victorian, like Kate's, but where Kate's house is an oversized, imposing Queen Anne, Cora and Dr. Ben live in a much smaller, daintier Folk Victorian cottage. Cora kept her decorations light and airy: The greenery—sweet-smelling cedar—didn't drape over the mantel so much as perch there, festooned with silver balls, like drops of water. The tree, slender and not overly large, was similarly decorated with silver and white balls, white bows, and strings of silver beads, as well as white candles. Real candles, not fairy lights. Real candles you could put a flame to.

"That looks scary," Kate commented.

Cora smiled. "It's just for the tour. We'll change them out for strings of electrical lights before Alice and Lon and the kids come for Christmas."

"It's beautiful."

It was. I nodded.

"Are you ready, Avery?" Cora asked me. I took a breath.

"I'm getting more and more worried the more houses we see. They've all been lovely so far. I'm afraid mine won't measure up."

"Don't worry about it," Kate said. "People will be coming just as much to see the inside of Inga Morton's house as to see your Christmas decorations. Nobody but her lawyer and that professor from Barnham College was inside that house for years before she passed. They're all curious now."

Probably so. And it did make me feel a little better about the whole thing. The house itself was beautiful. Derek had renovated it, after all, and he knows what he's doing. I smiled.

"That's better," Cora said approvingly, and changed the subject. "So where have the two of you been so far?"

I told her we had started at my house, and had stopped by the Fraser House Museum and the Silva house before coming here.

"I might leave Ben in charge of the open house for a bit tomorrow and run down to the Silvas myself," Cora confessed. "I've always wanted to see the inside of that place. Ben's been there, of course, and Derek, but I haven't. Is it fabulous?"

"It's . . ." I couldn't even find the words really. "Yes. It's fabulous."

Kate nodded. "If you have the chance to get away, Cora, you should. It's really something."

Just at that point my father-in-law stuck his head out of the room he uses for his painting studio, accompanied by the sound of Bing Crosby. "What's going on?"

"Just talking about the Silvas' house," Cora told him with a fond look. "How is it coming?"

"It's coming." He turned. "Kate. And Avery."

We both chirped back at him. "Are you painting?" I asked, although the answer was pretty self-evident, both from the stains on his fingers and the fact that he'd been in his painting cave.

Dr. Ben paints little watercolors. They were hanging all over the house, including the parlor, where we were standing. He especially likes to paint buildings and landscapes, and depictions of several Waterfield landmarks, including Kate's B&B, hung on the wall beside me.

"Trying to finish a few Christmas presents," he told me. "Not much time left."

No, indeed. Christmas was only a few weeks away. And

that reminded me I hadn't finished my own Christmas shopping and crafting. I still had Alice and Lon's kids to shop for, and Alice and Lon themselves, and Steve . . .

"How are things over at the Silvas'?" Dr. Ben asked, and pulled me out of my mounting panic.

"They're ready for the home tour, but Henrietta seemed more subdued than usual."

"I should give her a call to make sure she's all right. These shocks, one after the other, aren't good for her heart."

"For what it's worth," I said, "she didn't seem ill. Just out of sorts. Distracted maybe."

"It isn't always easy to tell," Dr. Ben said, "what's physical and what's mental. And better safe than sorry."

Of course. "You didn't notice anything the other night, did you?"

"Anything?"

"Anything . . . unusual?"

"The whole thing was unusual," Dr. Ben said.

True. "I was just thinking about that door that wouldn't open. Whether someone could have locked it deliberately."

"With Mamie inside?"

"Who would want to murder Miss Mamie?" Cora said. "Of all the people in Waterfield, surely she was one of the most harmless."

It was hard to imagine Mamie being a threat to anyone. She had no money, and a *crime passionnel* was surely out of the question.

"No," Dr. Ben said, "other than the door being stuck, I didn't notice anything unusual at all. She'd obviously gone there to have a tea party with her doll. As it got later and colder, the lock froze shut. Maybe she tried to open it, maybe she didn't. Eventually she gave up and went to sleep. At least that's my interpretation."

"She was on her way to have dinner with Henrietta. Why would she suddenly change her mind and decide on a tea party in the playhouse instead?"

"How do you know that?" Cora asked, and I told her what Wayne had told me.

"She probably got confused," Dr. Ben said, "and slipped back into childhood. She knew she was going to meet Henrietta, but in her mind, she and Henrietta were children, so she went to the playhouse."

Maybe so. It made sense anyway. In a way that might have made sense to Mamie.

"I spoke to Dr. Lawrence," Ben added, and I turned my attention back to him.

"Why?"

"Because I wanted to. Mamie was my patient on and off. I wanted to know cause of death."

"And?"

"Hypothermia," Dr. Ben said. "The toxicology screen showed no evidence of drugs or alcohol in her system. There were no external or internal injuries save for a bump on her forehead."

"What kind of bump?"

"You'd call it a goose egg," Dr. Ben said. "The kind of thing that might happen if she fell and hit her head, or ran into something. Maybe the lintel of the playhouse door. She is—she was a lot taller than when she was a child."

True. We'd both had to duck our heads to get through the door. Mamie may not have had the presence of mind to do so. "So nothing sinister."

"It wasn't what killed her," Dr. Ben said, "if that's what you're thinking. At worst, it might have made her dizzy and a bit woozy, given her age and frailty. If it had happened to you or me, we would have gotten a headache and kept going."

"So it was an accident."

"It certainly seems to have been."

Fine. "So there was no autopsy."

"Dr. Lawrence did an autopsy," Dr. Ben said. "There was nothing of interest."

"I don't suppose she happened to mention whether Mamie had ever had a child?"

This came from Kate, and Dr. Ben turned to her with his eyebrows hiked halfway up his forehead. "I'm sorry?"

"We thought," Kate said with a glance at me, "that maybe the skeleton in the attic wasn't Arthur Green. That it was left there years after Arthur disappeared. Maybe Mamie—or Ruth—had a baby out of wedlock, and maybe the baby was stillborn, and because they was afraid of the judgment of the town, they hid it."

There was a moment's pause.

"If either of the Green sisters was ever pregnant, I never noticed," Dr. Ben said. "Of course, it could have been before I started practicing. Most likely it was. They're ten or twelve years older than I am. But my father was the GP back then. I still have his old casebooks."

"Can I look at them?" I asked.

"No," Dr. Ben said. "Doctor-patient confidentiality, remember?"

Bummer.

"But I can check if there's any mention of it. And if not, I can call my father and ask."

Dr. Ben's predecessor and Derek's grandfather, Pawpaw Willie, was alive and well and living in a Florida retirement community. He'd been up to Waterfield just a few months ago, for our wedding, looking tan and healthy and in possession of all his faculties in his late eighties.

"Would you do that?"

"Not for you," Dr. Ben said. "That would be totally unethical."

"But . . ."

"But I'll check. And tell Wayne what I discover. We all want to figure out what happened to that baby."

I pouted, although really, it was better than nothing. And I could probably get Wayne to tell me what, if anything, Dr. Ben learned.

He added, "You have to realize, though, Avery, that if what you're thinking is true, it's much more likely no one knew anything about it at all. Including my father. If it wasn't Baby Arthur's skeleton you found, but a stillborn child of Mamie's or Ruth's, if my father had known either of them was pregnant, he would have wondered what was wrong when no baby was born. And it's not like he would have condoned hiding it in the attic."

That was true, and something I hadn't truly considered until now, although I should have. "Can you check anyway?"

He promised he would, and we took our leave, up the road toward Kerri's Brady Bunch house.

15

We walked past the house on North Street on our way to Kerri's house, and at Kate's suggestion, we detoured into the backyard for a look at the scene of the crime, as it were.

"You don't really think anyone killed her, do you?" Kate asked as we stomped down the now hard-packed trail between the two thin grooves of the baby carriage's wheels. In the light, they were easy to see, and I couldn't believe I'd missed them yesterday. "Are you sure you don't just have murder on the brain, Avery?"

I'd come up against more than my fair share of murderers in my time here in Waterfield, so she might have a point actually. Maybe I'd gotten to where I saw murder where none existed. Wishful thinking or paranoia, take your pick.

Then again, everyone had told me the same thing when Hilda Shaw died of anaphylactic shock in September, and it had been murder then. Maybe it was murder now, too.

"But who would kill Miss Mamie?" Kate objected when I said so. "Everyone wanted to kill Hilda Shaw, but Miss Mamie never did anything to anyone."

"Nor did my aunt Inga, as far as anyone knew. Except the one person who wanted her dead."

Kate conceded my point. "It's hard to imagine why anyone would want to kill Miss Mamie, though, Avery. I mean, half the time she didn't even live in the present."

"So maybe the motive is in the past." I brushed at the branches hanging low over the playhouse, and got a pint of snow down the back of my neck for my trouble. I wiggled as the snow melted and trickled down my back in little icy rivulets. "Maybe it has something to do with the skeleton. It had to be one of the Greens who put it in the attic. Maybe Mamie knew what happened. Maybe that's what ruined her mind. She saw her mother or father—or sister—kill her baby brother, and her sanity snapped."

The door was closed, but not locked. The busted latch dangled drunkenly from a bent nail, and the snow in front of the door was still dusted with little pieces of broken glass and fragments of metal. The late afternoon sun sent streaks of light through the branches of the trees to sparkle off the shards.

"The baby carriage is still here," Kate said, peering at it. "I didn't realize how old it was."

I nodded. "Baby Arthur's probably. Late 1940s."

"Maybe she thought the doll was her missing brother. How sad is that?"

Incredibly sad. "You're taller than me," I said, getting up on my toes to peer at the lintel above the door. "Do you see any blood? Or skin cells or anything?"

"Skin cells?" Kate arched her brows but came to stand next to me. "No," she said after a moment. "No blood. And no skin cells, not that I'm sure I'd recognize skin cells if I saw them. Or that I'd be able to see them without a microscope."

"You know what I mean. I want to know whether Miss Mamie hit her head on the door or whether something else happened."

"Like what?" Kate asked, reaching for the door. "You heard Dr. Ben. It wasn't what killed her. At most, she'd have a headache."

At most Kate or I would have a headache. Miss Mamie might have been quite woozy, according to Dr. Ben. Maybe woozy enough that she wouldn't notice someone jimmying the lock so the latch wouldn't open.

Kate ducked her head to cross the threshold into the playhouse, and I followed.

It looked just as it had the night before, best as I could tell. It had been dark then, and I'd been upset and worried about Miss Mamie. But there was the empty chair where the doll had sat, and the bench where Mamie had lain, and the tea set, arranged on the table, with the teapot and sugar and milk in the middle of the table, and three cups and saucers neatly arranged on three edges of the table. One for Mamie, one for her doll, and a third, where no one had been sitting.

I wandered over—it took all of three steps—and peered down at the tiny cup and saucer. "Who do you suppose this was for?"

"Henrietta?" Kate said in the process of looking around. "Maybe."

"We should go," Kate said, turning for the door. "We still have to stop by Kerri's place and the rectory."

I nodded and followed her out, carefully ducking my head again. The floor was full of dried footprints: the heavily grooved boot prints probably from Dr. Ben and/or the paramedics, and the smooth soles from Darren's dress shoes. Strange that he wouldn't have taken the time to change into something more suited for walking around the Village before joining us for the canvass, but maybe he'd been too preoccupied to think of it.

"Do you think maybe it was Mamie who killed Arthur?" Kate suggested when we were back on the road and headed up North Street toward Kerri's house. "She was small when he died, right?"

"Eight or nine, I think. Ruth is a couple years older."

"Maybe she tried to pick him up and couldn't hold him. Maybe he slipped out of her arms and hit his head and died."

"Or maybe she tried to set him on a chair expecting him

to stay, like one of her dolls would. But of course, he couldn't. Maybe he fell off and hurt himself. And then she tried to stop him from crying, and she ended up smothering him."

Kate nodded. "Something like that. And then she hid the body in the attic because she was afraid she'd get in trouble. Living with that secret all these years would certainly turn anyone's mind a little weak."

Indeed. The Green sisters had lived in that house their entire lives. Had they—singularly or together—known that their brother was rotting above their heads?

It was a deeply unpleasant thought, and I felt a shiver run down my spine.

"Cold?" Kate asked, glancing at me out of the corner of her eye. "We can walk a little faster if you want."

"Easy for you to say. Your legs are longer than mine." But I picked up my speed, and a few minutes later we got to Kerri's anomaly.

On one side of it stood a two-story farmhouse Victorian, pale blue, and on the other, a small 1930s cottage covered with asbestos shingles. The grouping looked something like a crazy family portrait: on one side, the stern Victorian father, leaning in, and on the other, a small dumpling of a mother. In the middle, the Brady Bunch split-level looked like a teenager thumbing her nose at both parents.

Not that the house in and of itself didn't look great; it was just the setting that left something to be desired.

No, Kerri's house looked wonderful. Nice and clean and spic-and-span, with fresh paint on the sided parts of the house, and fresh power washing of the brick. She had rows of dark green bushes—some form of evergreen obviously—underneath the first level, or basement, windows, and they were draped with netting and Christmas lights, so the bushes twinkled. There was a green wreath with a big red bow on each window—two shorter on the basement level, two taller directly above, and then two on the other side of the door, up a half-story flight of stairs. Another wreath, similar but even bigger, hung on the door itself.

"Very traditional," I told Kate, who nodded.

The inside was traditionally decorated, too. The Christmas tree was in the living room, topped by a star and draped with lights and strings of popcorn and American flags. A lot of the ornaments were made from stained glass: stars and angels and candy canes and reindeer.

"Are those Dab's work?" I asked Kerri, pointing.

She nodded. "She made a few sets of ornaments a couple of years ago. I bought some."

"They're beautiful. She's very talented."

"Yes," Kerri said, "she is."

"I was out at her studio this morning. She helped me make a lampshade."

She smiled. "Did you have fun?"

"It was interesting. I've never tried working in stained glass before. It's different from textile design."

"I imagine it is," Kerri said, just as a loud thump came from down the hall where the bedrooms were. The living room, dining room, and kitchen were on the main level. The basement had a family room or rec room and—according to Kerri—another bedroom she used for a painting studio.

Meanwhile, up a half flight from the main level was a hallway with two more bedrooms and a bath, and that's where the noise had come from.

I glanced in that direction and back at Kerri with a question in my eyes.

She blushed, almost as red as her hair. "Dog."

"Sounds like a big one." One upon a time, someone else had told me dogs were making noises in an upstairs bedroom. I had neglected to investigate, with consequences that could have been dire.

"Akita," Kerri said.

"You can let him out if you want. I'm not afraid of dogs."

"He's almost as big as you are," Kerri said, and managed a grin that didn't quite reach her eyes. "It's better if I just leave him where he is until you're gone."

"I'd like to see him. I don't think I've ever seen an Akita before."

She hesitated. Glanced from me to Kate and back before giving in. "Fine. Excuse me a minute."

She headed up the stairs to the second level while Kate and I stayed where we were.

"What's going on?" Kate whispered when Kerri was out of sight, inside a room down the hall.

"I just want to make sure there's really a dog. And that she doesn't have someone tied to a bed down the hall."

She shot me a look.

"Remember when Cora's daughter Beatrice was missing?"

Kate's face cleared, and she grinned. "I don't think anyone's missing now, Avery. If Kerri has someone tied to her bed, I'm sure he wants to be there."

I shrugged. "I'm probably just being silly, and it really is just a dog, like she said. But I haven't ever seen an Akita, so I wouldn't mind."

"Just don't say she didn't warn you," Kate said, and stepped back as the door opened and Kerri came down the hall with the dog. Or the dog came back with Kerri.

Yes, there really was a dog. And not just *a* dog, but the biggest dog I had ever seen. It came up almost to Kerri's waist, and would probably hit me at chest height. And it was furry to boot, so it seemed even bigger. It scrabbled down the hall, and it was all Kerri could do to hang on to the collar.

I jumped behind Kate while Kerri wrestled the beast past us and over to the sliding glass doors into the backyard. "He wants to go out," she told us over her shoulder breathlessly.

The dog must have understood, because he wagged his curly tail.

She shoved him outside and slammed the door, brushing her hands off as she came toward us. And although she didn't actually say, "I told you so," it looked like she was thinking it.

"Pretty dog," I said.

"He's a handful. But he makes me feel safe. And he's good company." She smiled.

"Thank you for letting us see him. And your house."

"You're more than welcome," Kerri said.

"You're all ready for tomorrow?"

She said she was as ready as she could be, and we took our leave.

By now, the sun had almost set and it was starting to get colder. I stuffed my hands in my pockets as we headed for the rectory and the last stop on our little tour.

I'd been inside the rectory before, of course. Barry and Derek had gone to school together and were good friends, so we'd been over to dinner many times, and we'd also gone to some sort of premarital counseling before getting married. Not that Barry was worried about us, but just because it was what he had to do before performing a wedding in the church. I hadn't seen Judy's Christmas decorations before, though, and I was curious to see what they were like.

The rectory itself was a big house, built of the same gray stone as the church. It had two stories and lots of dark wood inside, and had been constructed sometime between the Colonial and the Victorian eras. Antebellum, before the Civil War, but after the Revolutionary ditto. The ceilings weren't as tall as in the Victorians, and the windows were smaller and deep-set, probably because the people who lived back then were trying to conserve heat in the winter. There were several big fireplaces, and wide-plank floors. And whoever built it must have expended most of their attention and money on the church—God's house—and a lot less on the rectory, which would only house man, because it was a very simple house, which hadn't been updated much in the past hundred and fifty–plus years. The bathrooms were new, of course—or relatively new; there was running water and flushing toilets from sometime in the 1970s—and the kitchen had been updated, as well, but in every respect that mattered, the house was close to the original.

The tree stood in the middle of the parlor, decorated with lots of lights, a big star at the top, and chains of paper rings and little woven paper baskets full of raisins and nuts and popcorn.

"Norwegian Christmas baskets," Judy explained when I admired them. "My mother was Norwegian, like your aunt. These baskets are a traditional Christmas tree decoration over there."

"They're lovely." Heart-shaped, woven from two different colors of glossy paper. I immediately had a vision for a shoulder bag made in the same style, of two different-colored fabrics, and lined with a third. It would make a fun Christmas gift for someone—like Judy—and it looked like it would be fun to make, and not very complicated.

"Let me show you," Judy said and reached for a blue sheet of glossy paper. The big dining room table was littered with them; she'd obviously been busy. "You fold it over, like this. Cut it into a rectangle with a round top. This is one half of the heart. Then you cut a number of evenly spaced slits in the bottom, and make sure they're as long as the width of the whole thing."

I nodded, watching as her scissors flew.

"Then you do it again with another piece of paper." She folded a white piece of paper over and repeated the process, including the slits. "Then you weave them together, over and under, so you get a woven pattern, like a checkerboard." She was weaving furiously as she spoke, and I watched the checkerboard take shape, patterned in white and blue. "When you're done, you glue a handle on, and you're ready to hang it on the tree."

She held up the finished heart.

I reached for it. "Can I take it home?"

"Of course," Judy said, relinquishing it. "Would you like to try one?"

"I'd love to!"

I armed myself with paper and scissors and, under her tutelage, cut and wove a heart of my own. It wasn't as pristine and flat as Judy's, it was a bit lumpier, but it looked pretty good, if I do say so myself. "I saw a couple of these crumpled in one of Aunt Inga's Christmas boxes," I said, admiring my handiwork, "but I didn't know what they were. Thanks for solving the mystery."

"It's my pleasure." She smiled and reached for the scissors and paper again. "I learned how to make these from my mother, who learned from her mother, and so on. These are the most basic ones. My mother made them in all kinds of patterns. There were some that looked like owls, and some that spelled out words or had pictures of pine trees or bells on them."

As she spoke, she snipped and wove and, in a few minutes, held up a green and red heart with a green tree on a red background. It even had a trunk planted in the ground, and a star on top.

"Wow," I said.

She handed it to me. "When we have more time, I'll teach you how to make some others. Or you can take it apart and figure it out yourself."

I probably could. Although like a Rubik's Cube, there was the chance that once I took it apart, I'd never be able to put it together again.

I stuck both hearts in my pocket. "Thank you."

"My pleasure," Judy said and looked at Kate. "So you're making sure everyone's ready for tomorrow?"

Kate nodded.

"We're all set," Judy said. "I have a little bit of cleaning up to do around here," like removing all the big and small pieces of glossy paper from the dining room table and floor, I assumed, "but the church is ready. Barry will be there tomorrow, and I'll be here. We even have a full nativity scene again."

"You do?" I said, surprised. "The Baby Jesus came back?"

Judy nodded, smiling.

"When? It wasn't there last night. I looked."

She blinked at me, and I added, "Dr. Ben and I canvassed the section of the Village with the church, so we went through the graveyard before we set off. I looked at the nativity scene. The manger was empty."

"Of course," Judy said.

"So did it just appear overnight again?"

She shook her head. "Brandon brought it."

It was my turn to stare. "You mean . . . Miss Mamie was having tea with Baby Jesus?"

Kate choked on a laugh, and I frowned at her, which only made her laugh more. I turned on my heel and walked out, snagging my coat from the back of a chair on my way past and tugging it on while I walked.

I stopped in front of the nativity scene, just where I'd stood with Dr. Ben last night. There were the camels, and the sheep, and the three kings, and Mary and Joseph. And in the manger, Mamie's doll, looking up at me with big, blue, vacant eyes. For some reason, it was still wearing the blue knits, too. The same ones I'd found in the cubby in Mamie's room.

"It's Mamie's doll," I told Judy and Kate when they came up behind me, still pulling on their own coats.

Judy shook her head. "It's our Baby Jesus."

"That, too. But it's the doll Mamie had in the playhouse yesterday. She was having a tea party."

"She must have been the one stealing it from the manger all these years," Kate said, stuffing her hands in her pockets. "Poor old thing. She probably thought she found her brother, and that she had to bring him home. And then Ruth would bring him back in a day or two."

"Only this year Ruth couldn't bring him back," Judy added, "because she can't get around."

Probably so. "I'm glad you got him back," I said. "And from now on, I guess he'll stay, too."

A shadow crossed Judy's face. "Terrible about Miss Mamie."

It was, rather. Although she had had Baby Jesus watching over her, I suppose, and if she believed she was back with Baby Arthur, maybe she'd been happy.

"Do you know anything about the funeral?" Kate asked.

"Tuesday," Judy answered. "Mr. Silva called Barry yesterday. It's all set."

I looked over at her. "Just for family, or can anyone come?"

"He didn't say it was a closed service," Judy said, "so if you wanted to come, I'm sure that would be fine. She'd lived in Waterfield a long time. I'm sure she had friends who want to come see her off."

I made a mental note to mention it to Derek. "We should get home."

Kate nodded. "It was good to see you, Judy. The house looks great. Have a good time tomorrow. And remember to lock up anything you don't want to walk off."

"Most people think twice before they steal from a rectory," Judy said and headed off across the snowy ground. Kate and I turned and trudged back down the hill toward home in the direction we'd come.

By now it was almost full dark, and the lights were going on inside the houses we were passing. Kerri's bushes were lit up, and through the big window in the living room, we could see the Christmas tree, as well.

And we could see Kerri, walking around in the kitchen, probably putting together dinner. And then another figure walked on from stage left—the staircase—and she turned to him. Tall, with a head of thick, gray hair.

I stopped. "Is that—"

Kate stopped, too, and peered in the same direction I was. "Who?"

But there was no one to see anymore. Kerri and whoever she was with—a man who had looked a lot like Henry Silva—had passed out of sight.

"Nothing," I said and kept walking. Kate glanced at me, but didn't say anything.

I came home to a house smelling of tomato sauce, ground beef, and garlic. Derek, bless him, had taken it upon himself to make dinner. Again. He'd lived alone for long enough to learn how to cook in a halfway decent manner, too—better than I could—so it would probably turn out to taste as good as it smelled.

"So how do we stack up?" he asked when the food was

served and we were sitting across from each other at Aunt Inga's kitchen table.

"Your dad and Cora's house is beautiful. I'm sure you've seen it before. The Fraser House is the Fraser House, and very Colonial. Kerri's tree is decorated with Dab's stained glass ornaments. Did she have designs on you?"

He looked startled. "Kerri? Not that I've noticed."

"Dab. Is that why she moved to Waterfield?"

"If she did," Derek said, "she never said anything about it. We've never gone out."

"Oh."

"What makes you think she . . . how did you put it? Had designs?"

I shrugged. "Just something about the way she said your name. It's not like she fell on me and tried to kill me because I married you, or anything like that."

"Good to know," Derek said. His face was solemn, but his eyes were laughing. "I think you're imagining things, Avery. I'm glad you find me so desirable you think everyone else wants me, too, but I think you're worrying over nothing. So Kerri decorated with stained glass. And I've seen Cora's decorations before. So have you, for that matter. Last year."

"She did a little more this year," I said, "because of the tour. There are real candles on the Christmas tree."

"The kind with flames?"

I nodded.

"I hope she isn't planning to light those with Alice's kids around. They'll burn the house down." I wasn't entirely sure whether "they" were the lights or the kids, but I didn't suppose it mattered.

"She said she'd replace them before Christmas Eve. She did it just for the tour, she said."

Derek nodded, and I'm sure he was relieved to hear that.

"Your dad told me he'd look through your grandfather's medical records," I added, "to see if your Pawpaw Willie ever treated either of the Green sisters for pregnancy."

"You don't treat anyone for pregnancy, Avery," my husband said. "It's not an illness."

"You know what I mean. Kate and I thought maybe the skeleton isn't Baby Arthur. That maybe Mamie or Ruth had a baby at some point, and didn't want anyone to know."

"Big coincidence," Derek said, "but I guess it's possible. If my grandfather knew one of the Green sisters was pregnant, though, and then there was no baby, he would have wondered what happened."

"Maybe they lied. Maybe whoever wasn't pregnant told him the other one had gone away to have the baby, and someone had adopted it. I don't think adoption records were all that strict back then, so even if he'd checked, they might not have been there for him to find."

"They weren't there for him to find," Derek said, "if the baby was dead and in the attic."

"You know what I mean."

He nodded. "It's more likely it's Baby Arthur, Avery. A baby going missing and turning up in the attic sixty years later makes more sense than that the first baby went missing and was never found, and another baby, that no one knew about, also went missing—although no one noticed—and that's the one that's in the attic."

"I guess I just don't like the idea that someone did something to Baby Arthur. It's more pleasant—or less unpleasant—to believe that someone took Baby Arthur, and he was loved and cared for and had a happy life, while the baby in the attic was stillborn and the Green sisters just didn't want to deal with the shame of an out-of-wedlock pregnancy."

"Could you do that?" Derek asked. When I looked at him, he added, "Give birth to a stillborn baby and hide it in the attic?"

"No." The idea was abhorrent, and my response was instant and strong. "Never. But you always say how we can't judge other people by what we would do. One person's slight embarrassment might be another's motive for murder."

"True," Derek said and got up with his empty plate. While I'd been busy talking, taking a bite of spaghetti once in a while, he'd managed to polish off his dinner.

"On the good news side," I told him, "Barry and Judy got their Baby Jesus back."

"No kidding?" He sat back down across from me after loading his plate into the dishwasher.

I nodded and had to chew and swallow before I could continue. "Remember Mamie's doll?"

His eyes widened. "That was Baby Jesus?"

"It was." I twirled more pasta around my fork. "We think maybe Mamie got confused and thought it was Baby Arthur, so she brought him home. Dr. Ben told me the nativity was sixty or seventy years old. Do you think it's possible it was new the year Baby Arthur disappeared? And when Mamie saw the Baby Jesus in the manger a few months after losing her baby brother, she got confused?"

"It's possible," Derek said. "And then Ruth went back the next night and returned him. Only this year she couldn't, because of the hip. So he ended up in the play-house instead."

"And Brandon brought him back to the church. He's in the manger again now. Just in time for the tour."

"That's good," Derek said. "So at least that part of the puzzle is solved."

I nodded. "I wonder if we'll ever find out what happened to Baby Arthur." Or the baby in the attic, if it wasn't Baby Arthur.

"With Mamie gone," Derek said, "maybe not. It depends on how many people knew the truth back then. And whether any of them are still alive to tell."

I finished my pasta in silence.

16

The day of the Christmas Home Tour dawned fair and cold, with sunshine that sparkled off the snow crystals in the yard. We spent the morning putting the finishing touches on the house: making sure there were no dust bunnies or hairballs lurking in the corners, and baking dozens upon dozens of cookies. With Derek's help, the task wasn't as arduous as I had feared. It took a couple hours, but we had fun. Jemmy and Inky chose not to get involved, but Mischa kept an eye on us from the doorway. Occasionally, he'd venture into the kitchen to twine around our legs in an attempt to trip us up.

Dr. Ben called around lunchtime, to check in and to tell me that he'd perused Pawpaw Willie's medical records, and there'd been no mention of either Mamie or Ruth ever having been pregnant.

"I'm only telling you this," he informed me, "because it's essentially no information at all. And I called Wayne first."

Of course he had. Not that I had any complaints: He'd done what I'd wanted, and had even shared the results with me. "Thank you."

"We all want to figure out what happened. But it looks like this, at least, is a dead end."

It did look that way. "Did you ask your father whether he remembered anything?"

Dr. Ben told me he had. "He said that to the best of his knowledge, neither of the Green sisters ever dealt with a pregnancy."

I tucked the phone between my ear and shoulder so I could scoop cookies off the cookie sheet and onto a rack while we spoke. "Would he have known if they did?"

"Most likely he would," Dr. Ben said. "Waterfield's a small town now, and it was smaller then. I'm assuming we're talking about a time when the girls were young. Late 1950s, early 1960s, maybe?"

Probably. By my calculations, Ruth and Mamie would have been between fifteen and twenty-five, roughly, at that time, which seemed a good age for an accidental pregnancy. Not that older women don't get pregnant by accident, too, but hiding a dead baby in the attic for fear of judgment seemed something a young person would do. Surely someone older would have developed more of a conscience, or at least be less likely to panic.

Dr. Ben continued, "Back then, women in small towns went to their GPs with pregnancies. Home births were common, and Waterfield didn't have anyone specializing in gynecology or obstetrics. We still don't."

"So if one of them got pregnant, chances are your father would have been the doctor they went to. Unless they went to another town's doctor, just so no one here would know?"

"Anything's possible," Dr. Ben said, "but neither Dad nor I remember a pregnancy, or any rumors, or either Mamie or Ruth disappearing for any length of time and coming back, looking or acting different."

It had been a long shot anyway, the possibility that the baby skeleton in the attic was anyone other than Arthur Green.

I thanked Dr. Ben and went back to what I was doing.

At two o'clock, when we opened the doors, there were

people literally waiting on the porch, programs clutched in their fists, waiting to get in, and for the next two hours, we weren't alone in the house for more than a minute.

It was overwhelming, but fun, too, and they gobbled up cookies faster than we could get them out of the oven. Derek stayed on KP duty, while I hung out at the front of the house and praised his renovating abilities and handed out Waterfield R&R business cards. (Renovation & Restoration, not Rest & Relaxation. Rest & Relaxation were what we'd need once the tour was over.)

A lot of people had questions about Aunt Inga and what happened to her, and about the house itself, and I talked until my throat was sore, and then I talked some more.

About halfway through the afternoon, Darren Silva showed up, and walked through the house—the downstairs, since I'd strung a ribbon across the stairs with a sign forbidding people to go up to the second floor—looking at everything with a critical eye. I guess maybe Henrietta was busy with her own open house, and had dispatched him to check out the competition, or maybe he just wanted to see how the rest of us stacked up. (If so, he didn't have to worry. None of us came even close to the splendor of the Silva house, with the possible exception of Kate's B&B.)

Or maybe he wanted Derek. He disappeared into the dining room and from there into the kitchen, and stayed there awhile. I'm not sure how long, because I was busy myself and hadn't checked what time it was when he arrived, but he and Derek had time for a nice, long chat before Darren sauntered back out with a smirk at me. I made a mental note to ask Derek later what they'd been discussing. At the moment, I had too many other things to worry about.

The visitors kept coming until four o'clock, and then it took a while to get everyone out of the house, because of course you can't stop someone in the middle of a sentence, in the middle of a conversation, to say, "Sorry, but I have to close up shop now." And then there are always a few stragglers running up to the door at the last minute, begging to be let in and swearing up and down they'll be quick. They're usually not, although by four thirty, the house was empty of strangers, there was nothing but crumbs left of the eight dozen cookies we'd baked, and Derek and I were alone.

He looked like he'd been through the wars when he came out of the kitchen, with his hair standing straight up and his eyes wild. He peered from side to side suspiciously, as if expecting strangers to jump up from behind the furniture and yell, "Surprise!"

"They're gone," I told him, and he ventured a little farther out of the kitchen, raking his hand through his hair. That was probably how it had gotten into its current state in the first place.

"That was crazy."

I nodded. "Not sure I want to do that again next year."

"I'm sure I don't," Derek said.

We walked into the living room in silence and flopped down on the sofa, side by side. And sat there, wordlessly, for long minutes, just breathing and enjoying the solitude and the silence.

"I feel like I don't ever want to move again," Derek said eventually.

"Me, either."

"I just want to stay right here."

I nodded. "Me, too."

We stayed there. After a few minutes I turned to him. "It went well, I think."

"People seemed to have a good time."

"They were very complimentary of the house. The decorations, too—several people asked me how I made the Chinese lantern ornaments—but especially the house. I handed out a lot of business cards. Hopefully it'll turn into a lot of business."

"That'd be nice," Derek said. "Not that I wouldn't love to spend all my time on our own renovations, but it's nice to spend other people's money from time to time, too."

Definitely. "What did Darren want?"

"Not sure," Derek said, making himself comfortable against the soft pillows and propping his stocking feet on the coffee table. "Nothing in particular. He was just making small talk."

"He smirked at me when he left."

Derek turned his head on the back of the sofa to look at me. "Are you sure you didn't imagine it?"

"Positive. He smirked."

"Huh," Derek said. "I don't know why he'd do that. Your name didn't come up in the conversation."

"What did you talk about?"

He shrugged. "Just stuff. The house. The Green sisters' house. The home tour. Mamie."

"The funeral is Tuesday," I said. "Judy told me."

"Darren didn't tell me. Maybe he doesn't want us there."

"I don't care whether he does or not. I found her; I'm going to the funeral."

"Fine with me," Derek said with another shrug.

Silence reigned for another minute or two.

"You hungry?" he asked.

"Starving."

"You feel like cooking?"

I shook my head.

"Takeout? Or go out?"

"Pizza," I said. "I want to get out of these clothes"—the Christmas dress and high heels I'd worn for the home tour—"and into something comfortable, and I don't want to have to worry about looking good."

"You always look good." He glanced down at me. "Pretty dress."

"Thank you." I'd made it myself. Dark blue velvet with snowflakes and glitter on the skirt, so it looked like the snow was accumulating along the hem. Very festive, if I do say so myself.

"Need help getting it off?"

It slipped right over my head, so no, I didn't. However . . . "That'd be nice."

"Let's go upstairs and change," Derek said, pushing

himself out of the slothful grip of the sofa and reaching out
a hand for me. "C'mon, Tink."

I took the hand and let him lift me to my feet. We headed
up the stairs hand in hand.

.   .   .

It was an hour later by the time we left the house and got
into the little green Beetle. I was out of the dress and into
jeans and a comfortable sweater, and so was Derek. Comfortable, I mean; not out of the dress.

I drove down to the cul-de-sac at the end of Bayberry
Lane, Aunt Inga's street, and turned the car around. We
rolled down the hill toward downtown, picking up speed as
we went. The Christmas decorations along Main Street
were lit: outlines of bells and stars and anchors and ship
wheels hanging from the light poles.

As we crossed Cabot Street, I saw other lights in my
peripheral vision, but I didn't even have time to react before
Derek grabbed my arm, hard. "Turn around!" If it hadn't
been for the puffy down coat and sweater, it would have
hurt. And his voice was laced with panic, not something
I'm used to hearing.

"Hold on." I took a right on the next street and then
another right a block later. We ended up on the corner of
Cabot and Fraser, looking around.

The flashing blue lights were farther down, but not as
far away as Dr. Ben and Cora's house. I think we both let
out a relieved sigh when we realized it.

"Sorry," Derek said. "I thought—"

"Don't worry about it." I'd thought so, too, once I'd realized what was going on.

"I didn't hurt you, did I?"

I shook my head. "The coat took the brunt of it. If it had
been summer, it would have hurt."

"Sorry."

"No problem. Looks like everything is fine at your dad's
and Cora's house."

He nodded. "Drive down there to make sure anyway."

"Of course." I took my foot off the brake and slid around the corner slowly.

The closer we got, the more and more certain I became that the trouble—whatever it was—was at the Silvas' house. Two cars with flashing blue lights—one a police cruiser and one an ambulance—were parked outside the fence, and as we got closer, we could see several dark figures exit the house. As they made their way toward us, they resolved themselves into two paramedics—the same two I had seen three nights ago when the ambulance came for Mamie. A taller shadow behind them turned out to be Wayne, his face grim.

I slid the Beetle up to the curb on the other side of the street, and stopped.

The paramedics were wheeling a gurney with a form on it. It was dark, and the figure on the gurney was mostly covered with a blanket, so we couldn't make out who it was, but Darren was standing in the doorway of the house, watching, so at least it wasn't him.

Derek muttered a word I won't repeat, and I nodded. "The Silvas sure are dealing with a lot these days."

There was movement behind Darren in the doorway, and then another tall figure, this one with a head of silver hair, slipped past Darren and down the front steps, still in the process of wrapping a coat around himself. But instead of following the paramedics—and gurney—across the yard, Henry Silva made for the garage on the right side of the property. He must plan to follow the ambulance in his own car.

"It's Henrietta on the gurney," I said.

Derek nodded. "Must be. Unless one of the guests on the tour was taken ill suddenly, and surely they would have resolved that by now."

At this point Wayne had noticed us sitting there, and was on his way over. I rolled down the window.

"What are you two doing here?"

"We were on our way out to dinner," I explained. "Can't face cooking after baking eight dozen cookies this morning. We saw the lights on our way down the hill."

"And you thought you'd see what was going on?"

"Actually," I said, refusing to take offense at the hint of recrimination in his tone, "we couldn't see clearly in passing, and we were worried you might be outside Dr. Ben and Cora's house."

Wayne had the grace to look ashamed. "Sorry."

"It's OK. We were really just driving by. If I'd realized this was the Silvas' house, we would have just kept going."

Derek snorted softly, but didn't actually contradict me. Instead, he said, "Has something happened to Henrietta?"

"Heart attack," Wayne said.

"Oh, no. Is she . . ."

"Dead" was the word I couldn't quite bring myself to utter.

He shook his head. "She's hanging on. Barely. But I'm not looking forward to telling Kate about this."

"Why?" Not that it's ever fun to give somebody bad news, but I hadn't gotten the impression that Kate and Henrietta were all that close. No reason why it would be more difficult to tell Kate than it had been to tell, for instance, me.

"She'll blame herself," Wayne said. "For inviting Henrietta to take part in the home tour. For letting her do too much."

"It was her choice, wasn't it? She didn't have to accept."

Wayne shrugged. "Kate will still blame herself."

"So you think the stress was too much for Henrietta's heart? Is that what happened?"

"Something like that," Wayne said. "Dr. Ben is meeting the ambulance at the hospital. Her cardiologist will be coming up from Portland just as soon as he can."

"Is she going to make it?" Derek asked.

"Not sure. I don't have a lot of experience with heart attacks, but she didn't look good. It may have been too long before anyone found her. The tour was over almost two hours ago. It was more than an hour before Mr. Silva came home, and he didn't realize anything was wrong right away. Too much time may have passed." He shook his head. "I don't know."

"Is there anything we can do?" Derek asked as the ambulance took off down the street, lights flashing and siren wailing. The Mercedes with Henry Silva inside pulled out of the driveway and fell in behind. I caught a glimpse of his face as he passed, and his expression was grim.

"I don't think so," Wayne said. "Unless you want to keep Darren company."

We both glanced at the doorway, where Darren was still standing, outlined against the light. Either he was too much in shock to go inside and close the door, or he was wondering who Wayne was talking to.

"I'll go see if he wants company," Derek said and opened his door. "Just wait here, Avery."

I nodded. I had no desire to approach Darren. I didn't like him, and I was pretty sure he didn't like me. That didn't mean I wouldn't stay if he wanted us to. He and Derek went back a long way, even if they'd never been as close as Derek and some of his other friends. But if Darren needed company, I certainly wasn't about to refuse.

Derek headed across the street and into the yard, and I turned back to Wayne. "Poor Mr. Silva sure has had a lot to deal with this week."

He nodded.

"How did he take the news about the baby skeleton? And Mamie?"

"The same way anyone would," Wayne said. "Shocked. Dismayed. Upset."

"And of course he's upset about Henrietta."

"Of course."

"Does he have a bad heart, too?"

"Not that I've heard," Wayne said. "The heart problems are a Silva thing. Henry takes after his mother's family, I guess."

"Where was he this afternoon during the home tour? Here?"

Wayne shook his head. "Henrietta was alone. Darren was out looking at the other houses—"

I nodded. "He stopped by ours."

"And Henry has a lady friend he was visiting."

"Anyone we know?"

"It's personal information," Wayne said, "and none of your concern."

"Just answer me one question. Is he seeing Kerri Waldo?"

There was a pause. And although Wayne didn't answer, I could see the truth in his expression. "I thought I saw him there the other night," I said apologetically. "Yesterday, when Kate and I were out walking around."

Wayne didn't respond. Not to that. "Why are you so interested in where everyone was? Surely you're not thinking that there's anything suspicious about this? She had a weak heart."

"There's just been a lot of deaths lately in the Silva family."

"Henrietta isn't dead yet," Wayne reminded me. "And Mamie and Arthur were both Greens, not Silvas. And they were accidents, Avery. Mamie froze to death and Henrietta had a heart attack. Between the skeleton and Mamie's death and now the home tour, it's not surprising the stress may have gotten to her."

Maybe not. Although Derek and I had seen Henry and Henrietta having an argument—or at least a heated discussion—at the Waymouth Tavern a few nights ago.

Maybe Henrietta had disapproved of Henry's relationship with Kerri? Maybe she didn't like the age difference and thought her brother was making a fool of himself with someone so much younger? He must have twenty years on her, if not more. Kerri was closer to Darren's age than Henry's, and by quite a lot.

If they'd been together during the home tour, one of them could easily have snuck out and down the street to do something to Henrietta, while the other held down the fort.

Then again, Henrietta's disapproval surely wasn't enough reason for Henry to want to get rid of her. He was the one who had made her move in. He was the one holding the purse strings, too. If he wanted a relationship with Kerri, he probably wouldn't worry overmuch about his sister's opinion.

It was probably as Kate said: I'd gotten so used to murders and sinister happenings that I saw them everywhere, even in perfectly harmless occurrences.

I turned my head as Derek opened the passenger door again and slid in beside me. "He doesn't want company."

"Is he all right?"

"He's fine," Derek said. "He just said he had phone calls to make, and then he was going to drive up to the hospital, too, and stay with his dad."

"We should go," I told Wayne, and got a nod in response, so obviously he thought so, too. I thought about asking him to let us know if she pulled through, but I caught Derek's eye and realized it would be just as easy to call Dr. Ben and ask him. That way I wouldn't have to deal with Wayne telling me not to butt in where I didn't belong.

So we wished Wayne well and rolled off down the street. Dr. Ben's car was already gone from outside the Folk Victorian, so he must be on his way to the hospital. Wayne overtook us after a couple of blocks and zipped past us and around the corner, lights flashing but no siren.

"Still hungry?" Derek asked into the silence.

"I could eat." Although the thought of Guido's Pizzeria, with its hustle and bustle, had lost some of its appeal.

Derek must feel the same way, because he said, "D'you just wanna grab something quick somewhere nearby? I'm not sure I'm up for a lot of people right now."

"That's fine with me." The question was where to go. Waterfield rolls up the sidewalks pretty early, especially on a Sunday night.

"The cafés on Main Street usually stay open late the day of the Christmas Tour," Derek said, reading my mind again. "Maybe we can grab a couple of roast beef sandwiches or something."

Roast beef sandwiches sounded great. I made another

turn, and we were on our way back toward Main Street. Downtown was mostly quiet now, when the home tour was over and done. Just a few people walked the sidewalks. The greenery strung across the street swayed gently above us as we drove, and the seahorses and anchors lit our way.

We ended up in a little café and ate our sandwiches right there, on opposite sides of a little marble-topped table. Neither of us said much. There wasn't much to say.

"Was Darren rude to you?" I asked Derek, who shrugged.

"He wasn't warm. But then he had a lot on his mind. And we've never been close."

"Why not?"

"He's a snob," Derek said. "His family had money, so he'd only associate with certain of the kids. I was all right, because Dad was a doctor. And Zach was all right, because his dad worked for the bank. But Alex wasn't, because Alex's dad worked for the Silvas. And of course, Darren wouldn't have anything to do with Barry . . ."

I nodded. "I don't like him."

"I don't dislike him," Derek said.

I did, sort of. "I'd love for him to be guilty of something."

Derek's lips twitched. "Like what? He's my age. Born thirty years after whatever happened to Baby Arthur. And there isn't anything else he could be guilty of."

"I wasn't thinking anything related to this. Just something. Shoplifting maybe."

"He doesn't have to shoplift," Derek said. "He has money."

"I don't think people who shoplift do it because they can't afford to pay. I think they do it because it's fun. Like a game. Seeing if they can get away with it."

Derek shrugged. "I don't think he'd do anything like that, Tink. He gets his self-worth from his money—or I guess I should say his father's money, since Darren hasn't worked for any of it. Not that Henry has; he got it from Henry Senior. But I don't think Darren would risk the reputation of the wealthy and well-respected Silvas by doing something stupid like that."

Probably not. "I was just dreaming," I said.

Derek grinned and pushed back his chair. "How about we stop by Cora's house on the way home? Maybe Dad's called with an update on Henrietta."

A man after my own heart. "Let's."

"After you," my husband said, and gestured to the door.

.   .   .

I hadn't expected Dr. Ben to be there when we pulled up in front of the house on Cabot, but his car was back in the driveway, where it hadn't been when we drove by earlier. When we walked in, he was sitting at the table, indulging in food he had probably had to leave earlier, and which had been kept warm for him by Cora.

He looked up and waved when he saw us, but didn't stop eating. Cora turned from the sink, smiling. "Derek. And Avery. Good to see you."

Unlike Aunt Inga's house, which was still an unholy mess, the Folk Victorian was pristine. Cora was just finishing putting the dinner plates and pots and pans in the dishwasher and wiping down the counter. The floors were clean, the place was neat, and she didn't look like she'd been through hell earlier in the day.

"How many people came through here on the tour?" I asked suspiciously. Because I'd lost count at two hundred fourteen, and if she'd only had fifty or so, maybe that explained how her place looked so together while mine was such a mess.

"A few hundred," Cora said. "Brownie?"

"Don't mind if I do." My husband took a seat across from his father at the table. "Dad."

Dr. Ben nodded, still in the process of eating.

"You had time to make brownies?" I watched Cora pull a tray out of the oven. They were still warm, and when she put a scoop of ice cream on top, and drizzled caramel sauce over that, the ice cream started melting. My mouth watered.

She glanced at me. "They've been gone for several hours by now."

True. But . . . "I don't have the energy to do anything. Derek had to take me out for sandwiches, because I couldn't face cooking anything after baking eight dozen cookies."

"We did have enough energy for something," Derek reminded me, fork already halfway to his mouth. I blushed. Dr. Ben grinned, and so did Cora.

Derek turned to his dad. "We were on our way down the hill when we saw the lights outside the Silvas' house. How's Henrietta?"

Dr. Ben's face darkened. "She didn't make it."

Oh, no. My heart sank. "She died?"

He nodded. "DOA. Dead on arrival at the hospital. They tried to revive her, but there was nothing anyone could do. Her heart had stopped and refused to start again."

"I'm so sorry."

"It's hard," Dr. Ben said. "But at least it wasn't unexpected. I knew she had heart problems. So did she. So did her family."

"Was it the stress, do you think?"

"I imagine it was." He pushed his plate away, and nodded thanks to Cora when she swooped in and removed it to the sink. "There've been a lot of shocks in her life this week. The home tour on top of it may have been too much."

I pulled out a chair and sat down next to Derek, who was happily digging into his brownie à la mode. "Does that happen a lot? That stress brings on a heart attack?"

"Hard to say," Dr. Ben said judiciously. "Stress is a contributing factor to heart disease, we do know that much. Once the heart disease is present, a heart attack can come at any time. Stress won't always trigger one, but I wouldn't rule out that it could."

"There's no question that it was her heart, right?"

He shook his head, and smiled at Cora as she put a brownie in front of him. "No, no question at all."

Cora sat down beside Dr. Ben with her own brownie, and I lifted my fork and devoted myself to mine. We'd had enough sadness for one evening, and besides, my suspicions about Henry and Kerri were just that—suspicions—since I hadn't been able to convince even myself that if they were carrying on a clandestine affair, it was anything like a motive for wanting Henrietta out of the way.

— 17 —

Mamie's funeral turned into a double header when the Silvas decided to bury Henrietta at the same time. I'm not sure what the reasoning was, whether they got the two-for-one discount on the church, or whether it just made sense for the backhoe to dig both graves at the same time, since it was there pecking at the frozen ground anyway. Or maybe it was because Henrietta and Mamie were cousins, and contemporaries, and had the same friends and acquaintances. Maybe the family just didn't want to go through the sadness twice.

Whatever the reason, it was a double funeral. It wasn't until we got to the church on Tuesday morning that we realized they were also doing the honors for Baby Arthur. Between the two full-sized coffins at the front of the church sat a tiny one: white and with a spray of yellow roses on top, just like the others.

It was a full house, too. Half of Waterfield was there, or so it seemed. Derek and I sat with Dr. Ben and Cora. Kate was there, and so was Wayne. Josh and Shannon weren't; I figured they probably had classes. Kerri was there, and when we walked in, she was in earnest conversation with Henry Silva. Hand on his sleeve, gazing up at him adoringly. Or maybe the adoration was in my head. They did have their heads together, though, talking softly. Until John Nickerson walked in the door and made a beeline for Henry. Kerri withdrew then, and went to sit down, and then it was John who spent a few minutes talking to Henry. Like Dr. Ben, John and Henry were about the same age, and had probably grown up together.

John came and sat down next to me after he was finished, and I gave him a smile. A subdued one, given the occasion. "Hi, John."

"Avery." He smiled back, and reached across me to shake hands with Derek and to greet Cora and Dr. Ben. Then he sat back and shook his head. "Sad day."

I nodded. "I saw you talking to Henry Silva. Are you friends?"

He glanced at me. "We're cousins of a sort, but my mother was the black sheep of the family. Ran off to marry beneath her. So we didn't associate with the Silvas. Or they didn't associate with us."

"Goodness." I hadn't realized there was any other family, besides the Silvas and the Green sisters.

He nodded. "She's gone now, rest her soul. So is her brother. And the old man."

"The old man?"

"My grandfather," John said. "He never spoke to her again after she married my father."

"I'm sorry."

He shrugged. "My parents were happy. And we did well enough. And I don't think it was the old man's fault so much as my uncle's anyway. My grandfather would have come around, I think. It was old Henry who refused to talk to her again. Or let young Henry talk to me."

"Old Henry being Henry Senior, Henrietta and Henry's father?"

John nodded. "Nasty old bugger."

Quite so. "But you and Henry are talking again now."

"We lost touch for a while," John said. "I was caught in the draft, he wasn't."

John had gone to Vietnam in the late 1960s, and still had a limp to show for it. Henry had spent the Vietnam War here, it seemed. It crossed my mind to wonder whether his money had had something to do with that. Or maybe it didn't work that way.

John continued, "But after the old man died sometime in the 1980s, we got back in touch. We don't spend much time together—nothing in common really—but we're on speaking terms again."

"What about Henrietta? Did you know her?"

He shook his head. "She was almost a decade older than Henry, and a full decade older than me. And more like her father than he is." He nodded toward Henry, who was taking his seat in the front row beside Darren. "She'd nod when we met, but we didn't really talk."

"So are you Ruth and Mamie Green's cousin, too?"

"No," John said. When I must have looked confused, he added, "My mother was Henry Senior's younger sister. Henry Senior married Sonya Wikstad. Her sister, Lila Wikstad, married George Green. So my mother was only related to the Greens through her brother's wife. And since there was no contact between my mother and her brother, there was even less contact between my mother and the Greens."

I made a mental family tree in my head, with branches and twigs, and thought I understood. "So you didn't know Mamie."

"Only to look at," John said. "I mean, we've lived in the same small town for sixty-plus years. It's inevitable that our paths should have crossed. But like Henrietta, Mamie was a decade older than me, so we didn't have much in common."

Right.

"What's with the tiny coffin?" John added.

I guess word hadn't gotten around yet. "That's Arthur Green. Mamie and Ruth's little brother who disappeared when he was a baby. In 1949."

John arched his brows. He was a small, spare man with an Elvis cockscomb, who liked to dress in midcentury clothing, the same kind of thing he sold in his store. His funeral attire was a 1960s-style suit with narrow legs and an even narrower tie, paired with pointy-toed shoes. The pants had a knife's edge pleat that could have cut bread. "What's he doing here?"

"We found him," I said. "When we started renovating the Green sisters' house last week. In a crate in the attic."

"He'd been there all that time?"

"Must have been. It's a small crawl space, only accessible by a ladder nailed to the wall, so I guess nobody went up there much." Obviously the hiding place had worked exceedingly well, if no one had discovered the skeleton in more than sixty years.

"Wow," John said.

"I guess they decided, since they were digging graves anyway, they may as well put him in the ground, too."

John nodded, but before he had time to respond, Barry got to his feet and made his way up to the pulpit and onto the box he stands on, owing to his lack of height. "Good morning," he said, and as that wonderful, deep, warm baritone—the Voice of God—sounded through the room, all the rustling and whispers ended, and we settled in to listen.

I didn't actually pay attention to the words all that much, since I got caught up in listening to the cadences of Barry's voice and because there's only so much you can say about two old ladies in their seventies who die natural, or semi-natural, deaths. And as far as Baby Arthur went, the identification wasn't even certain, so Barry refrained from saying much at all about the miniature coffin.

It was hard to imagine who else it could be but Baby Arthur, though. Especially now that Dr. Ben and Pawpaw Willie had verified that to the best of their knowledge, neither of the Green sisters had ever been pregnant. I was back to my original theory, that Mrs. Green—Lila—had conceived Arthur with someone other than her husband, and when it became obvious—perhaps when the baby got old enough to start looking like someone other than his supposed father—one of them made up the story about the disappearance to account for the baby being gone.

The one stumbling block as far as that theory went was that they'd stayed together afterward. So far, no one had said anything about the marriage being in trouble. Then again, things were different fifty or sixty years ago, and divorce was a lot less common than it is now, so maybe that just wasn't an option for them.

Unless the innocent party really hadn't guessed that the guilty party was . . . well, guilty. If it looked like SIDS had killed the baby, maybe.

But if it was an accident, why hide the body? Why make up the story about the disappearance? Why not just report it as a sad but natural occurrence and go on?

With Mamie and Henrietta both gone, I wondered whether Ruth might be more inclined to talk about what had happened back then. She was the only one left who remembered, assuming she remembered, and she might be upset enough by her sister's and cousin's deaths to want to talk to someone. Perhaps I should make a trip out to the nursing home again soon. She was here—beside Henry in the front row—but now wasn't the right time to approach her.

I shifted in the pew, and Derek glanced down and reached for my hand. I let him twine his fingers with mine and rub the pad of his thumb over my palm. He must have thought I was getting restless. I settled back and did my best to focus on Barry and not on the thoughts in my head.

After Barry had finished speaking, Henry got up to say a few words. He got a little choked up over his sister's death, understandably, and he said some nice things about Mamie, too, and then he touched very lightly on Baby Arthur. Ruth didn't speak, maybe because it was hard for her to get around or maybe because she didn't want to, and when Darren got up, he merely thanked everyone for coming and informed us that there would be refreshments in the church hall following the service.

The church hall was the same place where Derek and I had had our wedding reception a month ago. That joyous occasion was the last time I'd been inside the big room. It was strange being there again now, for an occasion so much less happy.

Not that the mood was subdued really. The few family members who existed had followed the hearses to the gravesite to see the coffins lowered, so those of us who were left were really just incidental strangers. Not that we were having a party exactly, but we weren't grieving, either. None of us had known Mamie well enough for that, and it didn't seem as if Henrietta had had a lot of friends, either. Most of the people here were younger, just showing support for the family, or perhaps attending out of general nosiness.

The small coffin was a topic of conversation, of course. Most people had no idea who—or what—was inside. The craziest suggestion I overheard was a lady talking to Dab Holt, and explaining, very earnestly, that it was Henrietta's beloved shih tzu inside the coffin: a shih tzu which had died of a broken heart after Henrietta's passing.

"That's nothing," Derek said when I cornered him to pass on the joke. "I just overheard someone say that it's Mamie's doll, that they're burying it with her."

"In its own coffin?"

He shrugged. "It makes just as much sense as the shih tzu."

"Did Henrietta even own a shih tzu?" I hadn't seen one at the house on Saturday, when Kate and I were there.

"I don't really know," Derek said. "Although I think maybe she did. I think I've seen her walk a small, fluffy dog around."

I lowered my voice. "We're sure it isn't the shih tzu, right? In the coffin?"

"I'm pretty sure it isn't the shih tzu," Derek answered softly, "but when Barry gets back, we can ask him. Just to make sure."

We both jumped when a voice said, "What are you two whispering about?"

It was Wayne, closely followed by Kate, and he came

close to giving me a heart attack of my own. When I'd caught my breath again, I told him what we'd overheard, and watched him grimace. "It isn't the doll. That's back in the manger outside the church. And it isn't the shih tzu, either. It isn't dead, that I know of. Mourning maybe. It was a very unhappy dog on Sunday night. But it was alive and well."

"So it's the baby skeleton."

Wayne nodded. "They were burying family members anyway. It seemed a good time to put the baby skeleton in the ground without a lot of fanfare or attention."

"You don't think a little bit of attention might have helped?" I said. "Maybe someone who knew something about what happened back then might have come forward if they'd realized that we found the bones."

Wayne shook his head. "I think anyone who knows what happened is dead by now, Avery."

"Henrietta and Mamie?" Surely not.

"I was thinking more of Mr. or Mrs. Green," Wayne said. "Although I don't think we'll ever know anything for sure, and I, for one, am OK with that. Whoever is responsible is probably dead by now, too, and he—or she—has become God's responsibility, not mine."

. . .

"I'd like to go see Ruth," I told Derek when the reception was over and we were on our way home to change out of our finery and into jeans preparatory to going back to work.

He glanced at me. "Now?"

"She's probably still with Henry and Darren now. Don't you think?"

He nodded. "Probably."

"Maybe after we're done working tonight?"

"We could swing by, I suppose," Derek said. "What reason do we have for intruding on a grieving old lady on the day of her sister's, and brother's, and cousin's, funeral?"

Ouch.

"I just wanted to offer my condolences. I didn't get to talk to her in the church today, and she didn't make it to the reception."

Darren came back to the church after the graveside service, to shake hands and receive condolences, but Henry and Ruth didn't. He must have taken her back to the nursing home, I figured, while Darren did the family duty at the reception.

"Are you sure we shouldn't at least wait until tomorrow?" Derek asked.

"If it was me," I answered, "I'd want company today. As you said, she just buried her sister and brother and cousin. She must feel pretty alone. She might want to talk."

"So that's your grand plan." He didn't sound surprised, or even accusatory. More resigned really. "You're hoping the grief will loosen her tongue."

"More like, now that everyone else who could possibly be involved is dead, maybe there's a chance she'll want to talk about what happened." And—not to be too callous about it—now that she was the only one left, that she might want to unburden herself before it was too late.

"It's not your job to figure out what happened, Avery." He pulled the truck to a stop at the curb outside Aunt Inga's house. We'd driven it to the funeral instead of the Beetle because of the color: The Beetle is a bright spring green, while Derek's F-150 is somber black. It seemed more appropriate somehow. "Leave it to the cops."

"The cops aren't interested," I said, and waited for him to come around the car to help me down to the curb before I continued. "You heard what Wayne said. Or maybe you didn't."

"I heard." He closed the car door behind me and took my arm on the walk up to the porch. The path was slippery with ice and snow, and I was wearing heels, in honor of the occasion. "He said the case is closed."

"I'd like to know what happened," I said. "Even if whoever did it—whatever it was—is dead, I'd still like to know. That baby didn't get into the attic on its own. Someone put it there, and I want to know who and why. Even if it's too late to charge anyone with a crime."

Derek watched me fumble in my bag for the key to the front door. "Don't you think Ruth has had a bad enough day without bringing up that old tragedy? Asking her whether she thinks her mother or her father was a murderer, and who her mother was cheating with . . ."

"I wasn't going to ask her flat out," I said, offended, dropping the key back into my purse before pushing the door open. "I just thought she might want to talk rather than sit alone and grieve."

"Sure." Derek waited for me to walk into the house first. Mischa had pretty much stopped attacking him on sight, but this way, I was the one who had to stop and stand still while the kitten—who wasn't so much of a kitten anymore—spent a few minutes winding around my legs and complaining loudly about having been left alone. While I did that, Derek walked past me into the house and toward the stairs. "I'll see you upstairs."

I watched him disappear onto the second floor, and then I gave Mischa another minute or so of time, before peeling off the high-heeled boots and coat and leaving them in the foyer. Then I followed Derek up the stairs.

He had already changed into a pair of jeans and a snug T-shirt, and it was just as well, because we didn't really have time to indulge in any whoopie.

I gave my husband a regretful glance—one he didn't notice, because he had his back to me—and went to the bureau. A minute later I was dressed, too. "Ready."

"Let's go," Derek said. "We can still get a few hours' work done this afternoon."

I nodded and followed him down the stairs.

Over at the house, he went back to work on the downstairs bathroom. The ribbon tile on the floor looked great by now, but the bathroom had been built before the days of indoor showers, so there was no tile surround for the tub. And since someone at some point had added a showerhead to the tub, and finished the job off by gluing up a couple sheets of adhesive plastic wall, there was some work to be done. We had torn off the shower walls last week, while we were ripping out everything else that had to go, and all that was left was snaking stripes of dried glue on the walls. Derek had also unhooked the ugly showerhead, preparatory to replacing it with a new, much bigger and fancier one. Now it was time to start adding white subway tile to shoulder height, capped by a black border all the way around.

I left him to it and went into the dining room to hang my lampshade over the missing table. Derek had actually been pretty impressed with it, and assured me it didn't look anywhere near as amateurish as I thought. He had talked me into hanging it, just to see how it looked, and after struggling with the ladder and wires for thirty minutes, I finally got it up there and could step back and take a look. After turning the power to the dining room back on in the electrical panel, I flipped the switch and tilted my head.

"Derek?"

"Uh-huh?"

"Can you come here a sec?"

A few moments passed, and then he came wandering into the dining room, wiping his hands. "What's going on?"

I gestured to the lamp, all lit up and hanging.

"Oh." He tilted his head and contemplated it. "I like it," he said after a pause.

I glanced at him. "Really?"

"Sure." He glanced back. "What's not to like? It's a good size for the room. And while it isn't overly fancy, it looks very Craftsman-like. Tiffany did a lot of curved and colorful shades, but the Craftsman style is like this: square and simple. Like the furniture."

"Really?"

He nodded. "I promise. Leave it. It looks good."

He wandered back to the bathroom, leaving me happy and glowing. The lamp did look good. Or at least it didn't look bad. Now that I'd gotten it away from Dab's workshop, where I couldn't see it clearly next to the works of art she created, I was able to see it on its own merits and not just in comparison to hers. And Derek was right: The lamp I had made fit the room. It was a good size. And it looked better than I had thought it did.

I put the ladder away and walked into the living room to contemplate the fireplace. The other day, I'd seen a Craftsman-style sconce at the Silvas' house. Henrietta had told me it was original to the house; and remembering Henrietta made me feel bad, so I focused on the memory of the sconce instead. I had thought at the time that something like it might look good above the fireplace.

The fireplace was stone, pale gray, with a big slab of the same material making up the mantel. Unlike in my aunt Inga's house—or Kate's house, or Cora's house—there was no mirror above the mantel. The Victorians had fireplaces built of polished wood, often with tile surrounds and hearths, but during the Craftsman era, the fireplaces became bigger and more rustic, and they stopped with the mantel. There was nothing above but unbroken plaster wall, about five feet wide and almost as tall. On either side of the fireplace was an inglenook with a little casement window.

Two sconces would look wonderful on the wall above the fireplace. That would mean drilling into the brick of the chimney, though: both difficult and not too smart. Electrical wires and fires aren't a good combination.

I made my way over to the bathroom and stopped in the doorway. "Is it possible to use solar-powered lights indoors?"

Derek glanced over his shoulder at me. He was sitting on the edge of the tub with his feet inside. "Sure. As long as they soak up enough sunlight to work."

"How would you feel about mounting two solar lights above the fireplace? We can't very well drill into the chimney and string wires."

"No," Derek said, "that wouldn't be a good idea at all."

"That's why I thought solar lights might work. I've seen some that look like little lanterns. Very Arts and Crafts."

Derek wrinkled his nose, and I added, "Or not. Maybe

lanterns wouldn't look good inside. I could take the mounts and make my own shades. Maybe out of Mason jars."

"Mason jars?"

"Canning jars. The kind you put jam in. You know what they look like."

Derek nodded. "I just can't imagine them as lampshades."

"I saw it in a DIY magazine once. It's just a matter of cutting and filing and painting and hanging. Now that I've learned how to cut glass, I'm sure I can manage."

"Sure," Derek said. "What do you need?"

"Mason jars. Glass cutter. File. Paint. And some sort of light to attach the jars to once they're done. And a way to mount them."

"We cleared a bunch of Mason jars out of the basement, I think," Derek said. "We have files in the toolbox. You should be able to get a glass cutter and paint at the hardware store. Maybe solar lights, too. We can stop by on our way home."

"I can go now."

Derek arched his brows. "Looking for an excuse to go see Ruth Green?"

I shook my head. I wasn't actually. It was too soon after the funeral. I had figured on going over there around dinnertime. "I'll just go to the hardware store and back."

"Fine," Derek said. "Drive carefully."

I promised I would, and headed out into the afternoon sunlight. The hardware store on Main Street was a half-dozen blocks away, and in easy walking distance, but I took the truck anyway, to save time. If I stayed gone too long, he'd accuse me of sneaking off to interrogate Ruth, and I didn't need that.

It was a matter of four minutes to drive to Main Street and park in the lot behind the store, and another five before I was back out again, with my glass cutter, my can of frosted finish, and two wall-mount solar-powered lanterns with boring shades. Oh, and a bottle of cutting oil I was told I needed for the filing. I was on my way back to the truck with my bags when I heard my name and stopped.

And immediately wished I hadn't. But by then I had no

choice but to wait while Melissa James crossed the street, on knee-high suede boots just a few shades darker than her trademark off-white, and with a sapphire blue coat flapping around her calves.

Derek's ex-wife is gorgeous. Taller than me, with moon-light blond hair in a sleek cap around her face—while mine is the color of Mello Yello and frizzy—and with eyes so blue they're almost violet (while mine are a washed-out chlorinated aqua).

"Melissa."

I made no attempt to hide my lack of enthusiasm, and I'm sure she noticed, although she didn't let on. "Avery. Good to see you."

Sure. "You, too," I said.

"How's Derek?"

I chewed on my tongue for a moment while I debated the urge to say, "Married." But at the last minute, kindness got the better of me. I'd gotten a glimpse of what I wanted to believe was the real Melissa at my wedding two months ago, and the real Melissa had looked at my husband like she had just lost him all over again. Which she had, of course. While he'd been dating me, at least there'd been the chance that we'd get sick of each other and break up. Now that possibility was off the table. Forever, I hoped. So I bit back the word and resigned myself to being nice instead. "Fine. Working."

She brightened. "Are the two of you renovating something new?"

Did I happen to mention that Melissa is a real estate agent? I had actively resisted using her to sell our renovations during the first year I lived in Waterfield, but when our usual Realtor, Irina Rozhdestvensky, got married and moved to Florida, Melissa had talked Derek into letting her list the center-chimney Colonial on Rowanberry Island. We'd been stuck with her ever since.

"The Green sisters' house on North Street," I said.

"The big Craftsman bungalow?" She looked delighted.

"I'm sure you won't want to list it," I said, "now that you're living in Portland."

She looked down at me. "Portland's only forty-five minutes away, Avery."

Right. "So what are you doing in Waterfield? Slumming?"

She smiled. "Hardly. Just settling some business with Waterfield Realty. I was on my way there when I saw you."

"Don't let me keep you."

"I have a little time."

Of course she did. I was just about to say that I didn't when she added, "How did the Christmas Home Tour go?"

"Very well," I said, "although we missed you." Not personally, of course, but I couldn't resist a little jab at how she'd left us high and dry with too little time to prepare.

But either she didn't notice or she chose to ignore me, because she just smiled. "I knew Kate could handle it."

"She did. Very well. The only damper on the day was Henrietta Parker."

Melissa's perfect blond brows drew together. "What happened to Henrietta Parker?"

"Didn't you hear? The stress was too much for her. She had a heart attack and died. We buried her this morning, along with her cousin Mamie, who died last week."

"Oh, dear," Melissa said.

"Did you know Henrietta?"

She shook her head. "Not well, no. But I know her nephew."

"Darren."

She nodded. I wanted to ask whether they'd dated—he was the type she liked, or the type she seemed to have preferred after things didn't work out with Derek. Tall, dark, handsome, and rich, not to mention arrogant. Like Tony Micelli and my cousin Ray Stenham.

But then I didn't have to, because she volunteered the information. "We went out a couple of times after Ray . . . you know."

I did know. "Didn't you like him? Darren?"

"It wasn't that I didn't like him," Melissa said. "What's not to like? He's handsome, successful, well off . . ."

I didn't hold it against her that those were her criteria. From what Derek had told me, she came from a very different background than the one she aspired to. And rather than let her know that I knew, I just said, "So what happened?"

She hesitated, and it struck me that we were having an almost normal conversation for the first time ever. Two girlfriends gossiping about a guy. I wasn't quite sure how I felt about that.

"Nothing happened," Melissa said. "We just didn't click."

"So you clicked with Tony instead?"

She shrugged. Elegantly, the way she did everything. "Maybe I should stop by and offer my condolences."

It couldn't hurt. Especially now that Tony was gone. "Sure. Why not?"

"I should probably stop by the Green sisters' house, too. And see . . ."

I waited for her to say "Derek," but she didn't. "It," she said instead.

"Of course." Not like I could really refuse, was it? And besides, he was my husband now, and not hers. If she wanted to torture herself with what she'd lost, that was her business. She wasn't getting him back.

"Why don't you let Derek know to expect me in an hour."

I told her I would, and watched her undulate up the sidewalk toward Waterfield Realty before ducking into the parking lot myself.

"Couldn't you have headed her off?" Derek asked when I told him what had happened, which went a long way toward making me feel better about the impending visit.

"Not really, no. She just informed me she'd be stopping by to see the place. I guess she thinks we'll be giving it to her to list when it's finished."

"Who else do you want to give it to?"

"I don't know," I said since I didn't really have another Realtor in mind. "I just thought we were rid of Melissa when she moved."

"Portland's only forty-five minutes away."

"That's what Melissa said, too. I just thought I wouldn't have to deal with her anymore."

"She did sell the house on Rowanberry Island eventually."

No thanks to her own efforts. "That was luck," I said. "If you and I hadn't decided to get married, and Philippe hadn't decided to crash the wedding with Laura Lee, he wouldn't have come up with the idea of buying a house in Maine."

"She still got rid of it."

Whatever. "She said she and Darren dated."

I don't know what I had expected, but Derek didn't react beyond the lifting of an eyebrow. "Yeah?"

"After Ray dropped out of the picture and before she took up with Tony. She said they didn't click."

"I'm not surprised."

I lifted my own brows. "Why is that?" I would have thought they'd be perfect for each other. Darren was tall, dark, and wealthy, and Melissa was gorgeous.

"I can tell what you're thinking," Derek told me, "and you're wrong."

"About what?"

"She isn't that bad. I know I told you she wanted to marry a doctor, and when I stopped being a doctor, she left me. But that wasn't the only reason we got married."

"I'm sure it wasn't." And if he didn't mind, I'd just as soon not hear any of the details.

"We did get along well, too. At first. She wouldn't date Darren—or anyone—just because of money. She must have liked Ray. And Tony."

"I'm sure she did." As Marilyn Monroe said in *Gentlemen Prefer Blondes*, it's just as easy to fall in love with a rich man as a poor one. "Anyway, she might not get around to stopping by. She said she'd go see him and offer her condolences. If we're lucky, maybe she'll stay there."

"That'd be fine, too," Derek said. "In the meantime, let's get back to work. We still have a little time before we have to knock off for the day. I'd like to finish this wall, at least."

Sure. I left him to his tiling and dropped my supplies off in the kitchen before heading out to the Dumpster to dig for Mason jars.

Of course, Melissa showed up while I was crawling over and around the debris, trying to find two Mason jars that hadn't shattered on impact. I guess her meeting at Waterfield Realty hadn't taken as long as she'd thought. Or maybe she'd decided that seeing Derek trumped her need to see her former boss. It certainly must have trumped her need to see Kate and/or Darren.

At any rate, I heard the purr as an expensive car pulled up to the curb, and when I peeked over the edge of the Dumpster, I recognized Melissa's Mercedes, so I quickly ducked back down. Then came the sound of the door opening and closing, and the clicking of her heels on the snow and ice. She was muttering in annoyance as she moved past, whether because the snow was ruining her suede boots or because she was afraid the outside of the Dumpster would soil her cashmere coat.

I stayed where I was until she'd let herself into the house and I'd heard the door close behind her, and then I made my own way out of the Dumpster and up onto the porch.

I looked like hell, of course, with wet spots on my knees and drywall dust on my hands and coat. I'm sure my hair was a snarled mess, and my face was probably dirty. And because I was holding two Mason jars, I couldn't even do anything to remedy the situation. But I squared my shoulders and reminded myself that Derek was my husband now, not Melissa's, and he had married me after six years of singlehood, because I was the first woman he'd met who made him want to risk marriage again . . . so I had nothing to worry about.

I marched into the house with my dirt and my Mason jars, to find Melissa leaning on the bathroom doorjamb ogling my husband.

In fairness, all I saw was her back, so I can't say with certainty that she was ogling, but part of me wanted to think so. He's just so ogleable, especially when he's on his knees bending over the tub. So I slammed the front door a little extra hard and made Melissa jump. Derek straightened up and grinned, probably because he knew what I was thinking. "Hiya, Tink. Did you find what you were looking for?"

I brandished my jars and he nodded.

Melissa wrinkled her perfect nose, possibly at the state of my clothes and hair. "Canning?"

"Crafting," I said. "Sconces for the living room."

"Out of canning jars?"

I shrugged.

"Everything Avery makes ends up looking great," Derek said, which was nice of him, even if I might have taken issue with the "ends up," as if my projects didn't start out that way. Then again, maybe they don't. Some of my ideas have taken some getting used to, as far as Derek is concerned. He's always supportive of what I want to try, but not always confident that the result will match my expectations. So far I've managed to make him pleasantly surprised.

Melissa smiled politely and turned her attention back to Derek. "The place looks good."

I have no idea how she could tell, when we hadn't really started on any of the purely cosmetic fixes yet, but maybe she was just flattering him.

"Thanks." He went back to tiling, the muscles in his arms moving smoothly under the sleeves of the T-shirt.

"So did you see Darren?" I asked Melissa, as much to take her attention off Derek as because I wanted to know.

She shook her head. "I called. He said he was still with his family. We're going to catch dinner together later."

"I thought you didn't click," Derek said without looking up. I could hear the amusement in his voice, though, and I bet Melissa could, too. I'm sure she recognized it, after five years of marriage, even if that had been almost seven years ago.

She rolled those gorgeous Elizabeth Taylor eyes. "It's just dinner."

"No such thing as 'just dinner,'" Derek informed her.

She shrugged. Elegantly, of course.

"You settling in OK in Portland?"

We spent a few minutes talking about Melissa's new life in Portland—which sounded like it was going well, unless she was making things sound better than they were, and I wouldn't put it past her—and then she started making noises about leaving again. "I should stop by Kate's, too, before dinner, to see how the home tour went."

I could just imagine Kate's reaction to that, especially after getting the home tour dumped in her lap at the last minute. She'd liked Melissa about as well as I did before that—which is to say not at all—and I couldn't imagine she liked her any better now.

"Let me walk you out," I said, although she hadn't actually made a move toward the door. She smiled, or more accurately smirked, but pushed off from the doorjamb.

"See you later, Derek."

"Sure," Derek said without looking up.

She stopped just outside the front door. "How are you enjoying married life, Avery?"

"Very well," I said.

"Does Derek still snore like a buzz saw?" The question was accompanied by a fond smile, and the reminder that she'd shared his bed for five years or more, while I'd been married to him for only a couple of months.

"Not that I've noticed."

The look she gave me implied that she thought I was lying. I wasn't. If Derek had a snoring problem, it hadn't bothered me yet.

"Have a good time with Darren," I said and closed the door.

I stood and watched her mince back past the Dumpster to her car, and then I watched her get in before I left the window and headed back to the bathroom. "It smells like sulfur in here."

"It isn't me," Derek said.

I rolled my eyes. "I know that. Do you snore?"

He turned his head to look at me. "Wouldn't you know?"

I should. "You snuffle once in a while, but I wouldn't say you snore like a buzz saw."

"Thank you," Derek said, "I would hope not."

After a moment he added, "Did someone else say I snored like a buzz saw?"

I shrugged.

"That witch."

"She's just trying to cause trouble," I said. "Reminding me that she shared your bed for a lot of years before I did."

"Yes," Derek answered, "but I was married to Melissa

for only five years before I'd had enough. I plan to be married to you for at least fifty."

Awww. "You'll be eighty-five in fifty years."

"So? My grandfather's past that, and he's still going strong. We can play golf and ride dune buggies together in Florida when we're in our eighties."

I smiled. "I'll take it."

"It's a date." He winked and went back to the tile laying. I stood for a moment and watched his fingers deftly position and space the tiles.

"I'd really like to go visit Ruth."

He sighed. "Fine. Take the truck."

"I wasn't going to leave you here. I meant afterwards. After we're done."

"It'll be too late," Derek said. "I have another hour of work left, at least. Just take the truck and go out there. If you're not back by the time I'm done, I'll either walk home or go to Dad's. I'm sure Cora's cooking something edible."

No doubt. Derek's stepmother is a much better cook than I can ever hope to be.

"Maybe I should come with you."

He grinned. "I'll tell her to save you a plate. It'll be motivation for you to hurry back."

It would, at that. "Are you sure you don't want me to wait so you can come along?"

"I'm sure," Derek said. "You're not going to give up until you get what you want, and I'd rather just have you go than stand here looking over my shoulder and pecking at me."

"I'm not pecking!"

He looked at me. "Yes, you are. You want what you want, and you won't stop until you get it."

I pouted, and he smiled. "Just go, Avery. It's fine. I know you want to make sure she's all right. And I know you're curious. I am, too. But I want to stay here and finish what I'm doing. So just take the truck and get out of here. I'll see you at Dad's and Cora's later."

"I'll hurry," I said.

"Don't worry about it. Like I said, this'll take at least

another hour. Just enjoy yourself." He turned back to the wall. I grabbed my coat from the dining room window seat and headed out.

. . .

The truck was parked at the curb where I'd left it, and still warm from when I'd taken it out earlier. I slid into the seat and cranked the engine over, and away I went. It took only ten minutes to get to the nursing home where Ruth lived, and I parked in the lot and headed inside.

Like last time I'd been there, Derek's friend Wanda was manning the desk, and she dimpled when she saw me. "Good evening, Mrs. Ellis."

"Call me Avery," I said, even though I must admit it gave me a little thrill every time someone called me Mrs. Ellis. But I didn't know Wanda's last name, and if she called me Avery, I could get away with calling her Wanda.

"Are you here for Miss Green again?"

I nodded. "I'm just checking to see how she is. It's been a tough few days."

Wanda nodded, dimples disappearing. "Horrible about Miss Mamie."

Bad enough about Mamie, on top of the baby skeleton, but now there was Henrietta, too. Other than Henry, who was ten years younger, there was no one of Ruth's generation left in the family.

"Is she all right?" I asked.

Wanda moved her hand up and down in a rocking motion, like a ship on the sea.

"Is it OK for me to go back there?"

"Of course," Wanda said. "She's had time to rest up from the funeral this morning. Her cousin sat with her for a while, but he left a couple of hours ago. She might like some company."

Or she might not, especially from someone she didn't really know, and who had—to add insult to injury—discovered the remains of not only her baby brother, but her deceased sister, as well.

But nothing ventured, nothing gained, so I set off down the hallway in the direction we'd gone last time.

The doors along the way were all propped open, and I could see beds and some other furniture through the gaps. Not a lot of privacy in a nursing home, although I guess maybe it made it easier for the staff not to have to push the doors open every time they needed to get inside a room.

When I got to Ruth's door, I could see that she was sitting in the same chair she'd sat in last time, still in her black funeral dress and with a book on her lap. I stopped to take a breath before knocking on the half-open door.

Nothing happened, and for a moment—or two or three—I worried that something was wrong. But when I pushed on the door and stuck my head inside, I could see she was alive and well and looking at me.

"I didn't say 'Come in,'" she informed me.

"Sorry." I glanced over my shoulder at the hallway. "Do you want me to leave again?"

"What do you want?"

I took another step into the room. "I just wanted to see how you were. And give you my condolences. I didn't get a chance to talk to you in the church, and you weren't at the reception."

She nodded. "We went to the gravesite."

"I figured." I moved another few steps closer. "I thought it was a nice service. Barry—Reverend Norton—did a good job."

She hadn't kicked me out yet, and by now I was close enough to see that she hadn't been reading. The book on her lap, closed with her index finger between two pages, wasn't a book at all really. It was a photo album: big and brown and—in case there was any doubt—embossed with the word PHOTOS in gold print across the front.

"Are you looking at family pictures?"

She glanced down, as if she'd forgotten. There was a pause and then she sighed. More in resignation than annoyance, I think. "Yes."

"May I sit with you?"

This might be just the opening I was looking for. A perfect opportunity to talk about the past.

She hesitated, but then she pulled her finger out of the book and opened it at the beginning instead. I took it for an invitation and pulled up a chair, or rather, the ottoman, and made myself comfortable next to her.

"This is the house the way it looked when we were small."

It looked much the way it did now. The trees and flowers were different, and of course the picture was black-and-white, but it was clearly the same house.

"My father bought it when he and my mother got married," Ruth said. "In 1938."

She turned the page to a wedding photo. Mr. Green had been tall, with slicked-back hair and a flower in his lapel, while his bride was small and dark, her face half-hidden beneath the brim of a hat. She was clutching a bouquet of flowers.

I leaned a little closer, squinting.

"It was an afternoon wedding," Ruth said.

I nodded. That much was obvious. He was wearing a suit, and so was she. Tweed, it looked like. Midcalf-length skirt with darts, a belted jacket, and a blouse with droopy lapels. Plus the little hat coquettishly tilted over one eye. She was smiling, but I couldn't get a good look at her face. Something about her was familiar, but I couldn't place it. Maybe she just looked like her children, or they like her.

"Back then, most people didn't have cameras," Ruth told me. "All I have are pictures of special occasions. Here I am, at a year old."

There she was, a chubby baby in an embroidered dress, sitting on a pillow and brandishing a toy lamb to the camera, smiling with a few tiny teeth.

"You were beautiful."

She smiled. "Thank you. And here's my sister." She turned the page, and I saw an almost identical picture of Mamie, in what looked like the same dress, or at least one very like it. She held a rattle instead of a lamb, but the overall effect was the same. Even then, she had a softer look on her face, less aware.

I glanced at Ruth, wondering if it would be rude to ask whether Mamie had always been a bit simple . . . and then decided that yes, it would be.

"When was this?"

Ruth's eyes were a bit vacant, too, as she turned her focus inward. "I was born in 1939 and Mamie in 1941. This would be '42, I guess."

"During the war."

She nodded.

"Did your father serve?"

She shook her head. "He was too old by then. And married with children. He stayed here in Waterfield."

"Was he a local man?"

"He was from Boothbay Harbor," Ruth said. Boothbay Harbor was a little town slightly less than an hour up the coast. "But my mother's family was from Waterfield, so they settled here."

She turned the page. "Here we all are in the winter."

There they were, outside the house on North Street, all posed for another formal photo, surrounded by snowdrifts. The girls were maybe three and five, or four and six, and bundled to the eyebrows. So was Mrs. Green, so I didn't get a good look at her this time, either. The snow was almost as tall as Mamie.

"Here's my brother," Ruth said and pointed to a chubby baby on the next page. This one wasn't wearing the embroidered dress, not surprisingly, but was dressed in a little shirt and a pair of shorts, with chubby legs in ankle boots sticking out below. He was waving a building block at the camera and grinning toothlessly.

He was younger than the girls had been when they were photographed, only four or five months old, and still prone. The picture wasn't as posed.

"Cameras were more common by the late forties," Ruth said when I mentioned it. "Before, Mother and Father had to take us to the photographer to have our pictures taken.

But by this time, my father had bought his own camera. They took more photographs after this."

She turned the page, to a family grouping much like the one I'd seen in the Silvas' house the other day. Mother, father, and children, formally posed. Except here there were two girls and a baby boy, perched on his mother's lap, instead of just one of each. And suddenly I realized why Mrs. Green had struck me as being familiar.

"They're twins!"

Ruth looked at me as if I'd lost my mind. "No. I told you I was born in 1939, and my sister in '41."

I shook my head. "Not you and your sister. Your mother and hers."

"Oh." She looked back down at the picture. "Yes. My mother had a twin. Henrietta's mother. My aunt Sonya."

"I knew they were sisters. I just didn't realize they were twins."

Ruth nodded. "My mother was older by a few minutes."

"But neither of them had twins of their own?" Twins ran in families, from what I understood.

A shadow crossed Ruth's face. "Henrietta had twin brothers. But they didn't survive."

"That's sad."

She nodded. "One of them didn't thrive and lived only a few days. The other died a few months later. Crib death."

"That's . . ." Really sad. Horribly sad, in fact. I knew the child mortality rates were higher back then, but losing both of a set of twins must have been more than most people could handle.

We sat in silence for a few minutes while Ruth turned pages in the album. There were no more pictures of Baby Arthur, of course. And over time, the pictures turned from black-and-white to color. Clothes changed, hairstyles changed. Ruth and Mamie grew up, Mr. and Mrs. Green grew older. Eventually they disappeared altogether, but not until they were into what looked like their seventies or eighties.

"Were your parents happy together?" I asked.

She shot me a glance, and I admit maybe it was an intrusive sort of question to ask a virtual stranger. But the pictures made it very obvious that they'd stayed together for a very long time after Baby Arthur died—or disappeared—and they looked like they'd enjoyed each other's company, too. The stiff poses of the 1940s and '50s gave way to more relaxed snapshots in the late '60s and '70s. There were pictures of Mrs. Green and her husband walking on the beach, sitting in the garden, and driving a convertible with the top down.

"They look happy."

She nodded. Perhaps she'd decided I was just a harmless kook. "They had their problems, like most people. But they had a good life."

I took a breath before metaphorically plunging in. "Losing Arthur must have been hard on them."

Ruth stiffened perceptibly. "Of course."

"It's good that they were able to stick together through it. Something like that could easily tear a family apart."

"My mother married for love," Ruth said. "Unlike her sister."

"Sonya didn't marry Henry Senior because she loved him?"

Ruth glanced at me. "She loved his money more. Or so my mother always told me."

That didn't sound like something a twin ought to say about her sister, but what did I know? Not only did I not have a twin, I was an only child. "Were they close? Your mother and her sister?"

"They used to be," Ruth said. "Before."

"Before what?"

She hesitated, and I held my breath, afraid to jinx the flow of information.

"Henrietta, Mamie, and I were best friends when we were small," Ruth said eventually. "But after the babies were born . . ." She trailed off.

"The babies?" The twins who died, or Arthur and Henry?

When she didn't speak, I added, "Did something happen to change things?"

"Not at first. But when Arthur . . ."

"Disappeared," I said when she didn't finish the sentence.

She shot me a look, one I couldn't interpret. "Henrietta stopped coming by after that. And Aunt Sonya. We didn't see them as much."

"It must have been hard for them, too. They probably didn't know what to say. Or do." I knew I wouldn't. It was hard enough to talk about it now, sixty-plus years later.

"Maybe." Ruth turned the page, to a picture of Mamie in her forties. She had braids and was wearing a pinafore, holding a doll.

"Your sister kept stealing the Baby Jesus from the nativity outside the church," I said.

It was as if some of the air went out of Ruth, and her stiff spine slumped a bit. "I know."

"She probably thought it was her brother, didn't she? She wanted him back."

Ruth nodded.

"And you'd return him to the manger a day or two later?"

"When I found him." She glanced at me out of the corner of her eye. "She didn't mean any harm. She was just . . . confused."

Of course. "I don't think anyone minds," I said. "Chances are nobody will say a word about it. The baby is back in the manger now."

She nodded. "I saw it this morning."

"Of course. Your sister must have missed him very much."

"Mamie loved Arthur," Ruth said. "She was seven when he was born, and he was like a doll. But we weren't allowed to play with him. Only when Mother put him down on the floor. And we had to be very careful."

"Babies are fragile." My heart was beating hard in my

chest, and I was worried that if I said the wrong thing, she'd stop talking. So I said as little as possible.

But she stopped talking anyway, and we sat in silence. Time stretched. Eventually I figured I had nothing to lose, so I just asked straight out.

"Did Mamie have anything to do with what happened to Arthur?"

—19—

For a few seconds, I wasn't sure she'd heard me.

Oh, I knew I'd spoken loud enough. But she didn't react at all. Just sat there, staring at her hands, folded on top of the album. They were old hands, with thin skin and age spots, and with visible veins. They were shaking.

"I don't know," she said eventually.

"Can you tell me what happened?"

She didn't answer, and I added, "I found him. I'd like to know how he ended up in the attic. And how nobody knew he was there for so long."

Ruth drew a breath. It shuddered, and was painful to hear. "I knew."

I gentled my voice until it was just above a whisper. "Did you put him there?"

She nodded.

"Can you tell me about it?"

When she hesitated, I added, "Wayne—the chief of police—has told me he's closing the case. Even if someone did something to the baby, I don't think he'd file charges at this point."

She turned to look at me. "I didn't do anything to the baby."

OK, then. "So what happened?"

She shrugged thin shoulders inside the old-fashioned black dress. "We were playing. In the playhouse at the back of the yard. Mamie, Henrietta, and I."

"And Arthur was sleeping on the porch?" That's what the newspaper article had said.

She nodded. "My father was at work, and my mother went to the beauty parlor and left the baby with us for an hour. We were playing in the front yard . . ."

"Yes?"

"And Henrietta came and asked if we wanted to play tea party."

"So you went to the playhouse? Why didn't you bring the baby with you?"

"Mother said not to move the carriage unless he woke up," Ruth said. "We wanted him to stay asleep, so we left him on the porch." She glanced at me. "Things were different then. It was a small town, and everyone looked out for everyone else. He slept on the porch all the time with nobody watching him."

Sure. "So what went wrong this time?"

"I don't know!" Her voice was loud, louder than it had been so far—louder, I think, than either of us expected. Ruth looked surprised for a second before she continued. "I don't know what happened. Henrietta stayed for a while, and then Aunt Sonya called to her and she ran. I told Mamie to go see if Arthur was awake while I cleaned up the toys."

"And?"

"She came back and said he was still sleeping. So I told her to finish cleaning up so I could look, because he'd been sleeping for a long time by then. And when I got there, he was cold."

"You couldn't wake him?"

"He was cold," Ruth said again. "No, I couldn't wake him. And I thought . . ."

She trailed off, spots of color in her cheeks.

"You thought Mamie had done something to him? By accident? Or on purpose?"

She lifted her hands helplessly and let them drop back into her lap. "I don't know what I thought. I'm not sure I thought anything. I just know I panicked. Mother would be home soon, and she might think we hadn't taken care of the baby. That we shouldn't have gone and played with Henrietta. And I was afraid."

"Afraid?"

She looked at me, and I could see the echo of that frightened little girl superimposed on her old, wrinkled features, and in those faded blue eyes. "I was afraid they'd send Mamie away."

I leaned back a little, nonthreatening. "Had they talked about sending Mamie away?"

"Aunt Sonya and Uncle Henry were always saying that she should be somewhere where people knew how to take care of her. Where she couldn't hurt anyone. But she didn't hurt anyone! Aunt Sonya wouldn't let us come over to their house and play, though. And she wouldn't let Henrietta take Henry for a walk when we took Arthur, because she was afraid Mamie would do something to him."

"Mamie didn't hurt the babies, did she?"

Ruth shook her head. "Mamie loved the babies. Or at least she loved Arthur. She would never deliberately hurt him."

"So what did you do? When you realized that Arthur wasn't going to wake up and you didn't want them to take Mamie away?"

"I hid him," Ruth said.

"In the attic?"

She nodded. "I took him out of the carriage and went up to the second floor, and then I climbed up to the attic, and I put him in the crate and left him there. And when Mother came home, I told her that someone had stolen the baby."

"And she believed you."

"I told her that we'd gone to the playhouse, and that when we came back, the carriage was empty."

And she had called the police and everyone in town started looking for him. "Didn't anyone check the house?"

"They checked," Ruth said, "but not the attic. And they all thought someone else had taken him."

"But Mamie knew what you did, didn't she?"

Apparently not, because Ruth shook her head. "Mamie wasn't . . ." She hesitated. "Even back then, Mamie wasn't smart. She didn't always live in real life. It got worse after Arthur . . . disappeared, and then it got very bad when she got older, but I told her she didn't remember not seeing him in the carriage and she believed me. Everyone else did, too."

So she'd hidden her baby brother in the attic and sacrificed—in a sense—her sister's reputation, but in an effort to keep her sister with her, and to keep Mamie from being sent away to an institution. And she'd been a child herself, not really equipped to make these kinds of big decisions.

"How old were you?"

"Ten," Ruth said, her lips clamped together. "Mamie was eight, I was ten. Our mother lost a couple of babies between Mamie and Arthur, just like Aunt Sonya."

I must have been thinking especially loudly because she added, "Miscarriages. We didn't talk about it back then, but I found out later. There were two between Mamie and Arthur. Aunt Sonya had one, as well, plus the twins."

The twins who died. Sonya and Lila hadn't been very lucky in their pregnancies, for certain. Sonya had had Henrietta, the twins who died, a miscarriage, and then finally Henry. And Lila had had Ruth, Mamie—who, at least by those days' standard, was flawed—a couple of miscarriages, and then Arthur. Who disappeared.

"Thank you for telling me," I said, since there wasn't much else I could say really.

Ruth looked drained, her skin pale and thin as paper in the lamplight. "What will you do?"

I hadn't really thought about it, but . . . "I guess I'll have to tell Wayne, just so he knows what happened. But nobody committed a crime, so I don't see him doing anything about it."

"I hid my baby brother's body in the attic and told everyone he'd been kidnapped," Ruth said.

"You were ten. And afraid. And everyone else who was involved is dead now anyway."

Her face twisted and I remembered, just a second too late, why a little sensitivity on my part might have been nice. She'd buried her sister and her cousin today, along with her brother.

"I'm sorry," I added. "I just meant . . . your parents are gone. There's no one left who would remember what happened."

She nodded.

"Wayne will probably want to talk to you. Just to verify the facts. But I don't think you have to worry."

"It doesn't matter anyway," Ruth said. "Even if I do go to prison. As you said, there's no one left to care."

I hadn't meant it that way. "You're not going to prison." Wayne wouldn't put a seventy-five-year-old woman in jail for something that happened sixty-five years ago. Especially when her only crime had been fear for her sister's well-being. "What do you think happened to your brother? SIDS?"

"Crib death," Ruth said, "Nobody did anything to him. Nobody would."

I nodded. She looked exhausted, so I got to my feet. "I should go."

She glanced up. "Will you come back?"

"I can," I said. "If Wayne wants to talk to you, would you like me to be here? Or get someone else to come? Maybe Darren?"

She shook her head. "He's too much like old Henry. Nothing matters to him except money and family."

I blinked. "You *are* family."

"I'm not a Silva," Ruth said. "Just a Green. And just a woman."

"Is he that prejudiced?"

"His grandfather was. Henrietta wasn't good enough for him, because she couldn't carry on the name. Aunt Sonya was so upset when the twins died, because Henry didn't have an heir . . ."

She kept talking, but I missed the details, because a thought skittered through my brain and out the other side, and I was preoccupied with trying to chase it down for a closer look.

When she wound down, I said, "That's fine. I won't involve Darren. I'll just talk to Wayne, and if he wants to come talk to you tomorrow, I'll make sure I'm here, too."

Ruth nodded. "Thank you." She reached out a hand and I took it. It was cold and frail, a bit like holding a bag of bones. "I wasn't very nice to you the first time you were here. I didn't want you in the house. And when you found my brother, I was angry."

I gave her a gentle squeeze. "I understand. It must have been hard to leave the house where you've lived your whole life."

Her faded blue eyes filled with tears. "I don't know what I'll do now."

"Stay here?"

She looked around, and it was obvious from the look on her face that the idea didn't appeal. It wouldn't have appealed to me, either. She had always taken care of herself—and her sister—and once her hip was completely healed and she was back on her feet, she'd probably be capable of taking care of herself again. Especially if she didn't have Mamie to worry over.

But of course I didn't say so. "I'm sure it'll work out," I said instead.

She nodded and let go. "Thank you for coming."

"Thank you for talking to me," I said. "I'll probably be back tomorrow."

I headed for the door. By the time I was in the hallway and looked back over my shoulder, she had opened the photo album and was bent over the pictures again.

. . .

I called Wayne from the car and told him everything.

There was a pause. A long one. I must have driven a half mile, at least, before his voice came back on the line. "You're kidding."

I shook my head, even though he couldn't see it. "I'm not. I swear."

"Ruth hid the baby in the attic?"

"Because she was afraid Mamie would get blamed and that they'd send her to an institution. Yes."

"And it's been up there ever since."

"Until the other day. Yes."

"While Mamie and Ruth lived in the house and went about their business downstairs. While the parents were alive."

"That's what she said," I said. "The police checked the house at the time, but not very thoroughly because everyone thought the baby had been kidnapped. And they didn't crawl up into the attic. There was no need, since the baby certainly couldn't have made it there on its own."

There was another pause. "Did she say what happened? How the baby ended up dead?"

"She suggested crib death. SIDS. But I think she may have been afraid that Mamie did something to it. Accidentally. She said that Mamie loved the babies, and that she wouldn't hurt them. But if Mamie tried to play with Arthur and something happened . . ."

"I guess we'll never know for certain," Wayne said. "I'll have to go talk to her myself."

"I told her you probably would. I said I'd ask you if I could be there when you do."

"I'll have to call the Silvas."

Fine. "Try to get Henry. She doesn't like Darren. I don't, either." I slowed the car down to turn onto Cabot.

"I'll try," Wayne said. "Ten A.M. tomorrow?"

I told him that would be fine, and pulled the truck to a stop outside Dr. Ben and Cora's. But instead of getting out, I just cut the engine and continued the conversation. "She won't go to prison, will she? I'm sure it's a crime to hide a dead baby and say he's been kidnapped, but she was only ten years old, and scared that she'd lose her sister, too."

Wayne hesitated. "I don't see myself throwing her in prison, no. If the baby died of SIDS, there was no real crime committed, other than a scared little girl telling a fib to get out of trouble. She probably didn't think it through to even realize what repercussions a lie like that would have."

Probably not. And I was glad Wayne saw it that way, since I wouldn't have to lie awake tonight worrying.

"I'll see you at ten tomorrow."

"Ten," Wayne said and hung up. I stuffed my phone in my pocket, pulled the key from the ignition, and headed up the walk to the Folk Victorian.

. . .

They were playing Scrabble again when I walked in, at the family room table, and Cora waved in the direction of the kitchen. "Plate in the warmer."

I headed for the warmer, a special drawer of the high-end stove, where the brownies had been last time we'd been here, and found a plate of enchiladas waiting for me. After digging a fork out of the silverware drawer and grabbing a paper towel from the roll on the counter, I wandered back into the family room, plate in hand, in time to catch Derek score with the word "formication."

"You spelled it wrong," I informed him around a bit of enchilada.

He glanced at me. "No, I didn't."

"Well, then you got confused. And put two words together. Formica and . . . something else."

" 'Formica' isn't a word," Derek told me. "Not according to Scrabble. 'Formication' is."

"I've never heard of it."

"Dad has."

I glanced at Dr. Ben, who nodded. "It's a form of paresthesia. The feeling that insects are crawling on—or under—your skin. A tactile hallucination."

No kidding? "Being a doctor gives you an unfair advantage in Scrabble, doesn't it?"

Both doctors, the current and the retired, grinned. "Yes. But when it's two of us, it cancels out."

Not so for those of us who weren't doctors. But I wasn't even playing, so what business was it of mine?

"How did it go at the nursing home?" Derek asked, and I repeated what Ruth had told me. By the time I had finished, the Scrabble board was forgotten and my food was colder than I liked.

"You're kidding," Derek said, just like Wayne had earlier.

And just like then, I shook my head. But at least he, unlike Wayne, could actually see me. "No. That's what happened. Or so she said."

"That's crazy." He glanced at his father, who nodded.

"She must have been very frightened," Cora said in her soft voice, "to do something like that."

There was a pause while we all thought about just how scared someone had to be to hide her dead baby brother in the attic and then continue living in the house for the rest of her life. If it hadn't been for the broken hip and having to go to the hospital, she'd probably still be there.

"Wayne said he wasn't going to make anything of it," I said. "He has to talk to her, of course. She asked me if I would be there. At ten o'clock tomorrow." I glanced at Derek, who nodded. "But it's just to get the facts straight. He's not charging her with anything."

"I would hope not," Cora said indignantly. Dr. Ben reached out and put his hand over hers, smiling.

"Don't worry. Wayne will do the right thing."

"He only wants to talk to her," I said again. "Just to get the story straight. He said that as long as nobody committed a crime—nothing worse than we know about—he isn't interested in putting anyone in prison."

There was another pause.

"This is a first," Derek said at last. "Three dead bodies and not a single one of them murdered."

I shrugged. "It was bound to happen sometime."

He grinned. "Will you be able to handle the disappointment, Tink?"

I kept my own voice light. "You'll have to take extra special care of me tonight."

And I wasn't joking. Not entirely. The scene with Ruth had been difficult. Putting myself in her position, in the head of a frightened ten-year-old girl dealing with the loss of her brother and the potential loss of her sister, and doing the best she could in impossible circumstances, had left me feeling shaken. The fact that there'd been no murders wasn't the problem, not when what had actually happened had been so gut-wrenching.

Derek must have seen it on my face, because he got to his feet. "We should go."

"What about the game?" I gestured to the Scrabble board.

"I was winning anyway." He took the plate from me and carried it to the counter before coming back and extending a hand. "C'mon, Tink. Let me take you home."

I nodded and took it. "Don't mind if you do."

—20—

With everything that had been going on, part of me had been afraid I'd get out to the nursing home the next morning and find that Ruth had passed away overnight.

I was happy to see I'd worried for nothing. When I walked in, she was sitting in the same chair as the day before, in a housedress, slippers, and a cardigan, talking to Henry Silva. He was on the ottoman, facing her, and they were deep in conversation. Deep enough that they didn't notice me at first.

I stood in the open doorway, hesitating. I didn't want to interrupt what looked like a serious exchange, but I also didn't want it to look like I was standing there eavesdropping. And if I moved away again, that could be awkward, too.

They were nose to nose, with their heads close together, and it struck me just how similar they looked. Mirror images almost, allowing for the fact that Henry was ten years younger and a man. But the nose was the same, and the jaw. The shape of the skull and the ear. Henry's was bigger naturally—he was bigger overall, while Ruth wasn't more than an inch or two taller than me. But then their mothers had been identical twins, so maybe it wasn't surprising that they should look alike.

They noticed me then, and both turned to look at me. Two identical pairs of blue eyes.

I blinked.

"Hello," Henry said and got to his feet. "I don't think we've been properly introduced. I'm Henry Silva."

He extended a hand. I took it. "Avery Baker . . . Ellis. My husband and I bought Miss Ruth's house."

He nodded and let go. "Darren told me. He and Derek went to school together. He says you're doing a good job of renovating."

"Thank you." I hadn't noticed Darren coming through the house, but maybe he'd stopped by sometime when Derek had been alone. I'd been gone a bit lately, after all, and it made sense that he'd be curious. "It's a beautiful house. We're thrilled to be able to work on it."

I glanced at Ruth, who didn't seem quite as thrilled. And no wonder, now that her only home was this room.

"You're the one who found my cousin," Henry said, and I turned my attention back to him.

"Yes. I did."

Both of them. But since I didn't want to bring up the matter of the bones until I had to, I went on the assumption that he was talking about Mamie.

"I'm sorry," he said.

It was on the tip of my tongue to tell him that he didn't have to apologize, since he hadn't had anything to do with it, but I bit it back. "Thank you."

"And the"—he hesitated—"bones. You found them, too?"

I nodded.

"It's good that we know what happened," Henry said. "Closure is important."

I guess it was. And it was good that he could take that view.

On that note, Wayne appeared behind me, and we got down to business. And closure.

Since Henry was here as Ruth's representative, I guessed

I didn't really have to stay. She didn't need me. But I had promised her I'd be here, and besides, I was curious to hear how Wayne planned to handle the situation. So I did my best to fade into the woodwork while Wayne got down to interrogating Ruth—in the nicest manner possible—and Henry lent moral support.

He started by going over the same things I'd told him yesterday, and got all the same answers I'd gotten. Mr. Green had been at work and Mrs. Green had had an appointment at the beauty parlor. It was the baby's nap time, so she left him in the carriage on the front porch and told Ruth and Mamie to keep an eye on him while she walked down to Main Street. It wasn't the first time it had happened, and if something hadn't gone wrong on this particular day, it probably wouldn't have been the last.

"Everyone did it," Ruth said. "Things were different back then."

Wayne nodded. "What happened after your mother left?"

"Henrietta came," Ruth said. "She asked if we wanted to play."

"In the playhouse?"

Ruth nodded.

"So the three of you went back there?"

"And played," Ruth said. "Until we heard Aunt Sonya call Henrietta."

"Where was Aunt Sonya?"

She'd been on the road. With Baby Henry in his own baby carriage. Henrietta had gone to join her, and they had walked off. Arthur wasn't squalling, so Ruth and Mamie went back to the playhouse to clean up. Some of the toys had been left outside, and they wanted to put all the dolls and bears back inside before they left.

Very responsible, I thought.

Then Mamie went to check on Arthur and said he wasn't awake, and Ruth went to check on Arthur and found him dead.

"Where did the crate come from?" Wayne asked, scratching notes in his little pad.

"Shaw's Supermarket," Ruth said.

"You went to the supermarket for it?"

Of course not. "It was in the playhouse. We used it to keep toys in. But it came from Shaw's originally."

"So you put the baby into it and took it up to the attic."

Ruth nodded. I could see her throat move when she swallowed. She was so thin, her neck was barely bigger around than my forearm.

"That couldn't have been easy, on your own."

It hadn't been, and Ruth clearly had a hard time describing it. But eventually she'd made it up there with both baby and crate.

"And then you left him there?"

"I put the crate in the corner by the fireplace," Ruth said. "It was dark over there, and I thought even if someone climbed up, they might not notice it."

As indeed I almost hadn't. The rough wood of the crate matched the rough planks of the wall very well, and I hadn't noticed the crate until I was almost on top of it.

"Mamie didn't realize what you had done?"

"Mamie got . . . confused easily," Ruth said.

"Did you think she'd done something to the baby?"

"She said she didn't." Wayne didn't answer, and after a second Ruth added, "If she did, it was an accident. She loved Arthur. She'd never hurt him on purpose."

"Of course." Wayne made another note on his pad. "Were you afraid Mamie would get blamed?"

"They didn't know her the way we did," Ruth said with a pleading glance at Henry. "She was different, so they thought she might be dangerous. They thought Mother and Father should send her away."

"To an institution?"

Ruth nodded.

"Did your parents think about doing that?"

"She wasn't any trouble," Ruth said. "She wasn't hard to take care of. She just didn't think as fast as some people."

So no, probably not. The Greens hadn't considered

sending Mamie away. Not even with Sonya Silva telling them they should.

Or if they had, they'd decided against it. But if Arthur had turned up dead instead of missing, and they worried that Mamie might have had something to do with it, who knows what they might have done.

Difficult as it was to admit, even to myself, I thought maybe Ruth had made the right choice. I could certainly sympathize with her and grasp the difficulty of the situation she'd found herself in.

"Then what happened?" Wayne asked.

Ruth took a breath. "I went back to the playhouse and stayed with Mamie until Mother came home. She saw that the carriage was empty and came looking for the baby. I told her he'd been in the carriage when Mamie went to check on him. She called the police and then everyone started searching."

"And you never told anyone that you knew what had happened to him."

"I didn't know what had happened to him," Ruth said, her voice steady. "I just knew what I did. He was dead and I hid him in the attic so they wouldn't take my sister away."

Wayne nodded and closed his notebook. There was a moment's pause.

"So what happens now?" Henry wanted to know. He hadn't said a word through the whole ordeal, had just sat there and listened, looking strong and sober. He was a handsome man, and I could see why Kerri liked him, even with the age difference between them. Always assuming I hadn't lost my mind and it really was him I'd seen in her house the other night, of course.

Wayne hesitated, but only for a second. "Nothing. I write up a report and close out the case. The skeleton has already been processed through the system, released, and buried. There's nothing more to do."

"Thank you."

"Just doing my job," Wayne said, getting to his feet.

"Thank you for being here." His eyes glanced off me for a second, too, including me in the statement. "And thank you for telling me the truth, Miss Green. I'm sure it can't have been easy."

Ruth inclined her head. "Thank you, Chief Rasmussen."

Wayne took his leave, and I waited for him to be gone down the hall before I pushed off from the wall. "I guess I should go, too."

Ruth nodded. "Thank you for being here, Mrs. Ellis."

"Call me Avery. Please." Being Mrs. Ellis'ed by someone more than twice my age was weird. "And I didn't do anything. Just listened."

"Sometimes that's as much as anyone can do," Ruth said.

"Would it be OK if I came and visited you again?" I felt bad for her, being here all by herself. Henry would leave, and Darren probably wouldn't bother coming, and both Mamie and Henrietta were gone. Ruth would be lonely.

"Of course," she said.

I turned to Henry. "It was nice to meet you. I'm sorry for the loss of your sister. I didn't get a chance to talk to you at the funeral yesterday."

He inclined his head, in a gesture eerily similar to Ruth's. "Thank you."

His eyes, when he looked up at me again, were the exact shape and color of hers.

I tilted my head. "Did Henrietta have blue eyes, too?"

Henry looked nonplussed for a second before shaking his head. "She had the Silva eyes. Brown."

That's what I'd thought. "Your mother was the blue-eyed one. The twins."

He nodded, glancing at Ruth, who said, "My mother had blue eyes. And Aunt Sonya. And Mamie."

And Henry and Darren. But not Henrietta.

"Thanks," I said. "I'm glad everything worked out all right."

They both were, too, and on that note I made my escape into the hallway and from there through the lobby and outside. I waved to Wanda in passing, and stopped outside the doors to look for Wayne's cruiser. But he must have been in a hurry to leave, because I didn't see it anywhere.

Oh, well. I could always talk to him later. After I'd spoken to Derek.

.   .   .

He was busy grouting today. Yesterday, before he'd left, he'd hung all the subway tile, and now he was busy grouting it. Once that was done, and dry, he'd cap it off with a thin strip of black tiles at the top, to pick up the black in the ribbon tile, and then grout that. That'd be later today, I figured.

"How did it go?" he asked me when I came up to linger in the doorway.

"Fine." I stuck my hands in the pockets of my jeans and watched as he slathered grout over the tiles with a big trowel, pushing it into the grooves. "About as I expected."

"Learn anything new?"

I shook my head. "Same story as yesterday."

He shot me a glance over his shoulder, a flash of blue eyes. "Did you think it would be different?"

Not really. Although you never knew. "Your eyes are blue."

"You're only now noticing that?"

"Of course not," I said. "It was one of the first things I noticed about you. You have very pretty eyes."

He waggled his eyebrows. "The better to see you with, my dear."

I smiled. "Your dad has blue eyes, too." A little darker, closer to slate than cornflower.

Derek nodded.

"Did your mother, as well?"

"Recessive gene," Derek said. "So yes. Your parents were both blue-eyed, too, weren't they?"

They were. Or had been. My mother was blue-eyed. My father died when I was thirteen. I couldn't remember his eye color anymore. But if my eyes were blue, his would have had to have been as well, at least as far as I could remember from middle school biology.

"Yes and no," Derek told me when I said as much. "They've started rethinking that. Usually, two parents with blue eyes will have a child with blue eyes. But not always. If one of the parents has a latent brown gene hanging on, two blue-eyed parents could have a brown-eyed child. Just as it's not impossible for two brown-eyed parents to have a blue-eyed child. It doesn't happen a lot, but it can."

"So you and I would most likely have blue-eyed children because we both have blue eyes. All of Jill and Peter's kids have dark hair and eyes because Peter's coloring is dominant and Jill's is recessive. But if Pepper ends up with blue eyes, it's not because Jill had an affair with the milkman."

"Pretty much," Derek said. "Sometimes a recessive gene can crop up after generations of being latent. It's just the luck of the draw. And biology."

"Bummer."

He arched his brows. "What's going on?"

"Nothing. I just thought I'd discovered something that it turns out I didn't discover after all."

"What's that?"

I took a breath and marshaled my thoughts into what I hoped was coherence. "Henry Silva was there, at the nursing home, with Wayne. And I realized how much he and Ruth look alike. Same head shape, same nose, same ears. Same blue eyes."

"They're first cousins," Derek said, "so that's not surprising. And their mothers weren't just sisters, but identical twins. I'd say that isn't noteworthy at all."

Probably not. Nonetheless he'd asked, so I figured I'd better carry my train of thought through to the end. "Henrietta had brown eyes. I noticed it when I spoke to her. Henry said she had the Silva eyes."

"So?" Derek said.

"So Mr. and Mrs. Green both had blue eyes. And they had two blue-eyed daughters. And probably a blue-eyed son, although I didn't think to ask Ruth what color Arthur's eyes were. She probably wouldn't have been able to remember."

"Infants' eyes change color anyway," Derek said. "They're sometimes born with blue eyes that turn brown later."

"Really?"

"Yes, really. They say that all infants are born with blue eyes. That's not true. Black and Asian children are usually born with brown eyes. So are a lot of Hispanics and for that matter white babies. But some are born with blue eyes that change to brown or hazel later, too."

"So Henrietta might have been born with blue eyes that changed."

"Sure," Derek said. "Especially since her mother had blue eyes. But Henrietta inherited the dominant gene if her eyes were brown. Why are you so interested in this?"

"I told you. I noticed how similar Henry and Ruth looked."

"And it's likely to be because their mothers were twins. Identical twins even have the same DNA profile."

The tingling spider senses turned into a steady buzz, and the thought that had streaked across my brain last night slunk back in, and stayed long enough for me to get a good look at it.

"What if . . ."

"Yes?" Derek said when I trailed off.

"I'm still bothered by the fact that the baby's DNA didn't match Ruth and Mamie's. She told me—Ruth did— that her parents were happy together. They stayed together after Arthur went missing. Or died, I should say, although they didn't know that, I guess."

Derek nodded.

"I didn't ask her straight-out if she thought her mother might have had an affair, but I didn't catch any whiff of that in anything she said."

"She might not have known," Derek pointed out. "She was just a little girl."

It probably wasn't something Lila would talk to her daughters about. Or that they'd notice, at least if she were being careful. But children can usually tell when their parents' marriage is on the rocks, because of the arguing and such, and Ruth hadn't said anything about it.

"You may be right. But what if Mrs. Green didn't have an affair?"

"She had to have gotten pregnant somehow. She had a baby. And it wasn't her husband's."

"What if it wasn't her baby?"

"How could it not be—" He shook his head. "No."

"What do you mean, no? It makes sense, doesn't it?"

"Logically, maybe. But the rest of it . . ."

"Just listen to me," I said. "Sonya and Lila were identical twins, right? You said yourself they had the same DNA. And they both had blue eyes. Mr. Green's eyes were also blue, so he and Lila had blue-eyed children, but Mr. Silva's were brown, so Henrietta had brown eyes."

Derek nodded. "I'm with you so far. Those are facts."

"Lila had Ruth in 1939, and Mamie in 1941, and then a miscarriage or two before she had Arthur in early '49."

"Did Ruth tell you that?"

I nodded. "She also told me that Sonya had a miscarriage, as well as a pair of twins that died. Two little boys. One died almost immediately—it didn't thrive, Ruth said . . ."

"Failure to thrive," Derek said, nodding. "We've gotten better about that these days, at least in our part of the world, but sixty or seventy years ago, we didn't understand it as well. All it means is that the baby wasn't getting what it needed to grow and develop the way it should."

"Physically? Or mentally?"

"Physically," Derek said, "although failure to thrive physically can lead to abnormal intellectual, social, or emotional development later on. There are two kinds . . ." He trailed off, glancing at me.

"Go ahead." It was interesting, and besides, I just enjoy listening to Derek talk.

"Endogenous, or organic, failure to thrive means there's a physical reason the baby isn't getting enough nutrients to gain weight the way it should. Could be milk allergies or celiac disease or something obvious, like a cleft palate. Meanwhile, exogenous or nonorganic failure to thrive means that the caregiver isn't offering, or isn't able to supply, enough food. A mother might not be producing enough milk for the baby, or might not have the money for enough formula. Some idiots—excuse me—don't feed their babies enough because they don't want them to be overweight."

"That's crazy," I said.

Derek nodded. "We got off the subject there, though. Sonya's baby failed to thrive."

"Ruth said it died almost immediately. And then the other twin died a few months later. Crib death. And then Sonya had a miscarriage, as well. Ruth said she was desperate to give her husband a son, because Henrietta couldn't carry on the Silva name."

"Oh," Derek said.

"Yep. So finally she had Henry, and her sister had Arthur. They both had baby boys, and only a week or two apart."

I could see the light dawning in his eyes now, and knew he was coming around to agreeing with my point of view. Or at least coming around to the realization that maybe I wasn't as crazy as he'd originally thought.

"Henry Senior had his heir, after years of trying, and everything was great. How far do you think Sonya would have been willing to go if something happened to that baby?"

"Far," Derek said. "I don't know, though, Avery . . ."

"Just listen. Ruth said that there were no marks on the baby, and no signs of anything having happened to him, so let's just say the baby we found in the attic died of SIDS. Sudden infant death syndrome. Crib death."

Derek nodded.

"Imagine Sonya finding him and panicking, because suddenly her husband has no heir to carry on the name. She hasn't managed to give him what he wants, her babies keep dying, and there's only Henrietta left, and Henrietta is a girl. Ruth said that Henry Senior didn't care about Henrietta, only about Baby Henry."

"All right," Derek said.

"She isn't getting any younger. Her childbearing years are coming to an end, and there are no guarantees that the next baby will survive, either. Henry Senior might replace her with someone younger and more fertile."

Derek nodded.

"So there she is, with a dead baby. And there's her sister's baby, all rosy-cheeked and healthy. And so much like her own. Henrietta looked a lot like Mamie and Ruth, too, apart from the eye color."

Derek nodded.

"Lila was at the hairdresser's. There was only Ruth and Mamie at home, and the baby was sleeping in his carriage on the front porch. It would take less than a minute to make the switch. Chances were nobody would see her, or if they did, they wouldn't think anything of her being there, because she was the baby's aunt, and she looked just like the baby's mother. If anyone had seen her, they might even have assumed she was her sister."

I paused. Derek didn't seem inclined to interrupt, just kept watching me with a sort of horrified fascination. So I continued. "She sent Henrietta to play with Ruth and Mamie, to draw them back to the playhouse and keep them there—and they were probably happy to go, because Ruth said Sonya didn't like to let Henrietta play with them. She was afraid Mamie would rub off, I guess. Ruth said the Silvas were always telling the Greens that they should have Mamie put away."

Derek nodded.

"So Henrietta took Ruth and Mamie to the backyard, to the playhouse, and they played tea. Meanwhile, Baby Arthur was asleep on the front porch by himself, on the other side of the house. I imagine Sonya just walked up, put the dead baby in Arthur's carriage and Arthur into her own, and called to Henrietta that it was time to go."

"And nobody realized it was the wrong baby?" He sounded skeptical. "What about the clothes? Wouldn't they notice that the baby was wearing different clothes?"

"They were children," I said. "Mamie wasn't quite right in the head, even then, and Ruth was in a panic once she realized that the baby wasn't breathing. I don't imagine she looked at him all that closely. Arthur and Henry probably looked alike to begin with. Most babies do, and their mothers were twins. And nobody else saw him, remember?"

"I remember," Derek said. "But if you're right about this, Avery, Sonya couldn't count on Ruth putting the baby in the attic. That was Ruth's idea, and it turned out to be a big bonus for Sonya. But she had to have planned for the fact that her sister would see the baby. And having him wear the wrong clothes would be a—pardon me—dead giveaway."

He had a point. "Maybe she took the time to change him. It might not have taken long. It was September, and he was under a blanket, so she might only have had to change his pants. Baby undershirts are pretty much all the same, I think. If anyone asked, she could just say she was changing his diaper."

"Maybe." He didn't sound totally convinced, but after a few moments he added, "Then what?"

"Then Sonya took Arthur and Henrietta and left. And Ruth found who she thought was her brother dead, and hid him in the attic, and told everyone he'd been stolen."

"And Sonya managed to look her sister in the eye for the rest of her life?"

I shook my head. "I don't think so. Ruth said that Sonya didn't like to let Henrietta play with them even before that, and afterwards, I'm pretty sure she kept them apart. She couldn't risk anyone realizing that she'd stolen her sister's baby because her own died. And Lila might have recognized her own child, even if the girls didn't."

"Lila might have chosen to stay away, too," Derek said, getting into the swing of things. "She'd just lost her baby, but as far as she knew, her sister still had her own. It wouldn't be surprising if she'd want to avoid Sonya and Baby Henry for a while."

Maybe so. I hadn't thought about that, but now that he

mentioned it, it made sense. "So you think it could have happened that way?"

"It hangs together," Derek said. "How do you plan to prove it, though, Tink? Or don't you want to?"

"You don't know me very well if you think I don't."

"On the contrary," Derek said, "I know you very well. Where do we start?"

"We could exhume Henrietta," I said. "I don't think the ground's frozen again after the funeral. It should be easy to get down there. And I know the medical examiner has the DNA for the baby already on file."

"No digging up graves," Derek answered.

Fine. "I could sneak into the Silvas' house—now, before they start boxing up all of Henrietta's things—and grab a hairbrush or something, with her DNA on it."

"No breaking and entering."

"You're no fun."

"No," Derek said. "You're not thinking, Avery."

"I'm not?" It made perfect sense to me. If we already had the dead baby's DNA, matching it to Henrietta's to see if they had the same parents, would prove conclusively that the baby was Henry, not Arthur.

Derek shook his head. "We don't have to prove that the baby was Henry. All we have to do is prove that the current Henry Silva is Ruth's brother. They're both still alive, and they both have DNA we can get without breaking the law."

Oh.

"I didn't think about that," I said.

"I know," my beloved answered. "You're always looking to take the exciting way out. But this time we don't have to. We can just call Wayne and tell him what you think, and he'll get a sample of Henry's DNA to match to Ruth's, and then we'll know."

"It's more fun to dig something up."

"No," Derek said. "Not really."

He was probably right about that. I wouldn't mind sneaking into the Silvas' house to lift a hairbrush, though. It was a long time since I'd done any kind of sneaking.

But his way was simpler. So I stood by while he called Wayne and went through the conversation we'd just had. Like Derek, Wayne started out a little skeptical, but he was quickly won over. "That DNA match bothered me, too," he admitted. Derek had put him on speakerphone so we could both listen and talk.

"I thought maybe Lila Green had had an affair," I confessed, "and that her husband had found out and killed the baby."

That idea had occurred to Wayne, too, of course. "There just wasn't anything I could do about it. No way to prove that the baby didn't die a natural death, and I certainly didn't want to accuse a dead man of a murder that may or may not have been committed."

Of course not.

"It's good to have it explained. Assuming you're right and the DNA will show that Ruth Green and Henry Silva are brother and sister."

"How soon will you know?" Derek asked.

"We already have Ruth's DNA on file. We got that from the nursing home last week, when we were trying to match the baby's DNA. We have Mamie's, too. What we don't have is Henry's, but I don't imagine he'll refuse to give it to me if I ask. He's a law-abiding citizen."

"So you're just going to ask him for it?"

"Sure," Wayne said. "Why not?"

"You don't think he might refuse to give it to you? If it's

true that he's not Henry Silva, he's also not the heir to the Silva money." Or the Silva lumber business.

There was a pause while Wayne thought it through. "Who's the heir to the Silva money?"

"I suppose John Nickerson," I said. "His mother was Henry Senior's sister. He and Henry are cousins. If Henry isn't actually a descendant of Old Henry, I think John would be the closest living relative that can trace his lineage back to the Silvas."

Derek stared at me, wide-eyed. "You're kidding, right?"

I shook my head. "I spoke to him yesterday. At the funeral. He told me that the old man, his grandfather, cut his mother off when she married beneath her. Apparently Mr. Nickerson wasn't up to snuff as far as the Silvas were concerned. His grandfather would have come around eventually, John thinks, but it was Henry Senior who wouldn't have anything to do with his sister after she married John's father, so it wasn't until Henry Senior died that John and Henry started talking again."

"Wow."

I nodded. "I know. Some families are weird like that."

"I don't think he'll say no," Wayne said, yanking the conversation back on track. "Most people don't say no to the police."

"We'll leave you to it," Derek said. "Let us know how it goes."

He cut the call before Wayne had the chance to say anything else and, more important, before I could offer to help or be present or do anything else to insert myself into the situation. And then he grinned when he saw my pout. "Sorry, Tink. But I need you here."

"To do what?"

"You have sconces to make," Derek said. "Mason jars, remember? Plus, you've been going off so much lately I'm developing a complex. It's like, as soon as we got married, you couldn't wait to get away from me."

"I'm not trying to get away from you. I just get caught up in things."

"Well," Derek said, snagging me around the waist and pulling me closer, "today you can get caught up in me."

I supposed I could probably manage that.

When he let me go, after a suitable interval, he went back to his grouting and I went back to my Mason jars.

It isn't difficult to turn them into pendants. All you have to do is cut off the bottoms with a glass cutter, and then smooth the edges so you don't slice your finger open. I'd already done that in Dab's studio, and I wasn't eager to do it again.

So I cut the bottoms off and used a file from Derek's toolbox along with the oil I'd bought at the hardware store to make the jars safe to touch. The process was a lot less streamlined than how Dab had taught me, but it got the job done, if with a bit more elbow grease.

Attaching the jars to the solar lights was also a snap, since I could practically cut through the aluminum tops with a pair of embroidery scissors, at least after I'd pried the glass seals out. But before I did that, it was time to gussy up the Mason jars to make them look more Craftsman-like. In addition to the frosted yellowish paint I'd bought, I'd also picked up a tiny jar of thick black oil paint, and now I proceeded to slather it on the jars in precise stripes, to mimic lead strips. The result, once the paint was dry and the lights hung, was a sort of poor man's leaded glass: antique yellow pendants with dark edges and fake joins, rather a lot like some old carriage lamps I'd seen.

"Nice," Derek said, coming up to admire my handiwork and to slip his arms around me from behind.

I leaned back against him. "They turned out good."

"I didn't doubt it for a minute," Derek said. "Your crafts always turn out great."

He was so sweet. Even when his stomach growled practically in my ear.

I tilted my head back to look up at him. "Hungry?"

"Always," Derek said.

"For food?"

I could hear the smile in his voice. "That, too."

"Want to knock off early and go get something to eat? I'm done with the pendants."

"I'm done with the grouting," Derek said. "Although there are plenty of other things I could start on."

Sure, but— "What's the point of being your own boss if you can't leave work early once in a while?"

"None, I suppose." He dropped his arms from around my waist. "Grab your coat before I change my mind. Let's go."

I grabbed my coat from the window seat and went, just in case he was serious and did change his mind.

We ended up at Guido's, since we hadn't gotten there on Sunday night. And because it was still early, the place wasn't as crazy as it sometimes is. It was full, but nobody was hanging from the chandeliers, and we found a table right away. The same pierced and tattooed Goth girl as last time waited on us, and raised herself in my estimation when she remembered us and even remembered what drinks we'd ordered.

"Wonder how Wayne made out with Henry," I said while we were waiting for the pizza to arrive. Seafood, in case you wondered. Shrimp and mussels and mushrooms. Yes, I know mushrooms aren't shellfish, but they taste good with the mussels. And the shrimp tastes strangely good with tomato sauce and cheese, too.

"I'm sure he made out just fine," Derek said, taking a pull on his beer. "He's right. Most people don't refuse to cooperate with the police."

"But he had no real good reason to ask for Henry's DNA. It's not like he's investigating a crime."

"If you're right, he is," Derek said. "Kidnapping is a crime. Stealing someone's baby and keeping it for your own."

"Yes, but . . . do you think he told him that? That Henry's mother—the one he grew up with, whether she was his biological mother or not—was a criminal who stole her twin sister's son when her own died? I don't think I'd have wanted to tell anyone unless I was sure."

"Maybe not," Derek admitted. "I don't know, Avery."

"Should we call and ask?"

"He said he'd keep us updated." But he pulled his phone out and dialed anyway. "You know, it used to take weeks to get DNA results back. Six hours may be pushing it."

"I'm sure he's calling in favors," I said, sipping my Diet Coke.

"No doubt. But it's not like this is a priority. There are murders out there that need solving and unidentified remains that need to be identified. Figuring out whether two cousins are actually sister and brother is way down the list. Wayne?"

The phone quacked, and Derek winced. "Yes, I know who you are. I'm sure you're busy. We're just curious."

The phone uttered again and Derek listened. "I'll let her know," he said after a minute and put the phone down before turning to me. "He asked me if we know who he is."

"He's Kate's husband. And also the Waterfield chief of police."

Derek nodded. "I think it's the latter that's important right now. He said he'll let us know when there's something we need to know, and to leave him alone until then."

"That's a bit rude, isn't it?"

Derek shrugged. "He said he has other things to deal with. There's a car accident on the Ocean Road, and some kid at Barnham College went out last night and didn't come back."

Obviously those were more important than figuring out whether Henry Silva was actually Henry Silva, or whether he was Arthur Green.

The pizza came and we got busy eating. After a couple of minutes Derek added, "I spoke to Dad on the phone this morning while you were out."

"About what?"

"Henrietta Parker," Derek said.

"What about her?"

"He'd asked Dr. Lawrence, the ME, for an update, since he was Henrietta's GP."

"OK."

"Turns out she didn't die from a heart attack. Or rather, she did. Her heart stopped. But it was from an overdose of heart medication."

I stared at him. "You're joking."

"I wouldn't joke about something like that."

No, of course not. "Bad choice of words," I said. "So . . . did she take them on purpose? Or was it an accident?"

"No one knows," Derek said. "She could have gotten confused and taken too many. Or she could have done it on purpose. It goes along with your theory about the babies, though. If she knew what her mother did, but didn't know what had happened to the dead baby, the discovery of the skeleton must have given her a real scare. And when the DNA test showed that it didn't match Mamie and Ruth, she might have thought it was only a matter of time before someone figured out the truth. And since she was an accessory to the kidnapping, she might have been worried about going to jail."

"Wayne wouldn't have put her in jail. She was—what—nine back then? And doing what her mother told her to."

"Still," Derek said. "She did help her mother commit a crime. A meaner, less understanding chief of police might throw the book at her."

I suppose. "That's sad. I kind of hope she just got confused and didn't do it on purpose. Not that it makes a difference—she's dead either way—but at least she wouldn't have known it was coming."

Derek nodded. We ate in silence for a few minutes. The news didn't seem to have affected his appetite—then again, he'd known about it since this morning—but I found I wasn't hungry anymore. This whole situation was sad, and getting more so all the time. Now there were not only a dead baby and two dead old ladies on my conscience, but the possibility that Henry would have to give up his house and his wealth and his business to John Nickerson, too. And while I liked John and wished him well, I felt rather bad for Henry. What must it be like, after sixty-five years, to have to give up not only who he thought he was, but all the power and prestige—and money—that came with the Silva name?

People have committed murder for less.

I glanced up at Derek. "Any chance that Henrietta had help taking those pills? That it wasn't either intentional or an accident on her part?"

He stopped chewing. "What are you saying, Tink?"

"Work with me for a moment. Let's say that Henry is actually Arthur, and the baby switch happened the way we've theorized that it did."

Derek nodded.

"And let's say that Henrietta knew about it. Not about the bones in the attic, since that was Ruth's doing, but about the fact that her brother wasn't actually her brother; he was Mamie and Ruth's brother."

Derek nodded.

"And let's say that at some point she told him. Like last spring, when she had her heart attack and thought she was going to die. She wanted to unburden herself before she died, and so she told him what happened."

"OK."

"It didn't really change anything. Not right then. I mean, she didn't die, but she also wouldn't have wanted it to get out, so she wasn't really a threat to Henry. He moved her into the house on Cabot, so he could keep an eye on her and so she'd feel grateful to him for taking care of her, but he probably wasn't too worried."

Derek nodded.

"But then we found the bones, and suddenly things changed. Wayne determined that the baby's DNA didn't match Ruth and Mamie's, and Henrietta was probably freaking out. Henry thought there was only a matter of time before she spilled the beans, to someone other than him this time, and so he decided to do away with her."

"Wayne said he had an alibi for the home tour," Derek reminded me.

"He's been seeing Kerri Waldo. She lives just a few blocks away. It wouldn't have taken more than a couple of minutes to walk down the street to his own house to kill his sister. Kerri might not even have noticed. There were times during the open house when you could have left Aunt Inga's house by the kitchen door and been gone for fifteen minutes, and I wouldn't have known the difference."

Derek didn't say anything, just stared at me.

"It's a lot of money," I reminded him. "The house on Cabot. The lumber business. He'll lose all of it—to John Nickerson—if Wayne proves that he isn't really Henry Silva."

"They'll work it out," Derek said. "John isn't an unreasonable guy. And none of it is Henry's fault. Or Arthur's, or whoever he is. He was a baby when it happened. John won't cast him out in the darkness where there's weeping and gnashing of teeth. Henry doesn't strike me as much of a gnasher anyway."

"Does he strike you as a murderer?"

"No," Derek said. "Although you've made a good case, Avery. I suppose it wouldn't hurt to run your theory past Wayne. And maybe warn John, if Wayne thinks you may be right."

"Can we go do that? Now?"

"Sure." He started looking around for the waitress and the check.

"You know," I told him when we were in the truck on our way home, "I kind of wish I hadn't gone up into the attic."

He glanced at me out of the corner of his eye. "You didn't do anything wrong, Avery. This was all set into motion a long time ago. Whatever Henrietta chose to do— or Henry chose to do—isn't on your head."

"I guess. And I suppose it was better that we found the skeleton than whoever we sold the house to. Could you imagine what would happen if we renovated the whole thing and sold it to someone else, and then, a year from now, they go up to the attic and find a baby skeleton? We'd get sued."

"I wouldn't be surprised," Derek said, pulling up in

front of Aunt Inga's house on Bayberry Lane. He continued once he'd come around the car and had opened the door to help me down, "No, Tink. It was much better that it was us. We even managed to keep it fairly quiet. There's no stigma attached to the house. We'll finish fixing it up, and someone will buy it and love it, and pretty soon you'll have forgotten all about this."

That was going a little too far, I thought, but I didn't say so. Mostly because, when he put his arm around me and guided me toward the house, a shadow loomed up in front of us and the light from the porch glinted off the barrel of a pistol.

∎   ∎   ∎

"Whoa," Derek said and stopped so fast that he rocked back on his heels.

Darren—Darren?—glanced at him, but only for a second before he turned his attention back to me. That's where the pistol was pointed, too. "This is all your fault."

"Hold on," Derek said and pushed me behind him, "how is it her fault?"

"The chief of police came," Darren said, his voice tight, "to get Dad's DNA."

"So?"

"So when he figures out that Dad's really Arthur Green, we'll have to give Silva Lumber to that idiot John Nickerson."

"John isn't an idiot," I objected.

Darren snorted. "He's not a Silva, either."

Nor was Henry, it seemed, nor for that matter Darren himself, but it didn't seem politic to point it out. Not right now.

"Are there bullets in that thing?" Derek asked.

Darren nodded. "I'll use it if I have to."

I believed him. There was an edge to his voice, halfway between hysteria and anger, that made me feel quite uncomfortable.

Derek must have noticed, too, but I couldn't hear it in

his voice. "What is it you think we can do for you? If your father isn't Henry Silva, he isn't Henry Silva. Nobody can change that."

"I know," Darren said tightly.

"If the chief of police is checking your father's DNA, it's not like he won't find out."

"I know!"

"So what is it you're hoping to accomplish? If you can't change the outcome anyway?"

I didn't say anything, but my mind was ticking furiously. Derek was right, of course. There was nothing Darren could do to change the outcome of what was happening. If his father wasn't Henry Silva, and wasn't the heir to Silva Lumber, everyone would know about it as soon as Wayne got the results of his DNA test back. Shooting us—or me, since I seemed to be the focus of his anger; heck, even shooting Wayne!—wouldn't change the facts. The only difference would be that Darren would end up in jail for cold-blooded murder.

It seemed a stupid chance to take just so he could register his annoyance with me.

Granted, he probably wasn't thinking too clearly. But he wasn't stupid, so he had to know that shooting two people in cold blood wouldn't do him any favors.

Unless . . .

"I want her to pay," Darren said.

"You'll go to jail if you shoot her."

"I'll only shoot her if you don't do as I say. Turn around and walk back to the car."

Derek hesitated. I could feel it. "C'mon," I said, tugging on his coat. Darren might not want to shoot me—it seemed like he had something more unpleasant planned—but if he was determined to make me pay, he might not be too particular about shooting Derek to get to me. I'd rather keep my husband in one piece for as long as possible. Not only because I love him, but because, with two of us, we'd stand a better chance of outwitting Darren.

Derek muttered something, but he turned. He made sure

to keep himself between me and Darren on our way back to the truck, though.

"Get in," Darren said. "You drive."

He was talking to Derek. "I can drive," I said.

"No," Darren said. "You sit in the middle."

Fine. It wasn't like I particularly wanted to drive anyway. My hands were shaking too much, and I might not be able to keep the truck on the road.

I got into the middle and Derek got behind the wheel. Meanwhile, Darren crawled in beside me with the pistol. His thigh crowded mine, and his shoulder, too, but there wasn't anything I could do about in the close confines of the cab. I certainly didn't want to hamper Derek in anything he had to do.

"Drive," Darren told him and wiggled the gun.

Derek put the truck in gear and pulled away from the curb. "Where?"

"The house on North Street."

"What are you going to do when we get there?" I asked.

Darren smiled. Tightly. Probably at the wobble in my voice. "You're going to have a little accident."

"What kind of accident?"

"There's a gas leak," Darren said. "Very unfortunate."

Indeed. He'd probably arranged for the gas leak already. By the time we got there, the house would be filled with gas. A match would make it go up like a bonfire.

A memory of being locked inside my garden shed while flamed licked at the walls closed my throat for a moment, and I gulped. Derek reached out his free hand and put it on my thigh. I twisted my fingers with his.

"No touching," Darren barked.

I made to pull my hand back, but Derek held on. "What are you gonna do?" he asked. "Shoot us?"

Probably not. Not if he wanted it to look like we'd succumbed to a gas leak. And not if he wanted to keep the car on the road. I kept my hand where it was, too.

We got there sooner than I wanted to. It wasn't a long drive, after all. And by the time Derek pulled the car to a stop outside the house, I was no closer to a plan for how to disarm Darren. I'd risk the bullet if I thought there was any chance that he'd miss, but he had the gun stuck in my ribs, so I figured resistance was futile.

He opened the door and hopped out first, the ends of his fancy cashmere coat flapping. "Let's go."

I twitched my fingers out of Derek's hand and scooted across the seat as slowly as I possibly could. "I still don't understand why you're doing this. It can't be just that you're upset because your father isn't really Henry Silva. I mean, I know it's a lot of money, and I'm sure you're not looking forward to trading in the Mercedes and working for a living—"

"Shut up!" Darren growled.

"But it seems there ought to be something more than that."

If he wasn't trying to preserve his money and position—and for that he'd be better served by shooting John Nickerson than me—what was he trying to do?

There are only a few reasons most people commit murder. If you disregard the sickos, the ones who kill people because they like to, the others break down into three groups, generally speaking. The ones who kill for money, the ones who kill for revenge, and the ones who kill out of fear. Darren said he wanted revenge because I'd exposed his father and had probably taken away his inheritance, but that didn't make sense. He couldn't kill me for money, since me being dead wouldn't help him get his money back. His father wouldn't magically become Henry Silva if I were dead.

That left fear.

But what was he afraid of?

And that's when it hit me. That whole conversation I'd just had with Derek over pizza . . . it could equally well apply to Darren.

Darren, whom Derek had accused of only being interested in money. Darren, who stood to lose his fortune and his position, too, if Henry lost everything.

"You killed Henrietta," I said.

I knew I'd struck home when his lips thinned. "My aunt died of a heart attack."

"One brought on by an overdose of heart medication." I went out on a limb and added, "An overdose she didn't take herself."

"You can't prove it," Darren said, which was more of a confession than I'd thought I'd get, at least so soon. "She was distraught about the baby switch. She was afraid of going to jail."

So I was right about the baby switch. Darren probably didn't even realize he'd admitted it, and I wasn't about to clue him in. He already had reasons enough for hating me. "Did she tell you that?"

"She told me everything!" Darren snapped.

"Everything?"

Suddenly, the words started spilling out. It was as if I'd flipped a switch after he'd been waiting for an opportunity to talk to someone. Or maybe he'd just been simmering for so long that it finally boiled over. "It was when she had her heart attack. She thought she was dying, so she told me everything. Deathbed confession." His face twisted. "She told me how my dad isn't really her brother, and isn't a Silva, and how I'm not, either, and how her mother made her keep Mamie and Ruth busy while she switched her dead baby for their live one."

"She told you all of that?"

He nodded. "And then she didn't die after all. But I knew I had to do something."

"So you killed her."

"No." He looked at me like I'd lost my mind. "She said she didn't know what had happened to the dead baby. The Green sisters were just supposed to tell their mother that the baby was dead, and that was supposed to be it, but instead they told everyone it had been stolen. Henrietta said her mother went crazy for days, and wouldn't take the baby out of the house for fear someone would recognize him.

Luckily everyone in town was doing the same thing, because they were so afraid of the baby thief."

Luckily.

"So what happened?" I was fascinated, in spite of myself. Not quite fascinated enough to be able to disregard the gun pointed at me, but the story filled some of the gaps I'd been wondering about.

"Eventually things died down," Darren said. "The baby was never found. Henrietta said Ruth and Mamie must have done something to it. I needed to search the house, so I made Ruth fall down the stairs and break her hip, so she had to go to the hospital. A little grease on the stairs did the job nicely. And Mamie couldn't stay there alone, so I arranged to have them both live at the nursing home." He smiled, pleased with himself.

"That was nice of you," I managed, to keep the conversation going. But I must not have managed to keep the horror out of my voice, because he looked at me rather narrowly. I added, "So you searched the house?"

"I searched everywhere. The yard, the basement, the playhouse. I even stuck my head into that damn attic and looked around. I didn't find anything."

"The crate was there," I said. "You must have overlooked it. It was hard to see, up against the wall and wedged in beside the chimney."

He scowled. "I should have burned the house down then, instead of selling it to you."

That might have been better. Even if the word "then"—as opposed to now—sent a chill down my spine. "Why didn't you?"

He shrugged. "I'd already checked it out and hadn't found anything, so I figured it was safe. That way I could use that money to pay for Ruth and Mamie's bills, and I wouldn't have to spend ours."

"So why did you end up killing Henrietta after all? By then, we'd found the skeleton and everyone knew."

"I killed Mamie first," Darren said in the same tone as

someone might say, "I went to the grocery store first," "and Henrietta found out. She was going back and forth about whether to tell my dad. He might have cut me off, and I couldn't risk that."

Of course not. "Why did you kill Mamie? She had no idea what Ruth did with the baby. She probably thought he was kidnapped."

"She did," Darren growled. "But I couldn't have her go back and tell Ruth I'd asked about it. So I left her in the playhouse and jimmied the lock so she couldn't get out."

"So the story about her getting out of the car in front of the liquor store was just a story."

"Of course." He sounded impatient. "I took her to the playhouse and left her there. With a little knock on the head so she wouldn't think about leaving. And then I drove to the liquor store, in case the police checked that I'd been there. I got a bottle of wine and I made a big fuss in the parking lot about not finding my aunt. Then I drove around for thirty minutes looking for her before I called the police to report her missing."

"And by the time we found her, she was dead."

He shrugged.

"I suppose you went down there, to the playhouse, in your fancy dress shoes, because you were afraid you'd left tracks or DNA or something when you were there the first time."

He didn't answer, which I took as confirmation. I added, "So when Henrietta realized you'd helped Mamie along, you thought you'd better get rid of her, too?"

"She might have another heart attack," Darren said. "Any day really. Especially with all the stress. And who knows what she might say if she did?"

"Of course." She might decide to confess her sins again, and to someone other than Darren. Someone like Arthur. Or Ruth. Or the chief of police. "I still don't understand what you're trying to do, though. Killing us won't help. Your father still won't turn into Henry Silva, and someone else might realize that you killed Mamie and your aunt Henrietta."

"I have a plan," Darren said.

"What kind of plan?"

He grinned. "Once you're inside the house and the place is burning, everyone'll rush here to try to save you. Meanwhile, I'll go downtown and shoot John Nickerson. Without him, there'll be no one to take over Silva Lumber."

"You won't get away with that!"

"Sure I will," Darren said, "after I shoot my dad and make it look like he shot himself. It's his gun. And then I'll be the only one left. And who do you think'll get Silva Lumber then?"

I admit it, I was speechless. He'd killed Mamie and Henrietta, and had probably tried to kill Ruth in that fall down the stairs. That was two murders and one attempted. Now he was planning to kill Derek and me. Then he was headed over to Main Street to shoot John Nickerson. And after that he planned to shoot his own father and pin all those homicides on him?

And the worst part of it was, he might even get away with it. Because it made sense. He could make it look like Henry—aka Arthur—had done it all for him, Darren.

I felt sick to my stomach.

In the silence, Darren looked around, and I realized that while we'd been standing here talking, for the past several minutes, I hadn't heard a sound from Derek. Had he managed to sneak away while I was keeping Darren occupied?

Not that I'd been consciously trying to keep Darren occupied so Derek could sneak away. I'd pretty much just wanted to know why he felt he had to kill me. But if it had given Derek a chance to escape, so much the better.

Except it hadn't, it seemed.

"Get over here." Darren gestured with the gun, and my husband came around the truck to stand beside me. Close enough beside me that his hand could fumble for mine and give it a reassuring squeeze. "Move," Darren growled.

He herded us up the driveway toward the house. We skirted the Dumpster and climbed the steps to the porch.

"Open the door."

Derek took his time digging the keys out of his pocket and fitting one into the lock. Darren shifted from foot to foot, looking over his shoulder.

The door swung open. I could smell the gas seeping out.

"Get in." Darren waved the gun impatiently.

I balked. "I can't."

The gun swung in my direction again.

"C'mon, Tink." Derek put his arm around my shoulders. If he was worried at all, he didn't show it. "It'll be all right. We can die in each other's arms, just the way I've always wanted to."

Darren snorted.

"I'd rather not die at all," I said.

"It'll be all right." He winked.

Sure it would.

But there wasn't anything I could do really. I could make a break for it and have Darren shoot me in the back, I guess, but it wasn't that attractive of an alternative. And Derek didn't seem concerned. Maybe he knew something I—and Darren—didn't.

"Fine." I stepped into the house and tried to hold my breath as the gas assaulted my nostrils.

Derek stepped in behind me, and the door slammed. Darren got busy with a hammer, nailing it shut.

"C'mere." Derek pulled me close to him so I could bury my face in his sweater. He smelled of laundry detergent and Ivory soap and paint, and I breathed deeply, trying to chase the taste of the gas out of the back of my throat.

"How long can we last in here?" I asked against his chest.

"Long enough," Derek said into my hair.

"Should we break a window?"

He shook his head. I didn't lift my head out of the sweater, but I could feel the movement.

"Why not?"

"That's original glass. We won't be able to replace it."

If he was more worried about the windows than about our survival, I guess maybe we'd be all right.

Outside, Darren threw the hammer aside and fumbled in his pocket. I closed my eyes as he pulled his hand out and I saw a tiny little flame ignite.

The next second, everything lit up, and a booming voice told Darren to drop the gun and put his hands up.

—Epilogue—

We finished the house at the beginning of February. A few days after the For Sale sign went into the yard, while we were finishing up the last few details of the renovation, Henry Silva showed up, with Ruth Green and John Nickerson in tow.

The For Sale sign had Melissa's name on it incidentally. I hadn't come up with a good excuse why she couldn't list the house, since she seemed adamant that she wanted to, and since she, as Derek reminded me, was very good at her job.

"She'll phase out of wanting to work in Waterfield over the next year," he assured me. "She just doesn't have a lot of Portlanders clamoring for her business yet, and she doesn't want it to look like she's less popular than she used to be."

"Did she tell you that?"

He nodded. "She called the other day."

Of course she had.

"I don't like that," I said.

He shrugged. "What am I gonna do? Refuse to take her calls?"

He could, as far as I was concerned. I had never liked the fact that his ex-wife kept calling him, and I liked it even less now than he was married to me. But Derek is nothing if not loyal, and although they hadn't worked out as man and wife, he still cared about her. He had no plans, desire, or intention to get romantically involved with her again—he mentioned that proverbial ten-foot pole in connection with Melissa—but she had no family in Maine, and no close friends, and I guess he felt responsible for bringing her there. So he took her calls and gave her help when she asked. I guess I should be happy, because those were the qualities that made him a nice guy, and the qualities that had made me fall in love with him.

But I digress.

The sign was in the yard, and we were in the process of doing the final cleanup, like hanging light plates and wiping fingerprints off the doorjambs, when Henry Silva's Mercedes pulled up to the curb outside. He got out of the driver's seat, and John out of the backseat, and between them, they managed to get Ruth out of the passenger seat.

The big, unwieldy cast was off her leg, and she was able to move under her own steam, with the help of a sturdy arm. Her brother provided one.

Yes, it had been established that Henry Silva was actually Arthur Green. Not that there'd been much question really. But the DNA test had proved it beyond a shadow of a doubt. Henry's DNA was a perfect match to Ruth's, and just to make doubly sure, Wayne had checked Henrietta's DNA with the baby skeleton's, too, and had gotten another match. So it was definitely Baby Henry's bones I had found in the attic, while it was Arthur Green who was standing on our porch, tall and strong and very much alive.

He still called himself Henry Silva, though. After sixty-five years, it was too confusing to do anything else, both for him and everyone around him.

I hadn't had occasion to speak to either of them since the events before Christmas. I wasn't sure I wanted to.

What do you say to a man after his son has tried—and failed—to kill you, and you've been responsible for putting him in jail?

So no, I hadn't gone out of my way to track down Henry. I had stopped by the nursing home to visit Ruth again, because I had said I would, but that had been a little awkward, too, so I hadn't done it again. I had even stayed away from John, whom I normally enjoyed talking to, because he was caught up in the whole mess, as well.

And then we'd been busy with Christmas and family and the renovations, so it wasn't just avoidance, either.

Yet here they were, all three of them, on my doorstep, and I couldn't avoid them any longer.

"We saw the sign go in the yard," John explained when Derek opened the door. "Ruth wanted a look at the place before it's sold."

Another bit of awkwardness. She'd lived here her whole life and hadn't wanted to move, and Darren had sold the house out from under her.

I managed a smile. "Of course. Come in."

Henry assisted her across the threshold and they stopped to look around. I did, too, and tried to see it through their eyes.

It looked very different. The walls were a warm yellowy white now. A color wash technique I'd talked Derek into letting me try. It wasn't as opaque as paint—almost luminescent really—and it set off the dark wood of the windows and baseboards perfectly. My Mason jar solar lanterns hung above the fireplace mantel, and Derek had added bookshelves to the inglenooks on either side of the fireplace, under the casement windows, and stained them to match the dark wood trim elsewhere in the house. The built-in breakfront had been updated with new—or more accurately, vintage—glass knobs in lieu of the tarnished brass ones that had been there, and I had sewn a couple of brightly colored pillows to decorate the window seat, to match the curtains I had also sewn and hung. The expanse of oak floors gleamed with varnish and extended all the way into the kitchen, where we could see a glimpse of new cabinets and counters through the open butler door. We'd sprung for Shaker-style cabinets with glass fronts, and had stained them the same dark brown as the original wood-work and the breakfront, to look like they'd always been there.

When I looked back at Ruth, she had tears in her eyes. "It's beautiful."

It was. And I felt horrible. "I'm sorry."

She sniffed and shook her head. "Don't be."

"We took your house. You didn't want to leave."

"I couldn't leave," Ruth said. "Not with the bones in the attic. Not as long as Mamie was alive. She kept returning here from the nursing home. She would have tried to go back from wherever we lived. This was her home. She would never have been able to settle down anywhere else."

"But you don't mind that you don't live here anymore?"

"I'm happy not to live here anymore," Ruth said. "I would have left a long time ago if I could have. This wasn't a happy house for me. Too many memories."

Too many skeletons.

I glanced at Derek, who looked back at me. A corner of his mouth quirked, so he must be thinking the same thing.

"I'm glad to hear that," I said, turning back to Ruth, "because we've been feeling a bit guilty about it."

Ruth shook her head. "Don't feel guilty. I'm glad to be out of here. And you've done a wonderful job. It looks beautiful."

It did. If I do say so myself. "Let me give you the tour."

We toured, which took a while given Ruth's difficulty in walking. But she wanted to see everything, so between Henry and Derek, they even got her up to the second floor, to see the bedrooms and bath.

"Where will you go now?" I asked when we were finally downstairs again, and Ruth had been installed on the window seat with John next to her, to rest the leg.

She glanced up at Henry aka Arthur. "It's all worked out. I'm moving in with Henry."

"On Cabot Street?"

She nodded. "He's all alone now in that big house."

He was. And that was my fault, too.

"I'm sorry," Henry said, and when I looked up, I saw that he was looking at me. "About Darren. About what he tried to do."

For a moment I wasn't sure what to say. What Darren had tried to do to me, and to Derek, was nothing compared to what Darren had tried to do to his father. At least he'd only tried to kill us. He'd planned to kill his dad and pin all seven murders on him.

Derek got in ahead of me. "Darren's actions were his choice. You don't owe us an apology for Darren."

"He's my son," Henry said.

"And he's a grown man. He made his own choices. You can't take responsibility for those, any more than you're responsible for what happened when you were an infant."

Henry nodded, but he didn't look convinced.

"We don't blame you for anything Darren did," I said. "Derek's right. He made his own decisions, and he knew you wouldn't want anything to do with what he did, so he made sure you didn't know about it. You're not responsible for any of it."

There was a pause.

"So what's happening with Silva Lumber?" Derek asked, probably in an effort to break the silence. It might not have been the most diplomatic, or for that matter tactful, change of subject, but it worked.

"Henry's continuing to run it," John said. "I wouldn't know how, and I have my own business anyway."

"And the money?" The Silva fortune?

It was another touchy subject, and none of my business really, but I was curious, and I figured I'd earned the right to ask.

"We're sharing it," John said. "I don't need much. My business supports me just fine, and I have my parents' house to live in. And now I'll have a little bit to fall back on once I retire."

He grinned at Henry.

"So everything's been worked out."

"We've restructured the company," Henry answered. "The lawyers have had a busy few weeks. But for now, four of us own it together. The three of us here, and John's sister. When we're all gone, her children will inherit. But we're running the business as a board, with equal shares and equal rights. So will they. No more of this 'oldest son of oldest son' rubbish."

I wanted to ask whether Darren would be part of the board, too, whenever he got out of prison, but I decided that would be tactless, not to mention none of my business. And even if Henry and Kerri ended up together on a permanent basis, chances were there wouldn't be any offspring from the union. They were both too old for that. "I'm glad you got it all worked out," I said instead.

They all nodded. And then there was a little pause while we all tried to come up with something more to say, but couldn't. I thought about asking Henry about Kerri, but it wasn't really any of my business, and besides, as long as I stuck around Waterfield—and I planned to—I'd learn about anything that happened when it became official anyway.

They left after that, and Derek and I got back to our final polish.

It was later that afternoon that I finally straightened my aching back and surveyed the house. "I think we're done."

Derek nodded, stopping beside me. "I think so, too."

"I don't see anything else that needs doing."

He shook his head. "Me, either."

When he put an arm around me, I sagged against him and put my head on his chest.

"Tired?" His voice rumbled in my ear.

I nodded, rubbing my cheek against his T-shirt at the same time, because I couldn't bring myself to lift my head. "Beat."

"Want to go out and celebrate? Or do you just want to go home and put your feet up?"

I hesitated. Going home and putting my feet up sounded

great, especially if I could talk him into giving me a foot massage, but I'm not the girl to turn down dinner out. A dinner I didn't have to cook. "What did you have in mind?"

He put on a fake French accent. He'd spent a year in France once, in his teens, as an exchange student, so as accents went, it was a pretty good one. "A leetle food, a lee-tle wine . . ."

A little dessert? "Whoopie pie?"

"I could be talked into whoopie pie," Derek said.

"In that case, I could be talked into dinner."

"Or we could go home and put our feet up and order a pizza. I'll give you a foot massage." He smiled.

"You're on."

"Always." He picked me up and headed for the door.

—Home-Renovation—
and Design Tips

Make Your Own Tiffany-Style
Glass Lampshade

The do-it-yourselfer can construct two types of glass lamp-shades: panel lampshades and curved or free-form lamp shades. The latter require molds as a base for construction, and take much, much smaller pieces of glass, as well as more patience. In other words, they're difficult to make, especially for a beginner. Panel lamp shades are simpler to build, making them a good project for someone just starting out—like Avery, and most of us.

These instructions are for a simple panel lampshade, something most of us should be able to handle. However, to get used to the process and the tools, it's not a bad idea to start with something even simpler—like a flat stained glass panel—to hang in the window to look pretty, and then move on to lampshades and other things from there.

MATERIALS
- 2 copies of the pattern
- Scissors or pattern shears
- Wood or metal strips with straightedge
- Glass cutter
- Glass pliers
- Glass grinder
- Copper foil
- Wood or plastic burnisher
- Electrical tape
- Wood blocks
- Flux
- Flux brush
- Solder
- Soldering iron
- Vase cap
- Glass cleaner

DIRECTIONS
1. Attach one copy of the pattern to the work surface with the wood or metal straightedges along each side. Cut the other pattern apart with the scissors or pattern shears.
2. Cut the glass to fit the pattern pieces with the glass cutter and glass pliers.
3. Grind each piece as needed to fit the pattern exactly and smooth sharp edges.
4. Apply the copper foil all around the edge so that it falls evenly on both sides. Smooth it firmly into place with the plastic or wood burnisher.
5. Apply flux with the brush and solder both sides of each panel separately with the soldering iron. Form the solder into a smooth, rounded line. Make sure no solder is along the sides of the panels so they fit snugly together when forming the lamp.
6. Clean each panel as soon as it is soldered on both sides so that the flux does not etch the glass.

7. Place the panels flat on the work surface in a semi-circle with the tops lined up as closely as possible.

8. Connect the panels together at the top and bottom with electrical tape.

9. Apply a thin layer of solder to the vase cap.

10. Pull the pieces carefully upright and fit them together as evenly as possible, making sure they are symmetrical.

11. Apply flux and tack the pieces together, dripping a bead of solder on each seam.

12. Draw a thin line of solder along all the seams to hold everything together. Support the lamp as needed with the wood blocks as you rotate it to get the best angle for soldering.

13. Place the vase cap on the top of the newly formed lampshade, apply flux along the seam, and solder it in place.

14. Solder the outside and inside seams of the lamp with a finishing bead of solder, using the wood blocks to support the lamp at the best angle for soldering.

15. Clean the lampshade thoroughly with glass cleaner to remove all traces of flux.

Color Washing

Color washing is a painting technique that gives a subtle, undulating, almost translucent effect on walls. Something almost like rippling sunlight—yellow—or water—blue. It's perfect for anyone who doesn't want flat walls, but at the same time are unsure about faux finishes. It's a simple process that involves mixing latex paint with glaze and putting two layers together.

MATERIALS
- Satin interior latex paint (base coat, lightest shade)
- Satin interior latex paint (darker shade)
- Satin interior latex paint (darkest shade)
- Tintable glaze

- Paint roller
- Pan
- 4" brush
- Painters' tape
- Brush or sponge for blending

DIRECTIONS

1. Choose your color palette: 3 shades of the same color in a gradient from light (#1) to medium (#2) to dark (#3).
2. Roll on base coat—lightest coat; coat #1—and let it dry.
3. Mix a bucket of the medium coat—#2—and the tintable glaze. Use a 3:1 or 4:1 glaze-to-paint ratio. (The more glaze, the more translucent the mixture. The more glaze, the longer your "open" time, too—the time you have before the mixture dries.)
4. Mix a bucket of the darkest coat—#3—with glaze in the same ratio—or not the same ratio, if you prefer a more or less opaque finish.
5. Start with mixture #2 in the pan, and roll it over a manageable section of the wall, on top of the base (#1) coat.
6. While the glaze is still wet, use the brush to apply mixture #3 in large X's across the section of paint.
7. Use a cloth/sponge to blend the two shades of glaze together.
8. Repeat the process until the entire wall or room is complete. Let dry.

A Few Words on Solar Power

Solar powered lights are great for indoors, whether the aim is to cut down on electric bills or just to provide a softer mood lighting than lightbulbs can. The illumination from solar lights gives off a soft, warm glow, and there are many styles to choose from. The bulbs are available in a range of colors, too.

Consider placing a couple flat-bottomed lanterns on a night-table or shelf in a bedroom, maybe with amber bulbs inside, or hang them from hooks along a dark interior staircase to light the way. Garden bed lights—the ones shaped like flowers or bugs—look just as good inside, in a potted plant, as they do outside, too.

All you have to do is make sure your solar powered lights have plenty of opportunity to soak up sun during the day, either by being outside or sitting in a sunny window, and they'll give you hours and hours of soft, ambient light in return. They'll pay for themselves over time, and you can decorate with them without being tied to available electrical outlets, a definite plus in an older home, where there's often a limited number of outlets.

Or do what Avery did, and use them in places where electrical wires can't safely be used.

Mason Jar Pendant Lights

MATERIALS
- Mason jars
- Glass cutter
- Candle
- Diamond file
- Cutting oil
- Frosted spray paint
- Light fixture (solar powered or otherwise)
- Tools for hanging fixture, if needed

DIRECTIONS
1. Cut the bottom off the jar with the glass cutter. (You may find a designated bottle cutter easier than a pencil grip or fist grip cutter for this, but feel free to experiment.) Score the circumference of the jar several times to make sure the break will be clean.
2. Hold the jar with the score line directly above the lit candle and rotate it several times to heat and stress the glass.

3. Run cold water over the jar to crack the glass, or plunge it into a bucket of ice and water. The point here is to stress the glass by heating it and then quickly cooling it. If it doesn't crack completely the first time, repeat the process from the top, starting with the cutter. Canning jars are made of thick glass, and sometimes it takes more than once to cut one.

4. When the bottom of the jar is gone, use the file and cutting oil to smooth the edge, to make sure it's safe to touch.

5. Spray the inside of the jar with the frosted finish, from both top and bottom, and let dry.

6. Attach to the desired light fixture. The lid is useful for this. If it has a glass seal inside, you'll have to get rid of that first. Either pry it loose, or break it with a hammer and remove the pieces.

7. Drill a hole in the lid sufficient for mounting over a standard light socket, or wherever you need it to fit. Add the wiring—easy to do with a prewired fixture—and then screw the jar onto the lid.

8. For a bit of added punch, you can paint on the jar with glass paint, to give it a stained glass look. If you don't want to attempt freehand painting, this is somewhere else where small stencils come in handy and look great.

Scandinavian Christmas Heart Baskets

MATERIALS
- Scissors
- Glossy, scrapbooking, or construction paper; two different colors
- Glue

DIRECTIONS
1. Cut two rectangles 2½ inches by 9 inches from the papers.

2. Fold the rectangles in half, to make folded sheets 2½ inches by 4½ inches.
3. From the folds, cut three slits each three inches long.
4. Round the edge on the opposite side of the fold.
5. Lay the halves in front of you with the round edges closest to you, and mark the flaps from the left: 6, 5, 4 on the first half, and 1, 2, 3 on the second.
6. Weave the two halves together like this:

   – *Flap 1 goes through Flap 4, over Flap 5, and through Flap 6.*
   – *Flap 2 does the opposite: over Flap 4, through Flap 5, and over Flap 6.*
   – *Flap 3 does what Flap 1 did: through Flap 4, over Flap 5, and through Flap 6.*
   – *Flap 4 will be over Flap 1, through Flap 2, and over Flap 3.*
   – *Flap 5 will be through Flap 1, over Flap 2, and through Flap 3.*
   – *Flap 6 will be over Flap 1, through Flap 2, and over Flap 3.*
   – *The result should look like a 3x3 checkerboard heart.*

7. Cut a strip of either color paper and use the glue to fashion a handle. Hang it on a tree or on a string with others and fill with raisins, popcorn, or other small Christmas goodie.

Make Your Own Bookcase

MATERIALS
- ¾ inch birch plywood—enough for the project
- 1¼ inch poplar
- Wood glue
- Small decorative molding
- Finish nails
- Tape measure

- Table saw
- Miter saw
- Finish nailer/hammer
- Level
- T-square
- Router

DIRECTIONS

1. Measure the space where you want the bookcase to fit, and determine how much material you need.
2. Cut the plywood pieces to the right size.
3. The interior shelves should ideally be rabbited into the side panels of the frame to make them stronger. To make sure you router these rabbit grooves at the same position in both side panels, lay the two panels side by side on a table and screw a piece of scrap wood across both ends, effectively making them into one wide board. This will ensure that your lines are straight and even.
4. Determine the location of your first shelf and use a T-square to draw a ¾-inch stripe across both side panels at once. Draw another ¾-inch stripe at the location of the other shelves you intend to put in the unit.
5. Router out the grooves. Clamp a level or straightedge along your newly marked shelf lines to use as a guide.
6. Assemble the unit. Start by affixing the top to the two side panels using wood glue and finish nails. Then, install the shelves by putting glue in the rabbit joints and sliding the shelves into the joints, one shelf at a time.
7. With the shelves in place, add finish nails through the outside of the unit to hold the shelves in place.
8. Whether you want to add a base to your bookcase is up to you, but Avery and Derek did, to give their shelves a built-in look before mounting them in the inglenooks beside the fireplace. If you want a sturdy base, add that in the next step.

9. With the unit built, it's time to finish it off by covering the plywood edges with nice finished pieces of 1¼-inch poplar. Cut the poplar to the same dimensions as the exterior panels using the miter saw. The angles should be joined with 45-degree angle cuts for a smooth, tailored look. Use wood glue and nails to attach the framing to the bookcase. If you want to be fancy, you can add some decorative molding, too, and that heavy base we talked about.

10. Allow 24 hours for the wood glue to fully dry, and then sand it smooth and fill the nail holes with paintable or stainable wood putty. Use a tack cloth to wipe off any debris or sawdust created by sanding, and then paint or stain the unit to give it your desired look. Derek and Avery stained theirs to match the old woodwork in the Craftsman Bungalow, but you can paint or stain yours any color you want.

Have fun!

*Finding a property's hidden potential has
rewards and challenges—not to mention certain
unanticipated dangers. Like murder.*

FROM NATIONAL BESTSELLING AUTHOR
JENNIE BENTLEY

FLIPPED OUT
A Do-It-Yourself Mystery

Avery and her hunky handyman boyfriend are renovating a house belonging to a local news anchor who's
thrilled to be filmed as part of a home-renovation TV
show. But cable-TV fame proves fleeting when the
man is murdered and Avery faces the task of nailing
the killer.

Home-renovation and design tips included!

penguin.com
facebook.com/TheCrimeSceneBooks
jenniebentley.com

M1093T0412

FROM NATIONAL BESTSELLING AUTHOR
JENNIE BENTLEY

MORTAR AND MURDER
A Do-It-Yourself Mystery

Avery and her boyfriend, Derek, are renovating a magnificent 225-year-old Colonial on Rowanberry Island, just off the coast of Maine. The DIY is going great, even if a neighbor, a reclusive thriller writer, seems as strange and mysterious as his fiction. But his reputation seems in perfect keeping with what Derek and Avery discover next . . .

The body of an unidentified woman is found floating in the sea near the island with a piece of paper in her pocket bearing the address of Derek and Avery's Realtor. Then a second woman is retrieved like jetsam from the harbor. But it's not until Avery discovers a secret room in the house, and learns about Rowanberry Island's long tradition of smuggling, that a bizarre link is made between the dead women—and if it foretells anything, it's that things on the island are only going to get deadlier.

> "With plot twists that curve and loop . . .
> this story offers handy renovation tips, historical data,
> and a colorful painting of the Maine landscape."
> —Examiner.com

penguin.com
facebook.com/TheCrimeSceneBooks
jenniebentley.com

M1094T0412